TO RIDE THE WIND AND STEAL THE SUN

THE FOUR KINGDOMS AND BEYOND

THE FOUR KINGDOMS

The Princess Companion: A Retelling of The Princess and the Pea (Book One)

The Princess Fugitive: A Reimagining of Little Red Riding Hood (Book Two)

The Coronation Ball: A Four Kingdoms Cinderella Novelette

Happily Every Afters: A Reimagining of Snow White and Rose Red (Novella)

The Princess Pact: A Twist on Rumpelstiltskin (Book Three)

A Midwinter's Wedding: A Retelling of The Frog Prince (Novella)

The Princess Game: A Reimagining of Sleeping Beauty (Book Four)

The Princess Search: A Retelling of The Ugly Duckling (Book Five)

BEYOND THE FOUR KINGDOMS

A Dance of Silver and Shadow: A Retelling of The Twelve Dancing Princesses (Book One)

A Tale of Beauty and Beast: A Retelling of Beauty and the Beast (Book Two)

A Crown of Snow and Ice: A Retelling of The Snow Queen (Book Three)

A Dream of Ebony and White: A Retelling of Snow White (Book Four)

A Captive of Wing and Feather: A Retelling of Swan Lake (Book Five)

A Princess of Wind and Wave: A Retelling of The Little Mermaid
(Book Six)

RETURN TO THE FOUR KINGDOMS

The Secret Princess: A Retelling of The Goose Girl (Book One)

The Mystery Princess: A Retelling of Cinderella (Book Two)

The Desert Princess: A Retelling of Aladdin (Book Three)

The Golden Princess: A Retelling of Ali Baba and the Forty Thieves
(Book Four)

The Rogue Princess: A Retelling of Puss in Boots (Book Five)

The Abandoned Princess: A Retelling of Rapunzel (Book Six)

FOUR KINGDOMS DUOLOGY

To Ride the Wind: A Retelling of East of the Sun and West of the
Moon (Book One)

To Steal the Sun: A Retelling of East of the Sun and West of the
Moon (Book Two)

FOUR KINGDOMS FAIRY TALE NOVELLAS

To Ensnare a Prince: An Entwined Prince and the Pauper Retelling
(Book One)

To Entangle a Heart: An Entwined Prince and the Pauper Retelling
(Book Two)

TO RIDE THE WIND AND STEAL THE SUN

A COMPLETE DUOLOGY RETELLING OF EAST OF THE SUN AND WEST OF THE MOON

MELANIE CELLIER

LUMINANT PUBLICATIONS

Four Kingdoms
NORTHGATE
Northhelm
RANGMEROS
Rangmere
Arcadia
Kuralan
ARCADIE
The Great Desert
KAREMA
LANARE
Lanovre
SERRALA
CAVALIE DU INVERNE
Ardasira
LARGO
BANISHMENT ISLAND

TO RIDE THE WIND

*For my goddaughter, Teresa,
with the hope that you will grow to love
both adventures and happy endings*

CHARLOTTE

A flash of white caught Charlotte's eye, unnaturally clean and bright among the greens and browns of the forest. She turned to face it, but it was already gone.

"Elizabeth!" A surge of unease in Charlotte's stomach made her tongue trip over her sister's long name. "Odelia?"

She still remembered the childhood years when they had been Bettie, Dellie, and Charli. But it had been many years now since her older sisters had turned into prim young ladies who insisted all three use their full names.

She called again, more loudly, but heard nothing in return. The silence around her was deep—too deep for a forest in mid-afternoon. She opened her mouth to call again but was silenced by a piercing scream.

Launching into motion, she sprinted toward the sound only to run headlong into her middle sister. The two girls bounced away from each other, Odelia falling while Charlotte just managed to keep her feet.

Her sister glared up at her from the forest floor.

"What is it?" Charlotte asked, too frightened to worry about Odelia's irritation. "Why did you scream?"

Odelia stood and brushed off her dress. "That wasn't me." Her voice carried a note of superiority. "Elizabeth was the one who screamed."

But Odelia couldn't entirely hide the anxiety in her face as she glanced back the way she'd come.

Charlotte sucked in a breath. "Is she all right?"

She started in the direction of the scream, but she hadn't made it more than three steps before her eldest sister appeared, stalking through the trees with stiff dignity.

Charlotte raced to her side, grasping her arm. "Are you hurt?" She tried to examine her sister, but Elizabeth shook her off.

"I'm fine," she said shortly, glaring at Odelia. "I can't believe you abandoned me! I suppose you were hoping I would be eaten first, giving you a chance to escape."

Odelia turned pink but stuck up her chin defiantly. "Your legs work as well as mine. It's not my fault you froze."

"Eaten?" Charlotte asked, impatient with their bickering.

Both turned on her with a synchronized movement, glaring at the youngest. Charlotte winced. Elizabeth and Odelia might bicker at times, but they were barely a year apart and had always formed a united front when it came to her.

She sighed, but for once she was concerned enough not to back down. "Is there a dangerous creature about? I thought I saw something among the trees..." She trailed off, unable to think what predator might have been responsible for that flash of white.

"It was an enormous bear," Elizabeth replied in a small voice, apparently subdued by the memory. "A white bear."

"White?" Charlotte gasped. "I thought they only lived in

the far mountains! What was one doing down here in our valley?"

"As for that, who knows." Odelia looked at Charlotte with narrowed eyes. "But where were you?" She spoke as if she suspected her sister of setting the bear on them.

"I saw a flash of white earlier." Charlotte pointed toward a place between the trees. "I couldn't think what it might be."

All three young women turned to stare at the place she indicated, their earlier fear overwhelming their disharmony. Elizabeth and Odelia might have been pretending to be unaffected, but they were clearly still afraid.

Something moved between the trees, mostly out of view, but none of them could miss the glimpse of pure white. Odelia screamed, and all three sprinted away from the bear toward their house.

Elizabeth and Odelia soon outstripped Charlotte. Given her petite frame, she had never been a great runner. As she fell behind, she knew she should be afraid, but she couldn't help a surge of curiosity.

She glanced over her shoulder, scanning the trees for any glimpse of a snow-white bear. Did such a thing really exist? And, if so, what was it doing in her forest? In the five years her family had lived in the region, she had never heard tell of a brown bear in the area, let alone a white one. Could Elizabeth or Odelia have mistaken what they'd seen?

Her steps slowed even further, and she half turned. She knew she shouldn't look behind her while moving—she was going to walk into a tree if she kept it up—but she couldn't bring herself to blindly flee for home. It was rare for anything new or interesting to occur in this remote valley.

But her momentary courage fled the moment an enormous, white-furred shape lumbered out from between two trees. Her steps faltered and she stumbled to a halt, her mouth falling open. The creature was even larger than she'd imagined, and its fur seemed impossibly white for a wild creature. Charlotte herself never wore white, since the material didn't stay that way for long.

The bear lifted one foot to step forward, and her eyes caught on its long black claws. Her heart took off into frantic flight, and her muscles tensed, ready for her body to join it. But just as she sprang into movement, her eyes found the bear's.

Her breath caught. Objectively, they looked just like those of any bear, but there was something in the creature's expression that she couldn't dismiss.

She wanted to pause, even to reach toward the bear, but her body was already running. Within steps, trees blocked a clear view of the animal's face. She slowed, but the memory of the claws returned, and she shook herself. She must have imagined the look in the bear's eyes. There was no way an animal could display such sympathy, despair, and longing with a single glance.

She didn't look back again as she fled, and within minutes she had reached her family's wooden home. It was smaller than ideal for five people, and the paint was long since peeling, but at least the walls and door were sturdy. No wild animal had attacked the structure in the past, and there was no reason to think a bear would do so now.

She pulled on the door, meaning to fling it open and tumble inside, but it resisted her tug. Someone had latched it, although they didn't usually secure it during the day.

"Elizabeth!" she cried. "Odelia! Open the door!"

A shuffling sounded inside, and a crack appeared. Her

oldest sister's eye peered through, as if checking to see that Charlotte wasn't a bear speaking with the voice of a girl.

Charlotte huffed and pushed the door the rest of the way open, shoving her sister back. Lately her relationship with her sisters had regressed, and she had been restraining herself around them, but she was too irritated to hold it inside.

"You locked me out there? Are you serious? You were just going to leave me to be eaten?"

"I'm very thankful no one has been eaten." Her mother spoke with a faint trace of amusement. "But was there really such a need for concern? White bears in the forest sounds like one of your childhood tales, Charlotte, but I don't know what to make of it when all three of you claim you saw the creature!"

Charlotte winced. Her childhood claim that an invisible girl lived in a tower in the woods had been proven true in the end, but apparently she was never going to live down her reputation for being fanciful.

She directed an extra glare at her sisters, although neither of them was looking in her direction. It was partially thanks to her sisters that she had acquired the reputation in the first place. They had known the truth of the girl in the tower but had still taken delight in undermining Charlotte's claims. Her relationship with both Elizabeth and Odelia had seemed much improved in recent years, however, thanks to their leaving their old town behind and moving to such a remote area. But lately, it seemed as if nothing had changed after all.

"Perhaps you all imagined a bear," her mother said in a more comforting tone. "Sometimes the shadows among the trees can be positively fearsome."

The older two protested this suggestion, but their manner lacked the certainty Charlotte felt. Now that they were in the comfort and security of home, they were clearly both feeling ashamed of their reaction among the trees.

Charlotte shook her head stubbornly, however. "I saw it clearly. It was definitely a bear—and an enormous one too. I knew bears were large but not that large. And its color..." She shook her head. "It was such a pure white it would have hurt to look at its fur if the sun had been higher."

Neither of her sisters responded to her words, and her mother soon set them to chores around the house, separating Charlotte and her sisters in the process. It was an intentional act, Charlotte knew. Her mother was trying to give them space in the hopes it would soften the other two toward Charlotte. She had been doing similar things ever since the recent resumption of her sisters' old hostility—a change triggered by the celebration for their cousin's wedding.

But though Charlotte knew her mother meant well, she was tired of feeling alone and just wanted someone to take her side for once. It had been different in their old home. As young children, the sisters had been close enough, and by the time Elizabeth and Odelia pulled away from Charlotte, she had friends she could turn to in their place. When she was younger, she had solved the problem of her sister's growing animosity by escaping the house and them as much as possible, spending her time with her friends instead.

But it was different this time. When their father had first announced the family was moving to join his sister and her family in the far eastern valleys, Charlotte hadn't been too worried. Elizabeth and Odelia had complained that their destination was too remote, but the family had always lived in one of the remotest towns in Northhelm, so Charlotte had dismissed their complaints. The timing had even seemed perfect since her closest friend had just left the village.

But it turned out that the unscalable peaks forming the eastern border of Rangmere were even more remote than the forests of Northhelm. And while a number of secluded valleys were hidden in the lower part of the range, very few humans made those valleys their home. Charlotte had assumed they would at least have their cousins for company, but even they lived several hours' ride away. It had been a shock at first, and she had feared living in such an isolated way with only Elizabeth and Odelia for company.

But the isolation had worked to her advantage. It had been the presence of others that had first caused the issues in the sisters' relationship. First, the girl in the tower had chosen Charli as her closest friend, despite Elizabeth and Odelia being closer to Daisy in age. And afterward, the youths who caught her sisters' eyes had looked past them to their younger sister and the growing promise of her great beauty.

Elizabeth and Odelia, so close in age, had always been closer to each other than to Charlotte, and it had been easy for them to form an alliance against her. But in the valley, it was only the three of them, and her sisters had softened toward Charlotte, growing less distant and severe until she had even started to think of them as friends again, as they had been as children.

All of that seemed over, though. Their cousin had recently married, and everyone from three valleys had gathered for the occasion. There had been several new young men, recent arrivals to one valley or another, and it had also been the first gathering since Charlotte had turned eighteen. Since social customs decreed her birthday made her eligible for potential courtship, it had been a disastrous combination. Not one unattached young man had looked in the direction of either of her sisters, and in such an isolated living situation, that was too great a blow for them to bear.

Charlotte hadn't felt a connection with any of the young men, but it hadn't mattered. Before they even arrived home, all the progress of five years had been lost. Their memories of her supposed past crimes had reemerged, and Charlotte was back to being a source of resentment, an *other* her sisters could unite against. As the younger sister, she was supposed to wait her turn, not constantly steal the attention her sisters desired.

The door thudded open, and their father strode into the house, his cheerful smile banishing Charlotte's gloomy memories. If Charlotte had the qualities of a dreamer, she had inherited them from her father. It was no surprise he had followed the rumor of prosperity to a distant land—the true surprise was that he had remained settled in Northhelm for so long.

Looking back, Charlotte should have known it was the beginning of the end when a royal tour visited their old town. Not that her father bore any resentment toward King Richard or his heir, but a place visited by royalty was far too established to satisfy the explorer inside him—the one who wanted to carve order from the wilderness and uncover riches for his family in the process.

Her sisters still resented their father for ignoring their protests in favor of his own urge to go. But Charlotte couldn't maintain resentful feelings in the face of his obvious pleasure in their new home. He could never hide his joy after a day spent taming their land without another soul in sight, and she could rarely help smiling in response to his happiness.

His eyes fell on Charlotte first, standing closest to him. He immediately swept her into a hug, his bulky jacket emphasizing their size difference.

"Charli-bear!" He squeezed her as her broom dropped to the floor, and she buried her face in the soft leather of his jacket, barely holding back tears. Her father had his faults, but he was always warm and affectionate, and lately she had needed those qualities more than anything.

"You can't call her that anymore," her mother said in a tone of indulgent amusement. "The girls have seen a real bear in the forest."

"A bear?" Her father released her and stepped back, turning to look at Elizabeth and Odelia with a chuckle. "Here in the valley? It must have been a shadow you saw, although I'm sorry to hear you had such a fright."

He glanced at Charlotte, clearly as surprised as her mother that it was her sisters and not Charlotte spouting tales of a bear on the loose. And it was true that in the past she had shared her discoveries without first stopping to consider how credible they might seem to others.

A small, resentful part of her wanted to stay silent—or even to speak up in agreement that it had only been a shadow. She knew from bitter experience that her sisters wouldn't hesitate to undermine her in such a fashion. But the idea of being dishonest made her stomach squirm.

"Actually, it couldn't have been a shadow," she told her father. "It wasn't dark but white. I've never seen a creature with such pristine white fur."

She expected her father to protest, possibly even to laugh at her, but he did neither. Instead, a strange look passed over his face—an expression almost like fear. Charlotte frowned, but before she could question him, his smile returned.

"Well, well! I suppose anything is possible. These mountains must hold secrets unknown to any man. It is enough that he wasn't able to get his claws into any of you."

He gathered up his older daughters into the same hug he had given Charlotte, but they both protested and squirmed out of his grip.

"Tomorrow I'll check the closest sections of forest before you go out," he promised them. "If there is any sign of the creature, I'll drive it off."

He glanced at the enormous bow and arrow hung beside the door, and Charlotte felt an unexpected tug in her chest. The emotion she had imagined in the bear's face couldn't have been real, but she couldn't shake its lingering effects. It hurt with a melancholy ache to think of the majestic beast riddled with arrows, red blood marring his white fur.

"He wasn't aggressive," she said quickly. "I don't think he meant to hurt us."

Elizabeth and Odelia both shrieked protests at this suggestion, but her father looked at her with raised eyebrows.

"You don't wish me to drive it off?" He hesitated and then smiled. "I suppose you must feel a sense of kinship, Charli-bear."

Elizabeth sniffed loudly. She and Odelia had long ago insisted their father give up his childish nicknames for them, and Charlotte knew they looked down on her for allowing him to still use hers. But while she had submitted to the use of her full name in all other circumstances, she couldn't bring herself to reject her father's use of her old pet name. Every time she heard it, she felt warm, like being wrapped in a blanket made of affection and memories of happy times.

"I'll do my best to scare it away without harming it," her father said in a softer voice. "Indeed, I would prefer not to harm it. It is no small matter to fight a creature of that size, and who knows what the consequences would be."

He said the last part quietly, almost to himself, and he didn't seem to notice the odd look Charlotte gave him. Her mother's call for them to help prepare the evening meal interrupted the moment, and she lost the chance to question him further. But when she finally lay on her pillow, her ears full of her sister's even breathing, the image of the bear returned to her mind.

He had almost looked as if he would speak, and as she drifted off to sleep, she realized she would very much like to hear what he was going to say.

CHARLOTTE

She slept fitfully, her rest disturbed by strange dreams of snowy tundras and snarling bears. Consequently, she slept in, and by the time she woke, her sisters were fully dressed, bustling around their shared room while they muttered comments about lazy layabeds.

Charlotte rushed to catch up with them, stuffing herself into her clothes without even taking time to brush her hair. She rarely bothered to enhance her appearance in any way—her looks had been the cause of enough resentment as it was—but she preferred to present herself neatly, at least. She'd slept too late for that on this occasion, however.

But as she finally escaped into the forest, she acknowledged there was no need for tidiness. She wasn't likely to see anyone else all day. Especially since she was alone for once. Despite their father's reassurances, her sisters hadn't been brave enough to venture away from the house so soon after sighting the bear.

Her mother had looked once between her elder daughters and her youngest and declared she had plenty of tasks to keep

Elizabeth and Odelia occupied inside. And this time Charlotte felt nothing but gratitude for her mother's instinct to separate them.

She breathed in the fresh air deeply, glad to be free of the confines of the small house. But as she walked, she glanced back at her home and sighed. The only thing that had reconciled her sisters to their move was the promise that the family would be better off once they had land of their own in a region with plentiful resources. Her father had been full of stories of the wealth of the valley folk, as relayed by his sister.

But so far that wealth had failed to materialize. According to their father, it would be unlocked soon. He often claimed they just needed more time—time he gave cheerfully—before they would reap all the rewards the valley had to offer. But he was never clear about the source of the promised wealth, and the rewards had assumed a mythical status in Charlotte's mind.

For the moment, they were significantly worse off than they had been in the village. And this reality had likely only exacerbated the recent return of her sisters' resentment and ill temper. After days of celebration at the home of their much wealthier cousins, it had been difficult for all of them to come back to their own house, but her sisters had been the most affected. Elizabeth and Odelia might have directed their resentment toward Charlotte, but she was far from the only cause of their unhappiness.

Charlotte herself occasionally gave in to bouts of resentment, although she never seemed able to hold onto her irritation for long. She certainly didn't care about being wealthy—their family's needs were always met and that was enough for her. But she missed her old home and her friends there, and those feelings had grown hugely since the wedding and the subsequent alienation from her sisters. Would it have been so bad to stay in a village where they were known and valued, even if they were not among its wealthier inhabitants?

She tried to shake off the thoughts and instead enjoy her surroundings. Spring was finally shedding winter's grip on the landscape, buds poking up everywhere she walked. She watched them with pleasure, keeping a careful eye out for anything edible. After a winter of dried and preserved food, she was longing for greenery on their tables. She wouldn't be able to gather as much without her sisters, but she was determined not to come home empty-handed. Now that the last of the snow had melted, everyone was looking forward to a greater variety of meals again.

A flash of white once again caught her eye, and the jolt of excitement that shot through Charlotte made her admit what she had really been looking for. She froze, a distant part of her mind screaming to flee for the safe walls of home. Her feet didn't move, however. She knew she should feel fear, but curiosity burned more strongly. Despite everything, she had to know if she had imagined the expression on the bear's face the day before.

She barely breathed as he lumbered between two trees, moving in her direction. He hadn't seen her yet, and she rose on her toes, ready to run if he responded to her presence with aggression.

His large white head swung in her direction, his dark eyes fixing on her. Instantly he froze, reacting just as she had at the sight of him. It was such an unexpected reaction that the breath whooshed from her lungs, her muscles relaxing. More than anything, his surprise seemed so...human.

"You came back." The words were low and gravelly with a wild edge that hinted at their origin.

But even so, the sound was too shocking to be immediately understood. She opened her mouth, intending to exclaim in surprise, but only a squeak came out.

The bear blinked, still not moving closer.

"When I saw your father searching the woods with his bow this morning," the bear said, "I thought I had surely frightened you all away." Seeing his mouth move in time with the words made it impossible to deny the reality of what she'd heard.

The animal was speaking—and in perfectly intelligible words.

"You...you can talk," she said, her voice trembling.

The bear made such a terrifying rumbling sound that she nearly ran, but a certain brightness to his eyes gave her pause. Was he laughing?

"I'm sorry," he said. "I didn't mean to startle you, but I couldn't think of any other way to communicate."

"No," she said blinking, "I suppose not."

Silence fell as she tried to think what else to say. While she had never been excessively talkative like some children, she had rarely been at a complete loss. But what sort of conversation was one supposed to have with a bear? The entire interaction was inconceivable.

Or was it? Her thoughts stopped in their wild spinning as she remembered a story Daisy used to tell. The tale had been about a girl from a kingdom across the desert—a girl who had become a princess with the help of a talking cat.

According to the story, the cat had come from the High King's lands. It made sense, of course. Something as fantastical as a talking animal had to come from the Palace of Light. In fact, hadn't one of her cousins claimed to hear stories of a talking horse who had spent some time in Rangmere? Her cousin had never met the steed himself, but he had insisted the story was true. And in that tale, the creature had come from the Palace of Light as well. If the High King's lands contained a talking cat and a talking horse, why not a talking white bear?

She relaxed. It still didn't explain what such an animal was doing here, in their valley. But at least she was in no danger from a companion of the High King. However long his claws and sharp his teeth, no animal from the Palace of Light would eat a human.

At least, she didn't think one would.

She considered how to phrase a query about the bear's origins. She didn't want to offend him by appearing too suspicious.

"Aren't you afraid of me?" he asked while she was still debating the matter internally.

"Should I be?" she asked back, still marveling at the way his head cocked to the side in curiosity and at the intelligence in his dark eyes. It was no wonder she had sensed from the first that he was no ordinary bear.

"You have nothing to fear from me," he said promptly, and somehow his words comforted her, despite the deep, gravelly tone.

"Thank you." She offered him a small curtsy. She wasn't entirely sure if you were supposed to curtsy to anyone from the Palace of Light or only to the High King himself. But it seemed better to be safe than risk offending such a very large creature.

The bear dipped his head in response, seeming pleased with her action.

Silence fell again as she considered how she was going to tell this story to her family. She could already hear her sisters' ridicule. They would never believe the bear was friendly, let alone that it could talk. Especially not after their excessive—and apparently unnecessary—fear the day before.

She bit her lip.

"Does something trouble you?" The bear took several steps toward her before halting abruptly, as if he had suddenly realized she might not welcome his approach.

She smiled, touched by his thoughtfulness.

"It's nothing of importance," she said. "Merely that my sisters don't like me, and that's hardly new."

She blinked, surprised by her own words. Whatever had led her to blurt out her problems? She had to be badly starved of companionship if she was turning to a bear as her confidante.

He gazed at her with such quiet patience that somehow her mouth opened and more words poured out.

"I do nothing to antagonize them. Quite the opposite! But the two of them are so close in age and temperament, and they've always been willing to close ranks against me at the smallest perceived slight." She sighed heavily. "I thought we were making progress when we moved out here. I even began to think of them as friends. I guess that's why it hurt so much more when they turned against me this time. I've been doing my best not to provoke them, but it makes no difference when they're in this mood. They see fault in everything I do and say." Her voice dropped. "I suppose they don't need me. They have each other. But that leaves me all alone."

The day before, she would have said it was impossible for a bear to frown. But there was no denying his frown in response to her words. His intense gaze fixed even more closely on her face.

"I've been watching you all for days," he admitted after a

moment, making her start. "Even I, a stranger, have been able to see your sisters' feelings toward you." His eyes narrowed, and his voice dropped so low it was practically a growl. "Shall I teach them some manners?"

Her eyes widened, a strange rush washing through her—half fear and half imagined delight at the thought of the bear confronting her sisters. But she couldn't encourage the dark turn of his mood.

"Oh no!" she exclaimed. "You need to stay away from them! They're already afraid of you as it is. If you frighten them too badly, they'll never leave the house again."

"And then you'll have to gather food on your own," he said in a milder tone, looking disappointed. "I suppose that will only make everything worse."

She tried to hide her smile and didn't quite succeed. He sounded almost like a child denied a favorite sweet. But a moment later, he brightened, as if struck by a new thought.

He didn't speak, however, and her thoughts returned to his earlier words. He had been watching her and her sisters as they gathered food. Why?

She opened her mouth to ask him, but he spoke at the same time.

"What are the local wedding customs in this area?"

His unexpected words made her forget her own question entirely. She stared at him, unable to fathom what interest a bear could have in such matters.

"You want to know about our marriage customs?" she repeated, sure she must have heard wrong.

He shook his head slightly. "I don't care so much about the marriage itself, just the wedding. I know the customs differ in different regions."

She wasn't sure if his clarification made the question more or less strange.

"You really want to know how the people of the valleys do wedding ceremonies?" she asked, still unable to believe she'd understood correctly.

"Very much so," he said. "I've come here especially for that purpose."

She gaped at him. The bear had come all the way from the Palace of Light to research how different regions conducted wedding ceremonies? Was he traveling the entire Four Kingdoms, or only the remotest parts? Would he want to know about other ceremonies and celebrations as well?

She hoped he wouldn't ask her to explain a local funeral because she hadn't been to one since they moved from Northhelm. In fact, she only knew about weddings because of her cousin's recent marriage for which they had spent three days at her aunt and uncle's to join the celebrations.

Perhaps that was why the bear was asking her about weddings in particular. Had he overheard talk about a recent one in the area?

"Since the people of the valleys live so far apart," she said hesitantly, "we welcome reasons to gather together. Because of that, an occasion as joyous as a wedding is usually accompanied by a celebration of several days. That also gives the opportunity for young people to meet each other." She gave a small chuckle. "Otherwise there wouldn't be any future weddings."

The bear didn't smile in response, though. Instead, he looked disappointed. "The local weddings last for *days*?"

"Not the wedding itself," she rushed to assure him. "Just the celebration around it. The actual ceremony is short and simple. Valley folk work too hard to waste time and effort on weighty or expensive traditions."

The bear took another step forward, not seeming to notice he was doing so.

"A simple ceremony? What does it involve?"

She shook her head slightly, still utterly bemused. "The bride and groom hold hands in front of their family and friends and make their promises. They promise to support each other through life's joys and disappointments and to remain loyal. Then the parents each speak a blessing. And that's the whole thing. I know it's nothing like the elaborate ceremonies they hold in the cities, but it's accompanied by just as much joy and love."

"What if the parents don't approve?" he asked. "Or they're not able to be present? Can the ceremony happen without their blessing?"

Her forehead wrinkled. "Since the bride and groom have to be adults, it can still go ahead without the parents. It is merely customary to include them."

"An exchange of promises," the bear muttered to himself. "So simple."

Charlotte straightened, reading an insult in his words. "The people of the valleys might be simple folk, but they are good folk, for the most part. And they're certainly hardworking. Fancy gowns and elaborate speeches aren't the mark of good character."

The bear blinked at her, as if he was just as bemused by her as she was by him. Perhaps he hadn't meant his words as an insult after all?

"I know that well," he said in his rumbly voice. "It is merely the simplest wedding ceremony I have yet encountered. But I can assure you I am pleased to hear it."

He spoke as if he was well-traveled. Had he already been all around the Four Kingdoms for his research? Perhaps he had even been to the kingdoms across the desert or the ones across the sea. Although she couldn't imagine the white bear lumbering up a sand dune beside a camel string, nor could she picture him on the deck of a ship. Just the thought made her lips twitch upward.

But then an inhabitant of the Palace of Light probably had other means of transportation.

The bear seemed transfixed by the movement of her lips, and it occurred to her that he might think she was laughing at him. A twinge of guilt reminded her that she had been, in a way.

"Would you like to know about other local ceremonies?" she asked, contrite.

"Oh, uh, no, this is fine." He stumbled over his words for the first time since initiating the conversation. "I think," he added, "that there is someone else I need to speak to now."

"Oh, of course," Charlotte said, surprised at the strength of her disappointment. "I suppose I won't see you again, then. You'll be moving on to some other place soon." She peeped across at him, a little embarrassed, but not able to stop herself adding, "Won't you?"

"Yes," he said. "At least I hope so. I hope I may soon return home."

She nodded, telling herself she should be pleased for his sake. The note of longing in his voice told her he missed his home, and she could hardly blame him, given the tales of the Palace of Light.

"I hope your journey is smooth and swift," she said, giving a deeper curtsy than she had at the beginning of their conversation.

"And I hope all your troubles are soon resolved," he replied.

She smiled at him, once again touched. "Thank you, White Bear. It is kind of you to think of the troubles of an insignificant girl from the valleys."

"Insignificant?" He sounded thoughtful. "Are you? I wonder…"

For what felt like the hundredth time since meeting him, she was left in confused surprise at his words. But this time he moved before she could respond or question him further. With a final dip of his head, he swung around and disappeared back into the trees, moving faster and more quietly than she would have thought possible for such a large animal.

She stood watching the spot where he had stood far after the last glimpse of white fur had disappeared. Had she really just exchanged an extended conversation with a *bear*?

And what a strange conversation it had been.

She finally shook herself and turned north. She still had searching to do if she didn't want to return home empty-handed. And since she wasn't sure it was a good idea to tell her family about the bear, it would be better if she didn't provoke questions by coming home with nothing to show for her day's effort.

GWEN

Gwen stood in the doorway and surveyed the ballroom. It was full of people dancing and talking, and she wondered how it was possible to feel so alone while surrounded by so many people. Perhaps it was a special talent of hers.

"Gwendolyn." The sound of her full name on her mother's lips made her back stiffen.

She had vague childhood memories of liking her name. Princess Gwendolyn. It had sounded so elegant. But it had long since become a word that reminded her of responsibilities and unpleasant duties. And loneliness.

She knew all about how to behave properly as Princess Gwendolyn, but it felt like a role she slipped into in her mother's presence rather than something that actually belonged to her. And it was a role she always did alone. Was it really too much to ask that in this whole sea of people she might have one true friend?

She suppressed a sigh and pasted a smile on her lips. If she took any longer to enter the ballroom, her mother would say her name again but with an edge. And Gwen never liked what happened after Queen Celandine spoke to her with that edge.

If Easton had been there, he would have looked up at her from the mass of faces and smiled and just that would have been enough to drive back the loneliness. Gwen balled her hands into fists, hiding them in her skirts. Why was she thinking of Easton?

Usually she kept her thoughts under better regulation, but the errant memories of early childhood had brought him to the front of her mind. It wasn't that he ever completely left it, but she knew she had to keep him walled away from the surface of her thoughts. Otherwise she wouldn't be able to continue the grind of daily living without her mother throwing around phrases like *unnecessary melancholy* and *childish dramatics*. All said with the edge, of course.

Apparently, Princess Gwendolyn was not only not allowed to have friends, she wasn't even allowed to miss the one friend she used to have.

But now that Easton had pushed himself to the front of her mind, he wasn't easy to banish. She imagined the face of her lone childhood friend among the courtiers who smiled and bowed at her. She had to use her imagination because the last time she had seen him he had been only thirteen—on the cusp of manhood, but not yet with his adult face.

She had spent many solitary hours turning her memory of his childish features into an imagined adult face, and now it was haunting her. She should have listened to her mother and used her time more productively.

Except the responsibilities that fell to the princess of the mountain kingdom seemed to be universally dull. Her mother liked to talk of her duty and the position she would one day hold, but she never relinquished any actual power to Gwen.

Any decisions of note or consequence were made by the queen, and if she wanted to discuss them with someone, she always turned to one of her courtiers, usually Count Oswin, the most senior of her advisors. She would never ask Gwen's opinion—the princess wasn't even permitted to accompany her while she conducted royal business.

Which makes you wonder, what exactly is the point of it all? she thought, not for the first time.

At least Gwen was circulating in the crowd now which meant her mother was no longer looking in her direction with an expression that managed to convey expectant pressure without breaking a smile. Gwen had attended enough of these functions that she'd long ago mastered the art of moving through the crowd with an unhurried gait that still managed to convey a sense of purpose and direction. Not that she actually had anyone to seek out, of course. But looking as if she was moving toward a goal reduced the false pleasantries she was forced to exchange with people who would clearly rather have been talking to someone else. Anyone else.

She could hear their desire to escape the conversation in their strained voices and see it in the way their eyes darted to her mother after every few words. Even when her mother wasn't physically present, Gwen felt her specter hovering over every conversation she had with members of her mother's court. It was why she had long ago embraced solitude.

She passed a server circulating with a tray of drinks, and the briefest flicker of a smile from the older woman lightened Gwen's steps. She needed to remember that she wasn't entirely alone. She might not be able to talk freely with any of the courtiers, but they weren't the only people in the palace.

As if summoned by her disobedient thoughts, Queen Celandine appeared at Gwen's side.

"Would you like a drink, my dear?" she asked with a false smile.

Gwen gave a diffident response and accepted the drink her mother handed her. Why did the defiance in her mind never manage to translate to her words? No matter what her mother did, Gwen just went along with it, no matter how much she hated her own compliance later.

How many angry speeches had she composed in her mind, only to have them wither on her tongue? She tried to remember the last time she had truly spoken her mind, only to wince. More memories of Easton—and the worst sort this time.

She had never managed to entirely stop thinking of him, but she always tried to avoid remembering those awful days after he had disappeared. She had confronted her mother then, and the punishment had been terrible.

Before that, her mother had responded to defiance by confining Gwen to her room with only the barest of rations. Gwen had quickly learned that continued defiance meant she would be moved to smaller and smaller places of confinement and given less and less food, so even back then she had usually backed down quickly. But after the awful confrontation over Easton's disappearance, her mother had gone straight to a pitch-dark closet so small Gwen couldn't even lie flat, and she'd provided no food or drink whatsoever.

Gwen had believed she would die in there and might have done so if her mother hadn't relented and sent her a single glass of juice each evening starting from the second night. After several days in the dark, her mother believed she had succeeded in breaking Gwen's spirit, and sometimes Gwen thought her mother had been right. In the years since, she had certainly always capitulated at the first stage. Being locked in her room over a mealtime brought back too many memories of the closet for her to brave further escalation of the punishment.

But still, hidden deep inside, she protected a small flame of defiance. As long as it continued to burn, she could tell herself that Easton's Gwen still remained, not yet entirely subsumed by her mother's dutiful Princess Gwendolyn.

"You were late," her mother said, again without breaking the smile.

Gwen dared to give a small, audible sigh. Perhaps it was the effect of the memories.

"Why must we always have the balls in the afternoon?" she asked. "In the books I read, they happen at night. It would give everyone more time to prepare if we had them later, and they wouldn't interfere with the day's activities."

Her mother's eyes sharpened, and Gwen knew she had gone too far. Talk about nighttime always brought out the edge.

But her mother's response remained light. "But, my dear…" She ran gentle fingers over the frothy blue material of Gwen's gown. "You look so beautiful. Everyone does. What a waste to hide such magnificence in the darkness. You deserve to shine in the afternoon sun."

This time Gwen didn't let her sigh sound aloud. "Of course, Mother," she said dully. "I wouldn't want to prevent anyone gazing on their beautiful princess."

Her mother either didn't pick up or chose to ignore her irony. And when a courtier approached the queen, Gwen was able to escape entirely, considering herself to have gotten away from the interaction lightly.

Conversations such as those were the reason she couldn't indulge in thoughts of Easton. He had always brought out her true self—had made her feel brave—and there was nothing Queen Celandine hated more.

As soon as a small crowd gathered to talk to her mother, Gwen allowed herself to escape to the fringes of the room. She was tempted to hide behind one of the elaborate ice sculptures that decorated the edges of the ballroom, but it was safer if she remained in her mother's view. The queen always watched her most closely at this sort of event.

"I couldn't risk bringing my mother, of course," one of the courtiers said to another, catching Gwen's ear. "You know what she's like these days. She can't remember what she should or shouldn't say, and she keeps reminiscing about how things used to be before we were all—" He cut himself off.

His companion tsked, shaking her head. "Poor woman. You won't be able to bring her anywhere the princess might be now. Just imagine if she let the truth slip to Princess Gwendolyn! The queen would throw you all to the bears."

The original speaker winced. "One word on what has happened to this kingdom, and I tremble to think of the consequences. No, Mother will have to stay safely at home from now on."

Gwen stared at them transfixed. She knew the courtiers were uncomfortable speaking to her and that her mother was the reason for their discomfort. But it had never occurred to her that they might all be actively collaborating in keeping a secret from her. Or was it more than one?

What did the courtiers know?

She almost started forward, questions trembling on the tip of her tongue. But another courtier joined them, glancing at Gwen as he did so and giving a small, formal bow. The movement made the original two turn to look, expressions of horror transforming their faces when they saw how close Gwen stood.

They hurried into their own bow and curtsy, exchanging worried looks as they did so. Gwen attempted her warmest smile, trying to convey that they need not fear her. If they told her their secrets, she would never betray them to her mother.

Both of them responded to her expression, relaxing and shooting each other relieved looks. But her momentary swell of triumph died as they quickly turned back to their own small circle. Her smile had achieved nothing except to convince them she hadn't overheard after all. And from the alacrity with which they started another topic of conversation, she guessed they would never again risk saying something so revealing inside the palace walls.

As always, Gwen was left standing alone. But it felt different this time.

She looked slowly around the ballroom, heat bubbling up inside her. It started low in her belly and reached toward her throat. She had always been alone in crowds like this, and she had always wondered what was wrong with her to make it so. But suddenly she saw the scene in a different light.

What if the problem had never been with her at all? She had always known the palace held secrets, but she had never grasped the magnitude of the deception. It wasn't just the queen keeping things from her daughter but a conspiracy by the entire court. For so many people to keep a secret must have required a concerted effort of extreme proportions. No wonder the courtiers feared being caught in even a moment's conversation with her. They must have been living in fear of slipping up and saying something revealing.

Gwen had thought herself incapable of connecting with the people of her mother's court, but the fault hadn't been hers after all. It had been the courtiers who were actively working together to exclude her completely—from their friendships, their lives, even their simple conversations. Gwen might have lived in the palace and attended all the court events, but she existed in her own bubble, firmly outside the court itself. It must have been the only way to keep a secret so large.

She slowly turned to look toward her mother. She had no doubt about who had orchestrated her exclusion. But why? What was she hiding?

For a horrible moment, her stomach roiled as she wondered if it was because of her weakness and failings. The queen didn't want the court to know about the depth of her heir's flaws. But the face of Easton, which had plagued her since her arrival, flashed before her eyes again, and she stubbornly rejected the thought. Easton would never have befriended her if she was so terrible. Gwen might have faults, but she wasn't such a shameful heir that the queen would be forced to such lengths. Whatever secret lurked in the court, it was a secret being kept from Gwen, not from the courtiers.

Her feet kept walking as her mind worked, considering many things in a different light. Most of the courtiers had apartments in the palace as well as homes in the city, but she rarely saw children within the palace walls. She had always assumed the courtiers wanted to avoid bringing their youngsters to her mother's attention until they were old enough to be properly trained in respectful behavior. But perhaps they had a different reason for keeping them in the city where Gwen wasn't permitted to go. Children were notoriously bad at keeping secrets.

And the same explanation might account for why she never saw any of the mountain kingdom's regular citizens.

The palace was surrounded by a large city, but of its many inhabitants, only the courtiers ever visited the palace. Among her future subjects, Gwen knew only the courtiers, and her mother's guards and servants who lived inside the palace itself. She had always accepted that fact—initially because she was too wrapped up in Easton to care about anyone else, and later because she knew it would anger her mother to question anything. But the strangeness of it burned in her mind now.

Had her mother excluded her subjects from the palace because she feared what might happen if Gwen ever had a conversation with someone not utterly loyal to the queen? Did that mean Gwen was the only one of the mountain people not to know her kingdom's secrets?

The heat of fresh anger washed over her. What secret was so important that her mother had completely isolated her in order to keep it?

It's because you're too weak. It was her mother's insidious voice in her mind. *You're too weak to be trusted.*

But again, another memory swooped in to override it. *Come on, you can do it! If I can do it, so can you!* Easton's youthful voice was as clear as if he was speaking the words in her ear at that moment. She could even picture his easy smile, and the challenge in his eyes as he called her to match every feat of strength or dexterity that he attempted in the castle corridors. Gwen had sometimes doubted herself, but he had never done so.

Voices swirled around her, their words indistinct but alluring. The ball, which had seemed unutterably dull only minutes before, now sparked and fizzed. How many of the conversations hinted at truths she didn't know?

And most importantly of all—how was she going to uncover those secrets? She felt almost as alive as she used to when she ran, laughing, through the palace corridors, Easton always two steps ahead, and Nanny waiting for them with hot chocolate and warm cake. Discovering the conspiracy against her was the first step to laying it bare.

But for all Gwen's determination, and for all the conversations she sidled close enough to overhear, she learned nothing of note. No one else let any unwise words fall, and the topics that occupied them seemed even more dull than usual. She heard conversations about the weather—spring had started to reach the lower valleys, but it would still be a while before winter released their own vast basin, ensconced as it was by the deeper mountains. And she heard more than enough about who was dancing with whom and what gowns everyone was wearing.

Frustration filled Gwen, unalleviated by the frequent comments on her own beauty of both face and dress. It brought her no comfort to know the people of her kingdom admired her physical appearance even while they were afraid of speaking to her.

For once, the end of the ball brought disappointment instead of relief. Maybe if she had been able to hear more conversations, she might have stumbled on one of note. But at the same time, she was exhausted. Attempting to listen without appearing to do so was more straining than she had expected. Especially given how closely her mother watched her whenever she was among others. Gwen had always thought the queen was afraid of her daughter disgracing her, but that assumption, too, appeared in a different light now. Her mother wasn't afraid of Gwen—she was afraid of everyone else.

Had anyone ever tried to give her a hint? Gwen sifted back through a lifetime's worth of conversations, but nothing came to mind. In the early years she remembered only Easton, and in the last ten, her focus had been on avoiding her mother's disapproval. No one had broken through to her—she didn't even think anyone had tried. She wasn't the only one who feared crossing the mountain queen.

All through the evening meal—eaten in state with only the queen and her daughter present—Gwen racked her brain, trying to think of how she could uncover more information. Asking her mother outright was out of the question. Not only would that approach fail, but it would be far too dangerous. It had been years since she had been confined to the closet and left to starve, but she didn't consider herself safe from such treatment. Her mother would consider questions such as the ones that burned inside Gwen to be defiance of the highest order.

Gwen knew it would make no difference to her mother that she had officially been an adult for some years now. Gwen's age had never affected the punishments her mother meted out. And always there was the added horror of the unknown. Gwen still didn't know what had happened to Easton, and no one in the palace had ever been willing to speak of it. The queen had punishments Gwen didn't even know about.

No, talking to her mother was the last thing Gwen would consider.

And since the courtiers avoided conversation with her whenever possible, that left only one option. The servants.

Gwen shook her head in silent, stubborn denial of the title her mother gave to the people who served in the palace. In the privacy of her own mind, she would name them as they really were—captives.

She vaguely remembered a time when the palace had

employed regular servants from families in the city. But she could no longer remember any of their faces, except for Nanny who had been more family than servant. After Easton had left—when she had emerged from those terrible days in the closet, weakened and dazed—they had all been gone.

When she asked after them—dully, and without great interest—she was told they had been sent back to the city. But the palace couldn't function without servants, and so others had soon begun to appear. It was obvious from the beginning they were different. They spoke with unfamiliar accents, for one, and their faces shone with desperation and fear. It hadn't taken much to discover they were captives, valley folk snatched from their lives and carried off into the mountains to work for the mountain queen.

Gwen, cowed by her days of imprisonment and lost in grief at Easton's unknown fate, waited for someone else to protest this strange new state of affairs. But no one ever did. At least not anywhere that Gwen could hear.

Instead, the court buzzed with the news that a path had been found through the mountains. After generations of isolation, Queen Celandine's guards had forged the way, led by Count Oswin's youthful son. They had traded with the valley folk, bringing back delicacies and medicines that were entirely new to the mountain people, and the whole kingdom celebrated their success.

But as time passed, Gwen noticed it was only ever the guards and those most loyal to her mother who went on the trading trips, and it was only the queen who benefited from the new wealth coming into the kingdom. And every time her people returned, they brought new servants with them.

The mountain people traded with the valley folk in the open, but in secret they stole something from them worth more than goods and gold. Gwen could only assume the valley folk hadn't made the connection, since they continued to trade with her mother's people. Or perhaps there were so many valleys the mountain delegation could visit a new one every time? Gwen couldn't be sure, since the distant valleys were one of the many topics she was discouraged from asking questions about.

Thankfully the number of new arrivals had dwindled over the years, and there had been no new faces for the past two. As a consequence, Gwen knew all the captives by name and personality, but she still shied away from the idea of questioning them.

As captives, they could know nothing of her mother's secrets. There was no point in even asking. But even as she thought it, she knew it wasn't true. Servants had ways of discovering information never meant for their ears. She was making excuses to herself to cover her true fear. She didn't fear their ignorance, but rather the opposite.

It was one thing to think the courtiers had been conspiring against her—they were her mother's people and had been for as long as she could remember. But Gwen privately thought of the captives as her people. In a life of compliance, befriending the queen's captives was the one major defiance Gwen had managed to preserve, a secret that had escaped her mother's watchful eye. In the unwelcoming environment of the palace, Gwen had found the only people who had more reason to hate and fear her mother than Gwen herself did. And while she never openly defied her mother, it had comforted her to know that she had allies of her own.

If she found out now that her allies had been siding against Gwen and keeping their captor's secrets, it might break what little will she still had left.

So, even knowing the truth of her motivations, she still turned her mind to the courtiers instead of the captives. She determined to spend the whole night coming up with avenues of conversation that might trick the courtiers into revealing what she wanted to know.

But, as always, despite the most earnest resolutions, she had barely laid her head on the pillow before she was waking up to bright morning sunlight.

Groaning, she drove her fist into her soft mattress. Was the secret they were all hiding that their princess was gravely ill? She had always slept deeply, even as a child, and Nanny had assured her it was normal for children to be shut in their rooms before it even got dark and expected to stay there until morning. But what sort of adult still needed as much sleep as they ever had as a child? Was it even healthy?

She had tried raising the matter with her mother, but no topic related to nighttime was ever acceptable to the queen. She expected Gwen to sleep and to not ask questions about it. Given all the other things Gwen wasn't allowed to question, her mother's insistence had never seemed especially odd. But now it made Gwen even more suspicious.

On the other hand, if she really was ill—even dying perhaps—what purpose could her mother have in hiding it? If it was any other mother, Gwen might have suspected she was motivated by compassion. Nanny might have kept such a secret in the years before her passing. The elderly woman had been the kindest soul Gwen had ever met, and she wouldn't have been able to bear delivering such news to her beloved charge. But it was impossible to consider her mother in such a light. The queen considered compassion a failing. At least, she had always seen it as such in Gwen.

Which led her back to where she started. If the whole of

the kingdom was keeping a secret from her, there must be a reason for it. And if she was to discover that reason, she needed to find someone who could be tricked or cajoled into sharing it with her.

But after spending the daylight hours prowling the corridors of the palace, searching for people to gently interrogate, Gwen was forced to rethink her plans. She had spent so long doing everything possible to avoid the people of her mother's court that she had never realized how skilled they were in avoiding her.

It hadn't only been her melancholy talking when she bemoaned the emptiness of the palace halls. They truly were almost deserted. And when she did manage to corner someone, they slipped away like water between her fingers. She had planned some conversation gambits over breakfast, but she never even got as far as attempting them.

The stark gray stone of the walls and floor mocked her, reminding her inescapably of her mother as she walked dejectedly back toward her room. Gwen would have chosen to alleviate the cold bite in the air with warm colors and soft materials—both on the walls and underfoot. But the queen preferred an austere look.

"Are you all right, Your Highness?" a timid voice asked from behind her.

Gwen ceased her contemplation of the empty wall and swung to look at the newest addition to the palace captives. Not that Miriam could really be counted as new after being at the mountain palace for almost two years. But she still felt new since it had taken the girl over a year to work up the courage to address the princess. And, even now, she still looked around like a startled rabbit before daring so much as a word.

Not that Gwen could blame her. She sometimes felt like a startled rabbit who had wandered into the palace herself. But Gwen had been willing to persist because Miriam was the closest captive to her own age, only a few years younger by her estimate.

"I'm fine," Gwen said by habit before remembering she wasn't fine at all. But it seemed too late to take the words back, so she let them stand. "I was just contemplating how lovely this wall would look with a large tapestry hanging on it. And perhaps a carpet underfoot in matching colors? What do you think?"

Miriam cocked her head, examining both the wall and the floor with due seriousness.

"It would be more work to clean," was her eventual conclusion, the words delivered simply and without rancor.

Gwen blinked. "Yes, I suppose it would be. I didn't think of that."

She watched the younger girl vigorously scrub the window on the opposite wall for a moment before speaking impulsively.

"Miriam, am I ill?"

Miriam's rag stopped moving. "Ill, Your Highness? Are you not feeling well? Should I call for the royal doctor?"

"No, no." Gwen shook her head impatiently. "I feel fine right now. I mean something bigger."

Miriam stared at her as if she'd lost her mind, and Gwen couldn't help laughing at herself. She must sound unhinged. She started again, trying to talk with more sense.

"I feel perfectly healthy. But I'm concerned that I sleep so deeply every night and for so long. I'm wondering if it might be a sign of some illness of which I'm unaware? Perhaps everyone is keeping the truth from me in order not to upset me?"

Miriam's eyes widened. "Surely not, Your Highness! Could you really be so ill and not know it?"

Gwen shrugged. It was clear from Miriam's reaction that she had no idea what Gwen was talking about.

"I don't know." She sighed and slumped onto one of the chairs lining the inside wall. "Never mind. It was probably a silly thought anyway. I just hate the feeling that I've lost so many hours. I'm sure someone could steal into my chamber in the night and make off with every one of my possessions, and I wouldn't rouse."

Miriam frowned, her expression concerned. "I would offer to watch over your sleep, but…"

Gwen grimaced, feeling instantly guilty for her complaints. It was rare for one of the servants to speak of nighttime—it would be bad enough if they were caught talking to the princess, but much worse if it was of forbidden topics—but Alma had explained the full situation to Gwen once. The older woman had been among the first captives and had been the first to take pity on the numb, bewildered girl who had taken to roaming the corridors alone once she had lost both Nanny and Easton.

Alma had explained in a hushed whisper that the captives were given free rein of the palace during the day—they needed it to complete their duties, and it wasn't as if there was anywhere for them to run. Tall mountains encircled the deep valley that held the mountain palace and the city that surrounded it. No one in the city would hide the captives, and only the queen's people knew how to find safe passage through the mountains. Even Gwen herself didn't know how they had succeeded when previous generations had failed, and Alma said the captives were all drugged for the journey in, so they didn't know either. Without knowledge of the route or even appropriate provisions, the mountains would be a death sentence.

And yet, despite the natural forces that kept the valley folk captive in the palace, at night they were locked into a small group of connected storage rooms—ones that were built into the basement level of the palace and lacked even windows. Once the sun was down and the court was abed, the queen didn't want her captives roaming free.

During the day, the queen liked to pretend her captives were regular servants—a charade she expected them to uphold as well. But at nighttime, they were reminded of their true status. Perhaps it was why Gwen had always felt so connected to them. Since Easton's disappearance, she had often felt like a captive in the palace herself. But still, she felt bad to have compared her own experience to Miriam's, however unintentionally.

Miriam resumed polishing the window, but she continued to throw worried glances at the princess. And when she spoke, her words echoed Gwen's own thoughts.

"I wish I could help you at night, but I suppose we're both captives in the hours of darkness—me to a locked door and you to sleep." She paused, shivering. "Perhaps it's for the best, given the rumors."

Gwen bolted upright, her eyes fixed on Miriam. "Rumors?" she cried, only just remembering to modulate her volume. "What rumors?"

Miriam froze, her eyes widening and her expression growing terrified. "Wh...What? Rumors? I don't know anything about any rumors!"

"Miriam!" Gwen hissed. "You know something! Clearly you do! Tell me at once!"

Miriam stared at her, looking more like a startled rabbit than ever, except now she was caught in the gaze of a predator.

Gwen had the grace to feel ashamed, but she wouldn't let the dropped hint go. She couldn't. She needed answers, even if she had to press Miriam into giving them to her.

But footsteps around the corner shattered the moment. Their approach was rapid, and she barely had time to throw herself back into her chair before the newcomer appeared. Gwen smiled and nodded to the courtier, even as she watched Miriam out of the corner of her eye. Miriam had resumed polishing the glass at a feverish pace, her back to the princess, but Gwen still caught the telltale flush in her cheeks. Her eyes narrowed. Miriam definitely knew something she didn't want to tell the princess.

But the courtier paused, shifting uncomfortably as his eyes flashed from Gwen to Miriam. He might not have been comfortable in the princess's presence, but he clearly knew his duty. He obviously wasn't going to continue on, leaving the princess adjacent to such low company.

Gwen tried to wait it out, but as the man blustered through a series of increasingly terse attempts to get her moving, she gave up, putting all three of them out of their misery by agreeing to accompany the man in search of her mother. But once they found her, Gwen couldn't free herself again, and before she knew it, the evening meal had begun.

This time they ate in the presence of a select group of courtiers, including both the man who had *rescued* her and Count Oswin. Since the count was her mother's most senior advisor, he was always present at such affairs, but the other man was a surprise. Lord Rafferty, as he was apparently called, was a junior enough member of the court that Gwen couldn't remember ever meeting him before, although his face was vaguely familiar.

He had certainly never eaten with them before, and she could only assume his sudden inclusion was a reward for his meddlesome surveillance of her. The thought stung, although it shouldn't have come as a surprise given what she now knew about how her mother had been using the court against her. It wasn't much of a step from alienation to surveillance.

Gwen stuffed down her resentment, squishing her feelings away until there was no outward sign of them, as she had so often done before. She had no desire to attract her mother's attention, especially in the presence of guests. At least with the others present, she would be excluded from the conversation and could thus avoid having to converse with her mother.

As the meal progressed, her mind turned to more helpful topics, and she found herself extra grateful to be left to her own thoughts. In the corridor, she had been focused on Miriam's mention of a rumor—a topic she intended to pursue again at first opportunity. But in the time since, something else had occurred to Gwen, and as she ate, she was free to consider it from every angle.

Miriam had said they were both captives at night, and she was right. For the hours of darkness, neither the queen nor her courtiers watched them, believing both the princess and the valley folk to be safely shut away behind doors. But what if they were shut behind the same door?

If Gwen snuck into the storage rooms with the captives for a night, they could help keep her awake. Behind a locked door, they would have hours to talk freely without fear of discovery or notice.

The idea captivated her. Why hadn't she thought of it sooner? All she had to do was stay awake past sundown when the captives were locked away. Once darkness fell, she could creep through the palace to their prison. Given she and Easton had secretly appropriated a master key for the palace —to enable them to roam it freely—getting past the locked door shouldn't present a problem. Even if she eventually fell asleep—which she inevitably would, she was sure, even with assistance—Alma or Miriam could wake her before dawn so she could sneak back into her own room.

The hardest part of the plan would be staying awake long enough to sneak through the palace. She sometimes remained awake for a few minutes past her normal bedtime, but to succeed with her plan, she might need to last as long as half an hour.

As she considered the difficulty, she pushed her food around on her plate. How little could she get away with eating? A full stomach always made her drowsy, so perhaps hunger pangs would help keep her alert.

It wasn't as simple as not eating, however. She had long ago learned that her mother wouldn't permit her to boycott a meal altogether. She needed to walk a fine line—consuming just enough to satisfy her mother without coming close to filling herself.

Thankfully the guests took enough of the queen's attention that she didn't notice her daughter's tiny mouthfuls or how much of her movement was just shifting food around on her plate. And somehow the small amount she ate only made Gwen hungrier than she had been when the meal began.

She even limited the amount she drank, knowing the rich drinks favored by her mother would fill her stomach as easily as food. In a further stroke of luck, Alma was serving that night, and she seemed to pick up that Gwen was eating lightly on purpose. She whisked each plate and glass aside quickly before the queen could notice how full they remained.

Gwen wished she could whisper something of her plan to Alma, but she didn't dare try even the most subtle communication when she was at her mother's table.

Her fingers tightened around the handle of her fork, squeezing until her knuckles whitened. It didn't matter how many years passed. She might be a woman in her twenties now, but she was still trapped as a child beneath her mother's watchful eye.

But the surge of anger was accompanied with a familiar

impotence. Her mother wasn't merely Gwen's parent but the queen, and there was no one in the mountain kingdom who would gainsay her. The princess really was just as trapped as the captives, hemmed in by the same mountains that restrained them.

When the meal finally reached its end, Gwen surged to her feet and gave the necessary curtsy to her mother. The queen's eyes narrowed slightly at her daughter's hasty exit, but she let her go unchallenged. Gwen made it two corridors over before she put her back against the wall and sucked in several deep breaths.

Closing her eyes, she continued to breathe slowly, reminding herself that the walls of the palace weren't closing in on her. They remained exactly where they had always been. And her mother wasn't all-seeing. It might feel like it on occasion, but Gwen had successfully kept her connection to the captives a secret from her. She could keep other secrets too. She could defy her mother's iron reign.

A tug on her dress made her eyes fly open, her heartbeat skyrocketing with the irrational fear that her mother had somehow sensed her thoughts. But the girl tugging on her was unfamiliar, and she immediately fell back when she saw Gwen's wide-eyed expression, her own face flushing a deep red.

"I…I'm sorry, Your Highness," the girl stammered. "I didn't mean…That is, I didn't…" Her words grew so tangled that she stopped altogether.

"Who are you?" Gwen asked as her heart returned to a more normal rhythm.

The girl didn't look much older than fourteen, and Gwen didn't think she'd ever seen her before. She wasn't one of her mother's courtiers, but neither was she one of the captive servants.

With a start, Gwen realized she must be one of the mountain kingdom citizens—an inhabitant of the city who lived in one of the houses surrounding the palace but was never invited inside it.

Curiosity spiked inside her. The queen sometimes paraded through the city streets, her daughter in tow, and the populace obediently lined the streets to see their ruler pass by. But Gwen had never been permitted to walk through the city or interact with any of its inhabitants. Often she forgot about their existence altogether, except as a vague concept.

The girl shook her head, swallowing visibly as she began to back away. "I'm sorry," she said in a tumbled rush. "I'm sorry. I shouldn't have come. Of course I shouldn't have. I didn't mean any harm. I—"

"Stop!" Gwen surprised herself by producing the same commanding tone her mother employed so effectively.

Sure enough, the girl froze, her eyes somehow growing even larger and her face even redder.

Gwen softened her voice. "I won't hurt you." She added a stern note of warning. "But the palace isn't a safe place for you. You mustn't approach anyone else, and you mustn't let the queen see you. Can you do that?"

The girl nodded, her lips pressed together, and her eyes fixed on Gwen.

"What's your name?" Gwen asked gently.

The girl shook her head this time, still not speaking, and Gwen sighed. Given the warning she had just delivered, could she blame the girl for not wanting to identify herself?

"Very well," she said. "Don't worry about a name. I'm Princess Gwen."

"Gwen," the girl said, as if testing it out and liking how it sounded.

Gwen smiled at her. "It must have taken a lot of courage for you to come here. Surely you didn't come to find me?"

"Mother always told me stories about the mountain princess who lives in the palace and is more beautiful than any other. The one who will someday save us."

Gwen laughed uncomfortably. "Well, some of that is true, at least. I am a princess, and I do live in the palace."

"I thought…I thought surely a princess would have the power to help us," the girl whispered. "Mother doesn't know I'm here, but I had to come. Can't you help us?"

She stared at Gwen pleadingly as Gwen tried to make sense of her words. First the girl had spoken of being saved, and now she was asking for help. But for whom? Did she mean her family specifically?

"I…I would like to help you," she said cautiously. "I would like to help any of my people who are in trouble. But what exactly is the problem?"

"We've barely made it through the winter." The girl's voice trembled. "Spring will be here soon, but it will still be a long time before any crops can be harvested. And now the taxes are to be raised again? If the queen truly means to go through with it, we'll all of us starve!" She finished on a crescendo, only to look up and down the corridor nervously, her expression sheepish.

From her reaction, Gwen guessed she was dramatizing the situation, in the way that was common for children her age. From the look of her, she wasn't on the edge of starvation. But at the same time, it seemed equally clear that the people faced genuine hardship. The girl wouldn't have mustered the courage to sneak into the palace in search of the princess if that wasn't the case.

"Will you really starve?" Gwen asked, testing her.

As she asked, the small amount of food she had consumed roiled in her belly. It might have been the end of winter, but there was no shortage of provisions for those who lived in the palace. To her shame, she couldn't have even said when the new season's harvest would arrive. Autumn, winter, or spring, their tables were laden just the same.

"Maybe not," the girl admitted. "But soon we won't be able to afford mother's medicine."

"Your mother is ill?"

The girl nodded. "It's a chronic condition, and the medicine comes from the far lands."

It took Gwen a moment to realize she must mean her mother needed the medicine brought back by the queen's traders. It wasn't hard to guess that her mother charged the people high prices for anything that came from the valleys.

"I see." Gwen stared at the girl for a moment before reaching a sudden decision. "Come with me."

She led the girl down the corridor and into her room, moving quickly. It was best for the girl to be gone from the palace as soon as possible.

Rummaging through her cabinet, Gwen found the small leather pouch she had hidden at the back. For a few seconds, she hesitated, feeling the meager weight of it in her hand. The coins inside were few given how many years she had been collecting them—hoarding them against her dream of one day leaving the mountains. She had saved the first coin the year Easton disappeared, but her stash had only grown slowly.

But it was a hollow dream. In the depths of her heart, Gwen had always known that. She was never going to escape.

Never. So there was no point in the coins gathering dust in her cabinet.

She held the pouch out to the girl, a swift movement, as if she feared her hand might disobey her and snatch them back. The girl squeaked, staring at the pouch hungrily before reaching out tentatively to accept it.

"Thank you, Your Highness," she breathed. "You are as generous as my mother's stories always claimed."

Gwen smiled, but it was a tired expression. "I'm sorry I can't do more. I'll see what I can do about the taxes but…"

Even as she was speaking the words, she knew the dispiriting truth. There was nothing she could do. She hadn't even known her mother was planning to raise them—or that she had apparently done so several times before by the sound of it. She wasn't included in those sorts of decisions. She was powerless.

The girl curtsied deeply and thanked her again before moving to the door. Her hand was on the knob when Gwen called for her to stop, an idea striking her.

She hurried over to join her. "I'll help you leave. If someone spots you on the way out…" She trailed off, reading in the girl's face that she didn't need a reminder of the danger she was in.

What Gwen didn't add was that accompanying the girl out would benefit Gwen as well. Despite the late hour, she didn't feel in the least sleepy. Usually, her eyelids would be drooping by that point, but the surge of energy from the girl's unexpected appearance had driven away the fatigue. And surely creeping through the corridors and grounds would only continue that effect.

Gwen gestured the girl back and opened the door, peering outside into the corridor. There was no one in sight, so she slipped through, signaling for the girl to follow. She obeyed, tiptoeing behind with a thrilled look on her face that made Gwen want to laugh. How many of the girl's childhood imaginings were being fulfilled in that moment?

But Gwen was no longer prone to the dramatic swings of emotion that plagued children on the edge of youth, and she had a clearer idea of the danger. If the son of courtiers could disappear without a trace, how much more easily could the queen dispose of a girl from the city? Gwen couldn't let herself forget it wasn't a game.

They had almost made it to the closest exit when she heard voices. Sweeping the girl along with her, she fled through a nearby door. It led into a small storage space filled with cleaning supplies. Gwen knew the closet was there because she had seen the captives use it—she was just glad it hadn't been locked.

With the door closed, it was completely dark inside, and Gwen stood with her hand over the girl's mouth. It was probably an unnecessary move, but she couldn't help the tension flooding her. She had already been afraid for the girl, but being enclosed in the dark closet sent fear flooding through her at unmanageable levels. Only the contact with another person was keeping her from falling off the edge and plunging into uncontrolled panic.

Somewhere, distantly, she registered that the voices had faded. But her limbs remained locked in position, her mind too occupied with holding back the panic to manage proper thought. It was so dark, and she could feel the shelves pressing in tightly on her.

But she wasn't alone. She clung to that thought, hearing the scrape of the girl's breathing in the darkness and feeling the warmth of her presence. She wasn't alone. She wasn't being punished.

The girl pulled away, startling Gwen from her stupor. A crack of light appeared as the girl inched the door open, and Gwen's panic receded, leaving her feeling foolish.

"We need to keep moving," the girl whispered, sounding nervous. "I have to be home before dark."

Gwen nodded, hoping the girl hadn't noticed anything odd in her behavior. Shaking herself, she pushed the door the rest of the way open, taking the lead again.

The corridors stayed clear the rest of the way to the external door, and when she pulled it open, the girl rushed through. She paused to wave farewell to the princess, but Gwen shook her head and followed her outside. The girl wasn't safe until she was out of the extensive gardens that surrounded the palace. And the cool air of early evening would help drive away the sleepiness that had settled in the wake of Gwen's earlier panic.

As they walked along gravel paths between carefully sculpted bushes and beds of flowers, she glanced back at the building. Everyone always referred to it as a palace, but it had none of the lightness of the palaces in the storybooks of her childhood. It had the necessary size and turrets, but no bright flags waved at the top of them, and the dour gray stone gave it a stern look she had always hated. It seemed better named as a castle—or even a fort—than a palace. But her mother called it a palace and everyone else followed suit, playing into the fantasy her mother liked them all to enact—the one where she was a beloved monarch, her servants had chosen their positions, and Gwen was her loving, cosseted family.

Distracted by her thoughts, she nearly didn't hear the crunch underfoot as a patrol of guards neared their position.

They were so close to reaching the palace boundary, but they weren't quite there, and there was no time to conceal them both.

Acting without thought, she shoved her companion hard. Caught by surprise, the girl staggered sideways and fell between two bushes. The greenery grew close enough together that the shadows covered her in the darkness. Turning in the same movement, Gwen reached for an early rose bud, a smile fixed on her face.

The guards came into view, both halting for the span of a breath before hurrying toward the princess. Their hands rose to their sword hilts only to fall away again when they got close enough to confirm her identity. But their expressions didn't relax.

"Your Highness!" the older of them said, sounding disapproving. "You shouldn't be out here."

"But the first of the roses are starting to bloom," Gwen said as innocently as she could.

"Your Highness, you need to go inside," he said more firmly.

A slight rustle from the bush beside them made the second guard start to turn. She grabbed his arm, smiling inanely up at him.

"How could I sleep on such a beautiful night?"

The young man threw his superior a panicked look, and the older man pulled Gwen off more roughly than she had expected. But at least his firm hold on her arm drove off the sleepiness that had started to weigh her down.

She still threw him a shocked look, however. "Captain!"

He didn't loosen his hold. "It's nearly dark, and you need your sleep."

A stab of excitement sharpened her senses, driving the

sleep even further away. They had strayed onto the topic of nighttime, and though she was sure to suffer for this episode later, it would be worth it if she could reveal another piece of the puzzle.

"There's nothing dangerous about darkness," she said boldly. "I'm still within the palace grounds."

"Your Highness has no idea," the man said gruffly. "Nowhere is safe at night."

Gwen raised both eyebrows. He talked as if there were rabble at the castle gates waving pitchforks. Although given what she had just learned about the taxes, perhaps there soon would be. Gwen had helped one family today, but she was painfully aware there had to be many others with equally compelling needs in the city.

She pushed that thought down, however, focusing on the guard. "Please," she said as sweetly as she could manage, "enlighten me."

The younger man threw his superior another panicked look, this time encompassing the rapidly darkening sky in his glance.

"We have to hurry," he said, not speaking to her.

"Whatever for?" she asked brightly. "I don't feel at all sleepy yet. And I know the way well. I wouldn't lose my way even in pitch black." She smiled from one to the other. "And you two brave soldiers can accompany me to keep me safe."

They appeared not to hear her, too busy conducting a silent conversation comprised of their eyes and several expressive grimaces. At the end of it, they seemed to reach a consensus.

Still not addressing her, the other guard took her remaining arm in an equally firm grip as they hustled her along the path. When she exclaimed and tried to break free, they only tightened their hold, almost lifting her feet from the ground to hurry their passage.

Gwen managed a single glance back over her shoulder and caught sight of the girl slipping out of the bushes and running for the castle boundary. At least she had succeeded in distracting the guards. But she was going to have bruises to show for it in the morning. She had never expected castle guards to dare manhandle the princess in such a manner.

She swallowed down a lump of actual fear. Whatever had spooked them, it had to be more serious than she had realized. Just what happened in these grounds at nighttime?

She ceased struggling, but they didn't slow or even loosen their grip. Her fear increased, and she wondered if they meant to haul her straight to her mother. If so, she would need an excuse for going outside that was more believable than a sudden desire to see the roses.

But Gwen's mind had stopped working, frozen in a state of confusion and fear, as it had done in the closet. The morass only lifted when it became clear they were heading for her bedchamber. By the time they shoved her inside, she had gathered herself enough to at least recover her balance before she fell.

She turned, meaning to protest, but the door was already being firmly closed behind her. Angry, she stomped over and pulled it back open. The guards, already part way back down the corridor, didn't pause or even look back. Despite their cowardly retreat, Gwen didn't risk stepping out of the room. Instead, she contented herself with glaring fire at their backs.

When they had disappeared around a corner, she reluctantly closed the door. At least the trip outside had used up much of the wait before she could enact her plan. But it was still too early to leave her room—especially given what had just happened. The guards might yet be fetching her mother.

She waited, sitting bolt upright on the edge of her bed in expectation of the queen sweeping into the room at any moment. But as the minutes passed without the door opening, she couldn't maintain the alert expectancy.

She tried to hold onto the earlier thrill of creeping through the palace, but it had faded beyond her reach. She pulled up her anger instead, gently exploring the burgeoning bruises on her arms. But even the anger felt distant and hard to reach.

Her blinks became longer, the weights on her eyelids making them harder and harder to open. Her thoughts grew muddled, no longer following logical threads but jumping erratically and chasing down nonsensical tracks. Several times she jerked, her whole body jumping as she pulled herself back from the verge of sleep.

Defiantly, she forced herself to her feet, crossing over to open the curtains as wide as they would go, letting in a wash of moonlight. She pressed her cheek against the cold of the windowpane, the shock of it driving back the heaviness for a moment.

But the sensation lost its effectiveness too quickly, her limbs growing as heavy as her eyes. The sweet lure of sleep was harder and harder to resist with each passing second. Giving in to it would feel so blissful.

She slipped down to curl on the broad window seat, her hands reaching instinctively for one of the cushions and putting it under her head. Despite everything she had tried, she couldn't fight the sleep that always overtook her. It was a river, and she was drowning.

She woke with a start and the certain knowledge that something was different. It took her a moment to realize what it was. She had slipped off the window seat, landing on the floor with enough force to pull her out of sleep before the sun rose. Gwen couldn't remember the last time she had woken when it was still dark.

Excitement flooded her, fighting against the pull that tried to drag her back beneath the waves of sleep. There were still hours of the night left. She could still seek out the captives.

It was difficult to keep her eyes open, though, and she let them drift most of the way closed as she wrestled her sleep-heavy limbs into compliance. She felt as if she were fighting for control of her own body, but her determination drove her forward, and she crawled toward the door on all fours. By the time she reached it, her eyes had drifted shut again, but she was still forcing herself to move. It was too warm in her room. If she could just get out into the cold corridor, she would wake up enough to get to the captives.

Feeling blindly up the wood of the door, she found the handle. But it wouldn't turn. Her door was locked.

She slumped against the floor, despair filling her. Had the guards returned to lock her in? Was this the result of her small defiance?

A worse thought flashed through her mind. Had her door always been locked, and she had simply never noticed?

Following on its heels was another thought that rapidly grew into certainty when she combined it with the strange behavior of the guards. She had feared that everyone was keeping a secret about her, but whatever was happening was bigger by far. Something dangerous was happening in the palace at night. Something big.

She tried to hold onto the thought as sleep claimed her again.

CHARLOTTE

In the end, Charlotte did cut her foraging short but not because of her encounter with the bear. As the day wore on, gray clouds rolled in, and the afternoon became darker and darker.

She turned for home much earlier than usual, unnerved by the way day appeared to be descending into night hours too early. She was glad for her forethought when the heavy clouds released their wet load just as she ducked through the front door.

To her relief, her father was there ahead of her, although he had also planned to be out all day. He had probably read the change in the weather more quickly than she had and known what was coming. Even after five years, the sudden storms in the valley still took Charlotte by surprise.

"Charli-bear!" he exclaimed. "I was about to put my jacket back on and go out to find you. It looks like this will be a bad one."

She slipped her own jacket off and hung it on the hook by the door. "I should have turned back sooner, but I'd just found a pocket of wild mushrooms, and I wasn't sure I'd remember where to find it again."

She unpacked her load, laying it across their large wooden table. Her mother made several pleased sounds as she began to sort the delicacy, muttering to herself about what dishes she would make. Watching her made both Charlotte and her father smile.

"You turned back soon enough," he said. "All is well. And now we may enjoy a few snug hours together." He beamed, looking delighted at the prospect. While he never shirked the endless list of tasks waiting for him and seemed to genuinely love the valley, his favorite moments were ones like this, where the weather trapped them all together inside their cozy home.

Charlotte tried to feel the same enthusiasm. A few months ago, she would have at least been glad for the extra time with her father. But her sisters' frosty reception—they still hadn't even greeted her—reminded her that the painstaking ground she had won with them had all been lost, and her home was no longer a comfortable place.

Thoughts of her relationship with her sisters reminded her of her conversation with the bear. She knew she should tell her father about it, but she couldn't bring herself to speak of the strange meeting. Better her sisters be silent than speak up in ridicule.

She moved toward her mother, intending to help her with her food preparation, but Elizabeth leaped in before she could get there. Odelia followed with a contemptuous look at Charlotte, as if she had been lazing about all day instead of working hard like them.

Something bubbled up in Charlotte, and for once she wanted to speak up to defend herself, even knowing it would do no good. But her mother threw her a sympathetic look, clearly pleading with her to keep the peace, and Charlotte subsided, remembering they were all stuck inside together for the foreseeable future. As much as she would have liked to hear her mother defend her aloud for once, she was probably right that it wouldn't be worth it.

Sighing, Charlotte turned to the sewing basket instead. At least she had enjoyed her solitary wanderings, so maybe she really had enjoyed a nicer day than her sisters. She took a seat by the fire and was soon joined by her father, a block of wood and a carving knife in his hands.

He smiled at her, the quiet scene clearly filling him with contented joy. And glancing from him to the three women working in harmony on the other side of the large room, Charlotte could understand his feelings. She only wished she could share them. But while her father seemed not to have noticed the divide that had returned to his family, Charlotte felt it as a constant ache inside, a reminder of the pain of her childhood and their current isolation.

The sound of the wind grew, an eerie note to go with her melancholy thoughts. Her father had already fastened the shutters, but it was obvious the sky had darkened further. Night truly had come early, and the thunder of raindrops against the roof soon joined the wind. She usually enjoyed the sound of rain—as long as she was safely inside, preferably tucked in her bed—but the intensity of the storm turned the comforting noise into an assault. She kept glancing at the roof, wondering if it would hold.

"Don't worry, daughter," her father said softly, drawing her eyes. "It was stoutly made and will hold against storms worse than this."

She managed a tight smile and a nod. Her mind knew he

was right, but deeper instincts couldn't help responding to the ferocity of the storm. She was glad now that she had taken the extra time to harvest the wild mushrooms. Even if she could have found the spot again, who knew if they would have survived the downpour. It might be many days before she found anything worth harvesting now.

Her mother and sisters were just laying out the completed meal on the table when a sound made all five of them look up.

"What was that?" Elizabeth asked, sounding afraid.

"Probably nothing," her mother said quickly, but her voice was uneasy.

"It sounded like a knock," Odelia said doubtfully. "But it must have been a loud one to be heard above the storm."

"How could there be someone out there in this?" Elizabeth snapped, clearly wanting to believe her own words but struggling to do so.

"We shall have to look before they beat the door down," her father said, cheerfully. He stood, and Charlotte couldn't tell if he was really unbothered or if he was just pretending in order to reassure the rest of them.

She stood as well, and since she was closer to the door than he was, she moved toward it. Whatever her misgivings, she wanted to prove to herself that she wasn't like her sisters. She wouldn't give way to fear.

Taking a deep breath, she threw open the door in one smooth movement. A hard sheet of rain angled through the opening, carrying a gust of freezing wind with it. She gasped at the sudden assault, and before she could recover herself, her father leaped forward, thrusting her behind him.

Grimacing at her poor exhibition, she stepped to the side, looking past the rain to what stood outside. She gasped again.

Standing in the doorway, apparently impervious to the rain and wind, was the White Bear.

Her father raised the staff that had somehow appeared in his hand, his expression no longer calm. He looked equal parts afraid and determined, his gaze wavering only once, when his eyes flicked to his wife and daughters and then to his bow, still hanging to one side of the door.

"No!" Charlotte cried. "He isn't dangerous!"

"Not dangerous?" Elizabeth shouted in a half-scream. "It's a bear!"

"Quick, Father! Kill him!" Odelia called from where she was cowering behind their mother.

Charlotte leaped forward, placing herself between her father and the doorway, arms outstretched to hold him back. It was a futile gesture if he was truly determined. She was much too small to physically restrain her tall father. But surely he would turn away from any rash action once he heard the truth about the bear.

She stood with her back to her father, her face toward the doorway. Her eyes immediately locked with the bear's, and the expression on his face was hard to read. At least he didn't look angry at the outburst of her sisters. If anything, he looked...pleased.

"He isn't an ordinary bear," she said, the words tumbling out. She twisted her head to look back at her father. "He can speak."

"Speak?" Elizabeth's shrill cry was laden with disbelief. "You've lost your mind, Charlotte! Bears can't speak."

"This one can," she said stubbornly, keeping her eyes on her father. "We had a conversation in the woods this morning, and he showed no aggression toward me."

She turned back to throw a pleading look at the White

Bear. It would be the perfect moment for him to say something.

He gave the same rumbling sound she had earlier determined to be his laugh. "It's true I was raised to be polite in all circumstances," he said. "I wouldn't dream of offering any of you violence."

His eyes strayed toward her sisters, and for a fanciful moment Charlotte remembered his words in the forest and the moment when it had seemed he did want to threaten her sisters. But whether that desire had been real or imagined, he was firmly in control now, looking as civilized as it was possible for a bear to look.

"He...he spoke," Odelia gasped, the words barely audible above the wind and rain.

Charlotte rolled her eyes. Hadn't she just told them that?

"You conversed with him this morning?" her father asked in a slow, halting manner.

Charlotte lowered her arms and angled herself so she could see both her father and the White Bear. Her father's words didn't sound aggressive, and he had relaxed his stance, but his tone still made her frown. It was almost as if he was more concerned by her earlier encounter with the creature than by the appearance of a talking bear in the first place. Did he think she had been in danger? Surely her father must see the bear was a creature from the Palace of Light and therefore not a danger to her.

"I came to speak with you, sir." The bear was looking at her father. "Perhaps you might step outside so we can converse in private?" He glanced once more at the women by the table.

Charlotte squashed down a ridiculous feeling of hurt that he wished to exclude her from the conversation. It was foolish of her since the bear had already had the chance to ask her questions. Why would he wish to talk to her again?

"Outside?" Her father raised an eyebrow as he looked at the sheets of rain and the darkness beyond the house.

The bear grimaced. "Perhaps I do not have the best timing. I spent the day searching the forest for you but failed to locate you before the weather changed. Once the storm hit in earnest, I realized you would have returned here. Waiting for tomorrow might be more sensible, but I confess to a strong degree of impatience." He looked once at Charlotte, his gaze fleeting, but somehow the glance soothed her earlier hurt, although she couldn't explain why.

"I wouldn't dream of keeping you waiting," her father said respectfully, bowing his head briefly.

Charlotte expelled a breath of relief, glad her father had grasped the nature of their visitor after all. She would hate for her family to cause him any more offense than they must have already done.

"Wait!" her mother cried softly as her father stepped toward the open doorway.

He paused and glanced back at her.

"I must go, my dear. Surely you see that." He spoke only just loud enough to be heard over the storm. "We have no choice. But I believe all may still be well."

Her mother wrung her hands together before nodding reluctantly.

Charlotte frowned. There had been something strange in her father's manner since the first mention of the bear, and she now couldn't escape the certainty that whatever her father knew was also known to her mother. What secrets were they keeping?

She stood in place as her father took a waterproof wrap

from a hook and swathed himself in it. Only once he had stepped outside and closed the door firmly behind him did she move.

Racing forward, she placed her ear against the door. But there was no use in attempting to overhear the conversation. The noise of the storm was too great to allow any other sounds to permeate the solid wood.

Rushing over to her mother instead, she gripped her arm, ignoring her sisters who both appeared to be in too much shock to speak.

"Who is the bear?" Charlotte asked in an urgent voice. "Why has he come here?"

"I have no idea," her mother said in such bewilderment that she couldn't doubt her. "I never dreamed such a thing would happen."

"Who would?" Elizabeth finally managed to say. "It's a talking bear!"

"Daisy used to tell stories about a talking cat," Charlotte said. "And our cousins were telling us only recently about a talking horse. Is a bear so different?"

"Horses and cats don't eat people," Odelia said firmly, and Charlotte had to admit she had a point. There was no denying it would create a very different impression to meet a talking cat.

The thought only made her feel sympathy for the White Bear. How often was he met with distrust and fear just because of his form? It wasn't as if he was an ordinary bear who might attack a human.

The door swung abruptly open, and all four of them jumped. But it was only their father striding inside, shaking off water like a dog. Their mother raced to him, her eyes roaming over his body, as if checking for signs of injury.

"Is he gone?" she asked.

Her father hesitated and then shook his head. "Not yet."

"Oh!" Her mother clasped her hands together. "What does he want?" She sounded terrified.

Her father didn't answer for a moment. Instead, his gaze lifted and pinned itself on Charlotte. Her heart began to race, a strange feeling suffusing her.

"He wants Charli." Her father's words were almost too quiet to be heard.

"Charlotte?" Elizabeth screamed, sounding actually worried for her sister. "What can you mean, Father?"

"Does he wish to eat her?" Odelia asked, sounding ghoulishly curious.

"Of course he does not," their father said sharply, his face losing color. "Do you think I would talk with him if he wished to eat any of us?"

Odelia subsided, looking sulky.

"But what does he want, Father?" Charlotte asked in a much quieter voice that nevertheless drew her father's attention immediately.

"He wants…*you*," he said again, as if struggling to know how to communicate the bear's request. "He wants to take you away with him."

"Take her away?" Her mother gasped and rushed over to wrap a protective arm around her daughter. "How can you be sure he won't eat her later, once he's away from us?"

Charlotte stood motionless beneath her arm, unable to think clearly but free of the fear that gripped her mother and sisters.

"I'm certain he doesn't wish to eat me," she said in a faint voice, earning another sharp look from her father.

"Do you know his intentions, Charli?" he asked. "Did he speak of it this morning?"

She shook her head. "No. I am as surprised as any of you. I merely feel certain he doesn't wish me harm."

Her father nodded, a strange and almost calculating look coming across his face. "That is a good start," he said. "Perhaps it is not impossible after all."

"Does he wish…" Charlotte hesitated, trying to make sense of it. "Does he wish me to go with him somewhere? Does he need a companion?"

Her father glanced once at her mother, seeming to stumble over the word.

"Yes, I suppose it is a companion of sorts. He wishes to make you…part of his family."

"Part of his family?" Elizabeth asked, still sounding incredulous. "But he's a *bear*!"

"He may be a bear," her father replied, "but he is clearly also a person. Or do you think him a mere animal?" He spoke slowly, as if willing them to read between his words.

Charlotte nodded. It made sense to her. The inhabitants of the Palace of Light might not all wear human form, but surely they must all be considered people. They certainly couldn't be thought of as animals—not when they were thinking, feeling beings with as much intelligence and capacity for communication as she herself possessed. Probably more, in truth.

But even so, she couldn't help her thoughts mirroring Elizabeth's. How could she join the family of a creature from the Palace of Light?

"How could I do so?" she asked. "Surely it is impossible."

Her father cleared his throat, glancing once again toward his wife. "There is an established way."

For a second, Charlotte and her sisters merely stared at

him, confused. Then Odelia let out a gasping laugh, one that hung on the edge of hysteria.

"Marry him? You want Charlotte to *marry* a bear?"

"Of course not," Elizabeth said with a repressive frown. "That's ridiculous."

Utterly and completely ridiculous. They must be misunderstanding their father.

And yet, the bear had asked her specifically about marriage ceremonies. It had been the only thing he was interested in. She had assumed he was conducting cultural research, but...

"Of course she couldn't marry him in the normal sort of way," her father said quickly. "But a legal marriage would make her part of his family. It would make it all right for her to leave with him. They have different rules in..." He trailed off without saying the words Charlotte knew came next. *In the Palace of Light.* Was being tied together a requirement for the bear taking her there?

The idea caught at her, making her breath lodge in her throat. She had heard tales of the High King's domain, of course, but they were all fanciful ones. No one had ever been there—or even knew of anyone who had. Rumor said Queen Ava of Rangmere had traveled there once, but everyone seemed to agree she was the only one. Was it really possible she was to be given that opportunity?

The thought of visiting the Palace of Light had never even occurred to Charlotte. She couldn't say she had dreamed of it, but it was a captivating idea nonetheless. But why would the White Bear wish to take her of all people to such a place?

"This is madness!" her mother cried, rounding on her husband. "You cannot be considering this! We cannot give our Charlotte to a bear. He isn't...he isn't one of us!" Again Charlotte had the impression there was something more that her mother wished to communicate, but something was holding her back.

Her father cleared his throat uncomfortably. "The ceremony only requires that they speak the necessary words, so it is technically possible. As I said, all he wishes is to take her into his family. This is merely the mechanism of doing so. But of course I would never force Charli into it. That's why he's waiting outside. I said the decision belonged to Charli herself, as is only right."

"Decision?" her mother cried again. "What decision? You should have sent him on his way the moment he suggested such an outrageous thing!"

But even as her mother spoke, she looked uncomfortable, as if she knew the words were more easily said than done.

The suggestion was outrageous. Charlotte acknowledged that openly. But the strange request hadn't shaken her inexplicable certainty that the bear would never offer her any harm. And neither could she deny the strange pull toward him. He wished her to become his companion on a fantastical journey, and there was something enticing about the idea of leaving with him, of freeing herself from the valley's isolation and exploring places she could only imagine.

But at what cost?

"Even if it's only a legal marriage," she said slowly, "it would still turn me into a married woman. I would be barred from entering into a true marriage. I would never get to fall in love."

Her father looked pained, and she expected her mother to speak again in protest against the idea. But instead she was looking at her husband through narrowed eyes.

"What have you not said?" her mother asked. "Why would you even consider such a proposal?"

Her father looked from Charli to the older girls and then back again, looking more uncomfortable than she had ever seen him.

"Of course I couldn't entrust my daughter to just anyone," he said. "He's not an ordinary bear, that much is obvious to us all, but it's more than that. He has power and position. There is much he could do for her…and for us."

"Do for us?" Elizabeth asked, catching at his words immediately. "Whatever do you mean?"

Her father looked from his older daughters to his wife. "I know you've all been disappointed in our life here," he said softly. "You agreed to the move at my assurances, and so far it's not lived up to our expectations. It is a burden I bear daily. And while we are close to a turning point that will bring us greater prosperity, it will likely be a gradual change. However, if Charlotte agrees to undertake the wedding ceremony, the White Bear will reverse our fortunes. We will soon be as rich as we have been poor."

CHARLOTTE

"**R**ich!" Elizabeth cried. "Are you certain? He's just a bear."

Her father gave her a stern look. "I think we have firmly established that he's not *just* a bear. We would not be having this conversation if he were."

"A rich bear." Odelia's wondering tone didn't match the hard light that came into her eyes. She cast a quick, conspiratorial glance at Elizabeth before turning to Charlotte with a sickly sweet smile. "He must be in great favor with the High King. Perhaps he even has a title. You might discover after you marry him that you are Lady Charlotte!"

Her father threw a glance at her mother that Charlotte couldn't read. Did he believe Odelia's words and think the bear had some kind of official title? It sounded unlikely to her. Did anyone at the Palace of Light have a title other than the High King?

"A bride price?" Her mother frowned. "That isn't a common custom in any of the Four Kingdoms."

"I have told you," her father said quickly. "They do things

77

differently in…" Again he trailed off, giving her mother a significant look as if she would understand his meaning.

Charlotte frowned. Was her father awed at the idea that his daughter might one day dwell in the Palace of Light? Was that why he wasn't speaking of it directly?

Charlotte herself certainly felt awed. But not awed enough to agree to the bear's unexpected proposal. As much as she longed to escape her isolated life, she wasn't willing to entirely give up on the hope of romantic love in order to achieve it.

She had seen enough households in their old village, as well as here among the valley folk, to know that the happiest and most fulfilling lives were those built on love. It was clear that even the High King agreed since he had decreed that the kingdoms would prosper when ruled by love. It was the reason he sent out his godmothers to help the royal families to find true love. Not even the most powerful king or queen would deny their heir the chance to marry for love, so why should she be asked to marry a stranger—and one who could never truly be a husband to her?

She knew there were other types of love than romantic love, and that a life could be happily built on them. She even felt a connection with the White Bear that she couldn't explain. But it wasn't enough to give up her hopes of something more.

"I can't." She shook her head rapidly, feeling a little sick. "I'm sorry, but I can't. I don't want a legal binding but a real marriage."

"A real marriage?" Elizabeth scoffed, although Charlotte knew both her sisters dreamed of being swept off their feet by an eligible young man. "What man might you be thinking of? There's no one who wants to marry you!"

"I didn't mean anyone in particular," Charlotte said, saddened rather than offended by her sister's words. "Just that I would like to meet someone one day." It was painfully clear that Elizabeth was projecting her own disappointed hopes onto Charlotte, and her sister's next words only confirmed it.

"And who would you meet here?" Elizabeth asked poisonously, once again triggering a wave of sadness in Charlotte.

After hearing the tales of her aunt's success, her father had expected to find prosperity in the valleys. And in the early days, her mother had talked of future visits to the Rangmeran capital after Elizabeth turned eighteen. Given the proposed timing, Charlotte had always known what the purpose of such trips would be. But the expected prosperity had been slower to come than expected, and in the years since Elizabeth turned eighteen, there had been no trips forthcoming.

Elizabeth was right that it would be a struggle for any of them to meet a man they might be able to love here. But their father claimed change was just around the corner. It wouldn't take much of an improvement in their circumstances to allow the promised trips to happen. Couldn't they be patient just a little longer?

"We will none of us find husbands here," Odelia said on a sigh, echoing Elizabeth. "Is there even a point to being rich if we have to stay here, away from all society and comfort?"

Their father coughed. "Actually," he said, "the bear spoke of helping us establish ourselves in Arcadia." He sounded dispirited at the idea, and Charlotte knew what it would cost him to give up his dreams of forging a new life in this remote region. But he was clearly willing to accept a move for the sake of his family.

"Arcadia?" Her mother couldn't keep a longing note from her voice. "Everyone talks about what a wonderful kingdom

Arcadia is! The people lack the sternness of the Rangmerans and the formality of the Northhelmians, you know. And their royal family has led them to great prosperity. I've heard the old king is even thinking of retiring, as King Richard did recently in Northhelm. Everyone adores Crown Prince Maximilian and his wife, Princess Alyssa, and they say they will make excellent monarchs. It is better by far to have someone young and vital on the throne than someone declining in capacity. It seems a most sensible move."

Charlotte swallowed, trying not to feel betrayed by her mother's words. She could understand the appeal of riches and a life in Arcadia, but surely her mother wouldn't sell her own daughter to achieve it?

"Of course if you say no, it is not to be thought of, Charli," her father said, cutting through her sisters' excited exclamations.

He met her eyes across the room, and she told herself she was imagining the faintest shadow of disappointment at her resistance. It was merely exhaustion, and she couldn't blame him for that. Her father, at least, was always on her side.

"I only repeated the offer because I thought it might be of interest to you," he said, confirming her thoughts. "Someone so rich and powerful would change your life as well as ours, Charli-bear."

For the first time in her life, Charlotte winced at her old nickname. "I cannot trade love for riches, Father," she said softly.

He nodded quickly. "I will tell him."

As soon as he said the words, Charlotte felt a pang. She barely knew the White Bear, and yet she couldn't help but feel pain at the thought of disappointing him. But she comforted herself with the assurance that he would easily find a better companion than her. Plenty of people would be willing to sacrifice anything for the chance to travel to the Palace of Light.

Her father stepped outside, carefully closing the door behind him. Charlotte already knew it was futile to try to listen through the door, so she hurried to the window beside it and peered outside.

The storm still raged although she had barely noticed the wind and rain since the bear's arrival. The early darkness of the storm clouds made it hard to see far, but the whiteness of the bear's fur stood out, even through the driving rain.

She couldn't hear the words her father spoke to him, but she saw the moment the bear's demeanor changed, his shoulders slumping in a way that looked strangely human. Her stomach clenched, and she almost wavered. But she shook herself, remembering what was at stake. Something strange and magical was afoot, clearly, and she longed to embrace the strange adventure before her, but she could not sacrifice the chance of love and children and a home of her own one day. Not for adventure and certainly not for riches.

When her father slipped back into the house, unwinding his waterproof wrap, he looked subdued.

"He is gone?" Charlotte asked in a small voice. "I suppose he's already on his way to ask the next girl."

Her father shifted uneasily, pausing before answering. "Actually, he refused to give up hope. He said his offer had been sudden, and he could understand your hesitance. He asked me to assure you that he would never harm you and that anything you could wish for will be yours. He said he will return in a week for your final answer."

Charlotte gulped, her head spinning slightly. It had been a struggle to fight her impulse for adventure and escape, but she had succeeded and thought the matter finished. And now it wasn't finished after all? She could still prove weak and make a mistake that might throw away her life.

"No, no!" she cried. "You must tell him I do not mean to accept!" She ran to the door and pulled it open, poised to run out into the rain despite her lack of covering.

But there was no longer a patch of white in sight. The bear was gone, and she would have no hope of finding him in the downpour.

She slumped, slowly closing the door. As she turned, her eyes caught on her mother who had joined her older sisters by the stove. Her mother looked uncomfortable—as if caught between conflicting emotions—but Elizabeth and Odelia were openly exultant.

Charlotte's gut tightened again, but this time it was a dark, squirming feeling as if she might be sick. Her sisters had exclaimed in disbelief and even outrage at first, but the mention of riches had changed their minds completely. If there had ever been any doubt in her heart, she now knew for certain that they would sell her to the bear without a moment's hesitation.

The discomfort at her mother's reaction hit hardest, though. Since the wedding, her mother had been doing her best to smooth the way between her daughters, keeping the peace by separating them whenever possible. Charlotte had believed she was doing it for all of their sake because she didn't want the family marred by disharmony or to be forced to side with one child over another. But looking at her mother now, Charlotte saw her mother's silences and placating looks as something else entirely. By keeping the peace when Charlotte was being wronged, she had always been siding with her older daughters, even if she wasn't willing to admit it.

And now, despite her mother's bustling efforts to finish preparing the table for their meal, she couldn't hide her true feelings. She might feel guilty for it, but she was almost as tempted as Elizabeth and Odelia. She wanted a different life.

Just as she had chosen peace and an easier life over defending Charlotte in the past, now she was once again tempted to put her own comfort ahead of her daughter. Charlotte knew her mother loved her, but she didn't love her enough to choose her, and the pain of that constricted her chest.

A shiver ran through her, and she knew she couldn't possibly sit and eat the evening meal with them all as if nothing were wrong. Her family had shown their true colors, and although she had thought herself inured, it cut deep.

She managed to coax her legs into moving, pausing briefly beside the laden table. Snatching up a piece of bread, a wedge of cheese, and an apple, she hurried to her room.

Her father called after her, but she shut the door on his voice. She felt a pang of guilt for shutting out the only family member on her side, but her emotions were running too high, and the house was too small for all of them. Removing herself was the only way she knew to prevent an eruption.

She would eat, and then she would hide herself in bed. If she hadn't fallen asleep by the time her sisters came in, she would pull the blankets over her head. She couldn't face them. Not tonight. Not when she knew what they would say.

Tomorrow she would have new reserves. And surely a whole night would give her enough time to come up with a strategy—some way she could resist her sisters' blandishments without turning her life into a misery.

~

It turned out one night was not enough. Despite many sleepless hours, lying still beneath her blanket and listening to the wind, Charlotte could come up with nothing of use. That her sisters would try to convince her to accept the bear, she was certain. What she didn't know was how to hold firm in her refusal without stoking her sisters' enmity toward her.

Given how late it was before she fell asleep, it was no surprise that she woke late yet again. But this time she was greeted with bright smiles of welcome and two cheery greetings.

"We have breakfast laid out for you when you're ready," Elizabeth said in the warmest tone Charlotte had heard her use in months. "You must be exhausted after the terrible night we had. The wind was so loud! And that rain! I'm sure none of us slept a wink."

Charlotte managed a forced smile, remembering the gentle snores of both sisters, just audible above the storm.

Odelia nodded vigorously. "And of course you must not think of going out gathering today. Everything will be mud! We'll stay inside and have a comfortable time together. Perhaps you can advise me on the new dress I've been making?"

Charlotte struggled to come up with a response. She had expected some sort of campaign from them, but this was excessive. Did they really think she would find it sincere?

In the end, she remained silent, merely joining them at the table. At least she felt up to eating in company with her family which was an improvement on the night before.

The rest of the day progressed in much the same way. Her sisters were sickeningly kind to her, and every instance of their consideration felt like the twist of a knife blade in her gut. Even her mother's effusive kindness was hard to take, although in her mother's case it didn't feel entirely false. But it still made her feel tired, small, and sad. Her mother might love her, but her love hadn't been enough to make her stand up for Charlotte in the past, and it wasn't stopping her thinking of a new life in Arcadia now.

When she managed to escape outside with her father on the second day after the storm, she felt nothing but relief. Stretching, she sucked in a long breath, lifting her face toward the clear sky.

Her father chuckled. "Relieved to escape, hey?"

Charlotte threw him a grateful look. At least one of her family members understood her. Her father had always sensed when Charlotte had reached her limits, responding by inviting her to spend the day with him in the forest. And in the past, a day away from her sisters, with her father for company in their stead, had always set her right again. He was her solid foundation. He would never turn against her, and that knowledge enabled her to endure her sisters' pressure.

"Do I dare ask what you're thinking, Charli-bear?" her father asked with another chuckle.

She winced. It seemed the old nickname was ruined forever now. The thought dulled her enjoyment of being outside. Ever since their cousin's wedding, life had been growing increasingly insupportable, but how much worse was it going to get in five days' time when she stood firm and refused to sell her future for her sisters' enrichment?

But she didn't want to ruin the day with her father before it had even begun.

"I'm hoping there's still some edible greenery left after that storm," she said, forcing herself to respond lightly. "We've already eaten what we gathered from before, and I'm loathe to go back to a diet of only preserved food."

His smile grew. "If anyone can find something, it's you. You're almost as attuned to these forests as I am."

Her father was trying to compliment her, to buoy her up, but his words hurt. Did he really not know that it was a desire for escape that drove her from the house as much as a love for the forests themselves? In the face of her sisters' childhood dislike, she had aligned herself with her father from the beginning, always seeking his validation and approval. Had she taken it too far, leading him to believe she possessed the same love of the unclaimed wilderness as he did?

Charlotte did like the natural beauty and space of the valley—it was almost the sole positive in their second home—but it didn't light her up the same way it did her father. She explored because it was better than sitting at home with no break from her tense relationship with her sisters.

A cold, uncomfortable feeling swept over her. Did her one true ally in the family not actually understand her at all?

She shook the thought away violently. Her father loved her. Her father was loyal to her. He was the only one she had, and she wasn't going to undermine their relationship by focusing on hurtful imaginings.

She pinned a bright smile to her face. "I'll do my best."

They separated not long after, each off to pursue their own tasks for the day, and Charlotte tried to push all other thoughts out of her head. She really did want to find something edible to forage, and given the damage to the fledgling plants, it would take some concentration to achieve.

By the time the sun was seeking the horizon, she had succeeded better than expected. At the height of spring, she'd be able to fill the basket to overflowing, but given it was still the tail end of winter, half a basket was doing well.

Distracted by her success, she nearly missed the white

among the brown trunks. By the time she noticed the bear, he was already nearly close enough to touch.

Startled, she leaped back, only to freeze, staring at him. He remained carefully motionless, gazing back at her.

"I'm sorry," he said in his rumbling voice. "I didn't intend to startle you, but I wanted to speak with you directly." He shook his head. "Clearly I should have spoken to you from the beginning. I apologize for that as well. I thought it would reassure you if I went about everything in the proper, formal way, but I can see now that…"

He let out a great whuff of breath. "I am aware it's not a small thing that I'm asking. But I wanted to assure you of my sincerity, both toward you and with regard to the promises I have made. If you will agree to bind yourself to me, I will never harm you. Once we reach our destination, you need never even see me unless you wish it. And your family will live lives of comfort."

She bit her lip, the thought slipping through her mind that perhaps the bear had come to carry her off by force. But looking into his eyes, she couldn't believe it. Now that she was once again in his presence, she felt the same certainty as she had at their first meeting—he would not hurt her.

She felt something else too. The pull she felt toward him, the one that had made her consider running from her family to seek a grand adventure and the one that had made her sad at the thought of disappointing him, was even stronger than before.

"Thank you for your words, White Bear," she said slowly, trying to work out how to phrase her objections without disappointing him further.

"You may call me Henry," he said, cutting into her thoughts.

"What?" she asked, too surprised to formulate a more coherent question.

"Henry," he repeated. "It's my name. You may feel free to use it."

"Your name is…Henry?" she asked, still a little dumbfounded. She hadn't considered the matter of his name, but if she had, she would have expected something grand and foreign. "Are you sure?"

As soon as she asked it, she wanted to pull the words back. What a foolish question!

He made the rumbling noise that indicated his laughter.

"It is one of them," he said.

She nodded quickly, eager to make amends for her unthinking words. "It's a lovely name."

He laughed again. "I have always liked it well enough. It's a family name."

She raised her eyebrows. Did he have parents, then? Were they talking white bears like himself? Family was another thing she had never considered in conjunction with him. She didn't know how the magical creatures that dwelt with the High King came to be, but she had always imagined them springing to life at his command rather than being born in the ordinary way.

If he had once had a family and lost them, was that why he was so desperate for a family again—in any way possible? She softened, once again regretting the necessity of saying no.

If only he could have adopted her. But she was already eighteen, making that impossible. And she didn't think there was a single family in the valley that would send their minor child off with a bear, regardless of the promise of riches.

"I'm the one who is sorry," she said in a rush. "It's not that I mistrust you or am unwilling to accompany you. It's just…"

She hesitated. "Are you sure the wedding ceremony is necessary? Could I not just travel with you as your companion without it?"

He winced. She had become so used to impossible expressions on his face that she barely even noticed the strangeness of it.

"Unfortunately, the binding is crucial," he said. "But of course I understand your reluctance." He gazed at her longingly. "I would assure you with every bit of sincerity I possess that your future is safe with me, but I understand the heart isn't something that can be so easily governed."

He slumped down, hopelessness in every line of his fur.

Alarm at his extreme reaction made her start forward. "Does something ail you?" she asked. "Surely your life cannot be in jeopardy and requiring this binding to save it?"

He hesitated, as if considering her words. Did he know that he only had to say yes to compel her to agree to his bargain? The inexplicable connection between them was strong enough that she didn't think she could abandon him to die.

Eventually he sighed. "I fight for much," he said softly, "but not my life. There will be no blood on your hands if you refuse."

Charlotte knew she should have felt relieved, but she felt almost regretful instead. Had she wanted him to provide her an excuse to say yes?

She shook herself. She could not allow her thoughts to stray in that direction. She couldn't allow the impulse of a moment to destroy her whole future. She had to stay strong.

"I'm sorry," she whispered again. "I wish I could give you a different answer."

"Once again, it is me who owes the apology," he said,

seeming to gather himself together. He bowed his head even lower than he had on the previous occasion. "Even your sympathy is more than I might reasonably expect."

He turned as if to depart, only to hesitate and look back. "I told your father I would return in five days. I will be true to my word, but know that I will not pressure you. My offer, however, remains open until then."

She nodded, unable to summon the right words, and he disappeared into the forest. It was going to be a long five days.

CHARLOTTE

The five days proved even more difficult than Charlotte had expected. Her sisters grew more and more blatant with their hints and nudges. Their conversation was full of the possibilities of future wealth and luxury, and they exclaimed often over how they wished they were the ones being carried off to live like a princess. If Charlotte dared to comment, they quickly assured her that *of course* they weren't seeking to change her mind.

When it became obvious that they weren't, in fact, changing her mind, their syrupy blandishments grew sharper and sharper. By the day the bear was due to reappear, the knives were fully out.

Both sisters snapped at Charlotte, wielding their words as weapons and berating her for her selfishness and stupidity.

"Just know that every time we break our backs in hard labor in the days to come, we will be thinking of you," Elizabeth hissed. "For it will all be your fault."

Their mother looked up from where she stood over the stove on the other side of the room, her brows drawing together. Had she heard Elizabeth's words? Charlotte couldn't be sure. She told herself her mother couldn't have heard. If she had, she would have said something—rebuked her oldest and defended Charlotte.

Wouldn't she? Charlotte wished she felt more sure.

"Every time we're lonely," Odelia added, "and if we find no suitors, we will know you are to blame. We could have had everything, but you threw it away for the sake of a foolish dream. It's hard to comprehend such selfishness."

Their father stepped into the house in time to hear her final words. Both girls fell silent, looking at him guiltily. He frowned, giving them a sharp look.

"All three of my daughters are welcome under my roof for as long as they wish to stay," he said sternly. "None of you will ever be forced out while I am alive."

Gratitude rushed through Charlotte, only growing stronger when he turned to her. "Why don't you join me in the forest today, Charli? I don't expect the white bear to come until evening, as he did last time."

She stepped outside, embracing the familiar feeling of escape. Smiling at her father, she fell into step beside him, pleased he was allowing her to accompany him. He rarely did so when he was off to cut wood, since he worried about her safety. But he must have recognized Charlotte's need for comfort and companionship today. It was getting harder and harder to bear her sisters' dislike.

They walked in silence, and Charlotte relished it. No one was berating her or trying to convince her to change her mind. Utter bliss.

Once they were well away from the house, her father cleared his throat.

"Are you sure, Charli-bear?" he asked, the nickname once again setting her teeth on edge.

She forced herself to respond calmly. "About what, Father?"

He cleared his throat again. "About the white bear's offer."

She stiffened, disbelief filling her. Was this why he had invited her to come with him today? She had thought he was offering her a reprieve, but instead he was joining in the chorus?

He kept his face forward, his voice uncomfortable. "I don't mention it because of what the bear is offering us. He also wishes to offer you a life of luxury. I know you aren't swayed by the lure of worldly goods in the same way as your sisters, but I can't help wondering if you might still benefit from what he can provide."

She stared at her father, still too shocked to speak, and he finally turned to look at her.

"I do believe we are on the verge of turning around our fortunes here," he said earnestly. "Your aunt and the other senior valley folk are finally going to—" He cut himself off, shaking his head. "Never mind that. The point is that I haven't been lying to you all when I said better times are on the horizon for our family. But it's taken too long. I've taken too long." He looked so crestfallen that her instinct was to comfort him, but for once, she remained silent.

"With or without the bear's assistance, I think we're going to have to move," he said after a moment. "Your mother and sisters have been very clear about their feelings on the matter. I have to give Elizabeth a chance to..." He trailed off, grasping her arms as a new light came into his eyes. "But you don't have to come with us, Charli! The White Bear is offering you a chance to stay. And not just stay but seek out new frontiers." He looked in the direction of the mountains, his eyes still shining, and she wondered if he was seeing the Palace of Light in his mind's eye.

"You can have adventures the rest of us can only dream of," he whispered. "And perhaps, one day, when your sisters are settled, I'll be able to come and visit you."

Charlotte pulled herself free, stepping back. "Adventure?" she asked. "You think I should choose adventure over love?"

Her father frowned, as if confused at her reaction.

"There are different kinds of love," he said. "You can have a full life without romance. And your sisters might well be right. Even if we move, you might not find someone to match your girlhood dreams. With the bear you can have both security and new adventures. That is not a combination to be considered lightly."

He continued to speak, dropping his voice even lower, as if he was ashamed of his own words. But she couldn't hear him, the buzz in her thoughts drowning out his whisper, one line echoing over and over in her head.

Your sisters might well be right.

She had thought she had one ally in the family. One person who saw her and thought she belonged—who loved her for her and would never try to send her away. But she had been wrong. Her father didn't know her at all.

And what had he said earlier? That one day he might visit her at the Palace of Light? He might not have been motivated by riches, but he was still thinking about how Charlotte's marriage could benefit him, saving him from the future her sisters were hemming him into.

Tears rose up, clogging her throat and threatening to spill from her eyes. She stopped, desperately trying to hold them in long enough to get away.

"I should have known you would want to send me away, too," she managed to choke out. "How could you not when you have so much to gain? This is a rare opportunity, and I guess I am selfish to stand in all of your way."

Turning, she nearly tripped over her feet in her haste to run. She had to get away from him. She had to escape before she started crying in earnest. She couldn't bear to let her tears fall in front of him.

"Charli!" he called after her. "Charli, wait!"

But she didn't slow. She fled without thinking, horror overtaking her when she realized her steps were leading her home. But maybe it was a good thing. If she lost herself in the woods, the white bear wouldn't know where to find her.

She wrenched open the door, clearly startling the three women inside. Her mother exclaimed, speaking her name, but Charlotte ignored her. Brushing past them, she rushed into the bedroom she shared with her sisters, firmly closing the door behind her.

They got the message for once, and none of them attempted to follow her. She could hear them whispering to each other, no doubt speculating as to what had happened. Did they know the reason her father had invited her out? Had they been waiting with bated breath to see if he could succeed where they had failed?

The thought filled her with rage. How dare they all conspire against her! She was as much a part of this family as any of them. And yet, they would *sell* her for their own comfort!

She flung herself on the bed and cried until no more tears would come. Still no one tried the door. Eventually she heard her father return, the distant murmur of his voice deep and concerned.

His arrival provided the final bit of certainty to her decision, compelling her to action. Hurrying around the room, she took only what she most needed, wrapping the items into a makeshift bundle.

She would not stay where she was neither understood nor valued. She had reached her limit. Her mother and sisters thought she should be motivated by wealth and her father by adventure. But her true motivation—as it had been on so many previous occasions—was escape.

After years of sharing a home, not one of her family members saw her true self. And yet, with the bear, she had felt seen in only two interactions. Foolish it might be, but she would trust her future to the one person who actually wanted her around.

Several exclamations were heard from the main room, and then the front door opened. Charlotte drew a deep breath. The moment had come.

A tentative knock sounded on her door.

"Charlotte?" her father called through the wood, not attempting to open it. "The bear is here and wishes to hear your refusal from your own lips." Silence for a moment. "He will not hurt you."

Was he reassuring her that she need not be afraid of a brief moment of interaction, or was he making one last attempt to convince her? Charlotte didn't know, and she no longer cared.

Pulling the door open, she swept past her father without looking at him. Striding through the house, she continued straight out the open front door. The bear stood at a respectful distance, his eyes focused on the doorway. When she appeared, his gaze met hers, holding her eyes for a moment before his attention moved to the bundle over her shoulder.

She saw the moment realization hit him, his whole face lighting up. Peace swept through her, settling the frenzied desperation that had driven her this far. Here was someone who thought she belonged with him. There was one family in which she was welcome.

She was making the right choice.

Moving more slowly, she walked to him. Previously she had curtsied to him, but now she was to join his family. She nodded respectfully instead.

"I will come with you," she said in a voice loud enough to be heard in the house. "I will complete the ceremony."

The bear—Henry, she should think of him as Henry, as strange as it seemed—smiled, radiance emanating from him.

"I am honored, Lady Charlotte," he said. "And I will do everything in my power to ensure you never regret this decision."

"Thank you," she said more quietly.

"You're going to marry him?" her mother gasped from the doorway. "Are you sure?"

She nodded, not turning to look at her parents. "If you wish to see the ceremony, you should follow us to Master Harold's." As the only official across their valley and the two neighboring ones, Harold conducted all ceremonies. She was only fortunate he happened to be their closest neighbor.

"You mean to be married immediately?" her father asked, clearly shocked.

Was he upset at the thought of her departure or horrified about how it would look to Master Harold when she arrived unexpectedly and demanded immediate marriage to a bear? It didn't matter either way. Her decision had been made, and she had no desire to linger.

"Of course." Charlotte still couldn't bring herself to look

directly at any of them. "Henry has asked me to go away with him, and I see no benefit in delay."

"Henry?" her mother asked faintly.

"It is my name," the bear said in a deep voice.

Distracted by her swirling emotions, Charlotte hadn't noticed him moving. But at some point he had come closer, positioning himself protectively beside her.

Another band across her chest loosened. He wanted to defend her, to protect her from them. And he could clearly do it. She would be safe with him.

"We should leave immediately," she said. "The afternoon is already drawing on, and it's a long walk."

Henry looked at her, a considering light in his eyes. "If you would like to ride, we could get there faster."

"I don't own a horse," she said stiffly. And even if her father offered her one of his, she wouldn't accept it. She refused to accept their bribes, offered only to assuage their own consciences.

"I meant on me," he said with a smile. "But I understand if the thought is unpleasant."

"Ride you?" She stared at him, taken by surprise. People didn't ride bears, magical or not.

"We would get there much faster." He sounded apologetic.

A slow smile spread across her face. Her determination and sense of betrayal had been buoying her up, but she was dreading the long walk and the awkwardness of arriving in the middle of the night with such an odd request.

"If you really don't mind, that would be lovely," she said, already moving toward him.

He lowered himself as much as he was able, but he was still very large. She paused, unsure how to ascend.

"You can grip my fur," he said, the amusement in his tone reassuring her.

"I won't hurt you?"

"I will do my best to bear it," he said gravely although the amusement still leaked through.

She smiled at him and grabbed handfuls of his thick fur, using it to scale his side. The fur was soft—much softer than she had expected—and it was surprisingly comfortable sitting just behind the shoulders of his front legs.

"Charlotte!" Elizabeth's voice cried, her sisters both tumbling from the house to stand with their parents. "You can't get married without us!"

"We're supposed to have new gowns for a wedding," Odelia moaned. "And where is the bride price? We were promised a bride price!"

"You will have it," the bear said, all amusement gone from his voice. "Once the ceremony is completed."

"If you wish to be there, I can't stop you," Charlotte added stiffly. "But there is no time for new gowns. You will have to ride if you want to make it in time as it is."

Taking her words as a sign, the bear began to move. She had thought she would need to direct him, but he didn't ask any questions, moving with confidence in the right direction. She remembered that he had spoken of being in the region for some time. Perhaps he knew the homes of everyone who lived in the valley.

In what felt like an impossibly short time, Charlotte spotted the wooden house of their closest neighbor in the distance. And moments later they were lumbering to a stop in front of the door.

She hadn't expected him to move faster than a horse. Did bears usually move so quickly, or was it just the magical ones?

She glanced over her shoulder, checking for her family, but there was no sign of them.

Her last glimpse of them had been of all four of them rushing toward the small stable attached to their house, so she assumed they were on their way. But their horses couldn't have kept up with the bear. With a brief pang of guilt, she wondered if she should wait for them. But a moment later she swept the feeling aside. She was doing what they so desperately wanted her to do, and they deserved no further consideration in the matter.

She still climbed down slowly, however, her courage wavering now that the moment had arrived. Not that she was reconsidering her decision, but explaining it to near strangers was another matter. What would Master Harold and his family think of her?

"This is the correct house, isn't it?" the bear asked when she stayed motionless beside him.

Charlotte shook herself and nodded. "Yes, Master Harold is the official who conducts all the local ceremonies. Hopefully he doesn't mind being disturbed without warning."

She made herself move forward and knock loudly on the door. Movement could be heard inside, and then the door opened. The tall man on the other side looked from her to the bear standing beside her, his expression going slack.

Charlotte tried to think how to word her request and came up blank.

But Harold recovered himself more quickly than she expected, looking down at her with concern, rather than confusion, in his gaze.

"Good evening, Miss Charlotte," he said gravely. "I can't say I thought you would actually come."

"You were expecting me?" she asked, surprised.

He nodded. "Your pa came to talk to me yesterday. Explained the whole situation. Just in case..." His words trailed off as he looked back up at the bear, a crease between his brows.

"Father came yesterday?" Charlotte repeated in a breathless voice, struck anew by the sense of betrayal. Had he been so sure he could convince her?

"Aye, that he did." Harold ran a hand over his head. "He explained the whole situation and received my agreement to conduct the ceremony, but..." He hesitated again. "I believe it is incumbent on me, given my position, to speak to you alone for a moment first."

Charlotte glanced quickly at the bear, her first thought for him. Would he be offended by the implication of Harold's words? But the bear merely smiled, gesturing with his head for her to follow Harold into the house.

She swallowed and trailed him inside, giving a subdued greeting to his wife and young children as he closed the door behind them.

"You really came?" his wife gasped, making it clear Harold had already shared his neighbor's odd story. "You're a brave girl! Your family will owe you much. If the bear's claim is true, that is."

Charlotte gave her a tight smile. She wasn't doing it because of the rewards promised to her family, but she couldn't say that to this woman, who had always been kind to her.

"But are you sure about this, girl?" Harold asked. "It's not a light thing. You aren't being...coerced?" He winced as he said it, clearly as uncomfortable as she was but still determined to do his duty. "I can't conduct the ceremony if I think you're being forced into it."

A sudden influx of warmth made Charlotte soften. Harold was a good official, one who took his responsibilities seriously. He was attempting to protect her, as much as he was able, and she appreciated the efforts.

"It was my decision," she said softly, struggling to keep tears from her eyes at the look of sympathy on the face of Harold's wife. They had been at her cousin's wedding, like the rest of the valley, and must have some idea of Charlotte's position in her family.

"I understand, lass," he said quietly. "Although this seems a drastic step to take. Allying yourself with a white bear..." He shook his head. "I know his people have brought us great prosperity, but we know little about them, and there are some who think..."

He trailed off as his wife put her hand on his arm, her eyes wide as she shot a warning look toward the door.

Charlotte frowned. When people spoke of the High King and his servants, it was only to praise the great prosperity they had brought to all the Four Kingdoms. While it was true no one knew many details about the Palace of Light itself or the godmothers and creatures who dwelt there, that was hardly a matter for concern given all the good they had brought to the kingdoms. For herself, she couldn't believe the High King or his creatures wished any of them malice—especially given the inexplicable certainty she felt in Henry's presence.

"Of course it's unknown," she said, "but I don't fear the Palace of—"

"Hush!" Master Harold's harsh whisper cut her off. He glanced back at his children who were watching them with rapt expressions. "Of course I can see that you would need to know all about it given this unusual situation, but surely your father warned you of the necessity of discretion. It has been pressed upon him often enough. You shouldn't speak of such things aloud. Not around the valley folk, at any rate."

Charlotte blinked, utterly bewildered. In Northhelm, the people had spoken openly of the Palace of Light. She couldn't think why they would have a different custom here in the valleys. Unless there really were some people here who opposed the High King?

She frowned, wanting to ask the identity of such dissenters, but the sound of horses in the distance caught her attention. Her family was about to arrive to watch the wedding ceremony—her wedding. Did it really matter what the valley folk thought of the Palace of Light? She would soon be gone from among them anyway.

"Thank you for your concern," she said, "but I've made up my mind."

"I'll need a minute to gather the necessary papers then," he said. "Would you like to wait in here or…" He glanced at the closed door.

Harold's house was large, one of the oldest in their valley, and it was filled with cozy warmth. For a moment she hesitated, wanting to linger in the familiarity of ordinary valley life. But she straightened and shook her head. Her place was with Henry now and in whatever adventures awaited them outside the valley. She should wait with him.

Harold made no protest when she slipped back outside, leaving the door open behind her. All his children rushed to look, coming no further than the doorway despite their eager faces as they gazed at the enormous creature in front of their house.

"Has he talked you out of it?" the bear asked, saying it like a joke, although she could hear a hint of real concern behind.

"Of course not," she said. "I gave you my word, and I won't be so easily dissuaded."

"Thank you." He touched his great head lightly against her.

Her family's three horses pulled to a stop beside them, making her stiffen. Her sisters looked uncomfortable squeezed onto the sturdiest horse together, but at least all four of them had come. She couldn't help a sense of relief at their arrival. For all her bravado and hurt, it felt wrong to be married without a single family member by her side.

By the time Harold came back outside with a book in his hand, they had dismounted and stood awkwardly beside her and the bear. Charlotte's father moved quickly forward to greet Harold, and the two men exchanged some quiet words she couldn't catch. She kept her face steady, refusing to guess at what they might be saying. The only thing that mattered was that Harold had agreed to conduct the ceremony, which meant Charlotte was about to escape.

Harold's wife emerged, having somehow wrangled her children into staying inside, and she soon had Charlotte's family arranged to one side while Charlotte herself and Henry —she had to start thinking of him by his name, however hard it was—stood side by side facing Harold.

As she had promised the bear back in the forest, the cere-mony was a simple one. He lifted one enormous paw, and she placed her hand on it as Harold led them through an exchange of promises. She knew the solemnity of their words, and she wanted to take it seriously, but she was feeling strangely weightless and detached. Her mouth repeated the words whenever she was called on to do so, but she couldn't focus on what she was saying. Was this really her wedding? It was nothing like she had imagined as a girl.

When it came time for the parents' blessing, everyone kept

tactfully silent about the bear's parents, and Charlotte wondered again if he had any. When Harold turned to Charlotte's family, her mother instantly broke into gasping tears that left her unable to speak. But her father repeated the traditional blessing, sounding sad and broken in a way that twisted Charlotte's heart.

But she refused to soften toward him. His crimes against her had been the least, but they had hurt the most because she had trusted him.

His face crumpled when she wouldn't meet his eyes, but he finished his part, completing the ceremony. Harold would already have recorded their names in his book, along with those of all the valley couples who had been married before them. The next time he traveled to the capital, he would record them in Rangmere's official registries, but it might be years before that happened. It didn't matter, though. By valley law and social custom, Charlotte was married.

GWEN

For the second time, Gwen woke to find herself on the floor. This time she was slumped by her door, and the warm sunlight bathing her had driven away the sleepiness. But the exhaustion had been replaced with stiff muscles and aching bruises. This was why she usually slept in her bed, no matter how frustrating she found her long slumbers.

Standing slowly, Gwen gingerly tried her handle. It turned without resistance. Had she dreamed of the door being locked?

But Gwen refused to believe the night's discovery had been only the muddle of sleep. She could still feel the lingering indignation and fright at finding herself locked in. So why had she so tamely fallen back asleep? She had succeeded in waking in the night, but it had gained her nothing.

No, Gwen corrected herself. *It gained me knowledge.*

She had hoped to gain even more knowledge from an open conversation with the captives, but at least she had learned something. Between the guards and her locked door, she was now certain that something went on in the palace grounds at night—something she was being deliberately excluded from.

Gwen's eyes fell on her cabinet, now bereft of its small treasure. Other memories of the night before flooded back. Why had she never considered the regular citizens of the mountain kingdom? She had spent years pitying herself and the captive servants while overlooking a whole city full of people suffering at her mother's hands. Why had she never spared them a thought?

She could only conclude it was because she had no contact with them. To her, the people of the mountain kingdom were her mother's court—perpetual strangers who shut her out and kept her mother's secrets.

She knew better now. The regular people wore the face of a fourteen-year-old girl, full of the dreams of a child and the courage of youth. But while Gwen had gained knowledge the night before, she had acquired no extra power.

Still, she couldn't shake the thought of the girl all through breakfast. She ate well, hungry from her small meal the night before, but when she finished, she looked at her mother.

"I'm planning to go riding this morning," she ventured, holding her breath while she waited to see how her mother would react.

From the queen's calm behavior through the meal, she didn't seem to have received a report of Gwen's misbehavior the previous evening. But it was possible she knew and was just waiting for an opportune moment to bring down the hammer.

"Not today, my dear," her mother said, and Gwen's heart sank.

The only time she ever escaped the palace grounds was on horseback. Usually, she rode alongside her mother, but on occasion she rode with only two guards as companions. In the past, she had always headed to the edge of the valley on such rides, wanting to get away from everyone and as close to the wilderness as possible. But she had a different plan in mind this time. She wanted to ride toward the city and see if she could glimpse the ordinary life of its inhabitants.

But it seemed the guards had reported her after all.

Gwen could barely suppress her trembling as she looked at her mother, but Queen Celandine's smile didn't fade. And while it didn't reach her eyes, that was normal and not any cause for particular concern.

But somehow Gwen only felt more afraid. She almost wanted the punishment to fall just to escape the limbo of waiting.

"Really, my dear," her mother said, her voice sharpening. "Must you always look so diffident and uncertain? How many times have I reminded you that you're my heir and will one day rule the mountain kingdom? How can our people be expected to follow a girl who can't even string two words together in the presence of her own mother?"

Gwen swallowed. She knew she needed to answer, but she couldn't think of the right words. Her mother certainly didn't show any appreciation if Gwen ever spoke with strength or confidence. In that case Gwen was unattractively defiant and impudent and needed to learn respect for her elders and monarch.

"Yes, Mother," she said finally.

Easton would have known what to say—how to tread the exact line between diffidence and insolence—but Gwen's mind all too often froze in her mother's presence.

The queen sighed, as if she should have known it was futile to expect better of Gwen. "This is why you need me. Without me, you would be nothing. But you needn't fear. I will always be here for you."

The words should have sent a chill down Gwen's spine, but they were too familiar to warrant a reaction. Her mother rarely commented on Gwen's many deficiencies without saying something similar.

The queen surveyed her silent daughter and spoke again. "It's been too long since we spent time together."

Gwen stared at her, speechless. *Spend time together?* When had they ever done such a thing?

"I have some things to speak to you about," the queen continued.

When Gwen still didn't answer, the queen's brows contracted. She looked nettled by her daughter's obvious confusion, so Gwen schooled her expression and nodded obediently.

The effort satisfied her mother somewhat, so Gwen relaxed slightly. But as she trailed behind her mother all the way up to her room, her mind raced, even as she kept her face placid and calm. Was this some elaborate scheme to enable a new form of punishment? What was her mother planning to do to Gwen in the privacy of Gwen's room?

Her mother had never physically hit her—although her words often felt like blows—but locked away in the dark as a child, Gwen had understood her mother was capable of anything. When they reached her room, however, the queen's false smile was still firmly in place.

As Gwen followed her mother's directions and sat at her dressing table, she had to fight against terror. Gazing into the mirror, she met her mother's eyes where she stood behind her, and the longer they held, the more terrible the queen's smile grew. Gwen dreaded her mother's anger, but somehow this pretense of friendly affection was even worse. What lay behind it?

When her mother's fingers pulled at her hair, Gwen had to use every ounce of her self-control to hold herself still. With a few swift tugs, her mother released the hasty arrangement Gwen had managed before breakfast. Once her hair was flowing freely down her back, her mother picked up a brush and began to run it through her locks. While her hands moved, she smiled at her daughter in the mirror.

"You have grown into a lovely lady, my dear."

Was Gwen's panic showing in her eyes? She stared at her reflection, trying to see it the way her mother might. The face that looked back was strikingly similar to the life-size portrait of the previous king that stood in the line of monarchs that graced the throne room. Gwen might not have inherited the stunning, fair-haired beauty of her mother, but she still looked both beautiful and royal. A dark-haired princess with a pale, but otherwise composed, face. Her mouth was even curved slightly upward. The expression didn't touch her eyes, but perhaps her mother considered that normal.

The young woman in the mirror was Princess Gwendolyn, not Gwen. The reminder let Gwen breathe more freely.

"In truth, I've been remiss in my duties," her mother continued, not bothering to wait for a reply.

Gwen could barely keep her face still, unable to fathom what her mother could be referencing. The queen never criticized herself. She gave a laugh, a tinkling sound that never failed to grate on Gwen's nerves.

"I can see I've surprised you, my dear. I've been half-expecting you to ask me about it, but I'm gratified you're so content to remain here with only me."

"Ask you about what, Mother?" Gwen asked carefully, still with no idea what her mother was talking about.

"Why, your marriage, of course! You are old enough for it —and past age according to some." She laughed again. "But even the most impatient must recognize a mother's heart. What parent wants to give their precious child away to another?"

"You want to give me away?" Gwen asked, too dazed to filter her words.

The brush yanked downward, making her wince.

"Aren't you listening?" the queen asked, an edge to her voice. "I said I don't want to give you away."

"I...I apologize," Gwen stammered out, still lost. "But why are we talking of my marriage?"

"Because it is time, of course," the queen said calmly, her eyes meeting Gwen's wide ones in the mirror.

Gwen's mouth dropped open, not even fear of her mother enough to suppress her shock. "You want me to get married? To whom?"

While she had always dreamed of escaping from under her mother's eye, she had never thought of marriage as the answer. Surrounded by no one but the servants and the cold court, there was only one person who had ever occupied her heart. And he was never coming. She had given up hope of that a long time ago. She didn't even know if he was alive.

Her mind raced through the various courtiers, but she couldn't think of anyone eligible enough to appeal to her mother. She certainly couldn't think of anyone she could stomach marrying.

"To a prince, of course," the queen said. "Only royalty could be worthy of the princess of the mountain kingdom."

"A prince?" Gwen frowned. "But there are no princes here." Slowly the truth broke over her, and her eyes flew up to meet her mother's in the mirror. "You want me to marry a lowlander?"

It was inconceivable. She knew the valleys existed, of course, and the captive valley folk had assured her the lowlands existed beyond them. But the valleys had always seemed a part of the mountains—if a distant part—while the kingdoms beyond were as distant as a fairy tale.

She started to rise to her feet, but her mother's hand tightened on her shoulder, pushing her back into place. Gwen slumped into the seat, her mind whirling. A lowlander prince? Did the lowland royals even know the mountain kingdom existed? Which of them would want to brave the mountains and make their home there?

Gwen didn't fool herself for even a second thinking that her mother might plan to release Gwen, sending her off to a far kingdom. The idea was appealing, but she knew it to be nonsense. Her mother would never let her go. Even if she had another heir—and she did not—she wasn't the type to relinquish anything that belonged to her.

"I don't like that term," her mother said stiffly, showing more restraint than she usually did when they were alone.

Gwen murmured an apology. Her surprise had betrayed her into using the term of her childhood, although she had never understood what issue her mother had with it.

"Are not all lands equal?" her mother asked. "What is high that cannot be brought low and what is low that cannot be made high?"

Gwen kept her eyes lowered, not wanting her mother to see the skepticism in them. Queen Celandine was the last person to believe in the equality of all. Whatever her true objection, it wasn't over some imagined slight against the lowlanders.

"We must think of them as an extension of our own people," her mother continued in the gracious tones she usually used in company. "Indeed, after your marriage, they will be as much your people as our own citizens are."

Gwen frowned. Her mother's words sounded conciliatory enough, but there was something predatory in her tone. Did she hope to use Gwen's marriage to extend her own influence? That would be like her mother, but it seemed pointless when the mountains created a barrier that would forever separate them from the other kingdoms. Passage between the mountain kingdoms and the lowland kingdoms was difficult enough to keep them apart forever. Gwen's marriage couldn't turn mountains into valleys.

"You need not concern yourself with the details," her mother said, as if reading her thoughts. "You need only prepare yourself for your marriage."

Gwen looked up again. "Is it that soon? Who is the groom?"

"He will be here soon enough," her mother said, ignoring the question about his identity. "And when your prince arrives, we must not delay. This afternoon, the seamstresses will attend you and take your measurements. You will need an entire new wardrobe before you're married."

Gwen nodded silently, her mind still whirling too fast to engage on such mundane topics as dressmaking. Her mother had plans—advanced plans—to marry her to a foreign prince. It didn't seem possible.

But her mother never spoke frivolously. If she said it was

so, then she already had someone in mind. Knowing her, she must even have an agreement in place already.

Gwen wanted to press her to discover the name and kingdom of her supposed groom, but she couldn't shake off her unease from earlier. For some reason the queen was pretending affability, and Gwen didn't want to trigger overt anger.

She couldn't remain completely silent, however. "When?" she pressed. "How long before he's here?"

Her mother laughed. "So you are eager to be married after all. It is natural. But I cannot give you exact details on timing. We must wait for his arrival."

She finally put down the brush, meeting Gwen's eyes in the mirror in a way that told her they had finally reached the point of greatest importance to her mother.

"Once you are married, your duties and responsibilities will increase. You will find that the people look to you in a new way. But remember, the mountain kingdom is subservient to no one. Your future husband may be a prince, but that doesn't mean he'll be permitted to order matters here in the mountains. I am queen in this valley."

She held Gwen's eyes until she nodded. After all the years she had spent in her mother's company, she understood the underlying message. Marriage wasn't going to provide Gwen an escape. Single or married, she would still be under her mother's eye.

Her mother wasn't opening a gate and letting her walk free. She was merely luring another sheep into her pen.

Gwen felt a fleeting whisper of pity for the unsuspecting prince. But she couldn't hold onto the feeling in the face of her own discomfort. She had bowed her head and remained meekly in place for years in order to pacify her mother. But could she take it as far as marriage? Could she marry a stranger at her mother's order?

Everything in Gwen revolted, and she could no longer see her own reflection in the mirror. Instead, she saw curly brown hair and warm brown eyes with flecks of gold.

Was her mother leaving? She hoped desperately she was because Gwen couldn't lose her composure until her mother left the room.

Somewhere in the distance, she heard words that might have been a farewell. She must have managed a reply because she caught the sound of her door closing. Looking up, she confirmed she was alone.

Stumbling back from the dressing table, she collapsed onto her knees beside the bed, bracing her forehead against the soft mattress. Her breath rasped in and out too quickly, and she knew she needed to slow it down, but her body had stopped responding.

Tears leaked out, and the hands that gripped the bedspread shook. *Easton!* she cried silently. *Why did you leave without me? If you escaped from here, couldn't I have come as well?*

Her breath continued to rush in too quickly, and her head grew dizzy. What would she do when she didn't even have the sanctuary of her room? When the one space that was hers alone was filled with a stranger? Could she survive the palace when she no longer had even shreds of privacy left?

It was an unanswerable question, and she didn't try to count the minutes that passed until she finally steadied her trembling and took back control of her breath.

When she finally stood, she knew that even fear of her mother wasn't enough this time. She needed to find out the extent of her mother's plans, and then she needed to escape.

CHARLOTTE

The farewell exchanges between Charlotte and her family were stilted and awkward, and all she wanted was for them to be over. And yet, once they were, she hesitated. She knew it was too late to turn back, but her courage wavered in the face of departing everything she knew for a deep unknown.

She tried to remind herself of what was before her. The Palace of Light would no doubt be more glorious than she could even imagine. Her future might be unknown, but that didn't mean she needed to fear it.

Bolstering herself, she crossed to the bear, placing a hesitant hand on the soft fur of his shoulder. He stilled beneath her touch, but when she peered at his face, he seemed pleased. Did he still worry that she was afraid of him?

"Where do we go now?" she asked him, not quite managing to use his name.

"To my home," he replied, and she felt her first shiver of genuine excitement. Were they going to the Palace of Light immediately?

"Should I ride you again?" she asked, glancing toward the sky where the light was starting to fade.

"Yes," he said in his deep rumbly voice. "It is necessary if we are to reach our destination today."

She nodded. It made sense that she couldn't merely walk to another realm on her own feet. Murmuring an apology, she once again used his fur to haul herself into position on his back. From there, she sent a final glance toward her family who stood with Master Harold and his wife.

All four of them looked awed, and Charlotte allowed herself a moment of satisfaction. She was going to a bigger life, while they had merely made their world smaller. Then she remembered her family were to move to Arcadia and the feeling soured.

The bear took off with a lurch of movement that made her forget all about the people behind them as she clutched at his fur.

"Apologies," he called back to her. "But I will have to move faster this time if we are to make it before nightfall."

"Faster?" she gasped, remembering how swiftly they had traveled before. "Is that possible?"

He gave his gravelly laugh. "It is, indeed. If you lean forward and rest your head on my neck, you can wrap your arms around me in a more secure hold. You can even close your eyes and sleep if you wish. I will not let you fall, and we will be there before you know it."

Charlotte had intended to remain alert, curious about the journey itself, but as the bear picked up speed, she was forced to flatten herself or risk losing her balance. And pressed against his warm fur, it was easier to close her eyes than keep them open given the wind generated by their speed.

She wouldn't sleep, however. How could she sleep after all that had just happened and with all that was before her?

An unknown length of time later, she awoke with a start. It took her a disorienting moment to realize she was still clutching the bear's fur but they had come to a stop. When had she fallen asleep?

"We have arrived," the bear said in a deep tone she couldn't entirely read.

Shaking the remaining fuzziness from her mind, she slipped off his back and looked upward. The sight in front of her made her gasp.

An austere castle of gray stone had been built against a craggy mountain face. There were no lights in the windows nor any other sign of life, but it appeared to be in good condition and was by far the largest building she had ever seen. It had turrets but no flags—nothing to indicate which kingdom they were in. And given the rapidly gathering darkness, it didn't seem possible it could be the Palace of Light.

"Are we to stay here tonight?" she asked, bewildered, wishing she had stayed awake long enough to see the direction of their travel. The presence of the castle suggested they had moved westward, leaving the fringes of civilization and moving deeper into Rangmere. But the mountains that ringed them on three sides indicated they had rather gone east into the impassable mountains that bordered the Four Kingdoms.

"Of course," the bear said, sounding a little confused. "You would not want to sleep in the open."

"No," she rushed to assure him, despite the resurgence of her trepidation now they were truly alone in such a foreign place. "This is by far the grandest building I've ever seen. I will be honored to stay here. But...is this your castle?" She managed a small laugh. "Are you a prince among the bears?"

He hesitated for a moment, the air between them turning awkward. "It's true this is my home for now," he said at last, "but the castle doesn't belong to me."

She laughed again, trying to break the new tension. "Are you a squatter then?"

"More like a prisoner," he murmured, so quietly she almost didn't catch it. But when he looked up, he was grinning, and the coldness in the air had disappeared.

"Princess Charlotte suits you, though, don't you think? I'm sorry there isn't great fanfare awaiting you and a line of courtiers ready to pledge their loyalty."

She laughed back.

"I'm no princess, and I have no desire for such a scene. This is already far more than I expected."

Henry's face turned serious. "I hope that's true, and you didn't marry me because you thought I held some high position."

"Of course not!" she laughed. "And how could I complain when your home has turned out to be a castle? You said you would provide for me, and you're already doing so. It's clear you keep your promises." She said the last words with extra weight, and he nodded slightly, seeming to instinctively understand her sudden tension.

"You can be sure I will always endeavor to do so. And for now, you are princess of this castle, at least. Though I hope one day I may offer you more."

He spoke with a careful lightness that betrayed underlying tension.

"Truly, it isn't necessary," she rushed to reassure him. And even as she spoke the words, she realized she had no idea how he felt about their marriage. She had only ever considered the matter from her own perspective. Did it pain him to have to seek a human girl as a bride? What had driven him to do so?

"How long will we stay here?" she asked. "Before we continue on to your true home, I mean."

He looked shocked at her words, and his reply was slow and cautious. "My true home?"

Charlotte frowned. "The Palace of Light, I mean. That is where you are originally from, isn't it?"

Her clarification only seemed to shock him further.

"You thought I was one of the High King's creatures from the Palace of Light? And that I meant to take you there?"

"Aren't you?" She drew back, fear clogging her throat.

"Is that why you married me?" he asked, horror in his voice. "Is that why you trusted me?"

"Yes," she said in a small voice. But after a moment of heavy silence, honesty compelled her to continue. "Well, not entirely. That's the explanation I gave myself, but my instincts told me you were trustworthy and safe from the beginning. I was drawn to you from our first meeting in a way I can't explain."

She clasped her hands together, desperately hoping her instincts hadn't led her astray.

Henry drew back, his expression conveying a level of distress that shouldn't have been possible on the face of a bear.

"I'm truly sorry," he said. "I did not intentionally deceive you. If I had dreamed—" He shook his head abruptly. "No, I should have guessed it. It was a reasonable assumption. It is my fault for not foreseeing that you would—"

"No, indeed, you can't blame yourself!" Charlotte cried, moved by his concern. Clearly it had not been a duplicitous deception. Her heartbeat slowed again, the momentary panic receding. It might not have made logical sense, but she still trusted him.

Their current situation was another matter, however. Was this castle more than a temporary home for him? Had he really muttered something about being a prisoner? She stared at the castle with new eyes.

He wanted her to live here, in this cold and lifeless place, deep in the mountains? Who else lurked behind the castle walls? Were there others like him?

The thought filled her with horror, and she couldn't entirely keep the emotion from her face. The bear looked from the sky—which was clinging to only the last vestiges of light—to her face, desperation in his eyes.

"This is a truly terrible misunderstanding," he said, "but night is upon us. Shall we go inside at least?"

The pleading in his voice made her nod, and she followed him silently inside. There was certainly nothing to be gained by standing on the castle's doorstep as darkness descended.

The great double doors creaked as they opened, revealing a cavernous entryway that was as dark and cold as she had feared. From the outside, the edifice had looked lifeless, and inside it appeared no less so.

She tried to reassure herself that at least there were no fearsome beasts, but the shiver that rocked her made it hard to cling to any positivity. Was she really to sleep—to live—in such a place?

The bear still seemed concerned, but he moved quickly, his actions verging on frantic. Crossing to the mantelpiece over the vast and empty fireplace, he delicately lifted a silver bell, clasping the wooden handle in his jaws.

Shaking his head, he rang the bell, the sound echoing against the stone all around them. Instantly a roaring fire sprang to life in the dead fireplace, and all around her light bloomed as hundreds of candles began to glow.

Charlotte gasped, spinning to take in the whole entrance-way. Filled with light and warmth as it now was, the space felt entirely different. Even welcoming.

But how was it possible? Even if the bear had been able to instantly start a large fire, it should have taken time to warm the air.

Her eyes fixed on the bell, and she spoke in reverent tones. "Is that a godmother object?"

She had heard legends about such objects—gifted to worthy humans by the godmothers who served the High King, they were often passed down through generations.

"It is," the bear said, although he still seemed distracted and hurried. "And a powerful one."

"You have a godmother, then?" Charlotte asked, some of her earlier hope rekindling.

The bear hesitated before finally saying, "It wasn't gifted directly to me. I…acquired it from someone else. I don't know how old it is."

Charlotte frowned. The tales she had heard included some that involved nefarious people twisting godmother objects to their own ends. Surely the bear was not such a person? His presence couldn't fill her with such a sense of safety if he was.

Unless that was part of the enchantment that surrounded him.

She drew back, trembling as she realized yet again how isolated and alone she was. She didn't even know how far or in what direction lay her home valley.

No, she thought miserably, *not my home any longer. This is my home now.*

It was a painful thought.

The bear had always been sensible of her moods before, but he didn't notice this time, approaching her without regard to her new emotions.

"Who are you?" she gasped, needing answers. "If you are not a creature from the Palace of Light, how can you talk?"

The bear halted abruptly, shifting from side to side. Placing the bell carefully on the flagged floor in front of him, he opened his mouth as if to speak but ended up groaning instead.

"Please, just tell me," she said, her voice shaking.

The bear glanced at one of the long windows that framed the doorway. "There isn't time now. I will explain it to you later—it will be easier then anyway. For now, you should hurry and take this." He gestured toward the bell with his head.

"The godmother object? You want *me* to take it?" Charlotte stared at him.

"Of course," he said. "It's my wedding gift to you. You need only ring it and anything you wish will appear. You can use it to turn this place into a comfortable home. Please feel free to make any changes to the castle that you desire."

He glanced at the window again before muttering something hurried and dark. When he started to move, fresh horror filled Charlotte.

"But wait!" she cried, grasping for the first time that he meant to leave her. "Where are you going?"

"I'm sorry," he growled, not looking back in her direction. "There is no more time. Use the bell, and you will be able to sleep in comfort. I will explain what more I can…later."

"Wait! No! Stop!" she cried, but it was too late, he was already through one of the doors that opened off the entranceway.

Belatedly, she ran after him, pulling open the door that had swung closed in his wake. But although the door opened into a long corridor, he was nowhere in sight. He had already disappeared. Charlotte was truly alone.

She swayed for a moment, fearing her legs might give way. But despite herself, the warmth and light of the entranceway drew her back inside. Her eyes fell on the bell, discarded on the floor where they had been standing, and she hurried back to it.

When she reached it, she paused, gazing down at it. She couldn't doubt it was a godmother object—not after seeing its powers displayed. But did she dare pick it up—claim it? Who was she to possess something so rare and valuable?

Princess Charlotte. The echo of the bear's words made her chuckle, something she would have thought impossible only minutes before. Why shouldn't she claim it, after all? She was mistress of a vast castle now—empty though it might be. The bear had said it was a wedding gift. If so, it was the only one she had received, and she would not spurn it.

Drawing a deep breath, she wrapped her hand around the wooden handle. It was smooth to the touch, the whole thing weighing less than she expected. She laughed at herself. Had she thought its value would increase its weight? It was a small thing and should be light.

Holding it carefully motionless, she considered the world of possibilities in the bear's earlier declaration. By ringing this bell, she might have anything her heart desired.

Any material thing, an unwelcome voice whispered. *It cannot create love for you or companionship.*

She shook the thoughts away and considered what she wanted. She knew what her sisters would wish for. Gowns, jewels, chests of gold. Her mother might wish for a feast. Her father for sturdy walls.

Holding those thoughts in her mind, she rang the bell. Nothing happened. Or rather, nothing she could see. But she had been wishing for something far away. Was it possible the power of the bell worked at such a distance, and she had just gifted her family the bride price they had sought?

A vindictive part of her wanted to wish it away again, just in case. But for all her lingering resentment, she would gain nothing by wishing misery on her family. If the bell had done something for them—as impossible as that seemed—she would leave it be. Her thoughts were better spent on her own immediate needs.

Her eyes traveled the stone of the castle entryway. She had sturdy enough walls to keep out an invading army. And she doubted her ability to eat—not with her emotions in such turmoil. Fancy gowns and jewels would be equally wasted. Who was there here to see them?

She considered again. Her family's wishes would do her no good. What did *she* want?

The answer came immediately. After everything that had happened, she longed for nothing so much as the comfort of her bed and blankets she could pull over her head. She wanted to collapse into a soft mattress and enjoy the oblivion of a few hours' unconsciousness. Surely this strange new home would be easier to accept in the light of day.

Smiling at herself, she rang the bell. "My own room with a warm bed," she said, knowing it wasn't the sort of thing the bell could provide.

But to her astonishment, a door in the far wall swung immediately open, lights springing up in the corridor beyond it as candles flared into life along its length.

Charlotte hesitated for only a moment before picking up her discarded bundle and hurrying toward the door. Once in the corridor, she could see that the lit candles created a pathway, guiding her through the castle. She followed where they led until a second door swung open for her, creaking with a reminder that the castle was old and abandoned despite the lack of dust.

She paused in the doorway, peering inside. An enormous room emanated warmth and light. A large fireplace crackled with a cozy fire and deep, forest green carpet enticed her to step inside. The heavy brocade curtains were a lighter shade of green, while the green of the bedspread was enlivened with intricate gold embroidery. The curtains of the enormous four-poster were tied back with heavy gold cord and tassels, beckoning her to slip between the crisp white sheets.

"But it's huge," she gasped aloud as the door swung closed behind her. She had never seen or imagined such a large bed. "I'll be lost in that!"

She glanced dubiously at the bell in her hand, but another look at the room made her discard the idea of attempting to use it again. The enchantment might have miscalculated the size of the bed, but everything else was perfect, and she didn't want to risk changing anything.

Cautiously she placed the bell down on the walnut side table that was placed conveniently beside the bed. She didn't want to risk ringing it by accident. What if the bell attempted to make something out of her confused thoughts?

Although her meager things seemed laughably out of place in the room, Charlotte unpacked her bundle, changing quickly into the long nightgown she had brought with her. The material felt rough against the softness of the sheets as she crawled between them, and she suspected she would soon be requesting new clothes from the bell.

But she would wait for the next day. Surely the bear would return in the morning, and she would have the chance to ask more specifically about how the bell worked.

Wistfully she considered how he had run from her. What had been so urgent that he needed to abandon her like that?

A memory popped into her head of words he had spoken to her previously. He had said that once she reached her new home, she might choose never to see him. Surely he didn't think that was what she wanted? He didn't mean to abandon her alone in this enormous place?

She shook off the thought. He had promised her an explanation, so he hadn't left for good. She would have to hold on to that assurance until morning.

Sighing, she leaned over to blow out the candelabra sitting on the side table. She didn't relish lying alone in the dark, but the fire in the hearth would provide enough light for reassurance, and she didn't want to risk accidentally setting the bed curtains alight.

But the second the candle flames winked out, the room was plunged into complete darkness.

Charlotte gave a terrified cry, too startled to exercise restraint. Her heart pounded as she sat up in bed, trying unsuccessfully to peer into the black around her.

She told herself her reaction was unwarranted, but she wasn't convinced. What might be lurking unseen in this strange place? And what had happened to the fire? She hadn't made a request—she hadn't even been holding the bell.

The bell! Grasping blindly with both hands, she knocked over the candlestick before she finally felt the curved shape of the bell.

"Start the fire again," she gasped out, her fingers curled around the wooden handle as she made the bell peal out.

Nothing happened.

"Light the candles," she said in growing desperation, ringing the bell louder.

Still nothing happened.

She could feel the tears gathering, her panic threatening to take over and send her blindly fleeing. But where to?

She could try to use the bell to wish herself out of this room and back in the entryway, but it no longer seemed to be working. And what if the lights had gone out there as well? At least here she was snug in a bed, and she knew the room was empty and the door closed. Could she bear to be in the dark in the vast emptiness of the entryway? Or worse—wandering lost among the castle corridors?

No, it was far better to remain where she was. And her eyes would adjust to the darkness any minute, and she would see it wasn't as complete as she thought. There had to be traces of moonlight seeping around the curtains if nothing else.

But the minutes dragged out and nothing changed. No matter how closely Charlotte waved her hand in front of her face, she could see no flicker of movement. The darkness was absolute.

"It's still better to remain here," she whispered to herself. Morning would come eventually. Even the bell couldn't change that.

And at least she was alone in her room. She had even seen inside the wardrobe when she was putting away her clothes.

She slowly lowered herself back down to lie flat. But just as her heart was slowing to a more normal rhythm, the door to the corridor creaked open.

Charlotte only just bit back her scream, clapping both hands to her mouth. She felt sure she should do something—get up and fight perhaps, although she had no idea what she was facing and would be more likely to end up tripping over the side table than intimidating the unseen creature.

At the very least, she should call out to whoever had opened the door—assuming it had not been the work of the bell. But instead, she disgraced herself. Primal terror overcame her, and she scrambled beneath the bedcovers.

CHARLOTTE

*P*ulling the blankets firmly over her head, Charlotte lay there, trembling from head to toe. Her breath rasped in and out, the only sound in the heavy silence. She strained to hear footfalls, but the lush carpet absorbed any sound that might have reached her ears.

"Is…is someone there?" she mustered the courage to say, just as something tugged at the blanket.

For a second she feared it was being pulled off her entirely, and she gripped it harder. But it was merely rippling as someone touched the far side of it.

The mattress dipped slightly as someone climbed in beside her, although the size of the bed meant they were still out of reach of her arm. She scrambled away, nearly falling out of the bed before soft words made her freeze.

"Wait," the voice said. "I won't hurt you."

It was a deep voice, masculine and commanding, but it still had an edge of youth, and she would have guessed its owner to be only a few years older than herself. Strangest of all, the sound of it, although unfamiliar, filled her with the same sense of safety she always felt in the presence of the white bear.

Even so, she couldn't possibly accept the current situation.

"This is my bedchamber, sir!" she exclaimed, putting as much indignation as she could into her voice without making it waver. Better to show this stranger anger than fear. "This is my bed! You cannot be here!"

She remained poised on the edge of the mattress, ready to leap out if he came any closer. But there was no movement from his side, just words that carried a disconcerting layer of amusement.

"I think even the strictest matron would find it acceptable for a bride and groom to sleep beside one another on their wedding night."

"What?" Charlotte gasped. "What are you saying?"

"I am your husband," he said with more solemnity. "I am Henry in my true form."

"You're *human?*" Charlotte asked, dizzied. Part of her wanted to protest that it couldn't be true, but this latest shocking revelation was no more extraordinary than anything else that had happened to her in the last twenty-four hours.

"Yes, I am human," the voice that apparently belonged to her husband said. "I was once quite an ordinary human, in fact. But now I'm under an enchantment. At night I am allowed my true form, but during the day I become a white bear."

"You should have said as much!" Charlotte cried, and he was silent for a moment.

"That too is part of the enchantment," he said at last. "I cannot speak of my enchantment while in my bear form. I thought you would know of it anyway, however. From certain things your father said, he seemed aware of such enchantments."

Charlotte wanted to protest hotly, but the words died in her mouth. Her father had been so insistent that the bear was a person, and Master Harold had spoken of secrets that couldn't be shared. Clearly her father knew something—something he had been sworn to secrecy over.

"What is your business with the valley folk?" she asked, some of her anger at her father's secrets tingeing her voice. "What do they know of you?"

"Nothing," Henry said. "Your family is the first I ever talked to there. Whatever your father knows of my enchantment, he didn't learn it from me."

Charlotte frowned, but it was too late to pry the truth out of her father or Master Harold now. She felt the bed shift slightly and tensed, but Henry stilled again.

"In truth, I don't like to speak of my enchantment anyway," he said in a low voice. "It is because of my own foolishness that I've found myself in this situation, and though I hope to gain my freedom again, I cannot guarantee it. Even if I had been free to do so, I don't know if I would have spoken to you of my true identity. I needed a wife of strength and courage, and I didn't want to marry someone under false pretenses. After all, it is possible I'll spend our whole marriage as a bear."

"Except at night," Charlotte said softly, glad for the darkness that hid the warmth in her cheeks. Henry had promised her a legal marriage and nothing more, but now it turned out he became a man at night, and he had come here to her bed. Was he expecting a proper marriage between them after all?

"Don't worry," Henry said, once again picking up on her emotions. "There are other reasons for my silence. The same reasons that bring me here to this room. But while there are things I can't fully explain to you yet, I meant the promises I made. All I ask is for you to accept my presence beside you at night. I will not harm you, and neither will I impose any further upon you. You may go all day without seeing my bear form if you wish, and we can sleep side by side in silence at night. I ask only for you to stay true to the promises you have made and to endure it."

Charlotte let out a relieved breath. There was no doubt the request was strange. But was there anything about the entire affair that hadn't been strange?

Even the bed they slept in was large enough that two could occupy it without ever coming into contact. It occurred to her that the size of the bed hadn't been a mistake by the bell, after all. Apparently her husband had gifted her the use of the silver bell, but ultimately it still belonged to him and obeyed the parameters he had set.

She wished Henry could have explained it to her ahead of time, but she couldn't help but soften now she knew he had done his best to consider her comfort despite the oddness of the situation. Touched to once again see the signs of her new husband's consideration, Charlotte spoke, her voice coming out quiet and shy.

"I thank you for your kindness, and I have no desire for you to stay away from me or to stay silent. I'm sure I should be lonely if you were to disappear." She gathered her courage. "In fact, if you give me a moment, I will relight the candles. I should like to see your true face, and we will be more comfortable talking with a little light."

"No!" he said so sharply that Charlotte started and nearly fell out of the bed. "You can never turn on the light. You will find, in fact, that you cannot. None of the candles or fires here will permit such a request."

Heavy silence wrapped around the room for nearly a full minute before Henry sighed.

"I'm sorry. I know this is a strange marriage, and I have done little to earn your trust. But I must ask that you give it to me anyway."

Charlotte lay there, her heart beating erratically in her chest. She couldn't even see his face? He did ask a lot.

And yet, did he really? So far, he had met every promise he had made. If she had carried different expectations, that was her error, not his. He had given her a vast mansion for a home and even gifted her the use of a godmother object that would grant her every whim.

And in return, he asked only that she allow him to sleep in the same room as her at night without the comfort of illumination. Technically, they shared a bed, but it felt wrong to think of it that way when he lay so far away. She could thrash around in her sleep, or even reach for him on purpose, and she wouldn't make contact.

No, his demands were strange, but not onerous. As her husband, he could have expected far more and provided less.

"I don't understand," she said at last. "But I can accept it." She hesitated. "You said you can't explain the situation to me yet. Does that mean one day you will?" *Once I have gained* your *trust,* she added in her head.

"If you will trust in me, it will be a greater gift than any I have been given," he said, not quite answering her question.

She sighed quietly. He had said he couldn't give further explanations, and obviously he meant it. Was the enchantment physically restraining him from speaking? At least one of her cousin's stories had included something of that nature.

Silence fell between them again, but it was laced with

awkwardness, and Charlotte couldn't imagine sleeping in such a strained environment.

But just as her nerves were stretching taut, Henry laughed. A rich chuckle that pulled an answering smile from her, although she didn't know the source of his amusement.

"I know I said we could lie here in silence," he said, "but I didn't realize it would be so awkward. And yet, somehow, the harder I try, the less I can think of anything to say."

Charlotte laughed. "I'm glad it's not just me. I used to have an invisible friend, you know, but I've never had a stranger for a husband nor conducted any conversation in the pitch dark."

"An invisible friend?" he asked with another chuckle. "I didn't picture you as a fanciful child."

"Oh, she wasn't *imaginary*," Charlotte said calmly. "She was just invisible, although not to children. Of course that meant the adults all assumed she was imaginary, so you can guess how infuriating that was. But I'm sure my imagination couldn't produce someone like Daisy." She laughed again.

"You were friends with Princess Daisy?" Henry asked, clearly shocked. But after a moment, he added, "I suppose you would have been the right age. But I didn't realize you used to live in Northhelm."

"*You* know Daisy?" Charlotte asked in even greater astonishment. How did a man cursed to spend his days in the mountains in the form of a bear come to know a princess from across the sea?

"Not personally," he said hurriedly. "But I've heard the stories, of course."

"Oh, of course." Charlotte relaxed. "I suppose half the Four Kingdoms have heard the tale by now. It's a strange thought, even if I don't feature in the tale by name."

"I'm surprised the valley isn't abuzz about having a

celebrity in their midst," Henry said, and she thought she could hear a smile in his voice.

"My sisters didn't like me to talk about it," Charlotte said heavily. "They didn't take it well when Daisy's true identity was revealed."

"Because she was more your friend than theirs?" Henry asked shrewdly. "And they didn't like that she turned out to be someone important?"

Charlotte nodded, only to remember he couldn't see her. "Yes, that was part of it. And beyond that..." She hesitated, loathe to reveal the extent of her sisters' behavior.

"You can tell me," he said in a gentle voice. "I'm your husband now, so you don't need to hold back any of your story. Your past is safe with me."

Lying beside him, she realized he was already far more her husband than she had ever thought he could be. She had already pledged her life to him, so why would she withhold her past? She finished the thought she had held in.

"It wasn't just that I was closer to Daisy," she said. "Once Elizabeth and Odelia grew too old to see her, they sided with the adults, pretending they had never seen her at all and she was just a game I played with the younger children."

"They wanted to make you look foolish," Henry said with unexpected savagery in his voice. "Because even then they could see that you would outshine them both."

"I never wanted to believe that was the reason," Charlotte said softly, "but..." Given everything that had happened in the years since, it seemed almost certain. "It's a difficult time in those years between childhood and adulthood," she said softly. "We all make foolish choices we regret later."

"You're kinder to them than I would be," Henry said, still with that note in his voice.

It made her shiver, and she was once again glad he couldn't see her. Not that she was afraid of him. It was her own responses she feared. She was pleased enough at the way he leaped to her defense that she felt guilty.

She should try harder to understand her sisters, not delight in hearing them disparaged. But she couldn't help her pleasure at Henry's support. For some reason he seemed to genuinely care about how she was treated. Not since Daisy's friendship so many years ago had Charlotte had someone so actively on her side.

The cold, empty castle had frightened her, promising a future far different than what she had been imagining. But now Henry's words reminded her that she hadn't married him because of the Palace of Light. That had merely been an exciting possibility. She had married him because she wanted a place—a family—where there was space for her.

And here, lying in the darkness with a bodiless voice that burned in outrage on her behalf, she had found that sense of belonging.

"Goodnight, Lottie," Henry whispered, the unfamiliar nickname seeming to slip out without him realizing.

"Goodnight, Henry," she whispered back, his name comfortable on her lips for the first time.

The silence that fell between them no longer felt awkward or tense. Instead, it was filled with warmth and connection. She couldn't see the man who had become her husband that day, but she could feel his unquestioning support. It cradled her in a feeling of comfort and security that enabled her to sleep as peacefully as she had ever done in her own bed.

But when she awoke, daylight glowed around the edges of the curtains, and the long stretch of bed beside her was empty and cold.

GWEN

Gwen endured hours of forced stillness while a team of seamstresses dressed her in gown after gown, exclaiming over designs and materials and measurements. She couldn't enter into their excitement, but they didn't seem to notice her lack of it, treating her more like a doll than a bride-to-be. Had they known of her mother's plans for a royal marriage before this? Had everyone but Gwen known?

She told herself it didn't matter, and she tried to use the time to make plans. Part of her wanted to run straight for the mountains to the west of the valley—the ones that eventually led to other kingdoms. Surely, with enough provisions, she could find the passage through that was used by her mother's people.

But she couldn't leave just as she was uncovering the mystery at the heart of her home. And she must still have some time, going by the number of dresses her mother had commissioned. If they were intended to be finished before the mystery prince arrived, he must still be a way off. She would uncover her mother's secrets first, and then she would devise a plan to flee. Maybe she would even find something that could aid in her escape.

By the time she was finally released from the dress fitting, it was almost time for the evening meal. And after her experience the previous night, Gwen knew she wouldn't be able to stay awake for any nighttime wanderings.

She had the secret master key that should let her out of her room, but the locked door wasn't her primary hurdle. A key was no use to her if she couldn't stay awake long enough to use it. And worse—if she made it out into the corridor and then fell asleep there, she would alert her mother to her possession of the key.

So Gwen endured a normal evening meal, even forcing herself to eat as usual, and when she grew sleepy, she went to bed. At least the mattress was soft on her bruises.

But the next morning she arrived at breakfast filled with determination. She wasn't getting caught up in meaningless activities for another entire day.

On the threshold of the dining room, she paused, however. While they often had guests for the evening meal, having anyone but her mother at breakfast was unusual.

Count Oswin rose instantly to his feet on seeing her, bowing respectfully. "Good morning, Your Highness."

He smiled and held out her usual chair, waiting for her to take a seat.

"I apologize for intruding on your remaining family time," he said once she had begun her meal.

Gwen's hand froze, the knife halfway to the butter. He knew about her mother's plans?

She shot her mother a look and caught the strain around

her eyes as she held her smile in place. The count definitely knew, but the queen didn't like him mentioning it.

Count Oswin also glanced at the queen, hurrying into speech at sight of her expression. "Not that I mean to imply you'll be losing each other, naturally. But it will be different to have someone else join the family."

Seeing her mother relax, Gwen experienced again the familiar feeling that she was missing an underlying meaning in the words spoken around her. In the past, she'd allowed the sensation to wash over her, but now it sent energy crackling up her spine.

She could smell the secrets as clearly as she could smell breakfast. If only she could pluck them off the table as easily.

She forced herself to eat her toast, carefully chewing and swallowing each bite. But her ears were sharp, straining to catch any double meaning. The conversation had moved on to safer topics, however. The count and her mother discussed the weather and an upcoming picnic as if they were perfectly natural topics for a ruler to discuss with her most powerful advisor.

Gwen forced herself to drink her tea. This conversation couldn't be the real reason he had joined them for breakfast. And from the way he kept stealing glances at her, it was easy to guess that he wanted her gone so he could move on to his true agenda.

As disappointing as that might be, it was for the best. She wanted to escape as much as the two of them must want her to disappear.

Swallowing the last of her meal, she stood. When she tried to think of an appropriate excuse for her abrupt departure, her mind went blank, so she settled for a half curtsy to her mother before hurrying out of the room.

Alone in the corridor, she could finally breathe. And the further she got from the dining room, the more she recognized the unexpected windfall in the count's presence. Not only had her mother not given Gwen any tasks for the day, but she was likely to be occupied with Count Oswin for some time. The combination of those two things allowed Gwen to start her investigation somewhere she might actually find answers.

She forced her shoulders straight and her face into an expression of detached confidence as she approached her mother's exclusive wing of the palace. The guard who was always stationed at the door gave her a curious look but didn't stop her. Apparently the queen's one family member was allowed into her domain.

Once past the guard, with a door shut safely between them, Gwen's legs trembled slightly, but she couldn't risk slowing down.

She considered the options open to her. She could search her mother's office, but her instincts steered her away from there. Her mother sometimes mentioned having meetings there, and Gwen suspected anything the queen had hidden would be somewhere more private. Somewhere like her bedchamber. Not even Gwen was ever invited in there.

When she tried the handle, it didn't turn. She had expected as much and come prepared.

Somewhat to her surprise, the master key turned in the lock. She'd feared her mother might have an individual lock for her own chamber.

Inside, she found a room that looked like a mirror image of her own, down to the location of the bed and coloring of the carpet and curtains. She frowned. The castle might have been austere, but what little decoration it had was tastefully diverse. She'd never seen two identically decorated rooms before.

The unexpected appearance of the room gave her a disconcerting feeling of familiarity and wrongness at the same time. She shook it off and began a methodical search.

It didn't help that she didn't know what she was searching for. It was ludicrous to think she might come across a paper titled *My Evil Plans for my Daughter Gwendolyn*, or *A List of the Secret Things that Happen in the Mountain Palace at Night*. But if she didn't do *something*, she might spend another day shaking and crying by her bed.

Her mother's possessions were as luxurious as you would expect from a queen, but it struck Gwen that they were oddly impersonal. Nothing in the room gave any real sense of the owner's identity.

When she had examined each piece of furniture without finding anything of note, she turned her eyes to the walls. It would be just like her mother to have a hidden door in her bedchamber.

Her gaze lingered on a pair of closed, floor-length curtains. They would have been unremarkable except for the fact they were positioned on an internal wall.

Gwen pulled them open with a sweeping movement, gasping at what they revealed. Rather than a door as she had hoped, they concealed a large and striking portrait.

A stunningly beautiful girl stared into the distance, her golden hair matching her gown of golden satin. But more impressive still was her hand, which rested on the shoulder of an enormous white bear.

The pose was affectionate on her behalf and protective on his, although Gwen couldn't have put into words what gave her that impression. The painter had placed them in a spring setting, in a forest, although Gwen could see the edge of a gray stone building that reminded her unpleasantly of the stone that always surrounded her.

She stood still for several minutes, taking in every detail of the painting and trying to make sense of its existence. Why did her mother possess such a portrait—it matched no one Gwen had ever met—and why was it concealed in her bedchamber?

Something about the fanciful idea of a girl with a bear as a companion reminded Gwen of a fairy story. And nothing could match her mother less. Her mother didn't waste time on imagination or stories for children.

Unless the portrait itself hid something? It wouldn't explain the subjects of the painting, but it could possibly explain the concealing curtains.

Gwen stepped close enough to touch it, hesitating for a moment before carefully running her fingers along the edge of the frame, feeling behind it. Sure enough, she found a small lever that she managed to pull upward with a single finger.

As soon as she touched it, a creaking sounded, and the entire life-size portrait swung forward. Gwen only just jumped out of the way in time, gaping at the dark space revealed behind. She had been looking for hidden doors but had only half expected to actually find one.

She stepped to the edge of the space, peering into the black. Just as she was considering going in search of a candle, her eyes adjusted. It wasn't completely dark inside after all—she could see the rim of sunlight around at least two sets of closed curtains.

Within moments, her eyes had adjusted enough to allow her to step inside without any further illumination. Whatever she had expected to find, however, it wasn't what awaited her.

Several chests rested against one of the walls, their lids thrown open to reveal the sort of riches you might expect to find in a secure treasury. But they weren't what drew Gwen's attention.

Scattered around the middle of the room were a series of plinths, each proudly displaying a single item. She had seen an illustration like this in a book once. It had shown a royal treasury, with the positions of honor reserved for godmother objects that had been passed down within the kingdom through generations.

Gwen gasped as her gaze roamed over the room. There were so many of them. And yet, she knew of no recent stories about the godmothers visiting the mountain kingdom. Where had they all come from?

She stepped closer, fascinated. Her fingers reached for the nearest object, but she pulled her hand back. These weren't like the treasures in the chests. They had power she didn't understand, and a single touch might be enough to unleash something.

She wanted hours to slowly look through the room, guessing at the powers and original purpose of each object. But she didn't know how much longer she had. Her fruitless search of her mother's room had already taken too long. She should have looked for a hidden door first.

Her attention was drawn to a plinth that held two items. They both appeared to be made of gold, but they had a soft, pliable look that didn't match the metal. She knew why she had been drawn to them—the miniature version of a halter and whip were unusual items to see molded from gold, but they were also familiar. Just looking at them brought back the sensation of wind in Gwen's hair as she galloped away from the palace.

Without meaning to do so, her hand rose, reaching to finger the halter. The whip made her shudder—she didn't like them and had never used one—but the halter felt like freedom.

As her skin touched warm, supple metal, the air pressure around her changed. Someone had just entered the room. She jumped, whirling to face Queen Celandine, standing in the doorway of her secret treasury.

Gwen's face and hands went cold, her breath catching. How had she been so careless? She should have noted what she could and already left. She should have—

"Well done, my daughter!" The queen smiled at her, and for once she actually looked pleased.

"I'm sor—What?" Gwen asked, caught off guard in the middle of her half-formed apology.

Her mother gestured for her to exit the hidden room, but Gwen hesitated. Was there some reason why her mother didn't want to unleash her anger in this room full of powerful objects?

But staying would only increase her mother's wrath. So Gwen stumbled out in her wake, watching numbly as the queen closed both the portrait door and the curtains, shutting the girl and bear from view. Gwen almost blurted out a question about the girl's identity, but she held it in.

When her mother turned to her, Gwen's surprise grew, however. She still had the unfamiliar look of actual pleasure. If it had been on anyone else's face, Gwen would have called it pride.

"I wondered when you would find your way here," the queen said. "Perhaps I should have had that conversation about your marriage with you earlier."

"You're...pleased I'm here?" Gwen asked, analyzing her mother's face for any hint of her true emotions.

"Soon you will be married," her mother said, "and to an outsider. Some spine and spirit will be necessary if you are to keep him in line. It is a skill you must learn because your husband will not be the last you must control."

Gwen swallowed. She was not only to have a stranger thrust on her as a husband, but she would be responsible for his subservience to her mother as well? And what was this talk of others? Her mother surely couldn't mean more lowlanders, could she?

The queen approached her, cupping Gwen's face in what might have been a loving, comforting gesture from a normal mother. From Queen Celandine, it sent a chill racing down Gwen's spine.

"Of course, my daughter," she said, dropping her voice low, "independence shouldn't be taken too far or else it might grow displeasing."

She emphasized the last word in a way that made Gwen want to shrink from her hand. She forced herself to remain as still as a statue, however.

"I understand, Mother."

The queen regarded her for a long moment more before giving a slow smile. "Yes, I think you do. My expectations were low when you were younger, but you have turned out well enough, after all."

With a satisfied nod, she let her hand drop and stepped away. Her eyes flicked to the room's door, and Gwen recognized the dismissal with relief.

Picking up her skirts, she all but fled into the corridor, not slowing until she had passed the guard and escaped her mother's wing entirely. She kept her face down on the way past, not wanting to see the man's expression. Had he let her past on her mother's orders? How long had the queen been waiting for her daughter to go snooping in her chambers?

When she reached her own room, she closed the door and leaned against it. But even with its support, her hands were still trembling. She thrust them both into her pockets, wanting to hide her weakness, even with no witnesses.

She instantly stilled, distracted from the lingering echo of her mother's words and manner. Her right pocket wasn't empty.

Pulling out the miniature golden halter, she stared at it. Running the events in the secret treasury back through her mind, she remembered the moment when her hand had reached—almost of its own accord—to touch the halter.

It had been just at that moment that the queen had appeared, surprising Gwen. She had no specific memory of it but, when startled, she must have instinctively seized the halter and concealed it in her pocket.

She stared at it, so innocent looking in her palm. Slowly her heartbeat picked up its earlier terrified rhythm.

She had entered her mother's rooms to look for information, but somehow she had stolen a godmother object. This was undoubtedly taking the matter to a level the queen would find *displeasing*.

But slowly Gwen's fingers closed over it in a gesture of possessiveness. She had acquired something of unknown power, and she couldn't let it go. Not now.

If Gwen was ever going to break free from her mother, the time had come. And she needed all the power she could get.

CHARLOTTE

Charlotte considered trying to find a dining room of some kind, but her courage failed her. Instead, she rang the bell and requested a hot breakfast in her room. It would be easier to face exploring the empty castle with a full stomach.

At first she thought nothing had happened, and the bell really was broken, but then a delicious smell reached her nose. Turning, she saw a tray resting on a walnut table by the window, a padded chair in front of it and steam rising from the dishes.

Smiling, she rushed over and fell on the food. How many hours had it been since she had last eaten? She couldn't remember, and she didn't want to calculate it. Her life had changed so completely since her last meal that she didn't like to think how little time had actually passed.

She would have to thank the bear—no, Henry. She would have to thank Henry properly for the bell. It was clearly going to make life in an empty castle much more enjoyable.

Henry. She stopped eating and placed her hands against

her warm cheeks. Her husband was a human, not a bear. It was a shocking new reality, one she still hadn't fully absorbed.

Who was he? And what was he doing living in this empty castle? Surely he hadn't lived here alone before the enchantment? It was a strange enough home for a talking bear, but it would be stranger still for a lone human.

She'd never even heard of a castle in the mountains, but they couldn't be too far from the valley where her family lived. Even though the bear moved quickly, they had arrived at the castle before dark.

And now she understood the necessity of their speed. No wonder he had hurried them home given night was falling.

Thinking of her home made her wonder about her family. Had they received the bride price promised to them? Had her wishes from the night before reached them? It was strange to imagine her sisters and parents preparing for a move to Arcadia without her. It didn't really matter how close the castle was to the valley when her family wasn't going to be there anymore.

When she'd finished the food, she hesitated for only a moment before using the bell to fill her new wardrobe with gowns. When she flung open the walnut doors, she gasped at the array of luxurious material and beautiful designs. She could barely bring herself to touch them and choosing one to wear felt like an impossible task.

She had never obsessed over gowns and wealth like her sisters, but she still appreciated beauty, and she had never seen such dresses. Eventually she forced herself to choose one of the simpler ones, only to be delighted all over again at how easily she was able to get it on without assistance. Apparently the power that resided in the bell was of a practical as well as beautiful nature.

She blushed in earnest as she admired herself in the mirror, noticing how the folds of the dress enhanced the elegance of her shape. Here in the privacy of her room, she admitted that her request for new gowns wasn't solely about enjoying beautiful things. She had discovered her husband was really a man, and overnight she had become conscious of how she appeared to him.

Did Henry think her beautiful? Is that why he had chosen her? Or was it some other quality he saw in her?

The dispiriting realization that it might have been neither crept over her. She had quite possibly been the only girl in close vicinity who was miserable enough to consider such a proposal.

She didn't like that idea, but there was a good chance it was true. The valleys didn't offer a huge range of choice when it came to marriageable females.

Staring at herself in the mirror, Charlotte shook her head. It didn't matter what his reasons might have been. He was her husband, and he had already demonstrated his consideration and willingness to defend her against others. It was her turn to show him the same care he was showing her.

And to start with, that meant braving the castle that was his home. She cautiously opened the door of her new bedchamber, relieved to see that the stone corridor looked far less intimidating with daylight streaming in through a large window.

The overall effect was still stark and cold, though, and she remembered Henry's words from the day before. He had told her to restyle the castle to her taste, and with the bell, the task was simple. She didn't even have to worry about making mistakes, since she could easily fix them later.

Dashing back into the room, she retrieved the bell before

gazing up and down the corridor, considering her options. Finally, she gave a decisive nod and rang it.

"Give all the corridors a central runner of thick red carpet, and add tapestries to the walls. Also some comfortable chairs."

Instantly, the space around her transformed. She gazed up at a stunning tapestry of geometric shapes in complementary shades of red and gold. It matched the carpet beneath her feet and the red upholstery on the elegant wooden chairs that had appeared beside the tapestry.

She smiled. Practicality and beauty. She could get used to having the bell at her disposal.

"Lottie?" The sound of her new nickname in the rumbly voice of the bear shot straight through her heart.

She had been afraid that in the light of day, seeing his enchanted shape, she would lose the sense of him as Henry. But the sound of the single word was enough to tie the two together. He might be wearing a different shape, but he was still her husband underneath.

"When I suddenly found myself walking on carpet, I real-ized you must be awake," he said with amusement in his voice.

"Do you like it?" she asked, knowing her tone made it clear she was proud of her initial effort.

"It's an instant improvement," he said promptly. "I don't know why I didn't do it a long time ago."

A draft sent shivers through Charlotte, and she lifted the bell again. "Warmth please, as well." She glanced at Henry as the crackle of a distant fire reached her ears and the air temperature rose around her. "I suppose you don't feel it with that thick coat. Please let me know if it gets too hot for you."

He shook his large head, his eyes intent. "I've taken you away from your home and your family. I want you to be comfortable here. Please don't worry about me."

"But how can I not?" she asked softly. "You're caught in a terrible enchantment." She straightened her shoulders. "I don't have any particular experience or skill, but we're family now. There must be some way I can help you."

"You are helping me. More than you know." His intent gaze speared into her, and she felt a flush of warmth that had nothing to do with the change in air temperature. Did her presence and companionship mean so much to him?

"I can do more," she said stubbornly. "Surely there's something more I can do."

Henry blinked and looked away, as if considering. Finally he nodded and turned back.

"If you really mean it, then there is something." He hesitated again, a smile spreading over his head. "Come with me. There's something I want to show you."

Holding back her curiosity with difficulty, Charlotte followed him down several corridors and up a flight of stairs. He stopped in front of a set of double doors that rivaled the front doors of the castle in size.

When he looked at her, she realized he wanted her to open them. Hurrying forward, she had to exert her full strength to pull them apart.

"I suppose having paws must make lots of things difficult," she said, breathless from the effort.

"I've worked out I can manage door handles. But it's difficult and awkward." He took several paces into the room and then turned to look at her. "But I can't handle books."

Charlotte gasped when she saw what filled the room inside. Despite her best efforts, a laugh burbled up inside her.

She turned to Henry. "That's a lot of books for someone who can't even pick them up."

Everywhere she looked, stacks of books were piled

haphazardly, many of the piles taller than her. It was a large room—large enough she couldn't see its far reaches—but the entire thing seemed to be full of books.

Henry grinned ruefully. "I asked the bell to lead me to the library, and then I asked it to fill the room with a copy of every book found in any of the royal libraries. This is what I got."

If there was furniture in the room, it was too covered in books to be seen, with a single exception. The lone clear spot stood out like an oasis in the mess. A circle of lamps surrounded a small but thick rug, and the piles of books scattered around its edges were a much more manageable height. Realization filled her, followed by a pang of sorrow.

"This is where you usually spend your time at night," she said. "When you're a man."

The space was already cramped and unwelcoming, but she could imagine it was even more so at night. It pained her to think of the many solitary hours he must have spent there.

He nodded. "As I said, large paws with even larger claws aren't ideal for holding books and turning pages."

"So you spend your nights reading and your days sleeping —or roaming the forest and valleys."

He nodded again. "I hope that somewhere in this vast trove of knowledge is a secret that will break my enchantment or aid me against the person who trapped me in it."

Charlotte raised her eyebrows at the mention of his enchantment—it was the first time he had spoken of someone else's involvement. But she was more immediately struck by a different aspect of his words.

"Except now you're spending your nights with me," she said. "You can't continue your research."

"Unless you're willing to help me," he said, sounding

boyishly hopeful. "Not that you should feel any obligation to spend your days here. Even an hour or so would be an assistance."

"Of course I'll help you," Charlotte said quickly. "The bell meets all our practical needs, so there's nothing else demanding my time. Of course I should help my husband."

She gazed around the room again, her nose wrinkling. "But I think we need to make some changes first."

She paused, looking at him for permission, and he made a gesture of encouragement. Wrapping her hand around the bell in her pocket, she took her time shaping what she wanted in her mind. Once it was clear, she shook the bell.

From one blink to the next, the library in front of them transformed. The full length was now visible, the long space larger than any ballroom and stretching to enormous heights about them. Tall windows let in plenty of light, but every other inch of wall was covered in bookshelves, and at least three levels could be seen, accessed via a series of delicate stairs and layered balconies. The piles of books were gone, all the titles in neat rows on the shelves instead.

Charlotte's eyes lingered on the brocade curtains on the windows and the cozy reading nooks scattered around the main floor, many of them lit by lamps.

"That's better, don't you think?" she asked with satisfaction.

Henry's mouth had fallen open. "Infinitely!" He shook his head. "I think the godmothers like you better than me. Look what I got when I asked for a library, and you got this!"

Charlotte's lips twitched. "You should have been more specific in your request." She wandered to the closest shelf. "I directed that the books be arranged according to their piles, with the ones closest to your reading space at the front. So hopefully I haven't destroyed whatever organization system you were using."

"That was clever," he said approvingly. "I spent many weeks just finding titles of interest, so I'm glad all that work isn't lost."

"Do you know where I should start then?" she asked, gazing at the multitude of shelves and feeling overwhelmed at the task, despite the more welcoming environment.

Henry padded over to the closest shelf and examined it. "These are all the titles I had chosen to review next," he said with satisfaction. "We should start here."

Charlotte winced to see the number of books he was indicating.

The bear grimaced in response. "It's a wide range of topics. I didn't want to risk missing anything that might be of use." He gazed down the long room. "Although I'm sure I have. There are just so many books."

"To say the least." Charlotte ran a hand along one of the shelves before adopting a positive tone. "So it's a good thing you have me to take over for you." She glanced sideways at him. "Will you stay here with me?"

"If you'll have me." He gave her a look that seemed almost as uncertain as her own. "I don't wish to make you uncomfortable, but I would love to be part of the search still. Perhaps you could even read aloud if you find anything that might be of interest. Even if it's only distantly related. There might be some clue hidden somewhere that will mean something when combined with what I've already read."

Henry was clearly as uncertain as she had been as to whether his bear shape would change the rapport they had started to build the night before. She smiled at him as brightly as she could, hoping to convey that he was welcome to stay at her side no matter what his outside appearance was.

As she looked from the shape of the enormous white bear to the closest reading nook, her smile grew. Nothing about this scene fit her vague expectations from their wedding, but it was all so much more appealing than she had thought the evening before.

Logically, she was even more isolated than she had been in the valley—her company reduced to a single person. But it didn't feel the same. Being around Henry made her nerves fizz even as it filled her with a sense of contentment. There was no comparison with the presence of her sisters who had so obviously wished her elsewhere.

Soon they were settled in place, her in a comfortable armchair, and Henry curled up on the rug at her feet. He asked her to look particularly for any mention of people transformed into animals or the mythical mountain kingdom. She wanted to tell him that her cousins considered the mountain kingdom to be nothing but legend—as befitted a place that was supposed to lie east of the sun and west of the moon —but she couldn't scold him for seeking fairy stories when he was apparently living one. Those tales might be the exact ones that would hold a hint to his current situation.

The day passed easily, especially given the bell's prompt provision of requested food. It even cleared away the dishes.

"Where do you think they go?" Charlotte asked Henry from where she sat, her legs tucked beneath her.

He lifted his head from his place on the rug beside her.

"Are you afraid there's some hardworking soul somewhere receiving a steady supply of our dirty dishes?" he asked with a grin. "I'm fairly sure it's not anything like that. I think they just…cease to exist. They're not real plates. They're all part of the bell's power."

"Does that mean this isn't a real castle?" Charlotte wrinkled her brow. "That hurts my head."

"I recommend not giving it another thought," he said cheerfully. "Real or not, the castle keeps out the rain and wind."

"And it provides enough reading material for a lifetime," Charlotte added, gazing around them.

Henry gave a rumbling growl. "I don't have a lifetime."

Charlotte winced. "I'm sure we'll find something soon." She picked up another book. She had been skimming them, stopping when she found anything of potential interest and reading it aloud. But other than a story about eleven brothers who were turned into swans, there hadn't been anything that seemed relevant.

She had been excited by the story of the brothers, but according to the legend, they had been freed when their sister took a vow of silence and knit them all shirts from stinging nettles. The whole thing sounded hideously unpleasant, and she was afraid Henry might ask her to try it. But he rejected the idea before she even mentioned it, seeming certain it wasn't the answer to his situation.

As the light outside the windows finally began to fade, Henry excused himself. Charlotte didn't want to be left alone, but she was conscious that he had barely eaten all day, subsisting mainly on water which he had to lap from a dish. She didn't know what he ate in his bear form, and she didn't want to ask too many questions. Whatever practical life matters he needed to tend to, it was best he did them away from her.

She also could use some time to take care of the practical

necessities, although she had never washed and changed into her nightgown so quickly in her life. Once again she was grateful for the bell's provision since the nightgown she found in her new wardrobe was far softer than anything she had worn before. Unlike the night before, she felt no discrepancy between her garment and the sheets as she slipped into bed.

This time, she didn't linger in bed with the candles lit. As cozy as the crackling fire was, she felt only eagerness to blow out her candle and be plunged into darkness.

CHARLOTTE

Charlotte lay in bed, filled with anticipation, despite an entire day spent in Henry's company. And sure enough, within only a few minutes, her straining ears heard the sound of the door opening.

"Henry?" she called, the name slipping out before she could stop it. Despite her newfound knowledge, it was hard to shake the fear of such complete darkness.

"It's me," he said reassuringly. "I would never allow anyone else to come into this place and frighten you."

She felt instantly at ease, remembering that the darkness itself was a sign of the control he exerted over the castle thanks to the bell. Real or not, this castle was his domain.

During the day, they had spoken of the books and the things they discovered in them, their attention on his enchantment—although he had refused to give her details of how he had come to be trapped in it.

But she felt instinctively that those weren't topics for the night. Here, in their shared bed, they were just Henry and

Lottie, beginning a marriage the wrong way round—getting to know each other after their vows instead of before.

Haltingly, she asked him about his childhood, and he spoke with warmth of loving parents and a younger sister. A pang of longing hit her at the way he talked about his sister. She had always dreamed of feeling that way about her sisters.

But she reminded herself that she had at least had Daisy, and when Henry returned her questions, she spoke of her old friend rather than her sisters by blood.

When their talking drifted slowly off, Charlotte lay there and listened to Henry's breathing shift to become slow and rhythmic as sleep claimed him. She had shared a room with her sisters for years but lying here beside her husband felt entirely different. Even if they were separated by the expanse of the bed, she could still feel his electrifying presence.

Only the previous night, the distance between them had felt safe, but now she found herself wishing she could roll closer. She could hear his breathing, but she wanted to feel the warmth of his body as well, as he lay close enough to touch.

She forced down the foolish thought. It was enough that she wasn't alone in this strange place. She would sleep, and in the morning, she would be reminded that far more than a stretch of empty blanket lay between them.

Eventually she slept, waking alone as she had the first morning. This time she hurried through her morning routine, however, eager to return to the library and Henry.

When she stepped into the corridor, he was waiting for her in his bear form.

"I wasn't sure if you knew the way to the library yet," he said in his deep voice, and she gave in to instinct and wrapped her arms around his broad neck, resting her cheek against his soft fur.

He stiffened for a moment before relaxing and pressing back against her, which she took as a bear's version of returning the hug.

"Thank you," she said, wishing she could find the words to express everything in her heart. From the first moment of their meeting he had shown more consideration for her than her own family.

When she let go and stepped back, she wondered if she should feel embarrassed by her display. She couldn't muster the emotion, however. Somehow it was much easier to express affection to Henry in this form than in his true one.

They spent another companionable day in the library, although they found nothing of import. Charlotte knew she should feel impatient to free Henry, but it was hard to maintain a sense of impatience in the face of such contentment.

As on the previous day, Henry disappeared before the sun set, and she was able to watch him go without a qualm. Already the castle was becoming a warm and friendly place, and she struggled to remember why she had found it so unwelcoming at first.

Again he appeared quickly at night, and again they spoke of their lives and dreams, speaking as if there was no enchantment or mountain isolation. They might have been any two people getting to know one another.

He told her he had always dreamed of a big family, and although it made her cheeks furnace hot, Charlotte agreed. By silent agreement they kept the topic abstract—for all the intimacy of their nights together, the barrier of Henry's enchantment still lay between them. But it still thrilled her to know they agreed although their motivations were different.

Henry wanted multiple children because of the love he had received from his parents and sister—he wanted more of the warmth that had saturated his childhood. Whereas Charlotte wanted the chance to make a different family from the one she had grown up in. She was determined she would never stand by and see one of her children excluded.

Days and nights passed in the same manner—so many days that Charlotte was vaguely conscious her wedding had been weeks ago and spring had reached the valleys in earnest. Spring had certainly bloomed inside Charlotte.

She hadn't dreamed her strange marriage could bring such joy and contentment. From the beginning she had felt seen and known by Henry, but the nights of sharing their hearts in the darkness had deepened that sense into a surety. The only thing that marred Charlotte's happiness was her growing desire to be rid of the barriers that still held them apart. The gulf in the middle of their vast bed had never felt so large.

Eventually there came a morning when Henry waited outside her door with a different air from usual.

"I'm sorry, Lottie," he said without preamble, "but I can't read with you today. I'm heading into the forest, and I fear I'll be gone most of the day. Will you be all right on your own?"

Charlotte wanted to protest that she didn't want to be alone. For a second she even considered asking if she could accompany him. But no matter how comfortable she had become with him as a person, her husband spent his days as a bear. There were parts of his life she couldn't share.

"Of course I'll be fine," she said instead. "I don't want to risk missing anything important in the books, though, so I'll wait for you to return to resume the research."

He thanked her, but he seemed distracted and eager to be gone. After his departure, Charlotte wandered listlessly, realizing her feet had taken her along her usual route. But when she arrived in the doorway of the library, she couldn't bring herself to go in. The library was her haven within the castle—a place of comfort and enjoyment—but it felt empty without Henry.

"Stop this," she said aloud to herself. "Since when have you become someone uncomfortable in your own company?"

Many of her most enjoyable days in the valley had been the ones when she slipped away and roamed the forest alone. She refused to become a person who couldn't cope with being alone.

Turning her back on the library, she decided to go exploring. With the bell safely in her pocket, she knew she could always find a way back if she needed one. But it was past time she discovered the extent of her new home.

Everywhere she went, she found the same red carpet underfoot, and the corridors were lined with variations of the same tapestry and sprinklings of identical chairs.

"Beautiful and practical, but limited," she muttered to herself after viewing the same tapestry for the fifth time. Apparently the bell's power wasn't as vast as it had seemed.

The carpet and decorations still achieved a positive effect, however. Even impersonal, repetitive decoration was better than a whole building full of nothing but stark, cold stone, so she was far from complaining.

"But why is it so large?" she mused as she looked into yet another empty room. "If Henry used the bell to create a home for himself after the enchantment, why did he ask for such an enormous one? Or had the castle sprung into being as part of the original enchantment? Did it mirror a real place, like when Henry had asked for a copy of the books that already existed in the royal libraries?"

The thought stilled her steps, and she gazed at the walls around her with new eyes. Was she roaming a copy of a real place that had once featured in Henry's life? If so, what had brought him to a castle? Was it the castle of his home kingdom?

She had always heard that both Rangmere's capital and its palace were austere places of gray stone. Never having visited them herself, she had no idea if she was now living in an enchanted version of Queen Ava's castle.

She continued her exploration, but everything she saw had a new fascination. It became a game to guess at the original purpose of the rooms. Bare of furniture, many of them looked foreign, but she could make guesses from their shape and location.

Opening another door, she stepped into the first room that wasn't empty. Stretching along the length of the room was a long dining table of heavy, dark wood. It stood alone except for a single elaborate chair at its head.

Charlotte stood transfixed, but it wasn't because of the unusual presence of furniture or even from the mental image of Henry eating alone after sundown each evening, the long table stretching emptily before him. Her attention was caught by an enormous portrait hanging on the far wall, facing the head of the table.

The brunette woman was both young and beautiful, and she was dressed in a filmy gown of blue. Her face shone with a gentle strength that gave her an appealing quality that was hard to put into words. She evoked a protective instinct that was unfamiliar to Charlotte as the youngest in her family.

She wanted to shake off the feeling, to laugh at herself. After all, this woman looked several years older than Charlotte and from the quality of her dress, she didn't need anything that a girl from the valleys could supply.

But the woman wasn't so easily put aside. Her stomach

churned as the image of Henry's solitary meals soured in her mind. Before her arrival, the entire castle had been unadorned. Henry hadn't added a single piece of furniture or decoration outside of the library—except for this table and this single painting.

How many nights had he sat here, gazing at the woman in the portrait? What sort of protective instincts had she roused in him?

Charlotte ran from the room, slamming the door behind her, her heart pounding. But the image of the painting had been burned into her mind. She might have closed the door, but she could still see it in front of her eyes.

Charlotte was playacting as a princess in this empty castle, but the woman in the painting clearly belonged in such a setting. The painter had captured a poise that Charlotte envied but also a light of kindness that only made her feel sick.

The woman in that painting was one it would be easy to love. She pressed her hand against her stomach, her nausea surging.

She knew something had compelled Henry to marry her. Even without knowing his secrets, he had hinted as much. There was something he needed from her, and it was more than mere companionship.

Had this enchantment separated Henry from the woman he loved? And then, even worse, had it forced him into marriage with someone else? Had he sat here, night after night, longing for his lost love and trying to strengthen himself to put her aside and marry another?

Before their marriage, Henry had been earnest in assuring her that it was a legal marriage only. And even after she discovered the truth of his enchantment, he had repeated those promises. She had assumed his words were for her sake, and they had been gratefully received. In the growing relationship between them, it had been easy to forget about their early intentions. She had even started gathering the courage to tell him she no longer needed such distance between them.

But now the words took on a different light. Was Henry's determination to keep his distance not about Charlotte's comfort but his own emotions?

She stumbled down the corridor, heading back to more familiar parts of the castle. But now everywhere she walked, she was followed by the specter of Henry's life. The curious interest from earlier was gone, replaced with a burning in her chest as she imagined Henry walking identical halls with the woman by his side.

She stopped in the middle of a corridor, recognizing the sensation for what it was. Jealousy.

"He's mine!" she growled at the empty air around her. "Henry is my husband, and I'm his wife."

The words brought her little comfort, however. Henry had committed his life to her, but she admitted to herself that she wanted more. She loved him, and she wanted his love. She wanted a real marriage. But Henry had never promised her that. They had never so much as touched each other while he was in his human form.

Her queasiness grew as she realized what she had to do. If he had only married her because of the enchantment, then once it was broken, she would have no choice but to offer him an annulment. She couldn't allow him to be tied to her for the rest of his life just because he had been trapped in an enchantment. She cared about him too much to do that to him.

She told herself she was overreacting and leaping to

assumptions. But no matter how hard she tried, she couldn't shake the thoughts free.

All the time she had been exploring, she had been listening with one ear for Henry's return. But now she dreaded the sounds of the bear's arrival. She needed time to settle her emotions, to find a way to mask the sickness that swirled in her stomach.

She wandered slowly back to more familiar parts of the castle, running her hand along the small pieces of furniture that lined the way. The backs of the chairs somehow always remained dust free, although she never cleaned them, and the small side tables that paired with some of them remained equally spotless.

Still listless, unable to marshal her thoughts into a proper course, she slid out the small drawer in one of the tables. It would be empty, of course, but she couldn't keep her restless fingers still.

Except it wasn't empty. Charlotte froze, her heartbeat speeding up in contrast to the stillness of her limbs. Inside the drawer was a small oval frame protecting an unfamiliar painting. But while Charlotte had never seen that particular artwork, she instantly recognized the face and shoulders depicted. The woman from the full-length portrait in the dining room.

Slamming the drawer closed, Charlotte staggered backward, stopping only when she collided with the opposite wall. She wanted to scrub her mind clean and forget she had ever seen it lurking in there on the route between her room and the library—the route she had walked so many times with Henry and that he must have walked so often alone, coming to wait for her.

The full portrait had been painful enough, but it was a

relic of a time before she came to the castle. Henry did not sit there alone at night anymore. But this was different. The side table had only appeared after she had requested it with the bell. And yet, secreted inside it was a remembrance of this woman.

Unable to help herself, Charlotte hurried down the corridor, making for the next side table. Was it really possible that of all the drawers in the castle, she had happened to open the one containing the picture?

As soon as she pulled open the next drawer, her nebulous fears crystallized. In this one, too, sat a small portrait showing a woman's head and shoulders. She slammed that drawer closed as well and hurried to the next one and the next. In every drawer she opened, she found the mystery woman's eyes smiling kindly up at her.

The sickness in her stomach surged, and she sank to the floor against the corridor wall, tears running down her face. Earlier that day she had recognized the castle must be a copy of a real place—it made no sense otherwise. But she had only thought of Henry at the center of it. She had been wrong, though. It was this strange woman who lived at the heart of the castle Charlotte thought of as home. Even now, she had to be out there somewhere in the castle's original.

Part of her wanted to confront her husband immediately and demand the truth of the woman's identity. But the rest of her shrank from the idea. Even in her head, she sounded shrill and ungrateful. He hadn't demanded she reveal her own painful past—he had merely provided a safe space and waited until she opened up of her own volition. She owed it to him to offer him the same courtesy. His past was his own until he chose to share it, and despite what her feelings shouted, there was no betrayal to confront him over. The fact he might once have had feelings for another woman—in the past before he ever even met Charlotte—indicated no act of disloyalty to his marriage. And how could she accuse him of loving someone else now, when he spent night and day by her side, doing everything possible for her comfort?

She would have to ask him eventually. She couldn't live not knowing. But she couldn't do it while her emotions were so out of control. If she did, she would say something she would later regret. She would hurt Henry and that thought was the most unbearable.

Even as a bear, he was kind, his gentleness only broken by the strength of his protective instinct toward her. He treated her with respect, valuing her taste and opinions, and seeking out her company. And despite the direness of his situation, he laughed and joked with her, making it easy to spend time in his presence. Of course she was in love with him. She'd been a little in love with him ever since that first night when she'd discovered he was a man.

In these past nights, when they had lain side by side and shared their hearts, she had secretly longed for more. If he had broached the expanse of bed that lay between them and reached for her, she would have reached back.

But he had not done so.

Charlotte had assumed it was his promises holding him back. She had taken comfort and joy in the camaraderie and understanding growing between them, assuming it would gradually lead to more. But now she faced the reality that her husband might have no desire for a true marriage between them.

Time passed although she didn't track it. Eventually the growling of her stomach roused her, and she managed to get herself back to her room, even forcing herself to eat as the sun began to set. But as the last of the daylight faded, there was no sign of a white bear, and for the first time, Charlotte faced the possibility of a night on her own.

The prospect pulled her emotions into line more effectively than anything else. She couldn't endure this life without Henry. Just the thought of it was horrifying. But if she was going to continue to spend her days and nights at his side, she had to talk to him about her discovery. And to do that, she had to first master her new emotions.

She crawled into the sheets with steely determination, but she felt her control tremble as she blew out the candle and solid darkness descended. Every part of her was tense, listening for the sound of her door opening.

And, sure enough, it came as expected, only minutes after she had extinguished the candle.

"I'm sorry I'm so late back," Henry's now-familiar voice said into the dark.

Despite Charlotte's resolutions, her eyes immediately overflowed, silent tears tracking down her cheeks. The mattress moved slightly as Henry climbed into his side of the bed.

He said something else, but Charlotte didn't hear it over the beating of her heart. Her tears increased, betraying her into a small sob.

Henry instantly froze.

"Lottie?" He sounded worried. "Did something happen while I was gone? Are you hurt?" He shifted slightly toward her and then away again. "Curse this darkness!" he muttered with violent emotion.

More sobs escaped, Charlotte's emotions flowing out of control.

"Lottie," he said helplessly. "Talk to me! Please!"

She tried to form words, but the attempt only made her cry harder. Finally, with a muttered exclamation, as if driven past bearing, he closed the space between them.

Cautiously his hands reached out and, as she had predicted, her own reached back of their own volition. His fingers found hers, and he squeezed them, seeming to take courage that she wasn't drawing back.

"Lottie," he said again, sounding almost as pained as she felt.

Her heart expanded, the fresh sign of her husband's care only making the pain worse. She sobbed more loudly.

With another exclamation, he closed the last of the distance between them, gathering her into his arms.

Shock stopped Charlotte's tears, although a few sniffles still escaped. The feel of his strong arms around her was like nothing she had experienced before, enclosing her in an immediate sense of safety. But at the same time, it also made her senses thrill, sensation running through every part of her.

"Don't cry, Lottie," he whispered into her hair. "It hurts me to hear you cry. I'm sorry that I left you."

She rested her head against his shoulder and tried to master the shudders that were all that was left of the sobs.

"Did something happen while I was gone?" he repeated. "Did you injure yourself?"

She shook her head against him, knowing it still wasn't safe for her to speak of either her feelings or the woman in the portrait. Her tears might have stopped, but her heart still raged out of control.

"It's just foolishness," she finally managed to say. "Please ignore it."

His arms tightened, and she was secretly glad he hadn't ignored her tears. After the revelations of the day, she knew it was wrong of her, but she couldn't help the way she thrilled at being held in his arms.

If she lay still, she could imagine for a moment that theirs was an ordinary marriage and Henry was truly hers.

"It's all right, Lottie," he murmured against her hair. "You're safe here. I won't let anything happen to you."

She didn't doubt his words. That was the character of her husband. He might be full of secrets, but they were not ones of his making, and he would never swerve from the promises he'd made. He had promised to take her into his family and protect her, and he would never stop doing that. If he was ever going to be free, she would have to give him his freedom.

But still she couldn't bring herself to pull away from him. In that moment, there was no future, only the present. And in the present, she was his wife, she was in need of comfort, and she would accept the comfort he was offering. Perhaps tomorrow she would have gathered herself enough to speak to him safely.

Falling asleep within the circle of his arms was far easier than she could have imagined, and her sleep was deeper and more peaceful than she had anticipated after the upheavals of the day.

But, as always, when she woke, the bed was cold, and she was alone.

GWEN

aution told Gwen she should wait at least until the next day before doing anything else that might draw her mother's attention. But that instinct was balanced against the object that seemed to burn in her pocket.

How often did her mother visit the secret treasury? And if she did visit, would she notice something was missing? Would she know Gwen had taken it?

The fear of discovery overcame her sense of caution.

Mother and daughter had never been in the habit of eating the midday meal together, and so Gwen took it on a tray in her bedchamber. She found sitting at the small table by one of her windows less depressing than eating alone in a formal dining room. And that meant a servant always arrived at midday to deliver the meal.

It wasn't always delivered by the same servant, so she waited by the window, shoulders tense as the minutes ticked by on her clock. She was much closer to some of the servants than others, and there was only one she wanted to see that day.

The door finally opened, causing Gwen's anxiety to peak. Alma appeared, carefully balancing the tray as she closed the door behind her.

Gwen slumped down in relief before her eyes zeroed in on the closed door. Her eyebrows arched.

None of the servants ever shut the door when delivering the lunch tray. If Alma was doing so now, it was with a purpose. Which meant it wasn't coincidence that she was the servant who had appeared on this of all days.

"What did you hear?" Gwen asked as Alma approached and deposited the tray on the round table.

The servant woman looked briefly back at the closed door before sighing.

"You were outside? In the evening? What do you think your mother will do if she hears?"

"She hasn't heard?" Gwen should have felt relieved, but she already had larger misdeeds hanging over her head.

"Princess Gwen." Alma sighed, her manner more motherly than Queen Celandine's had ever been. "You are fortunate. If it had been different guards that found you..." She shook her head.

Gwen's brow creased. "Are you saying they had a reason not to report me?"

"Did I say they didn't make a report?" Alma snapped, only to rub a hand against her forehead as if overcome with exhaustion and anxiety. "How do you think I know of it?"

"I don't understand," Gwen said slowly, trying to make sense of Alma's cryptic words. "You said my mother didn't know of it yet, and now you're saying they did make a report."

Alma straightened and gave a rough chuckle. "Do you think the guards who patrol the grounds report directly to the queen? For someone who grew up here, you have an odd notion of how a palace works."

"Oh." Gwen frowned. "Yes, I suppose…"

The situation still didn't make sense to her, but Alma seemed irritated by the questioning, and she didn't want to put her in a bad mood before she got to much more important questions.

"My mother intends to marry me off," Gwen said, getting straight to the point. "Do you know of that too?"

Alma's eyes widened. "She told you about him?"

Gwen gasped, clutching Alma's arm. "You know who it is? She wouldn't tell me, except to say that he's from beyond the mountains."

Alma grimaced, her expression suggesting she had made a mistake. Gwen's suspicion hardened into certainty. The captive servants—her only allies in the palace—knew a great deal more than they had ever revealed to her.

She pushed aside the feeling of betrayal. There would be room for that later. For the moment, she had to make the most of this brief opportunity. She tightened her hold on Alma's arm, not letting go when the woman tried to gently tug herself free.

"What do you know, Alma?" she pleaded. "You have to tell me!"

Alma's expression of unease morphed into one of sorrow and compassion.

"Please, Alma," Gwen whispered, tears coming to her eyes.

She didn't have to dig for the emotion—it was already there. Her desperation for answers went deeper than even Alma could guess.

Alma opened her mouth and then closed it again, her eyes

sliding away from Gwen's before coming back to her face. She was clearly torn.

"We didn't like to do it," she whispered, making Gwen's fingers dig tighter into her arm. "The few of us who know have often debated if we should…" She sighed. "But it's dangerous, and you're not the only youngster we have to consider."

"Youngster?" Gwen managed a smile although it felt distant and strange on her lips.

Alma smiled softly, finally removing her arm from Gwen's grip and taking her hands instead.

"To one as old as me, you're young still, Princess. But so is Miriam, and others like her. Surely you can understand our hesitance. We have seen all you endure, but you are still—"

"My mother's daughter." The words slipped from Gwen's lips, burning on their way out.

"That doesn't make it right!" Alma said with muted ferocity. "What sort of mother drugs her own child? It's almost enough to make the rumors about the mountain people seem true."

"What?" Gwen stared at Alma. "My mother drugs me?" Her voice rose on the final words, and she glanced guiltily at the closed door.

Alma bit her lip. "I didn't…You mustn't…Princess, you mustn't say anything! There's no one else who knows about it, so if the queen finds out you know the truth, she'll know who told you. You must promise me—"

"She drugs me!" Gwen repeated, at a quieter volume but with no less heat. "How often? Why?"

But even as she asked, she already knew the answer, at least to the first question. Her unnaturally deep slumber every night had seemed unnatural. But even knowing her mother, she had suspected illness rather than deliberate poison. Why had she never drawn the connection with the sleepiness that always overtook her after the evening meal?

She could only conclude it was because it had been her reality for so long. And she sometimes felt sleepy after a large lunch as well.

It was all excuses, though. She should have been able to feel the difference.

"Where is it?" she asked, new steel in her voice she'd never heard in it before. "Where does she have you put the drugs?"

Tears ran down Alma's cheeks. "I never wanted to do it, Princess Gwen. I swear it. But if I refused her order, she would punish the others. You do understand, don't you?"

"Never mind that." Gwen still spoke in the hard new tone. "Where are the drugs?"

"In your drink," Alma admitted softly. "It's always in your drink."

Gwen groaned. All her efforts to eat less had been pointless.

"What else aren't you telling me?" she asked, suddenly remembering the rest of Alma's words. "You said something about a rumor about my people. What rumor?"

Alma hesitated, clearly nervous, but Gwen could see she was wavering. The fevered light in Gwen's eyes wasn't scaring her—quite the opposite. The longer she gazed at Gwen's determined expression, the more hopeful her own face grew. Gwen just needed to convince her old friend that she was serious this time.

"I have to get away from her." Gwen's voice came out hoarse, although she'd been aiming for strong. "I always dreamed of escape, but I always thought it was nothing more than a fantasy. This is different, though. This time I'll do anything to get away."

Alma stiffened, her face closing up. Whatever she had wanted to hear from Gwen, it wasn't that.

But it was too late for Gwen to take back the words, and she didn't know if she wanted to do so. She had made the declaration as much for her own sake as to convince Alma, and she had no idea what the woman had been hoping to hear instead.

Alma let Gwen's hands drop, stepping back and bowing formally. "I apologize, Your Highness. I hope you can forgive me for my role in this. And I hope you will see fit to keep our secret."

"Alma," Gwen cried. "Please! Will you not help me?"

Alma hesitated. "I think that's all the help I can provide. After all, I'm securely locked away each night. Just like you."

For a second she held Gwen's eyes, a message in her gaze that the princess didn't understand. Then she left, gently closing the door behind her.

Gwen stared at it for at least a minute, trying to make sense of the interaction. Her thoughts were too muddled to think clearly, and her emotions were even more of a mess. Should she feel gratitude to Alma for telling her about the sleeping potion or anger at her betrayal in keeping it a secret all these years? And why had she refused to tell Gwen anything further?

Or had she…? What had she been hinting at?

Gwen's circling thoughts slowed, focusing. Something in Alma's eyes had been pleading with Gwen to understand, but what exactly had she wanted her to grasp?

Just like you. The words echoed in her mind, and Gwen drew in her breath sharply as she realized she hadn't spoken of her recent discovery. Alma knew Gwen was locked in every night. Were the servants the ones to turn the key, just as they were the ones to place the potion in the drink they served?

Betrayal surged up again, but Gwen tamped it down once more. If they locked her room, it was at the queen's command. Her mother was the one hiding things from her, not Alma. Alma was locked up herself.

Gwen's mind circled around that thought. Alma had mentioned it specifically, although she knew Gwen was well aware of the captives' predicament. Almost as if she wanted to remind Gwen of their limitations.

What was it she had said at the start? She had mentioned rumors of the mountain people as if the servants didn't know the truth of those rumors—even after so many years in the heart of the mountain kingdom.

The two thoughts came together in Gwen's mind, making a conclusion that seemed so obvious she couldn't think why she hadn't seen it from the start. Alma hadn't been refusing Gwen information so much as goading her to go in search of it for herself. And she had been telling her where to start. Nighttime.

Everything pointed to the hours of darkness. And now Gwen knew why those hours were always lost to her. Which meant she could reclaim them. The answers were finally in front of her—she just needed to work out how to make it through an evening meal without drinking and without her mother noticing it.

Her fork clattered against her plate, and Gwen could barely restrain a wince. Years of discomfort during the meals she shared with her mother hadn't prepared her for her current level of tension. At any moment she expected her mother to stand up and accuse her of not drinking. Would she turn on the servants immediately or wait to order Gwen's punishment first?

A hundred times she had reconsidered her plan, wondering if she could truly put others at risk alongside herself. But no matter how many times she hesitated, she always returned to the same truth. Knowing what she did now, she couldn't sit there and drink the sleeping draft. She couldn't placidly accept a forced marriage and a lifetime of misery.

A curly-haired face appeared in her mind, the warm eyes laughing at her. She drew strength from Easton's encouraging expression, even if every part of his image in her mind was imagined. She hadn't dreamed up his personality and character, and she knew he would tell her to fight. He would never passively accept the queen's schemes—the evidence of that was in his disappearance.

But he also couldn't be dead. Gwen couldn't believe it—she wouldn't. If this worked, if she succeeded in escaping at last, she would find him, whatever it took.

The thought bolstered her as nothing else had done, and she lifted her goblet to her mouth, tipping it back against her firmly closed lips before taking another bite of food.

Her stomach roiled, but she forced herself to eat well, clearing her plate. If her mother saw how much she was eating, she was less likely to notice she wasn't actually drinking.

Alma appeared to remove the dishes after each course, taking Gwen's cup away and replacing it with another. She was protecting Gwen as she had on the night when the princess had attempted not to eat, and Gwen recognized it for the apology it was.

She didn't know which course's drink held the potion—maybe they all did—so she drank nothing. Her mouth was growing drier and drier, but she ignored the discomfort, intent on her purpose.

When her mother finally signaled the end of the meal, rising with her normal goodnight platitudes to her daughter, Gwen could hardly believe she had succeeded. Was she really about to experience the night hours?

Walking back to her room, she could already feel the difference. Her overly full stomach gave her a slow feeling that could be described as sleepy. But it was nothing like the irresistible pull to sleep that she usually felt. How had she mistaken that sensation for the ordinary response to a full stomach?

But she already knew the answer. Lack of experience. Gwen might have lived for more than twenty years, but she lacked experience in far too many things. Her life had been bound by walls of stone for far too long.

Waiting in her room felt impossible—at the lightest jump she might bounce off the walls or ceiling. But somehow she endured, even lying in her bed and feigning even breaths. She didn't know if her jailer usually checked on her before turning the key.

But when the grating sound of a key turning in a lock finally sounded, it came without the sound of the door opening first. After so many years, no one doubted the effect of the drugs.

Gwen leaped out of bed and laced on her boots, fumbling with the ties thanks to her trembling fingers. It only took seconds to retrieve the master key from her dressing table, but she made herself wait longer, peeking out at the darkening sky. She preferred not to wait until full dark, but she didn't want to risk running into whoever had just come by.

Finally she let herself turn the key in the lock, slipping out into the corridor before locking the door behind her. She doubted anyone rattled the handle in the night, but if they did, they would find it locked as it should be.

She had thought her heart was beating fast when she snuck through the corridors with the girl from the city, but it was nothing to how she felt now. While it only took her minutes to reach the outside, it felt like hours, and she was surprised to discover the last of the light lingering in the sky still. It felt as if enough hours had passed that it should have been midnight already.

Hurrying down the familiar paths of the garden, she considered the best place to conceal herself. Recent experience told her the palace grounds were actively patrolled, even at this hour, and she needed somewhere to conceal herself until the early hours.

Deciding on a place where tall hedges hid a bench seat from view, Gwen settled herself to wait. With the sun beneath the horizon, the last of the light was leaving the sky fast.

An itch made her scratch her leg, but it was immediately followed by one in her other leg. She scratched at that one, too, but it did little to reduce the strange ache which lingered just below her skin.

Her left arm took up the sensation, followed by her middle, and Gwen jumped to her feet. Almost dancing in her efforts to scratch herself all over, Gwen writhed and squirmed until a deep tearing made her freeze.

She was coming apart—she could feel it—tearing all the way up her body in a horrible sensation no person should ever feel. Why wasn't it hurting? She should be in agony as her final moments passed too quickly.

But no blood appeared, and no pain either. Instead, she dropped to the ground, landing on all fours as her eyes involuntarily closed. Dizziness made the world around her grow distant, her ears ringing and skin tingling.

And then, just as suddenly as it had begun, it ended. All that was left was a strange feeling of being far too large for her own skin. She felt…enormous.

Her eyes snapped open. Sure enough, she was looking at the garden from an unfamiliar vantage point. She looked down at herself and would have screamed if shock hadn't robbed her of all sound.

She was white. And covered in fur. And a bear.

CHARLOTTE

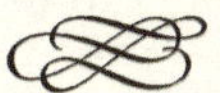

When Charlotte left her room, there was no white bear waiting in the corridor, and her heart contracted almost as painfully as it had the day before. On trembling legs, she ran to the library, but when she pushed open the door, he was waiting there, one of his unnaturally human smiles on his face.

"It feels an age since we were here together, Lottie," he said, "instead of just a day. I hope your throat is feeling better for the rest. It must be tiring to read aloud so much."

She blinked away tears, trying to find the words to reassure him that she didn't mind the reading. But all she could focus on was the way her heart leaped and fluttered in her chest when he called her Lottie—the name that belonged only to him.

She had once responded warmly to her father's affectionate nickname for her, but that had been a feeling of familiarity and the comfort of family. For weeks she had told herself she felt similarly for Henry, but now she had accepted the truth. When he spoke her name, it was an entirely different type of warmth that she felt—all fast heartbeats and a flush that made her turn her face away in case he saw the red in her cheeks.

He was in his bear form now, but all she could think about was the way it had felt to have his arms around her, and she longed for darkness to arrive so he could hold her again. But would he do so?

He had responded to her pain with comfort—something she could see he had done from the beginning. She would be foolish to read more into it than that. And she didn't want to compel his affection through pity.

One thing was clear—if just hearing him speak her name could overset her so badly, she hadn't yet gained the equanimity she needed before raising the topic of his past and what it meant for their future together.

"You're still unhappy," he said softly, making her startle.

"How could I be?" she asked. "You give me everything I ask for." It was a non-answer, and they both knew it.

"My godmother object provides any physical item you desire," he said, "but can possessions make a person happy? It has never seemed so to me. The bell cannot provide you with friends or family. You are lonely."

He had seen her grief the night before after a day alone in the castle and come to the wrong conclusion, but she didn't deny the charge. He was right in one way—just not in the way he thought. She did feel an aching loneliness, but not for the lack of family and friends. It was a different relationship with him that she longed for. She was lonely for his love.

"It's my fault," he continued. "I brought you here and have kept you day after day in the library with nothing to do but read. It's not the life you thought I was offering when I proposed. The Palace of Light must be nothing like this castle."

She remembered with an effort that she had once thought her marriage would take her to the fabled home of the High King. It felt like a long time since her dreams had changed.

"I know you can't take me there," she said, needing to say something. "I don't hold it against you."

"No, I can't take you there." He sounded defeated and sad, and she wondered with horror if he'd lain awake the night before trying to think how to fix her sadness. "But that doesn't mean you can never leave here," he concluded.

Shocked, Charlotte stared at him, frozen in place. "L… Leave?" she asked, horrified. Was he sending her away?

"Certainly." He sounded even sadder, as if he had mistaken her horror for shocked delight. "Not permanently, of course. I need you yet a little longer. But I can see no reason why you couldn't visit your family for a short while." He managed a smile although it looked strained. "I understand it's a common practice for new wives."

Her heart slowed, no longer feeling as if it would beat out of her chest. He wasn't sending her away forever. But she couldn't be entirely easy either. He had said he needed her only a little longer. Was the time she could stay by his side already drawing to a close?

"I…I don't know," she said, her mouth dry and her thoughts tangled. "I…I should think on it."

"You don't need to feel bad about going," he said gently. "It need only extend our situation by a few days, and there's nothing in that."

A few days? She tried to make sense of his words. He spoke as if he needed her for a specific length of time. So if she left, she wouldn't be losing any time with him.

Her first reaction had been to reject his suggestion, fearing what might be behind it. But now that he'd explained more fully, it didn't seem like such a bad idea. She desperately needed to sort out her emotional turmoil so she could have a frank conversation with him. Wouldn't it be easier to calm the raging storm inside her if she could have some space from him?

"Yes," she gasped, meeting his concerned eyes. "Yes, please. I would like to go to my family."

He nodded slowly.

"Can we leave immediately?" she asked.

"Leave now? This morning?" He came closer, his expression growing even more concerned.

At the hint of pain in his eyes she nearly crumpled and said she wouldn't go. But she couldn't weaken. She had to leave. She couldn't stay near him while there was such a weight between them, but neither was she ready for the necessary conversation. This was the best option open to her. She would leave him briefly and when she returned, she would be honest with him, even if she still didn't feel ready.

"If it's possible," she said. "Will you take me?" She suddenly remembered they had to be in Arcadia already. "Or can the bell send me to them?"

"I will carry you to them," he said. "And we can leave as soon as you're ready."

"I'm ready now. There's nothing I need to take. If my family has disposed of the things I left behind, I can easily borrow items from my sisters."

He hesitated still, but after another glance at her troubled expression, he nodded. "Very well. Let us leave."

The minutes that followed Gwen's transformation were hazy. But eventually reality intruded over the panic and shock that robbed her of coherent thought. As impossible as the situation seemed, she had to accept the truth. She was no longer a human but a white bear.

She had discovered the secret concealed by the darkness, and it was nothing like she had imagined. Her mother must have been concealing Gwen's condition from not only Gwen herself but the entire court. She wouldn't want the kingdom knowing her daughter and only heir transformed into a bear at night. And if Gwen herself had known, she would have told someone—it would have been her ticket to escape from the virtual prison of being her mother's heir.

Or perhaps she wouldn't have mentioned it to anyone. Perhaps she would simply have made for the mountains at sunset one evening. As a human, the snow-covered peaks promised only death, but in her new form, she could find a way across.

The thought stilled her involuntary pacing for a moment.

Her huge gait and heavy paws made small work of the constrained section of garden, but she couldn't hold herself still for any length of time.

Her first assumption had been that her transformation was the secret. But if that was true, why did the captives need to be locked away at night? And why did the courtiers talk of keeping a secret from the princess? If she was the secret, why would a girl from the city speak with fear in her voice of needing to be home by sundown? And how had her mother's guards found a pass through the mountains when the generations before them had failed?

Gwen took off through the gardens, her new shape making subtle movement difficult. She lumbered down the paths no matter how delicately she tried to step, but she had to test her theory. If she was right, then…

Her new ears picked up the sound of footsteps far earlier than her human ears would have done. And her nose detected a scent she didn't recognize. Someone unfamiliar was approaching her down one of the gravel paths.

Pushing through several bushes, she retreated until she found a place where she could watch the path while keeping her giant frame out of sight. As she waited, fresh fear washed over her.

She felt entirely like herself, her normal mind and personality merely trapped inside a new body. But what if the instincts of a true bear lurked beneath the surface? How would she react to the sight of another person? Would she be overcome by a desire to attack them?

The sounds reaching her ears made her frown, her thick lips pulling strangely against uncomfortably sharp teeth. The footsteps didn't sound as she had expected. The gait was off and the sound too loud.

She surged forward, peering between branches as two shapes came into view. Sight of them froze her in place, her breath stopping as her theory was confirmed.

She had suspected what she would find, but it still took her breath away to see two white bears—looking just as she knew she must now look—walking toward her, one after the other.

The two bears stopped, the one in front twisting to frown at the one behind.

"Did you hear something?" he asked in a gravelly voice that still sounded strangely familiar to Gwen's ears.

"Just one of the other patrols," the second bear answered, and Gwen instinctively knew their identity.

The two guards who had forced her back into her room were now patrolling the grounds in the form of bears. The earth beneath her feet felt soft and unstable, and she looked down to make sure she wasn't sinking into quicksand. But the gravel beneath her feet was steady. It was only everything she knew of her world that was shaking.

It wasn't just the princess who turned into a bear at night. Others did as well. Potentially the entire palace.

This was how her mother's people had found a way to get across the mountains and why no one from the city could make use of the path they had forged. The trading delegations must have traveled at night, their frailer human forms using the day to sleep.

What had triggered such a terrible enchantment? And how long had it been in place? It couldn't have existed for generations or some hint of it would have found its way into the storybooks and the kingdom's lore.

Easton's disappearance. The answer appeared in Gwen's mind already fully formed and obvious. As a young child she had been fully human—she must have been because she had the occasional memory of waking in the night or staying up past sundown. And she had definitely been human that first night locked in the dark closet.

Gwen shivered. Memories of that night weren't easy to forget. She'd barely slept, and the hours had felt like days. When the glass of juice arrived on the second night, she hadn't known if her mother had given way to compassion or if she was merely prolonging Gwen's suffering. When she slept so soundly after drinking it, she had assumed it was due to the exhaustion and weakness from her long ordeal.

But it had been neither compassion nor malice that had driven her mother. Her mother had sent the drink because she needed a way to deliver the sleeping draft that would hide the enchantment she had just unleashed. Knowing her mother hadn't been motivated by emotion—either positive or negative—but by cold strategy made sense. Gwen should have guessed as much.

The rest of the timing fit as well. It was only after her days in the closet that she had begun to hear talk of a new mountain pass.

But was it coincidence it had happened just after Easton's disappearance? Gwen couldn't credit the idea. Before the court stopped speaking Easton's name entirely, she had heard whispers about his fury as he marched to confront the queen. If anyone had seen the confrontation and heard the source of his anger, they didn't speak of it, but he had disappeared immediately afterward. And the next day an enchantment had taken hold of Gwen and the court.

Gwen didn't need anyone to confirm what she knew in her bones. Her mother had been the one to unleash the enchantment—her mother with her hidden room full of godmother objects. Gwen just didn't know why.

Knowing her mother, she had reasons wrapped within reasons. Queen Celandine was a master at turning any situation to her advantage and always thinking two steps ahead of her enemies.

Whatever her intentions, she had ended up with an army of enchanted bears at her disposal. Did she send them out to patrol the city at night?

The fear shown by the girl from the city hinted at the answer. The people had to contend not only with large and fearsome beasts in their streets but with the reminder of a power that was both foreign and terrifying in its strength. What limits were there for a queen who could turn people into animals and then command their obedience?

Did the city's inhabitants all lock their doors and windows and stay inside from first dark until morning light? A part of Gwen wanted to join them, to go back to hiding from the enormity of the truth. But there was no going back. She had to face the reality her mother had been hiding from her.

After enchanting her own people, the queen had orchestrated an enormous deception to ensure her daughter's ignorance. She had done it to preserve total control over Gwen and to keep her a prisoner at her side. She had known the truth would fuel Gwen's escape. It had been true when she was fourteen, and it was equally true now. Whatever political games her mother was using her daughter to play, they would all end now Gwen knew about the enchantment.

But she still needed to confirm her theory that the whole palace was affected. Employing her newly heightened senses of smell and hearing, she crept through the gardens unseen. She dodged another two patrols before she reached one of the wings housing palace apartments for the courtiers. Many of the courtiers would be in their city homes, but some always remained in the palace overnight.

Most of the curtains were tightly closed, although the occasional one was rimmed in light. But finally she found one set that had been thrown open, the window wide to let in the night air.

Inside, the room glowed with warm light, making it easy to see the large white form pacing up and down. Despite her own shape, despite seeing the guards earlier, the image still sent instinctive fear through Gwen. There was something different about seeing the hulking shape of a bear inside a room decorated with fine furnishings, and it was even more unnerving to see the animal conversing with a young boy. Even knowing everything, her instinct was to rush in and pull the boy away.

She kept herself frozen in place, however, her ears straining to hear. The bear spoke in a low voice, but as his pacing brought him near the window, she caught a few words. It wasn't enough to follow the meaning, but it was sufficient to bring the same shock of recognition as had hit her with the guards.

The voice might have been lower and rougher, but she could still recognize the words of Count Oswin. Which meant the boy must be his grandson—the seven-year-old child of the son who had led the first team through the mountains.

Count Oswin's son was obviously a white bear as well given his mountain exploration, but apparently his son was not. Whatever enchantment existed, it didn't affect children born after it took effect. Perhaps it hadn't affected many children at the time either, since most of them were kept sheltered in their homes in the city.

Although Gwen had known the count had a grandson, it was her first time seeing him. Had anyone ever mentioned that he walked with crutches, one pant leg pinned up due to the loss of his right leg below the knee? His face was calm, so if it was the result of an injury, it must have been an old one.

His whole bearing suggested he was comfortable with his grandfather in his bear form, and the sight of it reassured Gwen. Surely this scene wouldn't happen if those under the enchantment risked losing control while in their animal form.

Even so, anger swept through her. Her mother was the mountain queen and responsible for her people. How could she enchant some and terrorize others without qualm?

And what of Gwen's supposed new husband? The revelations of the night had been so shocking that Gwen felt only bewildered amusement at the thought of the unknown prince. How did her mother intend to hide Gwen's nighttime form from a lowlander husband? The entire plan went beyond foolhardy.

Gwen wanted to charge into her mother's wing and demand immediate answers. But enough caution remained to hold her back. As soon as her mother saw Gwen awake in her bear form, she would know her daughter had undertaken the ultimate defiance. It was wiser by far to approach her during the day.

Her best choice, however painful, was to go back to her room and wait until morning transformed her back again. But what about her clothes? In all the shock she hadn't given them a thought.

Remembering the moment of change, however, she was sure they hadn't torn as she grew. They had simply... disappeared.

Dismay swept through her. Presumably they would reappear when she turned human again—she had always woken in the same nightgown she had gone to sleep in—but what about the key concealed in her pocket? That had disappeared along with the clothes. Would it reappear with them? And even if it did, what would she do in the meantime? She was trapped outside her room for the remaining nighttime hours.

She looked down at her huge paws, unsure if she'd even be able to work a key or turn a handle in the form of a bear. With a wince, she remembered she had tried to turn a handle with bear paws once before without much success. On the night she'd discovered her room was locked, the drug had been so strong in her system that she'd barely been able to open her eyes as she dragged herself to the door. She'd been so dazed, she hadn't noticed the strangeness of her body, attributing her heavy, cumbersome limbs to the pull of sleep. But how could she have woken—however partially—and not noticed her change of shape?

She had plenty more hours to berate herself as she waited for the first sliver of dawn. When it came, she welcomed the crawling, itchy sensation and the tearing which she had found so unnerving the first time. When she was driven to her hands and knees, she felt only relief thanks to the sight of her usual shapely hands.

As she jumped to her feet, her hand flew to her pocket. Relief flooded her as her fingers closed around the key. Running through the corridors, she favored speed over concealment in the race for her door.

She dropped the key in her haste to fit it into her lock, but finally she got the door open and herself inside. She even remembered to re-lock the door, although climbing back into bed was more than she could manage.

Thankfully when she heard someone outside unlocking

the door, the unseen jailer made no effort to look inside and check on her. She had time to compose herself before the appointed hour for breakfast and her upcoming confrontation with the queen. Time she greatly needed.

She dressed slowly, choosing her clothing with care as she slipped back into the role of the stately, elegant Princess Gwendolyn—the royal heir who always knew how to look the part of a princess, even when she was screaming inside. She had never been so neat and well-dressed for breakfast before, and she entered the room with her head high. It was empty.

Taking her place behind her chair, unable to bring herself to sit, Gwen waited.

GWEN

When Queen Celandine appeared, she paused in the doorway, regarding Gwen with raised brows. "You're here early, my dear." Her tone didn't indicate whether she thought it a good or bad thing.

"I'm here," Gwen said through gritted teeth, trying to hold onto her courage now she was actually facing her mother, "for real answers. You cannot possibly mean for me to marry a lowlander prince."

The queen's brows rose even further. "Really, my dear, must you use that language?" She walked unhurriedly to the table and sat. "I'm not sure why you find the idea so impossible. Who else should you marry if not a prince?"

Something in the look she gave Gwen—as if she knew who Gwen would rather marry and was mocking her for it—sent anger searing through Gwen's veins. The emotion overpowered the instinctive fear she felt in her mother's presence.

"Oh really?" she spat out. "So you're intending to tell the lowlanders the truth about us? Or do you think you can

201

excuse why a husband and wife need separate chambers at night?"

The queen's hand stilled, her knuckles growing white around her fork.

"What do you mean?" she asked, the words coming out a fraction too quickly.

Satisfaction surged through Gwen. For the first time she had succeeded in rattling her mother.

"Oh, I don't know, Mother. I suppose I'm thinking that my husband might be a little surprised to discover his bride turns into a bear each nightfall! And when he finds out I'm not the only one, he may suspect a conspiracy against him."

"Silence!" The queen leaped to her feet, sending her chair clattering to the floor behind her. "How dare you!"

She reached Gwen in two strides, slapping her hard across the cheek. The blow sent Gwen staggering back, her hands flying to her face. Her mother had never hit her before, and the shocking pain brought her fear rushing back.

It was too late to back down now, though. She had revealed her knowledge to her mother, and she couldn't take it back.

"Never say that aloud," the queen hissed. "Anyone might have heard you!"

"So you *are* keeping me a secret from everyone." Gwen tried to keep her voice from shaking. "But why? If the whole kingdom knows the palace's inhabitants become bears at night, why can't they know their princess does as well?"

Her mother clapped a hand over Gwen's mouth, silencing her. Gwen pulled back.

"But why?" she cried. "What difference does it make?"

"It makes all the difference!" the queen growled. "Are you trying to ruin everything?"

For a moment the two stared at each other, both of their chests heaving and their eyes blazing. Distantly Gwen felt curious. Why had her mother kept the condition of the court a secret from Gwen and Gwen's inclusion in the enchantment a secret from everyone else? The two guards who had found her in the garden must have been genuinely worried for her, thinking she was an ordinary girl about to be confronted with something horrifying.

But sharper than the curiosity was the anger, laced with the inevitable fear that underlined every interaction with her mother. Despite her shaking knees, Gwen wasn't going to back down. Not this time.

The queen's brows drew closer, her eyes narrowing. "So you have discovered the truth at last, pathetic girl. I suppose you had to know eventually. But I will not allow you to ruin plans that have been years in the making."

She grabbed Gwen's wrist, holding it tightly enough that Gwen cried out in pain. The queen didn't loosen her grip.

Dragging Gwen behind her, she strode out into the corridor. Gwen struggled to free her arm, but despite her efforts, she was pulled along in her mother's wake.

When they began climbing the winding stairs of the west tower, Gwen considered throwing herself down them, pulling her mother with her. Surely the queen would have to release her hold then.

But Gwen was as likely to be injured in the attempt as her mother. She would have little chance to escape with two broken legs.

She kept struggling, though. It might be futile, but now that she had unstoppered the dam, she couldn't suppress the years of bottled anger and resentment that were flowing out.

It made no difference. Her mother maintained an iron

grip, proving herself stronger than she appeared. Only when she had opened a door at the top of the tower did she finally let go, and only then so she could throw Gwen into the room beyond.

Gwen flew forward, losing her balance and landing hard enough on the stone floor to bruise. She scrambled to her feet, wincing, but her mother stood in the middle of the doorway, barring the exit.

Tears sprang to Gwen's eyes. "Why, Mother? Can you really not tell me why?"

"What a fool I was to think you had finally matured into the tool you need to become." The queen regarded her with disgust. "How the court and kingdom can put their hope in you, I'll never understand."

"H…hope? What do you mean?" The queen's unexpected words drove back Gwen's impending tears, a strange echo of those spoken by the girl from the city.

"It's all your fault, you know," the queen snapped. "If it hadn't been for that fool boy, I would never have felt the need to—"

"Fool boy?" Gwen surged forward, grasping at her mother's shoulder. "You mean Easton? What did you do to him?"

"Far less than he deserved!" The queen thrust Gwen backward again, sending her to the floor in a second heavy fall.

But Gwen barely felt the pain. She stared up at her mother. "So he's alive then?"

"As I said, better than he deserved! But I couldn't risk killing the son of a courtier. Not after everything went wrong."

Her eyes snapped and burned, pouring the load of her own anger and frustration onto Gwen. "But how was I supposed to know the object worked in such a way? It was supposed to bind my people to me—ensure their loyalty. How could it turn us into bears and bind us to the mountains instead?"

Gwen slowly stood, giving a shaky laugh. "So it was a mistake, then? The high and mighty Queen Celandine made a mistake, and now you must spend your nights as a bear?" She laughed again, a stronger, colder sound. But her mother was finally talking, giving her answers, and she had to goad her into continuing.

"Silence!" her mother cried. "It may have been a miscalculation at the time, but I can turn any situation to my advantage. Haven't I used it to keep the population quiet? I even found us a way through the mountains—I bought us a future!"

"But it was still a mistake," Gwen said softly. "And every night you're reminded of it. But why did you have to involve me?"

The queen gave her a satisfied look. "That was a master stroke, and I came up with it on the spot. Obviously I couldn't confess I'd made a mistake. I needed to assure my people the enchantment wasn't permanent, but since I had no idea how to reverse it, I needed to give myself time. And thankfully you were safely out of sight."

Gwen sucked in a breath at this description of her torturous imprisonment.

The queen smiled in response. "A humorous fantasy, is it not? But hope is as powerful a tool as fear. A careful wielder of both can hold more power than you can imagine."

"You've been using me to control the court all this time?" Gwen stared at her mother. It was far beyond what she had imagined.

"I'm only surprised they swallowed the notion of a virtuous princess so easily," the queen said with a mocking smile. "A girl so pure, the enchantment couldn't touch her.

One who must be protected at all costs because only she could save her people." She chuckled. "But it does sound like something the godmothers would contrive, does it not?"

"But you haven't found out how to reverse it," Gwen said slowly. "It's been ten years, and we're all still trapped. How can the people still look to me with hope?"

The queen's smile turned hard. "Who said I didn't know how to reverse it? A prince is the answer, of course."

Gwen gaped at her. "That's why you're bringing a lowlander prince here? Marrying him is supposed to reverse the enchantment?" She frowned. "But love is usually the key when it comes to godmother objects. You can't possibly think I love this stranger or he me?"

"Love?" The queen's brows rose. "No, who could ever love you?"

Gwen froze, icy tendrils creeping over her. She didn't know why the words shocked her after everything her mother had said over the years. But they hit her in a part of her heart she didn't know was still unguarded.

"A prince was just the excuse at first," the queen continued, "since I hadn't found a way to reverse it by the time you came of marriageable age. I told them it could only be a prince and that stalled them for a while. And then somehow they found..." She broke off, clearly seething too much to finish the sentence.

Gwen frowned at her mother, trying to understand what she wasn't saying. Had it not been the queen herself who had chosen the prince and insisted on Gwen's marriage? Had someone actually called her mother's bluff? Had it been one of her trading teams? Gwen almost wanted to laugh at the idea of her mother's horror when her people returned in triumph with a prince in tow, expecting to be rewarded.

But if they had found a prince and brought him into the mountains, where was he now?

The queen looked up at Gwen, her eyes narrowing. "As always, I turned the situation to my advantage. You would do well to remember that no matter what happens, I will always find a way to control the situation. The time had nearly come in any case, and the princeling has proven useful and will have further uses still. Including him in the enchantment produced unexpected results, but the boy has his own godmother, and her words were far more interesting than the boy himself." She scoffed. "He will soon fail, of course, that much is inevitable. But he will still free us in the process, and then I will have one final use for him."

"Marrying me," Gwen said, the words dull. She couldn't follow half of what her mother was saying, but anything that brought the queen so much satisfaction had to be bad for Gwen.

"You may think you're defying me right now," the queen said. "But it is as pointless as everything else you've attempted. The prince will return to us soon—the painting has shown that clearly enough. So I merely need to keep you sequestered here until then." She tapped her chin. "I will say you're sick and resting so as to be recovered for the prince's arrival." She nodded. "Yes, that will work well enough."

Gwen's heart leaped as she realized her mother meant to lock her in the tower room and leave her there. But it wasn't fear that stirred her. Not when she had the master key still resting in her pocket.

The queen stopped halfway through the doorway, however, turning back with a mocking smile. "I am not such a fool as you apparently think me, daughter. The key to this room is one that only I hold. Your master key will not open it.

And so I recommend you reconcile yourself to your stay here and use the time to prepare for your future. Soon our curse will be broken, and you will be married straight after. You will soon be the princess of two kingdoms, and we will begin a new and glorious future for the mountain throne."

"What do you mean?" Gwen asked, her mouth dry.

The queen's lips curved upward. "I've always promised you would one day rule, haven't I? But how could I leave you such a small kingdom, trapped behind walls? The throne I will pass to you will stretch all the way to the ocean. There is no mountain I won't level for your future. Don't worry, my dear. You will be Queen Gwendolyn sooner than you think—but I will always be by your side."

With those haunting words, she disappeared, the key turning in the lock. Gwen threw herself at the door anyway, pounding on it and screaming as she tried to open it.

It remained sturdy, however, and she knew she was too high in an unused tower to be heard by anyone. Even her servant friends wouldn't know to look for her in such an unlikely place.

She had thought her mother might lock her in her room—had even thought she might try a closet again—but she had been overconfident in her possession of a master key. Failing that, she had thought Alma and the others would find some way to reach her. Now that both possibilities were stripped away, she felt raw, exposed, and desperate.

Her moment of defiance had been so long in coming and had failed so spectacularly. She had known her mother had some scheme underway, but she hadn't realized the scope of it. Did she really think she could put her daughter on the throne as a puppet queen, hailed by the court as their savior but powerless in everything but name?

Looking around the barren room, it seemed all too possible. And what had her mother said about leveling mountains? A week ago, Gwen would have dismissed it as grandiose talk. But now she had seen the godmother objects her mother had amassed. Was it possible they had the power to change the geography of the region itself, laying forth a path for her mother to conquer the surrounding kingdoms in Gwen's name?

She looked down at her empty hands, remembering how they had looked as the paws of a bear. Nothing seemed too far-fetched any longer. And her mother would already have a foothold in the lowlands if Gwen's marriage made her a legitimate princess in one of their kingdoms.

Her mother wanted to fool the mountain people into following Gwen as the one who had saved them from the curse. And she wanted to fool a lowland kingdom into accepting her by marriage, opening the door to her planned conquest. But all her plans revolved around her daughter. Her mother had made Gwen the key to all of them.

A different level of desperation sank into her. She couldn't stay in the tower to meekly accept her mother's planned future. Escape wasn't only necessary for her own sake anymore. Her mother said the curse had trapped her and her people in the mountains—explaining why they had never traded beyond those who lived in the valleys of the foothills—and as far as Gwen was concerned, her mother could stay in the mountains for the rest of her days.

Gwen looked wildly around the empty space. The unused room wasn't even furnished, so there was nothing she could use to try to batter down the door.

Her eyes fell on the windows. Rushing toward the closest

one, she tried the latch. When it swung open, she had a brief moment of triumph before she remembered where she was.

One glance downward sent her staggering away from the open pane of glass. She wasn't in her room any longer. There was no friendly ground waiting for her, only a fall of several stories.

But desperation still had its fingers deep in her heart. Not even her fear of the drop could compare to her fear of her mother. And if she did fall, at least her death would foil her mother's plans.

Knowing she couldn't wait until her false courage faded, Gwen swung one leg over the windowsill. There were no sheets to make into ropes or anything equally fanciful. She would either scale the rough stone of the castle wall or she would fall.

Her bravado wavered when she reached the point of releasing her death grip on the windowsill. But she had already gone too far to turn back. She was dangling down the side of the wall, and she didn't possess the strength to pull herself back up. There was nowhere to go but down.

The wind whistled past her, making her shiver, although she didn't feel cold. If anything, she felt unnaturally warm. One small slip, and it would all be over.

She wished for a calm day without so much as a breeze that might disrupt her climb, but the wind mocked her, blowing more strongly in response. It curled around her, catching at her hair and dress.

She licked her lips, testing the position of both feet. She had wedged her toes into cracks provided by the uneven stones of the tower wall, but there wasn't much grip. She would have preferred a better foothold, but it was the best she'd been able to find.

She let go with one hand, holding even more tightly with the other as she searched for a lower hold. When she found one, it felt painfully insufficient. Her fingers could barely grasp the slight lip of stone.

You can do this, she told herself, forcing her mind to override her terrified body. She released her final hold on the windowsill above.

Somehow she remained in place as her second hand sought another uncertain hold. Once she'd found it, she froze, her whole length pressed against the stone, her breath coming in desperate gasps.

But the longer she took, the weaker she'd grow. She had to keep moving. She removed one foot and cautiously lowered herself, blindly feeling for another toehold.

The change in position upset her balance, and her fingers slid. There was no time to recover herself. One second, she was still held in place by three points of contact, the next, she had lost them all, and her body was falling backward, drawn irresistibly toward the ground.

She only had time for an awareness of her impending death and the thought of a single face. And in the utter helplessness of that moment, she felt peace.

Except she wasn't falling as fast as she should have been. The wind curling around her had grown more solid, winding its way around her legs and supporting her fall.

Could she even use the word fall? Impossibly, she seemed to be not so much falling as flying. Except it didn't feel like flying. It felt like…riding. An uncontrolled, tempestuous ride, but she could have sworn she felt an invisible mount beneath her.

She glanced over her shoulder and saw the palace

retreating behind her. She was actually being carried along by the wind, moving parallel to the ground.

Her invisible mount lurched upward and then dropped abruptly, making her stomach sink to her feet although the wind caught her before she hit the ground and lifted her again.

The warmth she had felt earlier grew, reaching an unpleasant level of heat which seemed to be emanating from one of her pockets. She thrust her hand into it, distracted and confused as she sought the source. It was the opposite pocket to the one holding the key, but her fingers closed around a small metal object.

Gasping, she pulled out the golden halter she had accidentally stolen from her mother a lifetime ago. Given all the revelations since, she had forgotten about the object whose purpose she hadn't been able to guess.

As soon as it was free, the miniature halter cooled. It also began to grow. Within seconds, it was as large as a real halter, and it had leaped from her hands to position itself as if she really were riding an invisible horse made of wind. A golden thread grew from the halter, connecting it with her hand like golden reins that glowed.

She tried pulling on one side, and the wind horse responded, moving in the direction she indicated. Somehow, impossibly, she was controlling the wind.

Whooping in elation, she looked up to see a mountain face bearing down on her. Given her impossible speed, she was already nearing the western edge of the valley. Gulping, she tugged on the reins, and the wind horse surged upward, carrying her higher and higher until she sailed over the mountain's peak.

A brief surge of elation gave way to concentration as the

wind raced her down the other side, another peak appearing in front of her. It took all her energy to control the wind horse as she rode it up and down the various peaks and summits that lay before her. Somewhere in the back of her mind, the steady beat of elation kept trying to break free, but she wasn't safe yet. She wasn't free yet.

Finally she rode down the final mountain face, reaching the first of the legendary valleys. They sat on the very fringe of the mountains, but they belonged to a different world—the border of the Four Kingdoms. Far below her she could see roofs and gardens scattered among the trees.

The wind raced her quickly past the first valley, but she angled it downward, and when the next valley appeared, she brought it all the way to the ground. She hit harder than she had expected, sending herself tumbling sideways.

As soon as her hands flew from the reins, they disappeared, and the halter shrank again, dropping to the ground beside her. She scrambled forward, crawling across the littered leaves of the clearing to grab it.

Thrusting it into her pocket with shaking hands, she lay flat, staring up at branches and blue sky. It took a long time for her trembling limbs to still and her heart rate to steady.

As soon as they had, tears took their place. She had done it. After all these years, she had succeeded. She was free.

CHARLOTTE

Charlotte stood in her room in front of her full-length mirror, regarding herself in her plainest gown. She had made her rapid decision without even considering what it would be like to meet her family again. What would they think of Charlotte now? Would they think her changed? She felt changed. The Charli who had left them had been a young, naïve girl.

She knew she looked beautiful—her beauty had caused her too much pain in her life to bother denying it—but she felt only listlessness. Her image held no appeal as it had done on the morning after her first night beside Henry. She could no longer see her own golden loveliness without seeing beside it the darker beauty of the princess in the portrait. The unknown woman—who Charlotte felt certain had to be royalty from her bearing alone—made Charlotte feel colorless and washed out.

She shook herself, turning from the mirror. It didn't matter what she looked like for the coming reunion.

Henry awaited her just outside the castle, and it took all

her willpower to make herself climb into position on his back, his soft fur gripped in her hands. It had been a long time since their first journey through the trees together, and everything had changed since then.

She stayed awake this time, marveling at the speed of his run. Even knowing how fast they moved, she was taken off guard when she began to recognize their surroundings and knew she was within minutes of her old home.

"We were so close all this time?" she whispered. Their months in the castle had felt so entirely removed from regular life that it seemed incredible the physical distance hadn't been greater.

But she was even more astonished when Henry took her straight to the location of her old home. Had her family not moved after all?

One look at the building told her it wasn't her old home, however. The house that stood in its place was at least four times bigger and more luxurious than any house she had seen in the valley. And the attached stable had been replaced with a free-standing building of significant size, and it clearly housed far more than their original three horses.

"I'll leave you here," Henry said. "I think it's best they don't see me."

Charlotte wanted to protest, but she remained silent. While her heart wanted every extra minute with him, the whole point of this visit was to give herself distance.

"There is one thing I must ask of you, though," he said in a voice turned suddenly serious. "Of course you will wish to talk to your parents of your new life. You may speak freely to them of our home, of our days in the library, even of the bell, if you wish. But our nights together—those belong to just you and me. Please swear to me you will not tell your parents what happens at night."

Charlotte's throat clogged at the way he spoke of their hours in the darkness. She felt in perfect agreement. Even though they maintained physical distance from one another through the night, that time was private between the two of them.

She nodded, managing to squeeze out enough words to reassure him. Her sudden emotion brought a resurgence of his earlier concern, and he hesitated. But voices from inside made him glance toward the house.

"I must be going," he said. "I'll come back for you in three days." He turned to go, only to stop and look back at her, his voice turned urgent. "You will return to me?"

She nodded. "I will be ready in three days. Thank you, Henry."

He examined her face for a moment before nodding and disappearing into the trees.

Charlotte watched him go, barely holding in her longing to call him back, to say she would return with him immediately. But she couldn't speak. She was doing this for both of their sakes, and she had to stay strong.

The door of the house opened, and an unfamiliar older woman came out. She regarded Charlotte with curious bemusement, her eyes growing wider as she took in Charlotte's gown.

Charlotte looked down at herself, recognizing that even the plainest of her new gowns was out of place in the valley. Even with her family's obvious new wealth, she clearly didn't belong.

"Surely you're not the daughter who married the bear!" the woman exclaimed. "Your parents claimed you were living in luxury like a princess, but I thought…" She trailed off, clearly not willing to voice her previous opinion.

"I am she." Charlotte cleared her throat. "Are my family here?" Seeing the unfamiliar face filled her with urgent fear. Had Henry left her on the doorstep of strangers?

"Oh, aye." The woman was still regarding Charlotte with amazement. "They're inside."

"Who's there?" the familiar voice of her mother called. "Do we have visitors?" She appeared in the doorway and let out a piercing shriek.

"Charlotte! Oh Charlotte! Quick, girls, come quick! Your sister is here!"

Falling forward, she wrapped her arms around Charlotte in a bone-crushing hug. Dazed, Charlotte embraced her back, embarrassed to feel moisture on her cheeks.

She had left in a storm of righteous fury, and all this time she had been happy to be far from her family. She had thought Henry's company was all she needed. But now that she felt her mother's arms around her, the walls she had built inside crumbled. She might have been an adult and a married woman, but she still needed support. And her family, for all their flaws, were the only ones she had.

Elizabeth and Odelia piled out the door, their own cries of surprise filling the air. To Charlotte's surprise, they also fell on her, enlarging the hug so it became an awkward mass of entwined arms.

Apparently her sisters had grown more fond of her in her absence. Or maybe it was merely that they now associated her with wealth and ease. Charlotte was grateful to maintain the peace of the moment, but she couldn't forget the way they had treated her for so long. She had thought their relationship changed once before, but it had all too easily reverted again after her cousin's wedding.

Having heard the stories about Henry's supportive and affectionate relationship with his sister, she wasn't going to be fooled again. Now that their lives were so separate, she felt hopeful she and her sisters could spend time together in peace. But they would never have the sort of close, loving relationship Charlotte had always wanted. Hoping for it would only lead to further hurt down the road. The acceptance and safety Charlotte had found in her marriage allowed her to accept her relationship with her sisters for what it was, instead of always seeing it through the lens of what she wanted it to be.

"Charli!" Her father appeared, and her mother and sisters melted away, leaving Charlotte free to greet him.

"Father." She had intended to speak in a steady, cool tone, but instead her voice broke.

His face crumpled in response.

Stepping forward, he also swept her into a hug, and just as with her mother, she responded instinctively, wrapping her arms around him. The hurt still lingered, but unlike with her sisters, there were years of warmth and affection behind it that she couldn't forget.

The shining, perfect father of her childhood had turned out to be flawed, and it had been hard to accept. But she had overreacted to his words that day in the forest. While he might have misunderstood her heart, he had still been trying to act out of love toward her.

"How have you been, Daughter?" he murmured. "Has the bear kept his promises to you?"

She clung on tighter as she nodded. She could hear the

worry in his voice, and all the resentment that had built up inside her washed away like a sandcastle before a wave.

"He gives me everything I ask for, Father," she said. "I live in greater luxury than even you." She pulled back and offered him a weak smile. "Though it looks as if you live in plenty of luxury yourself these days!"

He stepped back and smiled proudly, but she could see the truth behind his attempted good cheer. He had never wanted wealth for its own sake, and the family's good fortune was tied up with her departure and the end of his frontier dreams.

"Actually, it's not just from your bride price," her mother interjected, sounding proud. "Although we were all shocked when the house suddenly grew around us."

"Did it really?" Charlotte laughed at the image. "So my wish reached you after all." She had seen the bell work often enough to guess how shocking it must have been for her family, coming without warning or context.

"But it was only a short time later that your father's efforts to win his place with the valley elders finally bore fruit," her mother continued. "Even if you hadn't left us, our fortunes would have been looking up."

Sorrow tinged the pride as she finished her words, and Charlotte could easily read the message behind it. They could have kept their daughter and had eventual wealth as well, even if not as much.

"Oh, Mother," she whispered.

Her mother stepped forward. "I'm sorry, Charli," she murmured back. "I failed you as a mother. I was tired and weak, and I thought our poverty was the root of all our problems. But once you were gone, I realized I could never enjoy luxury and ease that came at the expense of one of my daughters. I shouldn't have let you go."

Tears filled Charlotte's eyes at the apology, but before she could reply, her mother continued.

"But that's not all I have to be sorry for. I've spent so many weeks thinking of you and remembering the past, and I realized I failed you long before I sent you away. I'm sorry I let our home become such a painful place that you would marry a bear to escape it."

Charlotte tried to smile, but her lips were trembling too much to manage it.

Her father slipped an arm around her mother's shoulders, although his eyes stayed on Charlotte.

"I realize much of the blame is mine," he said. "I moved us out here because it was what I wished. I convinced myself it could help you all, too, but that was only an excuse to justify what I wanted. When it took so much longer to establish ourselves than I expected, I should have moved us back to civilization."

Charlotte shook her head, sniffing as she held back the tears. She hadn't come home to hear their apologies, but their words healed something broken deep inside her.

"Be at peace, Mother and Father," she murmured. "I accept your apologies, and I'm even glad we moved here, as difficult as it was. I am truly well, and I don't regret my choice. If we hadn't moved here, I never would have found Henry."

Despite all the newfound pain, and the prospect that she might have to give Henry up in the future, she couldn't wish away her love or her months with him. When she had left home, she had believed herself fully grown up. And in some ways, she had been. But now, after only a short time away, she understood better how much growth still lay before her. She had already experienced so many new emotions, and with them had come an understanding of her parents she had never expected to have.

She knew what it was to hurt someone despite your love for them—even because of it. It was clear that her unhappiness and her abrupt departure pained Henry. And yet, she had left anyway. She had done it not because she didn't care about him but because of her emotional weakness. She needed space before she could discuss their future without heaping guilt and hurt on his head. And so she had chosen to leave not to cause him pain, but because it had seemed, in a collection of bad options, like the one that would hurt him the least.

She could see now that her father had only been doing the same thing. Faced with his daughter's unhappiness, he had looked at the selection of bad options before them and nudged her toward the one he thought would cause the least pain. He hadn't understood the true cause of her suffering—part of which came from him and his choices—and so he had worded himself badly. But as it turned out, he had been right about her potential for future happiness. So she couldn't blame him now for doing his best.

The weight that lifted off her shoulders as she let go of the last of her resentment toward her parents lightened the pain she still felt over Henry, and her tears started flowing again.

"Charli?" Her father gazed at her with worry.

"They're happy tears," she managed to say, smiling from him to her mother. "I'm so glad to see you again. I didn't realize how glad."

"Come inside, come inside," Elizabeth gushed, oblivious to the emotional exchange that had just taken place. "Let us show you all around our new house. It's the nicest one in all the valleys, and everyone has come to admire it."

"I was surprised to find you still here," Charlotte said,

entering the house in Elizabeth's wake. "Weren't you going to move to Arcadia?"

Odelia, who had followed them inside, pouted. "According to Father, the bear said we have to wait for that. But we're going to move still!"

Charlotte frowned, wanting to ask her to explain further but knowing Odelia wasn't the one with answers. Why had Henry told her family to wait?

Elizabeth began to show off elements of the house, but from the way she was preening and positioning herself, she clearly wanted a comment on the fine gown she was wearing. Charlotte bit back a smile and supplied it. She extended the compliment to Odelia who lit up in response. Her absence had forced her parents into self-reflection, but clearly the same wasn't true of her sisters.

"Your gown is very nice, too, Charlotte," Odelia said before leaning closer. "Wait, are those real gems?"

Charlotte glanced down. "Perhaps? You may have this one, if you like. I would prefer to borrow something plainer for my stay, if you have it."

Elizabeth and Odelia locked eyes over Charlotte's head, and she realized she might have spoken too carelessly. If her sisters understood the wealth she now enjoyed, would all their old resentment return?

"I would rather have my sisters than any gown," she added brightly, and the tension passed.

Both her sisters smiled again, sweeping her inside to find her a change of clothes. She was paraded through every room in the house where she forced herself to dutifully admire everything. Her family really was living in comfort, and with her new forgiveness of them, the knowledge brought her joy instead of a surge of resentment.

But by the time she had seen every nook, been fed until she was bursting, met the three helpers who lived in the rooms attached to the stable, reassured her parents again of her husband's kindness, and regaled her sisters with descriptions of her days spent reading, she felt as wrung out as the rag her mother was using to wipe the table.

"Do you really do nothing but read all day?" Elizabeth exchanged a look with Odelia. "What's the point of a fancy gown like yours if your only audience is books?"

Charlotte smiled, pleased that her story of the library—incomplete though it had been—had erased any lingering effect of her earlier careless words. Neither of her sisters would feel any jealousy toward her now.

"I do read all day most days," she said. "And so I must confess I'm longing for one of my old walks in the forest."

"Of course you would be missing your old haunts," her mother said. "Give your sisters a moment to change into something more practical and—"

Charlotte threw a beseeching look at her father, and he came to her rescue as he always had before on the worst days.

"Peace, my dears," he said. "Elizabeth and Odelia need not bestir themselves. Charli won't have forgotten her way in such a short time. She'll be safe enough on her own."

"Yes, indeed!" Charlotte said quickly. "I don't want anyone put out for me."

She leaped up and was out the door before her mother could protest. She hoped none of them took offense, but she desperately needed some solitude.

As soon as she lost sight of the house, she felt her chest expand. Breathing deeply, she turned her face toward the sun and smiled. Shut in the castle, she had registered the change of season, but she hadn't had a chance to experience it properly. Out in the forest, the ground was a riot of color, spring filling her senses.

The pain of her love for Henry and the uncertainty of their future still sat in her heart as a constant ache. But for the moment she was content to be alone with the flowers and the forest's new life.

Charlotte walked for what must have been hours, losing herself in the forest without ever actually being lost. She knew the ground too well for that.

She had seen no one the whole time—the one advantage of such distant neighbors—so she was shocked when she stepped around a bush and into a small clearing only to find an elegant woman sitting on the small patch of grass at its center.

The woman rose as soon as she caught sight of Charlotte, and Charlotte's astonishment grew far greater, hitting her with the force of a speeding arrow. For the face smiling a hesitant greeting was one she recognized, although she had never met the woman before.

Here, in the middle of her familiar forest, she had found the woman from the portrait. Henry's lost love.

INTERLUDE
QUEEN CELANDINE

Queen Celandine stared at the empty room and then down at the key in her hand. What she was seeing was utterly impossible.

Gwendolyn couldn't have escaped. Only the queen herself had the key for this room. And, if Gwendolyn had somehow tampered with the door, she would have at least left some evidence behind. But the door had been whole and locked when the queen arrived moments before.

She had prepared the remote room years ago, thinking it would be needed. But Gwendolyn had proven more biddable than she could have dreamed. Until now, when the girl had suddenly developed a new defiant streak, only to then vanish in a way that shouldn't have been possible.

A slight creak caught the queen's ear, and her eyes narrowed. Striding across the room, she pushed against one of the windows. It swung open.

Celandine sucked in a breath. The girl had gone out the window. The wind must have pushed it closed again afterward, but it had failed to completely latch.

She leaned out, peering downward with an unfamiliar spike of fear. If the pathetic girl had managed to get herself killed, all of Celandine's plans would be for nothing.

But no crumpled body lay on the ground beneath the tower. The queen's gaze moved across the western palace grounds, but no sign of movement caught her eye. She drew back inside and clicked the window shut, scowling.

Soon she would need to return and resume a mask of calm indifference. She had already told the court the princess was recovering from an illness, so nothing needed to change immediately. But she had to get her back, and quietly.

If only that fool of a count hadn't rushed matters. She ground her teeth as she slowly descended the flights of stairs that wound down from the tower.

When she had been pushed into declaring that only a royal prince was a suitable groom to marry the princess and lift the curse, she hadn't expected her courtiers to actually produce one. The enchantment wouldn't allow them to travel further than the valleys. What had the fool boy been doing there?

But it was the defiance of the action that made her seethe more than anything. After all these years, they thought they could push her?

She drew in a calming breath. Anger would get her nowhere. She had felt enough anger to drown a ship or level a village in the years she had spent in her father's home. And after she had found refuge—thinking herself safe with one more powerful than her father—she had felt its fire again. That second betrayal had been even worse than the one by her blood parent.

But all that impotent fury had won her nothing. It had been worse than useless, in fact, since it had blinded her to the valuable lessons to be learned. She could not trust to the power of others to save her. That power only enabled them to treat her as they wished.

When she set aside emotion for clear thinking and cold revenge, the answer was obvious. She had to seize her own power. She had to rise so high that no one could ever stomp on her again.

It had taken planning and effort, but she had succeeded. And those who had once made free use of their fists had been forced to kneel at her feet and pay homage.

Remembering that moment usually calmed and stabilized her, but now it only brought back the hated wave of anger. She returned to her breathing exercises, trying to drive back the emotions. She couldn't afford to crack now.

She pressed a hand to her head. Was it never to be enough? She had become queen—had ruled with a tight rein for twenty years. There should be no one with the power to assail her.

And yet...

She clenched her teeth. The breathing was no longer working. The court thought they could manipulate her, control her. They thought they could free themselves of the bindings she'd used to ensure their loyalty after that boy had questioned her rule.

She glanced back up the stairs, feeling the cracks in her wall widen. How dare that child flee from her! It was impossible. Unthinkable.

Had someone told her? Celandine stilled mid-step. But after a moment she shook her head and resumed her descent. After what had happened to the boy, no one in the court would be so foolhardy. It had been ten years, and no one had dared.

Princess Gwendolyn still believed Celandine to be her real

mother. She must. Given the girl's earlier tantrum, she would have thrown that in the queen's face as well if she had known.

Some of her secrets were still safe.

But her hold on power was slipping. She had kept it secure all these years with the promise that everything would change once Gwendolyn was on the throne in her place. If they discovered the princess was gone, what would they do?

No. She couldn't be gone. Even if she had managed to climb down the wall, she couldn't have gone far. Celandine would find her.

She stalked through the corridors, and her expression was enough to send anyone she encountered hurrying in another direction.

The guard at the entrance to her wing bowed deeply, avoiding eye contact. He was frightened too.

Yes. She drank it in, reveling in the reminder that her power hadn't cracked yet.

Inside her chamber, she flung open the curtains, pausing to check the portrait behind. It had changed yet again. The girl in gold was now turned toward the bear, her arms wrapped around his neck.

Hours before, Celandine would have been pleased. Soon she would have the prince caught in her snare. Her courtiers had thought to force her hand, but they didn't understand who they were dealing with. The queen had already turned their empty scheming to her own advantage. They thought the wedding would be their moment of freedom, but it was only the beginning.

She had thought the power she had amassed sufficient, but from the moment the count made his move, she knew it wasn't so.

She pulled on the lever and let the portrait swing open,

stepping through. As always, the hidden room calmed any lingering unease.

Her people had no idea of the power she had stored here—power she could use to gain even more. When they had seen her level the mountains, when she was seated as empress on a throne that spanned kingdoms, she would finally have climbed too high for anyone to touch her ever again.

She would be safe.

But for now, she needed to find the princess—the girl was still a tool she would need in her stepping stones of conquest. One of these objects would surely help her locate the runaway.

Her eyes flicked between the plinths until they came to rest on one holding a tiny golden whip. She sucked in a breath, her cheeks growing pale.

Instantly she could recall the earlier scene and the place where the princess had been standing. Gwendolyn had taken the golden halter. She had brazenly picked it up and walked out under the queen's nose.

The earlier storm of fury was nothing to the tidal wave bearing down on her now. How dared that girl enter Celandine's innermost sanctuary and steal from her! The queen had offered her grace when she had found her here, and the girl had laughed in her face.

But the wave bearing down on her could sweep away everything she had built. Celandine strode over to another object and placed her hand on it. Instantly the overwhelming and unwanted emotions disappeared, leaving stillness in their wake. The empty bliss of nothingness.

The queen drew a steady breath and assumed a serene smile. This had been her first object, the one that was the foundation of everything. Without her emotions, she was truly free. Without them, she could manage the cold calculation needed to ensure no one ever threatened her again.

The situation wasn't lost yet. The selfish girl had taken the halter and would no doubt be gone from the mountains already. She was probably in the middle of savoring her victory. But she had been more foolish than she realized.

She had left the whip.

INTERLUDE

EASTON

Easton stood on the seawall and gazed out at the endless stretch of ocean. He had always liked this spot. Standing here, he felt surrounded by the sea in a way that could only be rivaled by standing on the deck of a ship.

The wildness of it reminded him of his childhood home in the mountains. And thinking of his home reminded him of her.

There was little point in thinking of Gwen. When he had been cast out, it had been made very clear to him that he would never see her or his family again.

He had even accepted it, in his own way. Or at least he had made the necessary peace that allowed him to forge a new life and to continue on each day. But he hadn't been able to purge Gwen from his mind. He wasn't even sure he wanted to.

Was she all right? It seemed a foolish thought. Of course she wasn't. Nanny was already gone, and now Easton was gone too. She was alone in that castle of stone with only her stepmother.

He regretted that he hadn't told her the truth about her

real mother. If only he had run to Gwen when he found out instead of rushing to confront the queen like a hotheaded child.

But there was no use in such regrets. He couldn't change his actions now. He could only hope someone else would muster the courage to tell her the truth.

He didn't regret being free from under the queen's oppressive watch. He only wished Gwen could join him in his freedom. If she and his parents were by his side, he could happily make Ranost his home forever. The coastal town wasn't large, but it had work enough. And it had the sea.

He breathed deeply, tasting the salt on the wind.

He dreamed of the princess sometimes. And the Gwen of his dreams always wore the same face—a grown up version of the one he used to know. Sometimes, she was alone, looking sad and wistful. Occasionally she laughed with a friend, although the other girl always seemed to be cleaning on those occasions, as if the presence of soap and water lightened the princess's mood.

And other times she wandered beneath the moon, her hand resting on the shoulder of a large white bear. He liked those dreams the best. It comforted him to think of Gwen with a silent protector at her side. He had filled that role once—doing more to shield her than she had realized—but he was gone now, and he hated to think of his childhood playmate alone.

The wind gusted against him, caressing his cheek and rifling through his hair. If only it could bring him news of his old home.

Were his parents still alive and well? Had they suffered for his defiance? If they had been banished from court, he didn't think they would regret it. Life in the city was at least a little freer than life in the palace, if only because it wasn't so close to the queen. Neither of his parents had ever desired power. They had only escaped the purge of the king's old inner circle because they had never been close to him.

Familiar anger rose at thoughts of Queen Celandine. He let it come, let it wash over him. For a moment his hands balled into fists.

But then he gazed out across the ocean and breathed in the salty air. He let the steady pull and crash of the waves pull the emotions back out again.

"You are right and just, Anger," he murmured. "But you cannot serve me in this moment. I still have life and breath and work to sustain myself. That is what I must focus on in this moment."

He felt the calm of the ocean seep into him—the calm that came when he remembered that his was just one life among countless in the kingdoms and that even Queen Celandine's power was nothing compared to the vastness of the ocean.

The last time he had faced the mountain queen, he had still been on the threshold of childhood. But now he was a man grown. If he ever faced the queen again, he knew the anger would be there, ready.

It would take courage to face her, he knew that. And his anger at all the wrongs she had committed would spur that courage. If he had another chance to stand up for Gwen, he wouldn't fail again.

CHARLOTTE

The woman in the clearing smiled hesitantly at Charlotte. But as she took in Charlotte's obvious shock, her smile faltered. She stepped closer, staring more intently at Charlotte's face, and then let out a cry.

"You're the girl from the portrait!" she exclaimed, stealing the words from Charlotte's own mouth.

From the woman, they made no sense.

"I don't know what you mean," she managed to say through numb lips.

"Your dress is different, of course," the woman said, smiling at Charlotte in a friendly way. "And you're missing the bear." She laughed as if she'd made a joke, but tension shot through Charlotte at the mention of Henry.

"Excuse me?" she asked before remembering that the whole valley must know she'd married a bear. This woman couldn't know his real identity. "Are you saying someone here has painted a picture of me with…a white bear?"

The woman's eyes widened. "It *was* white! How did you know? Don't tell me you actually have a bear companion?"

Charlotte shook her head, trying to shake loose her brain. The whole interaction felt like a dream. Perhaps she'd stopped to rest somewhere and had fallen asleep. She'd spent enough hours thinking of this woman that it was plausible she would appear in her dreams.

Examining the woman again, Charlotte had to admit the scene felt too real to be a dream. And if it was one, shouldn't she understand—in the magical way of dreams—why something in the conversation had brought a shadow to the other woman's face? There was tension there that hadn't been there earlier.

"It wasn't in this valley that I saw the portrait," the woman said after an awkward moment. "Perhaps I shouldn't have mentioned it."

"Great." Charlotte sank down onto the grass. "So the story has spread to the neighboring valleys too."

What she really wanted was to run away, but her legs wouldn't let her. They wouldn't even hold her upright anymore, so there she was, sitting at the feet of the woman from the painting. Charlotte couldn't lie to herself and pretend it didn't sting.

But the woman immediately sat as well, resuming her original position so she faced Charlotte. Her expression was a mix of curiosity and sympathy, so she must have sensed something of her new companion's inner turmoil.

Of course, if she knew who Charlotte actually was, she would no doubt hate her. Unless Henry's love had been one-sided. Charlotte couldn't believe that, though. What woman could resist loving Henry?

"Are there a lot of...white bears in this area?" the woman asked after a long moment of silence.

The way she asked the question made Charlotte's head

snap up. She sounded hesitant and wistful and almost afraid. Before Charlotte could formulate an answer, the woman continued.

"I've been in the area for a few weeks now. I'm only passing through, but everyone has been more than friendly. The local official and his family have taken me under their wing and include me in their meals, although I prefer to sleep outside now the weather is warm enough." She looked uncomfortable, and Charlotte wondered if she was unused to sleeping in the company of strangers.

"I try to repay them by gathering what I can," the woman continued, gesturing at a half-full basket Charlotte hadn't noticed before. Her lips twisted in a self-deprecating way. "I'm not very good at it, though."

"You've been staying with Master Harold and his wife?" Charlotte asked.

The woman's brows lifted. "You know them? Are you a local, then?" Her brow furrowed. "I thought I met everyone from this valley when they celebrated the birth of the new baby from three houses over. I would have noticed you, though."

Charlotte wondered fleetingly why none of her family had mentioned Harold having an extended guest—an odd one who refused to sleep in his house. But she could hardly blame them for the omission given Charlotte had fled into the woods at the first opportunity.

"You probably met my sisters," she said dully. "Elizabeth and Odelia?"

"Oh yes!" the woman said, but she sounded cautious.

Despite herself, Charlotte's lips twisted upward. "Let me guess, they weren't delighted at the arrival of a new and beautiful young woman in their midst?"

The woman bit her lip and looked to the side, clearly uncomfortable. Charlotte winced. She shouldn't have said that, but she still felt so off balance. The woman was being friendly, but the last thing Charlotte wanted was to become friends with her. And yet, at the same time, she couldn't suppress an insatiable desire to know more about her.

"I'm sorry," she said softly. "Forget I said that. I'm Charlotte, by the way. I used to live here before my marriage."

Mentioning Henry, even in passing, sent a jolt of pain through her. The woman seemed to notice and frowned in response as if concerned, but she didn't comment on it.

"My name is Gwen. It's a pleasure to meet you, Charlotte."

Gwen. Charlotte regarded the woman in the painting who finally had a name. Gwen. She moved with the same elegance Charlotte had picked up from the portrait, and her gown looked like Charlotte's—too fancy for a walk in the woods.

Just seeing her image had been enough to plant the idea that she was a princess. Meeting her in person did nothing to erase that impression. But despite herself, Charlotte felt the same curiosity and sympathy growing toward Gwen that Gwen seemed to feel toward her.

They had met by chance in this forest, but neither of them belonged here—not anymore. On the outside, this place might be home for Charlotte—or an old home, at least—but inside she was lost, alone, and in pain. If she felt the pull of a kindred soul toward Gwen, did that mean Gwen felt as she did inside? What had brought her to this place? Why was a young woman traveling the kingdom alone?

"So you've returned from your new home to visit your family?" Gwen asked, clearly trying to inject some cheerful normalcy into the conversation. "You must be so happy to see them."

"Yes," Charlotte said, the answer surprising her with its honesty. "I am." She hesitated, but again she felt the unexpected pull toward Gwen and the desire to be honest with her. "We didn't leave on the best terms, so it's been a relief to reconcile with them."

A wistful look came into Gwen's eyes, and on impulse Charlotte reached out and clasped one of her hands.

"What about you?" she asked. "Have you left someone behind in need of reconciliation? I left my home once in anger and bitterness, so you'll receive no judgment from me."

Gwen shrank in on herself, but it didn't seem to be from offense at Charlotte's words. Instead, after a moment, she shook her head.

"The one I'm fleeing is beyond reconciliation." The stark look in her eyes shook Charlotte, and she knew instantly that if she could help Gwen, she had to do so.

Her jealousy didn't matter beside whatever horror this woman was fleeing. If Charlotte truly loved Henry, she would do anything she could to aid Gwen in finding escape and healing. It was what he would want.

Charlotte squeezed her hand, putting every bit of sympathy and compassion into her expression that she could.

"I hope you know that you're safe here," she said. "No one in this valley will hurt you. And though Rangmere isn't the warmest of kingdoms, it has changed greatly since Queen Ava and King Hans took the throne. If you head for the capital, I believe you will find assistance there as well."

She paused to consider. The one thing—the only thing— she couldn't do for Gwen was offer her a home. Not when Charlotte and Henry lived alone in an empty castle. The situation would be intolerable for all of them.

"Arcadia is well regarded as being a place of prosperity

whose people are warm and welcoming," she said in a rush. "My family has plans to move there. I could talk to them. I'm sure they would be willing to take you with them."

A guilty part of her wondered if she was trying to send Gwen as far away as possible, but she pushed it aside. Gwen was clearly fleeing something, so distance was likely what she wanted.

Gwen hesitated, however, pulling her hand free just so she could wring both hands together. When she looked up at Charlotte, she looked tormented, and Charlotte's heart seized.

"I don't know what to do!" Gwen burst out. "There's someone I have to find, but I don't know where he's gone. I don't even know if he's alive." Her voice dropped to a whisper that was almost a sob. "I have to believe he's alive."

Cold washed over Charlotte, robbing her of proper thought. She put her hands in her lap, hoping Gwen wouldn't notice them trembling.

"You've lost...*him*?" she asked carefully.

Gwen nodded, silent tears running down her face. "It's been so many years since I've seen him. Maybe he doesn't even remember me. But he's the only one I trust. Now that I'm free, the only thing I want to do is find Easton. But I have no idea where to even start looking." She wrung her hands together again.

Charlotte's thoughts, which had seemed mired in molasses, sputtered and flared back to life.

"Easton?" she asked. "Did you say his name is Easton?"

Gwen leaned forward, excitement sparking in her face. "Do you know him? Have you met someone by that name? Someone else without a home?"

Charlotte quickly shook her head. "No, I'm sorry. I don't know any Eastons."

"Oh." Gwen sat back, all the animation leaving her.

But Charlotte felt alive in a way she hadn't since discovering the portrait. It was all she could do to keep sitting still and talking to Gwen as if nothing had happened.

"Do you love this Easton?" she asked, holding her breath as she waited for the answer.

Gwen flushed, the color making her even more beautiful. "I haven't seen him for ten years. He may be married with children by now for all I know. But I certainly loved him fiercely as a child. He was my only playmate and companion."

"Did his family move away?" Charlotte asked.

Gwen's brows contracted, her face growing dark. "No, he just disappeared one day."

Charlotte gasped. Did Gwen think he had run away? Surely she had considered the likelihood of a more awful possibility.

"You…you don't think he met with an…accident?" she asked hesitantly. "Was he the type to run away?"

"No!" Gwen said fiercely. "He wouldn't have run away and left me without a word. He didn't leave by choice."

Charlotte bit her lip, and Gwen winced.

"I know how it must sound," she said. "Sometimes in my most despairing moments, I think he must have fallen down a ravine or met a wild animal and be dead. But he was strong and clever and resilient. When he was cast out, he would have found a way to live. I'm sure of it."

"Someone sent him away? As a child?" Charlotte asked horrified. "Surely not!"

Gwen shivered. "You don't know my—" She cut herself off. "You don't know the woman who rules my home. I used to fear she killed him, but she claimed not to have done so. Just removed him." Her voice dwindled. "I sometimes think she would have gotten rid of Nanny too if she hadn't died."

Charlotte's face paled. What sort of horrible situation had Gwen escaped from?

She had wanted to help before, but the rush of warm feeling had grown in the wake of Gwen's revelation. Gwen wasn't searching for Henry, but for Easton. He was the sole focus of her memories and hopes.

That knowledge gave Charlotte the hope she had been lacking. If Henry's love had been one-sided, it changed everything. She had thought his enchantment and Charlotte herself stood between Henry and his lost love. She had thought it might be her duty to remove herself so he could be happy.

But if a future with Gwen had never been possible, then perhaps she didn't have to leave. Perhaps, Henry was in the process of forgetting the past and growing happy in the new life he had created.

"Where are you from?" she asked Gwen, filled with determination to repay the gift Gwen didn't even know she had given Charlotte. "If you're right, and he was banished from your home, we can use it as a starting point and work out a search plan. There may be somewhere obvious he would have gone."

She gazed expectantly at Gwen. The other woman grew first pale and then red again, her hands tightening convulsively on each other.

Charlotte frowned, instinct telling her what Gwen feared. "Have you been keeping your home a secret? Because you're scared of the people you left behind? I promise I won't tell anyone anything about you unless you want me to." Indignation filled her voice. "And if the monsters you've left behind ever come searching for you, I certainly wouldn't reveal anything about your whereabouts."

Gwen smiled, a shaky gesture. "Do you think if I had been born here, we would have been friends? I've never had an ordinary friend before. But I always wished for one."

Charlotte reclaimed one of Gwen's hands. "Of course we would have been friends! I only wish you had been born here." She paused, examining the other woman's face. "Would you like to stay here? I'm sure I could find a household in the valley that would be willing to take you in permanently if that's what you'd like. Are you sure you want to search for Easton? You might never find him."

Gwen was already shaking her head before Charlotte finished.

"Logically I know the search is almost hopeless. But I can't just give up on him. Not without at least trying."

"Then you have to try," Charlotte said stoutly. "Which leads us back to making a search route." She gave Gwen a coaxing look. "Can't you tell me where you've come from?"

In the back of her mind was the thought that whatever community Gwen had left, it wasn't a healthy one. If she'd come from one of the valleys, Charlotte would have to convince her to report them to Master Harold. And if she came from somewhere further away…Perhaps Harold could still report them to Rangmeros. The capital had responsibility over the whole kingdom, and she doubted they would be happy to hear of a community that had gone as rogue as Gwen's clearly had.

"I come from the mountains," Gwen whispered, silencing Charlotte's thoughts.

"The mountains?" Charlotte looked instinctively toward the ranges that towered over them. "You mean one of the valleys that's deeper in? I've heard there are a couple..." She trailed off since Gwen was already shaking her head.

"I come from the mountain kingdom." She still spoke in a whisper.

Charlotte stared at her, struck silent by the claim. The mountain kingdom was just a legend!

But was it? Henry had asked her to look for information about them, and she had heard the occasional hushed whisper in the valley. But none of those instances had convinced her the mountain people were anything other than stories created by those who gazed up at the impassable mountains in awe.

Gwen's claim was another matter, however.

"You're saying you grew up in the mountains?" she clarified. "Not in one of the valleys but actually deep in the mountains? And there's a whole kingdom there?"

Gwen nodded, her face pale. She seemed to understand the import of what she was revealing.

Charlotte leaned back, trying to absorb it. Gazing at her new friend, she noticed her straight posture and thought of everything she had said—and not said. After seeing her portrait in Henry's castle, Charlotte had been certain she was a princess. But sitting in the forest with Gwen, it had seemed nothing more than fancy. Not only was she alone in the depths of Rangmere, but Charlotte had learned the royal families of all the kingdoms as a child and none of them had contained a Princess Gwen.

She had never learned about the royal family of the mountain kingdom, however. Her earlier certainty returned. She wasn't just talking to a girl from the fabled lost people. She was talking to the mountain princess. And something was terribly wrong in their kingdom if she had been forced to flee.

Charlotte swallowed down the enormity of the revelation

and nodded slowly. "Very well, then. Is it possible Easton is somewhere in the mountains? I have no idea how you would search the peaks for a lone person." She gazed again at the glimpse of distant stone visible through the canopy.

"It would be an impossible task." Gwen slumped before rallying with a determined look. "But the mountains are a death sentence, and the queen said Easton was banished. There are ways out of the mountains—we have a few traders who make the trek in secret—and I think she might have abandoned him on this side of the mountains."

Charlotte raised her eyebrows at this information, but it made sense. If the mountain kingdom existed, then the stories hadn't been mere fancy after all, and they must have originated somewhere.

"Do you have any idea where the paths exit the mountains?" Charlotte asked. "If we could work out where he came out…"

Gwen grimaced. "I wish I knew. But I came out by… another means." Her hand strayed to her pocket.

Charlotte waited, full of curiosity, but Gwen said nothing more. Charlotte would have liked to press her for more information, but it seemed rude, so she let it go. She had secrets enough of her own, so she couldn't fault others for keeping their own counsel.

"I think Harold might know something about the routes," Gwen blurted out. "It's why I've stayed with his family so long. I've been trying to convince him to tell me, but he won't talk about it. From what I can gather, only a chosen few valley folk are permitted to meet and trade with the mountain delegations. I think the queen's people might have threatened those valley folk that if word gets out more broadly, they'll lose their trade."

Charlotte's mouth fell open as several things clicked into place. Her aunt and uncle were clearly among the chosen few to be permitted to act as traders—it was the source of their extra wealth. And it must have taken her father all these years to gain enough trust to be included in their number.

But that new knowledge did nothing to help Gwen. "The most obvious place to look is the valleys," she said briskly. "So you've done well coming here. Have you asked Harold if he's met anyone by the name of Easton?"

Gwen nodded. "He says he hasn't."

"Hmmm…" Charlotte hummed to herself as she thought. "That rules out all the closer valleys. We should ask him for help, though. He could provide a map of the remaining valleys and mark off those where he knows all the residents. That will narrow the initial search a little. Unless Easton changed his name when he arrived." She looked to Gwen. "Would he have felt the need to do that if he was on the run from…your kingdom?"

Gwen frowned. "I suppose it's possible. But I did ask Harold if he knew of any boys who had arrived alone ten years ago, and he seemed certain there was no one like that in any of his valleys."

Charlotte nodded. "Good point. Even if his name has changed, it's a unique enough situation that people should remember him." She frowned. "But are you really going to travel through Rangmere alone?"

Gwen shivered. "What other option do I have? It's not that I want to be alone, but I have no one. As it is, I feel terrible for imposing on Harold and his family just because he's the local official."

"Don't worry about that," Charlotte said as cheerfully as she could. "I'm sure they're glad of the company. Society is so restricted out here that all newcomers are a matter of interest."

"That's what everyone keeps saying, so I've allowed myself to be talked into staying this long." Gwen didn't sound happy about that weakness on her part.

"They're not making excuses," Charlotte said. "They really mean it."

Gwen gave her a tremulous smile, and Charlotte wanted to give her a hug. How quickly her feelings toward the other woman had undergone a complete shift.

"You also haven't heard of an Easton," Gwen said after a pause. "So that might be another valley I can cross off the search. Which valley are you living in now with your husband?"

It was an innocent question, but it sent a surge of longing through Charlotte. Her thoughts and emotions had been trapped inside her, in such intense turmoil, and she hadn't been able to speak of them to anyone. Even now that she had returned home, she couldn't talk about the truth with her parents and sisters. Her husband had asked her to remain silent, but she would have known it was a bad idea anyway. Her relationship with her family was tangled enough, and they had only just reached a new place of peace.

But here in this secluded clearing, real life seemed distant. She had made a friend, and impossible as it had initially seemed, one who felt like a kindred soul. For the first time, she felt it was possible to talk about the incredible turns her life had taken since her wedding, and she couldn't help wanting to be honest even though she had known Gwen for less than a day.

Somewhere in the recesses of her mind, Charlotte felt a twinge of discomfort. Henry had only told her not to speak of their nights to her parents, but surely he had meant to keep it private in general. He knew her history, and he wouldn't have thought there was anyone else she would be tempted to tell. He couldn't possibly have guessed she would run into Gwen.

Charlotte ignored the small voice of caution. She was so full of emotions, she was going to burst if she couldn't get them out.

Or do you just want to make sure Gwen knows Henry is yours? a less pleasant voice asked.

Charlotte brushed that one aside too. Of course it wasn't jealousy motivating her. Gwen had Easton.

"Actually," she said, her voice trembling with a heady mix of excitement and nerves now that she was finally telling someone the truth of her strange situation, "my husband doesn't come from the valleys. I don't know where he comes from originally, but we have a castle in the nearby mountains."

"A castle? In the mountains?"

Before Gwen could ask any more questions, the story poured out of Charlotte. She told how the white bear had approached her family and about the wealth and escape he'd offered in exchange for marriage. When she mentioned his name, she watched Gwen closely, but there wasn't so much as a flicker of recognition or curiosity.

Charlotte's hope surged afresh. Gwen didn't appear to even know a missing man named Henry. If his love for Gwen was not only one-sided but had developed from afar, then surely such a hollow emotion might have already been supplanted by the wife he spent all his days with? Now she knew Gwen was the mountain princess, it seemed more than possible that Henry—who must also be from the mountain kingdom if he knew Gwen—might have loved her from a distance.

Charlotte had been too hasty in leaving him, and now the hours before his return stretched out far too long.

But in the meantime, she'd found a new and completely unexpected friend. Buoyed up by her relief and the heady excitement it created, she continued on with her tale. She described the castle he had taken her to, and the building provoked more questions from Gwen than the revelation that Charlotte had married a bear.

The more detail she gave on the castle, the deeper Gwen's frown grew. But now that Charlotte had begun, she couldn't stop. The rest of the story followed, culminating in her discovery that Henry was really a man and the way they spent their nights lying side by side in the pitch darkness.

When she finished, silence fell on the clearing. It lasted until Gwen spoke in a voice that trembled slightly.

"You're married to a man who turns into a white bear every day?"

GWEN

Fear nearly immobilized Gwen, but she wasn't sure if it was general dread or fear for Charlotte, who seemed so bright and lovely. Gwen had allowed herself to be swept up in excitement at the unexpected discovery of a friend and in their exchange of confidences. The feeling—however brief—of being part of a team, united in the search for Easton, had been heady. But reality fell far too quickly.

From the bright, almost tender, expression on her face, Charlotte had no idea of the danger she was in. Gwen guessed she even felt affection for her husband, despite his transformations. But Gwen couldn't brush aside the coincidence.

Away from her mother's sleeping drafts, Gwen had been forced to endure her own transformation every night since her escape. She hid in the forest, away from the valley folk until the sun rose each morning, and she had yet to meet another bear of any sort, let alone one who was actually human.

If there was a man in the mountains who turned into a white bear, he must be part of the same enchantment as Gwen herself. And the only people trapped in the enchantment were her mother's people—the mountain court and the queen's guards.

Bile rose in her throat as she put it all together. She had been swept up in their talk of Easton and forgotten where she had first seen Charlotte. It hadn't been in this clearing but in her mother's bedchamber—in a portrait that had also featured Charlotte's husband.

At best, Charlotte's husband was a member of her mother's court, loyal to someone unspeakable. But her friend claimed he was a bear during the day and a man at night—the opposite of the enchantment on the mountain court. The more she considered the strange anomaly, the stronger grew an even more horrifying possibility. What if this man wasn't a member of the court but the original owner of whatever object her mother had used to create the curse?

Was he even a man at all, or was he some creature of nightmare who had managed to assume the trappings of a man by night? It was entirely believable that her mother would be allied with such a creature.

Creeping fingers of cold slid up Gwen's spine. Her friend had said she only ever encountered her husband as a man in the pitch dark. She had never seen him, not once. Did his dread enchantments allow him to assume the voice and size of a man but not a proper appearance? Was that why he hid in darkness?

Charlotte's bright smile was fading in the wake of Gwen's long silence, and she knew she needed to speak.

"Charlotte," she gasped, "are you sure you've never seen his face?"

"No, never." Charlotte leaned forward, looking concerned. "Are you well, Gwen? You look ill."

"I...I'm well enough." Gwen exerted all her will power to push down the horror that was making her sick. "It's you I'm worried about."

Charlotte laughed and waved a hand as if to brush off Gwen's concerns. "I know it's an unusual situation—to say the least!—but Henry is everything considerate."

Gwen caught the soft glow in her friend's eyes when she spoke his name, and her heart sank. She had spent years forced to attend the events of her mother's court, always watching and listening from the sidelines. While she might have engaged in few conversations herself, she had long ago learned that sometimes the most charming of faces concealed a rotten core. This Henry had clearly won Charlotte over, but that fact provided Gwen little reassurance. He would show his true colors eventually, but when he did, Charlotte would be trapped alone in his castle.

What could Gwen do about it, though? Charlotte had known her for less than a day. Why would she listen to her speaking against her beloved husband? In any ordinary situation, Gwen would even have applauded Charlotte for that loyalty.

But her friend was caught up in a dark enchantment, and Gwen couldn't leave her to fight it alone. Especially when Charlotte didn't even know the danger she was in.

"Don't you think you should at least insist on seeing him once?" Gwen suggested tentatively.

Impatience crept over Charlotte's face, as if she was disappointed in her friend's reaction.

"I can't do that. Of course I'd like to see his face—I've imagined it too many times to count—but I trust him. He has a reason for keeping it hidden, and he'll show me his full self when the time is right."

But will you like that full self when you see it? Gwen pleaded in her mind.

Aloud, she said, "But surely it couldn't hurt to see him only once?"

Charlotte shrugged. "Even if I wanted to, it's impossible. The castle is Henry's, and he controls the sources of light. None of them work during the nighttime hours. It's not just a matter of taking a peek."

Gwen bit her lip. She could think of strategies that might circumvent the enchanter's machinations, but it was clear her friend didn't want to hear them. Already Charlotte had deflated at Gwen's questions. She feared that if she pressed any harder, Charlotte would close herself off from Gwen entirely.

Gwen couldn't risk that. Not when she had finally found someone who might become a friend, someone who would help her make a plan for finding Easton. And even for Charlotte's sake she didn't want to destroy the fragile beginnings of their friendship. If her suspicions were even partially correct, Charlotte would need every possible ally in the future.

"I'm sorry," Gwen said softly. "It's just such an...incredible story."

Charlotte relaxed, laughing. "Imagine what it was like living it! I wasn't sure if I was in a dream half the time."

The two chattered on a little until Charlotte noticed the afternoon sun waning. She leaped to her feet.

"We really must be getting back. Otherwise my family will start worrying, and you might miss your evening meal." She smiled at Gwen. "Shall we meet again?"

Gwen agreed eagerly, and the two began the walk back, staying together until they had to part ways to reach their separate destinations. As they walked, Gwen's mind raced, and when they paused for a final farewell, she made a suggestion.

"I could meet you at your house tomorrow, if you'd like. I remember where it is, and I'd be happy to have the chance to greet your parents and sisters again."

Charlotte paused for the briefest moment, and Gwen wondered if she'd rather keep their friendship separate from whatever complicated dynamic Charlotte shared with her family. Gwen could certainly understand that desire. In ordinary circumstances she wouldn't have dreamed of intruding. But the circumstances weren't ordinary, and while they were walking, she'd realized what she should do. She just needed a chance for a quiet word with one of Charlotte's parents.

Charlotte might not have a reason to listen to a friend of a few hours' standing, but surely she would listen to her own parents. Gwen just needed to convince them there was something terribly wrong with Charlotte's husband—something beyond the fact he turned into a bear each day.

CHARLOTTE

Although Charlotte had been hesitant at the idea, Gwen's visit to Charlotte's family home had been a success. With no one else present to provoke her sisters' sense of competition and comparison, they were welcoming to the visitor. And Charlotte's parents seemed delighted to hear she had a local friend, even if only of recent standing.

Gwen herself was everything that was charming and polite. She even graciously accepted a tour of the new stable, conducted while Charlotte was caught inside by her sisters. Elizabeth and Odelia had somehow talked her into helping with the food preparation their mother had assigned them, and Charlotte wasn't able to extricate herself before her proud mother swept Gwen off to complete the tour. Given Gwen's true status, Charlotte could only hope she wouldn't take offense. But she couldn't warn her family that Gwen was a princess when her friend hadn't even fully confided in her.

Thankfully Gwen's royal manners were more than adequate for Charlotte's absence. But she still felt guilty enough to stick closely to her friend for the rest of her stay. So it was only after Gwen left that Charlotte noticed how distracted her parents seemed. With the excitement of the visit over it was impossible to miss.

When her mother dropped her third bowl in a row, Charlotte asked what was wrong.

"Nothing, nothing," her mother said, but the look she cast at Charlotte suggested otherwise.

Charlotte sat straighter, frowning. It hadn't occurred to her that her parents' mood might be related to her, but her mother's expression suggested it was.

"Actually," her father said suddenly, "your mother and I were wondering if you would come for a walk with us, Charlotte?"

If her father was using her full name, then something was definitely wrong.

"Of course I'll come," she said, dreading the possibility that her parents might ask her to extend her stay.

She gathered her cloak with a heavy heart. It would be difficult to say no to them, but there was no question of staying longer. She was already counting the hours until she saw her husband again and was able to finally have the too-long deferred conversation about their future. She wouldn't delay her reunion with Henry for anyone.

Sure enough, as soon as they were away from the house, her mother cast a beseeching look at her father, and her father cleared his throat. Charlotte held herself silent, knowing it was only fair to allow them to have their say, even if she already knew the outcome.

But her father's first words took her completely by surprise.

"You seem happy, Charli," he said, "but your mother and I have some concerns."

"Concerns?" Charlotte looked between them, bewildered. "About what?"

"In retrospect, I can see that I took the matter of your marriage far too lightly," her father said. "I made certain assumptions that I have since realized are false."

Charlotte frowned. Where had these concerns been in their joyous reconciliation the day before? Her obvious well-being had seemed to clear away their lingering worry.

"I don't know what you mean," she faltered. "What sort of assumptions?"

"In truth," her father said, "I took certain hints dropped by the white bear—"

"Henry," Charlotte interrupted.

Her father exchanged a look with her mother. "Ah yes. Henry. I took certain hints dropped by Henry and combined them with information from your uncle to reach erroneous conclusions. It was on the strength of that understanding that we agreed to part with you."

"What can you possibly mean?" Charlotte asked, growing more and more incensed. "Henry promised me a life of ease and comfort, and he promised you riches through a large bride price." She glanced back in the direction of the new house, now hidden by the trees. "Can you deny he's provided exactly that for both of us?"

Her mother looked pained, but her father's stern expression didn't waver. "I admit he has so far stayed true to the explicit promises he made. It's the implications that have proven false that now concern me."

Charlotte felt her anger on Henry's behalf peak and then

suddenly abate. She let out the breath she'd been holding. Could she blame her parents for leaping to wrong conclusions about Henry when she had done exactly the same? And just like them, she had been concerned when she first learned she was wrong. But just as she had long ago forgotten her thoughts of the Palace of Light, they would soon realize their daughter had more than she could ever need.

"I'm sure I can ease your minds," she said softly. "What is it you were wrong about?"

Her father looked at her without any abatement of his obvious anxiety. "When we encountered a talking white bear, naturally we assumed he was one of the mountain people."

"Naturally?" Charlotte asked, astonished. "Whatever can you mean?"

"At the time I hadn't met one myself, of course," her father said, "but since the mountain people who visit these valleys transform into white bears, the connection was obvious. I told you as much."

"Told me?!" Charlotte stared at him in astonishment. "What are you talking about? I've never heard such a thing!"

Her mother looked from Charlotte to her husband, horrified, while he merely looked confused.

"Given I was working so hard to be accepted as one of the approved valley traders, your mother and I were extra careful to maintain discretion about their existence. Even after Henry first appeared, it didn't seem wise to mention anything in front of your sisters."

Charlotte frowned, remembering all the times after Henry's appearance when her father had hinted at something unsaid, or trailed off a thought half finished. Even his response to the arrival of a white bear hadn't seemed entirely normal.

"I can understand you not wanting to say anything to Elizabeth or Odelia," she said, incensed. "But how could you not tell me the full truth when I was about to marry one of them!"

"I couldn't say it in the house with your sisters around," he said. "But I did tell you out in the forest when we talked about his proposal, remember? Or at least, I started to tell you, but you became furious and cut me off, running back to the house."

Charlotte gaped at him. The memory of that day was burned into her mind, thanks to the high emotions that had marked it. And now that she thought back to that conversation, she did remember him whispering something that she hadn't heard, too caught up in her heartbreak to pay attention. How could she have guessed he was imparting secrets of such significance?

"I didn't hear you," she said, groaning. "You were whispering, and I was too..." She sighed. Perhaps it had all been for the best. She might not have gone through with the marriage if it hadn't been for her mistaken assumptions.

"But Harold said you knew everything," her father said, still frowning in confusion. "He gave me a whole lecture about how I should have warned you to be more discreet. He said you nearly blurted it all out in front of his children. I thought you must have already heard about it from one of your cousins and were protecting them by not mentioning as much to me."

Charlotte shook her head, her emotions shifting toward amusement. She remembered the conversation with Master Harold as well. She had been confused to receive a similar lecture to the one her father had been given and even more confused when he had spoken about some in the valley not trusting Henry's people. If she hadn't been so emotionally worked up, maybe she would have hesitated long enough to demand a full explanation.

"None of my cousins ever mentioned a thing," she said.

"You really didn't know?" her mother frowned. "But you can't have married him thinking he was genuinely a bear!"

"I thought he was one of the High King's creatures from the Palace of Light," Charlotte said. "I thought he meant to take me there!"

Her mother gasped, and her father's jaw tensed.

"What?" he asked. "You thought what?" He looked thunderstruck.

Charlotte shrugged. "It doesn't matter now. I'm perfectly happy in Henry's castle and have no desire to go to the Palace of Light instead."

Her parents exchanged worried looks.

"But what is this castle?" her father asked. "Is it not in the mountain kingdom?"

Charlotte shook her head. "Actually, it isn't far from here. It's certainly not up among the proper mountains—which is where I assume their kingdom must be. I've recently found out some information that makes me think Henry must have come from the mountain kingdom originally, but he doesn't live there now."

"You really do live all alone?" her mother asked. "I thought your stories sounded a little strange, but I didn't realize you were so totally isolated." Her expression was growing more and more alarmed, and Charlotte tried to think how to reassure her.

"Did Henry ever say he had come down from the mountain kingdom or that he meant to take me there?" she asked slowly.

Her father sighed. "No, he didn't. We assumed as much

because he was a white bear. How could we think anything else? But he was obviously wealthy, and he dropped certain hints that gave me the impression he was a prince among them—or a senior member of their court, at least. I know some in these parts mistrust the mountain people—it's why the traders wish their existence to remain secret so as to avoid any prejudice or hostility. But the mountain kingdom has brought new prosperity to the valleys. Its people aren't evil— they're just unknown. And if you were their princess, what danger could there be? Henry assured me you would have a life of luxury, privilege, and power, and that you would be free to come and go as you wished." He audibly ground his teeth together. "It sounds foolish now to say that his manner convinced me he could be trusted. I shouldn't have been so credulous."

Charlotte put a gentle hand on his arm. "I know what you mean. I sensed it from him myself. It's a large part of the reason I agreed to the marriage. And you needn't be so alarmed, Father. He may not be who either of us thought, but he has done nothing to betray our trust."

"I know now he's not a prince," her mother said, sounding eager, "but you said he is one of the mountain people?"

Charlotte bit her lip. Since meeting Gwen, she had concluded he had to be, but they had all been wrong in their previous assumptions.

"He has never said so," she admitted reluctantly.

"He hasn't taken you to visit the mountain kingdom?" her father asked.

Again Charlotte was reluctant to answer, but a lack of communication was what had caused the problem in the first place. "No. We've never been anywhere but his castle, which, as I said, isn't far from here."

"And you live there completely alone," her mother said slowly, looking at her father with eyes of concern.

"We may be alone, but it's still a life of luxury," Charlotte said quickly. "Henry's godmother object provides for all our needs."

She had thought mention of a godmother object would reassure them, but they merely exchanged another significant look.

"So this Henry is neither a resident of the Palace of Light nor one of the mountain people," her father said slowly. "And he keeps you isolated and alone, far from any communities. It seems impossible that he could be a white bear and not be one of the mountain people, but they have never mentioned one of their own living isolated within the valleys. If he isn't one of them, then we must know—who and what is he?"

Both her parents fixed her with such intense looks— compelling, anxious, and charged all at the same time, as if they were ready to wrench her away from Henry and never allow her near him again.

Fear made Charlotte's heart lurch and race, words falling out of her.

"Henry is a man! You're talking as if he's something horrible, but he's just an ordinary man under an enchantment."

Her father's stance didn't relax, but her mother slumped a little, the first hint of relief appearing on her face.

"You're sure?" she asked. "You've seen him as a man?"

Charlotte bit her lip. "I haven't seen him, but..." She fell silent, remembering her promise to Henry. Would he still want her to keep it in the face of this terrible misunderstanding?

Her mother let out a soft cry. "You haven't seen him! How can you know he's a man, then? Oh, my daughter!" She flung her arms around Charlotte. "We should never have let you go. This is all our fault!"

"Mother!" Charlotte struggled to free herself from the suffocating grip. "You really don't need to be so concerned. I'm happy in my life with Henry." She drew a breath as she finally extricated herself. "I love Henry."

Her admission, which felt so weighty and significant to her, seemed only to fuel her parents' unease. They exchanged yet another look, and this time she could read it. They found the idea discomforting—as if it were further evidence that she was under the thrall of someone malevolent.

"He isn't like that!" she cried. "He's kind and considerate, and he knows me—the real me. I belong with him." Tears ran down her face as she realized the truth of her own words and how foolish they made her doubt and uncertainty seem. Why had she been so overset that she couldn't even manage a conversation?

"Hush, my dear, hush." Her mother rubbed her back. "We'll find a way out of this marriage for you."

Charlotte pulled back. "Aren't you listening? I don't want to leave my marriage!"

"We should all calm down," her father said. "Charli, we're only worried about you. If everything is as you say, we will be delighted. But how do you know he's really an ordinary man? Do you have anything to rely on other than his own words?"

He looked at her so intently that she squirmed. She had to defend Henry. Surely she could do so without telling them the full truth of their nights together.

"It's not just his words," she said slowly. "I've talked to him as a man."

"I thought you said you hadn't seen him in any form but

that of a bear." Her father was watching her carefully and must have caught her grimace.

"I didn't say I've seen him, I said I've talked to him."

"That sounds like nonsense," her mother said. "If you've talked to him, why don't you look at him as well?"

Charlotte hesitated, worrying at her lip. "Because it's always dark," she finally blurted out. "He is only a man at night and the palace is shrouded in complete darkness then."

She didn't mention the specifics of their nights spent side by side in bed, but it was clear that even without those details, her words had confirmed her parents' fears rather than allayed them. She should have just remained silent as Henry had asked her.

Fresh tears threatened. She had only wanted to defend him, but instead she had terrified her parents.

Her mother's voice softened. "You say you love him. Don't you want to see his face? Just once, so you can be sure—so we can be sure—that he's really what he claims to be."

Charlotte scoffed. "What else could he be?" Even as she said the words, she could feel the warmth of his arms around her on the night he had comforted her, his heart beating so close to her own. Of course Henry was a man.

But she couldn't deny the insidious appeal of her mother's suggestion. She did want to see his face. She wanted it desperately.

"We don't really know anything about him," her father said. "But it would be reassuring to know he truly is an ordinary man. There are clearly strong enchantments at work, and you yourself have pointed out that not all creatures in this world are entirely...natural."

Charlotte frowned. The creatures that lived in the Palace of Light with the High King weren't something to be afraid of.

But then, neither were any of the godmother objects when they were first given to humans. And yet, some had been corrupted and misused.

Charlotte didn't believe Henry was someone who deserved her fear. But she wanted a future with him—one in which they could be fully husband and wife—and she longed to see her husband's face. Even if she only saw it once, for a moment, it would be enough for now. Once she had seen it, she would be able to picture him as he lay beside her in the darkness. Nothing else would need to change, but she would truly know him the way he knew her. And maybe if she truly knew him, their marriage could become real, the way she longed for it to be.

"But I can't," she said, sounding more regretful than she should have. "His object controls all the sources of light in our castle."

"I have an idea about that." Her mother gave her father a look that made Charlotte wonder about the source of her mother's idea. "I'll give you a candle from home and a way to light it. Keep it hidden on you, and when night comes, you can light it and see him for yourself. If that upsets him, then he's not being honest with you, and at least you'll know..." She hesitated. "Whatever there is to know."

Charlotte bit her lip. Her parents didn't know that Henry slept beside her at night. If she looked at him while he was asleep, he wouldn't even need to know about it. She could light the candle for a brief minute and then hide it again. She would even destroy it the next morning so she wouldn't be tempted again. Nothing would need to change.

"Fine," she said in a rush. "If it would relieve your mind, I'll do it."

Both her parents smiled at that, although it didn't quite

relax the tension in her father's frame. She could only imagine what he was thinking. If she did discover something terrible about her husband, what would she do about it alone in their castle? But she wasn't worried about that aspect because, unlike her father, she knew there was nothing terrifying to find. All she was going to see was the face of the man she loved. The face of her husband.

CHARLOTTE

By the time Henry arrived to collect her the next day, Charlotte was a wreck. The candle had been received and stowed carefully inside her gown, but she might as well have stored a nest of ants there. She could barely stay still, one minute seized by the certainty she should throw it away and the next by a burning impatience for night to fall so she could finally see Henry's true face.

She waited outside for him, but since her entire family waited with her, he couldn't avoid them this time. They greeted him politely enough—even with curious excitement on the part of her sisters now that he had provided the promised wealth. Charlotte just hoped he didn't notice the tension in her father's shoulders or the way her mother clung to her and avoided looking straight at the bear in front of her.

Henry himself said as little as possible until they had departed and were traveling through the trees.

"How did it go?" A world of tension lay beneath the words. Had he been worrying about her for the last three days?

Charlotte leaned forward, resting her cheek against the fur

of his neck. Had he been taking proper care of himself? What had he done alone at night in his human form? Without her to sleep beside had he roamed the empty corridors?

The only thought she couldn't stomach was the idea that he might have spent those nights alone in the dining room. But memories of the portrait—once so painful—led her now to thoughts of Gwen and her search for Easton. Even if Henry's feelings still lingered, she would find a way to drive them out. Now that she knew there was no bereft love waiting for him, nothing could make her give him up. Henry was hers, just like she was his, and she would hold onto him with every bit of her strength.

"Lottie?" he asked at her silence, and warmth rushed through her at the nickname. She had missed hearing it. She had missed him.

"Thank you," she said. "For suggesting I go home and for taking me there. I didn't realize how much I needed to reconcile with my parents. Even my sisters were kind to me like they used to be when we were small. Now that I'm gone and they're rich, everything is forgiven."

She couldn't keep a hint of sourness from appearing in the last sentence, but it was tempered with amusement. Her sisters were who they were, and there was nothing for Charlotte to do apart from accept that fact. She couldn't force them to change, and she would only make herself miserable hoping for it. They wouldn't be bothered in the least.

"It was a good time." Henry repeated, both relieved and pleased. "I was worried I'd done the wrong thing sending you to them. They have never treated you as you deserved, and I spent the whole time you were gone worried I'd only delivered you into further heartbreak. Perhaps you'd be better without them in your life at all."

"No," Charlotte said quickly. "My parents apologized for the past, and everyone treated me well. I know my life is with you now—I welcome that—but my past is still important to me. They're still important to me."

Henry grunted as if not entirely convinced.

"I'm sorry you worried, though," Charlotte said softly.

"I just hope it won't make you feel more lonely in the castle," Henry said, still sounding concerned.

"No," Charlotte said fervently. "As much as I liked seeing my family again, I missed home. Our home." Her voice dipped shyly on the last two words, and he rumbled in response.

"Our home," he repeated, in his deep, gravely voice, and the sound filled her with happiness. She was with Henry again, and they were going home.

And soon it would be night.

The trees flew past, and when the castle finally appeared, Charlotte felt actual tears at the sight of the sober gray stone. She never would have guessed how comfortable a home the castle would become.

They parted ways as usual, but Charlotte could barely make it through her usual evening routine. Food might as well have been paper in her mouth for its lack of taste, and the candle still burned beneath her dress, although it had never been lit.

When it came time to undress, she hid it carefully beneath her pillow. Almost as soon as she'd extinguished the normal candelabra—triggering the accustomed descent of pure darkness—the door opened. Henry had never arrived so promptly before, and she dared to hope he had missed her some fraction of the amount she had missed him.

He sighed as he slid between the sheets, keeping to their usual distance.

"It's nice to have you back," he said simply. "I managed alone here without you before our wedding, but now…"

Charlotte glowed at his words. He really had missed her. He wanted her here. Maybe she was right in hoping he had already started to forget his youthful interest in the princess and was turning toward his wife instead.

"I'm glad to be back," she murmured, wondering if the extent of her emotion sounded in her voice. "I won't leave you again."

"It was a fortunate day when I first saw you and your sisters in the woods." The sound of his voice told her he'd rolled over and was lying on his side facing toward her.

"You mentioned you'd seen us before," Charlotte said. "But how did you decide to propose to me? And why me?"

She asked the questions shamelessly, the fear she had felt before over his answers gone.

"From the moment I saw you, I couldn't take my eyes off you, Lottie."

She laughed, unable to help the glow of satisfaction.

"Do you not believe me?" he asked. "How could I look away? You're like sunshine itself. I knew I needed to find a wife, and as soon as I saw you, I knew I wanted it to be you. Seeing you made me feel like I'd spent the last months beneath solid gray cloud and the sun had finally appeared."

She considered his words. "You needed a wife. Because of your enchantment." She was skirting dangerously close to topics he had declared off limits, but she couldn't help herself. "And you picked me because you thought I was beautiful." She wasn't sure whether to be amused or offended.

Henry groaned. "That sounds terribly shallow, doesn't it? But it wasn't like that. Of course I noticed your beauty—it would be impossible not to. But I've seen plenty of beautiful women before. What drew me to you was something else. The brightness in you was in your expression and your words, not just your features. Even the way you carried yourself…"

He groaned again. "I'm not explaining it well. I'm just saying that your beauty isn't only physical. It shines out of you. I could see it in the way you approached simple tasks like gathering food and in the way you interacted with your sisters. I suppose, objectively speaking, they are attractive enough, but they seemed like gray clouds beside your sun. I know it sounds foolish, but I felt as if I knew you. And then after we talked…"

The rustle of sheets gave away his restless movement. "After we talked, I was really sure. If I hadn't managed to convince you, I don't know what I would have done. Thanks to the enchantment, I would still have needed a wife, but how could I have married someone else?"

Fresh warmth suffused Charlotte. Henry had seen her from the very beginning, just as he had seen her all these weeks in the castle. She had come home ready to fight for their future, but was it possible he was already won?

Her heart soared at the thought even as she cautioned herself. If he loved her as she loved him, why did he keep such a careful distance, never treating her as anything more than a friend and companion?

Unless he's just keeping his promise, a new voice whispered.

As soon as she thought it, Charlotte realized how likely it was. Her husband—her good and true husband—had made promises to her that he would consider absolutely binding. Promises he wouldn't break, no matter his feelings.

She let out a sound that was half sob, half laugh. Whatever Gwen had once been to him, his attention now seemed solely for his wife. Everything she longed for was in front of her. She just had to reach out her hand and grasp it.

"What is it?" he asked sharply, worry in his tone. "Are you all right?"

Charlotte was tempted to say no, just to see if he would cross the divide to comfort her again. But she couldn't bring herself to say something so untrue.

"I'm just happy," she whispered. "I'm happy to be back."

"Oh." He settled back, rustling the sheets at his movement. "Then we can be happy together."

"Yes," she murmured. "Together." She knew her voice sounded a bit watery, but she didn't care.

Soon she would tell him all her heart and admit her foolish fears. But she didn't want to mar this perfect moment with her confession. They had the rest of their lives to be together as husband and wife. There was no rush.

"I think I might actually be able to sleep tonight," Henry murmured in a voice that was already half slurred with sleep.

Her heart contracted. Had he lain awake without her beside him? Or perhaps he had prowled the corridors as she had feared. As much as her heart ached for him, it also rejoiced to know she had so much sway over his emotions.

"Sleep, dear husband," she whispered. "And in the morning, we will begin afresh."

And she would know his face by then. She would be able to picture him as his true self, and there would be no more barriers between them.

Swept up in her emotions, even the enchantment seemed like nothing. With their combined effort, how could they not find an answer to it?

His breathing evened, slowing into the familiar rhythm of his sleep. She lay for a long time, listening contentedly to the sound of his presence. But finally eagerness overtook her, and she stole out of bed.

With trembling fingers, she retrieved her mother's candle and flint. It took her several tries to light it, and part of her thought it wasn't going to work. But then flame blossomed in the darkness.

She squeezed her eyes shut, waiting a moment for them to adjust before cracking them open. She had never realized how bright a single candle could be until she had seen the depth of full darkness.

Shielding the single flame with her hand, she crept around the end of the enormous bed, approaching the far side where her husband lay. Her heart pattered far faster than her feet, sounding so loud she feared he would hear it and awaken.

But he slumbered peacefully, clearly deeply tired. When she had approached close enough, she leaned in, holding the candle so it would illuminate his face.

Her breath caught at sight of him. How was it possible that he was even more handsome than she had dreamed? He looked so peaceful in repose, giving her a full chance to admire his straight nose, strong jaw, and the riot of dark brown hair. The candlelight caught on his head, suggesting a hint that was almost auburn amid the brown. She couldn't see his eyes, but she didn't need to see them to fall even more in love with him.

Her body swayed toward him, pulled by something beyond conscious thought. But as she shifted position, a drip of candle wax fell. She only had time to gasp and jerk backward as it landed on the hand he had thrown over the blanket.

His eyes sprang open, and she forgot everything else at their piercing blue. With his eyes closed, he had been almost painfully beautiful, but the animation and intensity of his eyes only amplified the effect. The startling blue stood out against his dark hair, creating a whole that robbed her of breath. Could this man truly be her husband?

His expression, which had started out with the confusion expected from someone who had been woken from deep sleep by burning wax, softened at the sight of her. Their eyes locked together. Looking at his true face—at his unguarded response to her—she knew he already loved her as completely as she longed to be loved.

But the joy had barely registered when his expression changed. His thoughts had caught up with his instincts, and his gaze dropped to the candle in her hand. Instantly his face changed to a look of such profound horror that she fell back before it.

"What have you done?" he cried. "What have you done?"

"I…I just…" She moved to blow out the candle, panicked by his response, but he leaped forward and gripped her wrist in a steel hold.

"No," he said sharply. "There's no point now. The damage is already done. At least let me see you for these last moments."

"What do you mean?" she gasped as he removed the candle from her now trembling hold and placed it on the small table beside the bed. "What last moments?"

"Three months," he said. "That's all we needed. Three months' worth of nights. We were nearly there."

"I don't understand." Charlotte's trembling had spread from her hands to her whole body.

"When I left home to go adventuring on my own—a foolish notion I know now—I was captured in these valleys. The people who captured me wanted me to break their enchantment through my marriage. But something went wrong. I don't know why—I don't think they do either. I was supposed to be a bear at night, not during the day. It ruined their plans." He gave a harsh laugh. "Many marriage cere-monies are too elaborate to be completed between a human and a bear."

Charlotte swallowed painfully, putting together the pieces he hadn't said. "The mountain kingdom. They stole a husband for their princess. They wanted to marry you to Gwen!"

"Who?" he asked blankly.

"The mountain princess," she cried. "The one in the portrait."

"The portrait?" He frowned for a moment before his brow cleared. "Oh, you mean the one in the dining room? I never go in there."

"You...never go in there?" Charlotte whispered, trying to understand the seismic shocks that kept hitting her.

He laughed again, another bitter sound. "An empty castle except for one furnished room? This place didn't come from the bell—it's part of my enchantment, and it was a little obvious in its efforts to sway me with that one."

"They...they weren't your portraits?" Charlotte stammered.

"There were others?" He sounded genuinely surprised.

"In the side tables. And those came from the bell, after I arrived."

"When the bell interacts with the castle, it's affected by the castle's enchantment." He shrugged. "I never even met the princess. If they ever told me her name, I don't remember it. I certainly had no desire to eat my meals with her looming over me. She's the reason for my capture, my imprisonment in the body of a bear, all of it. Even if she didn't order it herself, she's still at the root of my involvement."

Gwen wasn't his lost love, she was his enemy—although she didn't know it. From her reaction to Charlotte's story, she clearly had no idea who Henry was or what had been done to him in her name.

"So you didn't create this castle yourself?" Charlotte gasped out.

"I came here from the mountain kingdom, and the castle already existed when I arrived. Even with the bell, I could hardly change anything until you arrived."

He spoke in a dead, hopeless tone, and Charlotte feared she might be sick.

"How did you escape them?" she asked.

"I didn't. When it all went wrong, she released me."

"Who is *she?*" Charlotte whispered.

"The mountain queen. The ones who captured me were her people, and she's the one who enchanted me. As I said, I was intended to marry their princess, but when the enchantment went wrong, she gave me the bell and told me that if I wanted to live, I had to find my own way to break the enchantment. She tied me to her with a second enchantment so that if I did break it, I would be forcibly returned to them. So I had two choices: live as a bear forever, or reclaim my true form and be forced to marry the princess as they planned."

"But why free you in the first place?" Charlotte asked, trying to make sense of the nightmare she had suddenly found herself in.

"The mountain court has been enchanted for as many years as we've been alive," he said. "If they had the answer to breaking the enchantment, they would have done so long ago."

"And they expected *you* to find a way free?" Charlotte asked.

Henry shrugged. "I'm a prince and uninvolved in their schemes. There are always ways for one such as me to free themself. All the stories say it."

"A...a prince," Charlotte gasped. "What do you mean? I thought—"

"That's another thing I loved about you," he said sadly. "That you didn't know I was a prince. You knew me only as Henry, not Prince Henry, soon to be crown prince of Arcadia."

Charlotte gasped again, remembering his promise that he would move her family and establish them in Arcadia. She had even known Crown Prince Maximilian and Princess Alyssa's only son was called Henry. But it had never occurred to her to put those things together. Had he been planning to move her family after he broke his enchantment?

"But if you're a prince, you must have a godmother," she said, clutching desperately at possibilities. "We need to call her!"

"I already did." He sounded grim. "She told me the mountain people were partially right about the way to break the enchantment. It was through a royal marriage. But it would take love as well as a wedding. The moment I looked into my wife's eyes with my own human eyes and felt nothing but love, the enchantment would be broken. But she told me something else as well. There was a way for me to break the second enchantment, the one tying me back to the mountain kingdom."

"What...what did you have to do?" Charlotte whispered although she could already guess at the answer.

"I had to find a girl to love who would marry me despite my being a bear—someone who didn't know my true identity or the details of my enchantments. A girl who would sleep beside me for three months' worth of nights and trust me without ever seeing my face. The queen's enchantment creates a false bond and forced loyalty, but it could be broken by trust that was freely given and a bond created by choice. If I could find someone who would believe in me and trust in me enough to sleep beside me in darkness without knowing why, her faith would win my freedom from both enchantments."

He smiled, but it didn't reach his eyes. "You married me, Lottie, and I can assure you I felt nothing but love when I looked into your eyes just now. You've freed me from my life as a bear. I will never be one again. But now I cannot escape the mountain queen. My godmother has already done as much as she can for me."

Charlotte stepped forward, fisting his nightshirt in both hands. "Surely there's a way! There has to be something I can do!"

"Can you find the mountain kingdom?" he asked in a voice that would have been mocking if it wasn't so gentle and full of love. "Can you find a place whose only direction is that it lies east of the sun and west of the moon? Can you tear me from the grasp of a queen who has spent two decades consolidating her power? A queen who spends half her time as an enormous bear?"

"Yes," Charlotte sobbed. "I can do anything! I will do anything to free you. I promise!"

He stared deep into her eyes, his breath coming ragged and fast.

"Lottie," he finally groaned and yanked her toward him.

For one breath, his blue eyes devoured her face. And then his lips descended on hers.

There was nothing soft about his kiss. It was demanding

and possessive and burned with the longing of all their weeks together.

She melted against him, glad for his strong arms pressing her close. She didn't want the kiss to ever end. She couldn't accept that he was about to be ripped from her.

But too soon he pulled back, gazing hungrily down at her face again. "Do you know how much I've wanted to hold you like this? To gaze human face to human face?"

"I'm sorry!" she wailed. "All I wanted was to see your face once."

"If only you'd waited!" he cried in tones of fresh anguish. "Do you know how much self-control it took to lie beside you each night—my wife!—and keep my distance? But I endured it in the hope of a future where I could stay by your side night and day in my true form. If only you could have waited as well, then that future could have been ours. But now everything is destroyed!"

"I'm sorry," she repeated, sobbing in earnest now. "I'm sorry. I love you, Henry."

He stilled, only the muscles in his arms jumping in response to her words. His face softened as he gazed down at her.

"I love you, too, Lottie," he murmured, and then he was gone.

CHARLOTTE

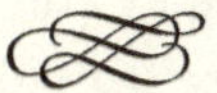

"Henry!" Charlotte sobbed, her empty arms reaching for a man who was no longer there.

"Henry!" she screamed more loudly, but it wasn't only her husband who had disappeared.

Her bedchamber was gone, along with the candle and the entire castle. Soft moonlight illuminated a clearing at the base of a mountain face, and nothing blocked the stars that twinkled uncaring overhead.

She fell to her knees, the sobs shaking her so strongly it hurt. But she couldn't master them. She had won Henry's love, had been held in his arms, only to have him ripped from her.

She couldn't accept it. She wouldn't.

She screamed again, wordlessly this time, shouting her defiance at the cold sky and the unmoving mountain.

Her anger burned against the mountain queen who had stolen her husband, but it also turned inward. Why had she been so impatient? Why hadn't she trusted in the man she loved so much?

From there, the spark of it leaped to her parents. It had all been their fault. They were the ones who had pressed her and given her the idea. They were the ones who had given her the candle. Why couldn't they have trusted her when she assured them of Henry's character and her own happiness? They had married her off, and yet they still thought of her as a child whose judgment couldn't be trusted.

Distantly, some part of her knew she wasn't being fair. They had acted out of fear for their daughter, whereas she had acted from selfish desire. She was the one who knew Henry, and yet she had been the one to accept the candle, the one to light it. But in that moment she didn't care. If it hadn't been for them, she wouldn't have lost Henry. The idea of the candle would never have occurred to her on her own.

Anger, grief, pity, fear, and fury bit as deeply as the night's cold, and she collapsed on the patch of grass where the castle had once stood. Consumed entirely by her tears, she cried until her exhausted body collapsed into unconsciousness.

When she woke, the emotions were waiting for her, prowling and circling while she slept, ready to pounce when she opened her eyes. But she fisted her hands, letting her nails dig into her palms, and wrestled them under control.

If it had only been for herself, maybe she would have succumbed to them. But she had made her husband a promise, and this time she wasn't going to let him down. It didn't matter how high the mountain or how impossible the task. She would find him and rescue him before he fell to the mountain queen's schemes.

He had trusted her with his hand, his heart, and his enchantment. She would not allow that trust to be entirely in vain.

Her first instinct was to stand up and start walking uphill, heading into the mountains. But her determination hadn't robbed her of all sense. She would find nothing but a quick death if she braved the mountains alone and without provisions.

East of the sun and west of the moon.

The words taunted her. She needed proper directions if she was to find the mountain kingdom.

She sprang to her feet. The mountain kingdom! She knew someone from the mountain kingdom. She knew its princess!

She hadn't pressed Gwen for answers about her home before. But somehow Gwen had traveled from the mountain kingdom to the Rangmeran valleys. She must know the way. And Charlotte would beg and plead without a trace of pride if it was necessary to pry an answer from Gwen. Surely her friend would help once she knew Charlotte's husband had been stolen by Gwen's own mother.

With an actual, achievable goal, Charlotte couldn't start quickly enough. But the trees passed much more slowly than they had when she rode a white bear. Her will was strong, but she was still bound by her short legs. It would take her more than a day to reach her home valley. She just hoped Gwen was still there when she arrived and hadn't already left on her search for Easton.

Eventually, as the hours passed, Charlotte had to give in to her hunger and spend some time foraging. As little as she wanted to waste any daylight hours, she would be slower in the long run if she lost her strength due to lack of sustenance.

If the moon had been full, she would have tried to keep going even when night fell, but it was too dark to make any progress realistic. As with the food, Charlotte knew a twisted ankle would only slow her down.

She slept fitfully, however, her arms always reaching for

Henry, only for her to start awake when they found empty air. And each time she woke, her cheeks were wet with tears.

As soon as the sun rose, she continued her journey. The forests around her had finally grown familiar—the very furthest reaches of what she had explored while she lived with her parents.

Back on familiar ground, she could take a more purposeful route—aiming not for her old home, but for that of Master Harold. Gwen was the one she sought, and Charlotte had no desire to see her parents—not while she was still lost in the height of her anger and grief. They had become inextricably entwined with her betrayal of Henry—the greatest mistake of her life—and the searing loss that had followed.

But long before she could reach Harold's home, she heard movement in the forest nearby. Her first instinct was to hide. But she was still too far out for it to be any of her family—they never came so far.

What if it was Gwen herself? Charlotte could think of no reason for her to be moving eastward toward the mountains, but she still raced forward, hope lending her speed.

And, sure enough, when she sprinted into view of the sound's source, it was the mountain princess herself.

"Gwen!" Charlotte gasped. "Oh, Gwen! You have to help me!"

"Charlotte!" Gwen paled, racing forward to take her friend's hands. "What is it? What is it? Is he after you?" She looked wildly behind Charlotte as if searching for a white bear in full chase.

Charlotte ripped her hands free, anger surging easily to the surface.

"Of course he's not after me! Henry would never hurt me." Her anger collapsed and her body collapsed with it, leaving her sitting on the grass. "He's gone, Gwen. He's gone, and I have to get him back."

Gwen knelt beside Charlotte, her face somehow growing even paler. "I don't understand. What do you mean?"

In halting words, devoid of all emotion, Charlotte told her the whole story. At some point, Gwen fell back, as if Charlotte had struck her. But she remained silent until she had finished.

"Henry—your Henry—is the lowlander prince my mother and the court wanted me to marry? That was the reason he was a white bear?" The thought had clearly never occurred to her.

All of Charlotte's animation returned, making her surge forward and grasp Gwen with both hands.

"You'll help me, won't you? You know how to get east of the sun and west of the moon?"

"I…East of the…" Gwen clearly had no idea what Charlotte was talking about.

"The mountain kingdom!" she exclaimed impatiently. "Your mother. That's where the stories claim it's located. You can help me get there, right?"

"Oh." Once again Gwen's hand went to her pocket. "I didn't know the stories described us that way. I don't know what it means. But I think…I think I might be able to get back there."

Charlotte fell back, relieved, her good sense finally starting to reassert itself.

"But what are you doing out here?" she asked. "Surely you can't be foraging so far, and so early in the morning?"

Gwen looked away. "As to that. Well…" She drew a breath. "I was worried about you. I wanted to come and check on you."

"You were coming to our castle?" The possibility hadn't

occurred to Charlotte. How happy she would have been to receive her friend's visit if only she had never lit that candle.

How different everything would have been if Charlotte hadn't acted like a fool from start to finish.

GWEN

*H*er friend fell into silence, lost in her own reflections. They were unhappy ones from the look of her, and the familiar sensation of guilt wrapped itself around Gwen.

She had been worried for her friend—worried enough to attempt to find the castle on her own. But she had never dreamed of the damage she herself had done. Charlotte must blame her parents, but that was only because she didn't know it was Gwen who had spurred them on to it. She had purposely maneuvered them outside without Charlotte or her sisters so she could tell them her concerns about Henry.

They had still believed him a mountain prince until she had told them there was no such person. She had even been the one to suggest the candle. She had let her fears consume her, had spread those fears to others, and now this was the result. How many lives had she ruined?

The thought of her mother's plans of conquest seized Gwen's throat, threatening to close it over. There were still so many more people who could be hurt as a result of her misjudgment.

Should she confess everything to Charlotte? Even as the thought occurred to her, she was already rejecting it. She wanted to help her friend, but would Charlotte let her do so once she knew the truth?

And under that, the uglier reality. She didn't want to see the hurt and disgust that would surely fill Charlotte's eyes once she heard what Gwen had done behind her back. Gwen had finally found a friend, and she couldn't lose her already. She couldn't be alone again.

"We'll go together," she said instead, the words surprising her. "Together we'll find both Easton and Henry." The thought of going back home, in reach of her mother, terrified Gwen. But she couldn't abandon Charlotte after causing her suffering. And if she was honest, the mountain kingdom was the most obvious place to look for clues as to where Easton had gone. She would have started there already if her fear hadn't gotten in the way.

"Yes!" Charlotte leaped up, her earlier despair evaporated, her face alight with purpose. "We'll go together and find them both." She paused, her brow creasing. "So where exactly are we going? You'll have to lead the way."

She flashed her friend a smile, and Gwen took strength from it, even managing a smile of her own.

"Actually," she said, "about that..." She drew the golden halter from her pocket. "I didn't walk here when I escaped, I rode the wind. And I think that's our best hope of getting back."

"You...rode...the wind..." Charlotte startled her by letting out a loud whoop. "That is far more amazing than I was expecting. You are amazing, Gwen." She shook her head. "You escaped your mother on the back of a wind horse. I think I picked the right ally."

She eyed the halter in Gwen's hand. "Although the horse that would fit that might be a little small to carry both of us."

Gwen chuckled in spite of herself. She didn't deserve Charlotte's admiration, but she couldn't help being swept up in the other girl's enthusiasm.

"It gets bigger," she said.

Charlotte laughed. "Of course it does. So how do we use it?"

She looked at Gwen expectantly, and Gwen's heart sank. "Um…that might be the hard part. I've only used it once, and then it sort of…well, it caught me while I was falling from a tower."

"You fell from a tower?" Charlotte eyes widened. "Someday you really need to tell me your whole story. But for now…" She looked around them. "Do you think that would be tall enough?"

Gwen followed the direction of her finger to a tree. "Tall enough for what?" she asked, her heart sinking.

Charlotte flashed her a challenging smile. "To fall from, of course."

"Of course," Gwen repeated weakly. She wasn't sure if she had the courage to throw herself purposefully from the top of a tree, but she also didn't know another way to activate the halter. "What if it doesn't work this time?"

Charlotte was already walking toward the base of the tree. "It'll work."

Gwen wished she had half her friend's certainty, but she could sense Charlotte was in no mood to be dissuaded. She would take any risk to rescue Henry, and Gwen owed it to her to offer what assistance she could.

When they stood on the highest branch, however, she was no longer so sure she could do it—even for Charlotte.

"Are you sure about this?" she asked, her voice coming out a squeak.

Charlotte threw her a mischievous glance. "No." She already had one arm wrapped firmly around the bark, but she wrapped her other arm around Gwen. "I think we'd better be connected, though. Do you have the harness ready?"

Gwen held it up. Her hands were sweating, but she had her fingers wrapped so tightly around the golden object they were white with the effort. Even the wind that tugged at them given their height couldn't pry it from her grip.

"Well, then," Charlotte said. "Here we go."

Before Gwen realized what she intended, her friend pushed herself off the branch, pulling Gwen with her. She had angled them away from the other branches, attempting to jump into clear air rather than lower boughs.

She had succeeded partially, but there was still one large branch beneath them—one they had both made use of to haul themselves so high. For a dizzying second, Gwen was sure they were going to collide with it. But then the harness in her hand began to grow.

A blink of the eye later, she had the golden reins in her hand, and the wind beneath her, as steady as any mount. A whoop in her ear and hands clutching at the back of her dress told her Charlotte was safely behind.

"Did that mad plan really work?" she murmured, but the wind snatched the words away before they could reach Charlotte's ears.

She didn't know the exact direction of her home, but on the way out, she had been able to steer the wind at will. If they circled high enough over the mountains, eventually they would catch sight of the mountain kingdom. It was too large to miss, especially from the air.

She tried to direct her wind mount upward and east, toward the nearest mountain peak, but it pulled north instead. She pulled harder on the reins, and the wind bucked in response.

Charlotte gasped, grabbing tighter to Gwen. "What's going on?" She had to shout to be heard over the rushing noise around them.

"I don't know!" Gwen cried back. "This didn't happen last time."

She tried again to direct their wind mount right toward the mountains, but it wouldn't respond. When she pulled harder, it suddenly disappeared beneath them.

They both dropped, screaming and flailing before it suddenly caught them again. Gwen only had a second to catch her breath before it surged upward, carrying them terrifyingly high.

"This is too high!" Charlotte shouted in Gwen's ear.

Gwen gritted her teeth and didn't reply. All her attention was focused on wrestling with the uncooperative reins. She couldn't understand why they were behaving so differently to the previous occasion.

The wind lurched, almost exactly like a bucking horse, and the reins nearly slipped from Gwen's grasp. Charlotte threw herself forward and grabbed them as well, the two girls holding on with everything they had.

And all the time they fought the wind, it carried them

northward at breathtaking speed, the mountains rushing past on their right. She didn't know how many valleys had passed beneath them, but they had long since left their starting place far behind.

"I…don't…understand…" Gwen forced out, her teeth still clenched.

"It's like someone's driving it with a whip and spurs," Charlotte gasped from where she was awkwardly squeezed against Gwen as they both fought the golden reins.

Charlotte's words sparked memory in Gwen and suddenly everything made horrible sense. There had been two objects on the one plinth—a pair. She had been repulsed by the whip and without thinking had grabbed the halter. It had never occurred to her that overlooking the whip might cause her a problem.

But if the halter controlled the wind, wouldn't the whip be a matching pair with it? The halter could tame the wind, and the whip could control and drive it. And her mother still had the whip.

"Is the wind getting stronger?" Charlotte cried as their pace picked up even further. "How do we get back to the ground? At this speed we're going to create a storm and destroy something!"

Gwen pulled on the reins as she had done last time, and the wind thankfully dipped in response. But almost immediately Charlotte cried a warning. Gwen craned to see what her friend was indicating and caught sight of a village approaching below at a terrifying pace.

She pulled their mount sharply back up again. If they went any lower, a wind as strong as the one they rode would rip the town to pieces. As it was, she could see the trees swaying and loose objects blowing wildly about.

She twisted in her invisible seat to see the town disappearing behind them. At least all the buildings looked intact.

Trying again, she pulled the reins up, and the wind lowered them toward the ground. It appeared her mother couldn't prevent them landing, at least.

But just as she was wondering what to do about the speed of the approaching ground, another cluster of houses appeared. She flinched, starting to direct them upward again, but Charlotte prevented her.

"No, it's too late!" she shouted. "We won't get high enough fast enough to miss them. We have to land!"

Gwen realized she was right. As they lowered, the wind was losing strength, so the lower they got, the less force would hit the hamlet.

She pulled with all her strength, no longer worrying about the speed of their own impact. She would have to trust in the object to keep them safe. All that mattered was to slow the wind as much as possible before it hit the defenseless houses.

She couldn't lower them fast enough, however. Their wind mount swept them between two houses, tearing the roofs off both as it went and filling the air with wreckage.

Gwen screamed, the sound seeming to echo around her as Charlotte also cried out. And then her shoulder, hip, and back hit the ground, and all she could do was breathe, the effort a frantic struggle.

When she finally managed to draw a proper breath, she realized the wind had disappeared completely. She looked down at the tiny halter still gripped in her fingers and quickly thrust it into her pocket.

Charlotte recovered a second behind her, leaping up and offering her hand to pull Gwen the rest of the way to her feet.

"We have to find the people," she said breathlessly,

ignoring the disarray of her hair and the dirt smeared down her nightgown. "They might be trapped or hurt."

Gwen nodded, scrambling upright. She had brought the wind to this hamlet. Whatever had happened here was her responsibility, and she would do what she could to help, little as that might be.

CHARLOTTE

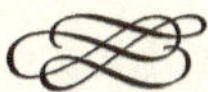

Charlotte followed at her friend's heels as Gwen raced back toward the destroyed houses. She could see from Gwen's expression that she was feeling tormented, considering herself responsible. But neither of them had foreseen the possibility of the wind turning against them and becoming an unchecked weapon.

"What made the wind fight you?" Charlotte asked Gwen as they ran.

"My mother," Gwen panted back. "There was another matching object that I left behind. A whip. I didn't know what it did, but it's obvious now. She must be able to tell when I've activated the halter, and she started using her object to interfere."

The hard ball that burned inside Charlotte flared up. Another crime to lay at the feet of the mountain queen. It seemed there was no end to them, and Charlotte meant to hold her accountable for every last one.

"Help!" A desperate voice called, directing their steps.

They raced around a wall—one that stood starkly upright, no

longer attached to the building it had once supported—and Charlotte crashed into her friend's back. Peering around her, she saw a woman attempting to lift a large beam off a young man.

Charlotte and Gwen hurried forward in unison, one on each side of the woman.

"I'm all right, Ma," the man said, although he looked pale to Charlotte's eye and his breathing was strained. "It's just a pity our roles aren't reversed—I'd have this off you in a moment."

"Hush now," the woman said sternly, "and save your breath." She sent a desperate look at Charlotte. "It's on his chest, and it's getting harder and harder for him to breathe."

"We'll help," Gwen said from the woman's other side. "If we all pull together..."

The three women reached down, all three of them straining with the effort to pull up the beam. But they couldn't shift the heavy bar of wood.

The mother kept trying even after Charlotte stepped back, so she pulled her away. The woman fought, trying to get back to the beam, so Charlotte snapped at her, trying to pierce the mother's mounting fear.

"We're not giving up! We just need to try something different. Is there anything we can use as a lever?"

"Over here," Gwen called, and Charlotte turned to find her already dragging a wooden post toward the other two women. It looked as if it might have been a fence post before the wind ripped it from the ground.

She ran forward to help her friend carry the post.

"Where do you think...?" She didn't need to finish the question before Gwen was placing the shorn-off tip underneath the beam, just above the man's head.

The mother realized what they were doing and ran

forward to help. The fence post was only just long enough for the three women to all get a secure hold at once, but as soon as they had, they all pushed downward.

For a second, Charlotte thought it wasn't working, and then the beam lifted slightly, raising one inch and then another.

As soon as they had it high enough, the trapped man rolled sideways, freeing himself. The moment he was clear, the mother let go, and the beam clattered to the ground.

She ran to her son, pulling him up.

"Wait!" Charlotte called, rushing after him. "He might be injured. We should check him first."

"No, I'm fine." The man managed a pained smile. "Thanks to your assistance."

Charlotte exchanged a guilty look with Gwen. He would never have needed help if they hadn't accidentally brought a gale to his home.

Fortunately for Charlotte and Gwen, the mother and son were too relieved at his rescue to ask where the two young women had come from.

"There might be others in need," Gwen murmured, and Charlotte followed her to the next house.

Once they had rounded a particularly large pile of rubble, they got a proper look at the rest of the hamlet. None of the houses were untouched, although they weren't all as shredded as the one of the mother and son.

Several people were still being retrieved from two of the houses, and Gwen rushed to help. Charlotte was about to follow her when she noticed an old lady standing on her own at the edge of the chaos.

She crossed over to her, concerned.

"Are you all right, Grandmother?" she asked. "Are you injured or missing someone?"

"I'm not your grandmother," the gray-haired woman snapped, but there was an amused twinkle in her eye that softened her tone.

"No, indeed," Charlotte said politely. "But I would offer you aid anyway if you're in need of it."

"Aid, is it?" The woman raised her eyebrows. "And here was I, thinking you were the one who brought this on them."

Charlotte paled. So someone had noticed them riding in on the wind after all.

She bowed her head. "It wasn't our intention. We ride in rescue of others, but the person who has wronged us is a powerful foe." The fire in her belly flared up again. "She is the one truly to blame for this catastrophe."

The woman chuckled. "I'm glad to hear you see things clearly. So what do you intend to do about it?"

Charlotte glanced back at Gwen, who was ferrying a bucket of water toward a small fire that had sprung up in the wake of the various collapses. Others rushed to help her, and they soon appeared to have the fire under control.

"We'll do everything we can, although I fear we're ill equipped for this sort of work."

"Not about the hamlet," the grandmother said, exasperated. "About this powerful foe."

Charlotte winced. "I'm not sure what we'll do about her either." Her eyes narrowed. "But we'll find a way."

The woman patted her on the arm. "That's the spirit." She leaned close as if about to impart a secret, and Charlotte responded instinctively, also leaning in. "You have to be in the fight if you want a chance of winning it."

Charlotte pulled back, fighting a smile. From the old

woman's air of great significance, she hadn't expected such a familiar saying.

"Very true, Grandmother," she said. "I'll keep it in mind."

The woman gave her a tart look, as if she could read Charlotte's thoughts. "See that you do."

Charlotte turned to leave. "If you're truly uninjured, I should see if there's someone who needs my help."

"Wait a moment, wait a moment," the woman cried testily. "You young things are always in such a rush. Give me a moment."

Charlotte waited obediently, trying to hide her impatience to join Gwen and do something to help.

"It's here somewhere," the woman muttered before giving a cry of triumph and producing a golden ball.

Charlotte stared at it, bewildered. When the woman held it toward her with an imperious gesture, she reached out her own arm, and the woman dropped it into her hand. She stared down at the ball, which fit comfortably into her palm.

It looked and felt as if it were made of real gold, but it was far too light to be solid.

"I don't understand," she said. "What is this?"

"It's a gift," the woman said with satisfaction. "Rumor says it will help you find your true love."

Charlotte looked up sharply, and the woman smiled. "You are looking for your true love, aren't you?"

"Yes, but—"

"Don't bother me with silly questions," the woman said with a return of her earlier tartness. "Don't they teach young people manners in this part of the world? If you receive a gift, you should thank the giver, not pester them."

"Thank you," Charlotte said obediently, still shocked.

A moment later the woman's words registered, and she

frowned. She spoke as if she wasn't a resident of this hamlet after all. And neither did she look as if she'd just been caught in a gale.

"No more nonsense from you, youngster," the woman said with a knowing look. "I'll look after these people, so you can focus on what you must do."

"And what is that?" Charlotte asked, watching the woman closely.

But despite her attention, she couldn't help blinking, and in the half-second her eyes were closed, the woman disappeared.

Charlotte gasped. In the second before she had gone, she could have sworn she saw something shimmering behind the woman's shoulders.

"Were those wings?" she whispered, although there was no one near enough to hear the question.

The woman couldn't possibly have been a godmother. It wasn't as if Charlotte was a princess.

Except…she was. The thought hit her for the first time. If Henry was a prince—one in the direct line to a throne—and also her husband, that made her a princess. The thought was enormous. Too enormous to be grappled with in the moment. But it was enough to make her believe in the identity of the woman who had disappeared before her eyes.

Her fingers closed around the ball. It had been a strange enough gift already, but it had just become infinitely precious. Even after her marriage and residence at Henry's castle, she had never imagined she would someday receive a godmother object directly from the hands of an actual godmother.

Reverently, she placed it in her deepest pocket. Turning toward Gwen, she was about to call out to her friend in excitement, but something snatched at her dress before she could speak.

The sharp wind pulled at her again, making her stomach tighten. The wind that had died when they landed was returning.

She ran toward Gwen and the others, shouting for everyone to take shelter. She didn't know how she knew it was necessary, but the certainty filled her.

Gwen looked up, frowning, and Charlotte called only two words. "The wind!"

Gwen's eyes snapped upward, although there was nothing to see in the sky. Her hair whipped around her face, though, and her skirts flapped. It wasn't just Charlotte's imagination. The wind had returned and was growing stronger by the second.

"It's back," she panted as she finally reached Gwen. "And it's going to destroy what's left of these houses if we don't do something."

"But what can we do?" Gwen wailed.

The grandmother's earlier words—increased in significance in Charlotte's memory now she knew they were the words of a godmother—came back to her.

"You have to be in the fight if you want a chance of winning it!" She grabbed Gwen's arm. "Your mother has sent the wind against us again, but we can't fight it from down here. We have to be riding it if we want a chance at controlling it."

Gwen wanted to argue. Most of all, she didn't want to return to the sky to be buffeted and thrown about at her mother's whim. But she couldn't deny the logic of Charlotte's words.

A particularly strong gust made a child cry out in fright, and Gwen's fingers plunged into her pocket.

"Hold onto me," she said grimly as she pulled out the halter. She didn't think they were going to need to fall from a height to be caught in the wind this time.

Sure enough, Charlotte barely had a hold on Gwen when the halter grew and the reins appeared. The next second, both girls had been swept into the sky.

"Go higher!" Charlotte shouted in her ear, ignoring the cries of shock and fear from below them.

Gwen pulled on the reins, relieved when the wind responded and leaped skyward, taking them high enough not to touch the houses or even the trees.

"What now?" she cried, but Charlotte didn't know how to answer. When she had directed them to resume their journey, she'd been thinking of the villagers below and following the directions of the godmother. She didn't know how to control the antagonistic wind.

"Forget about the mountains," she cried as loudly as she could. "Just try to keep it away from people and anything it could damage."

Gwen nodded, her attention focused on the reins as the wind lurched first one way and then another, trying to throw them off.

Charlotte held onto Gwen, but she kept herself poised ready to grab the reins as she had done before. If the wind grew strong enough, it would take both of them just to keep hold of it.

The land raced beneath them, so distant Charlotte hardly noticed it. But eventually a bright light ahead of them caught her eye. It took her a long moment to realize what she was seeing, and when she finally caught on, she gasped.

Spread from one side of the sky to the other was the ocean, reflecting the sunlight so that it winked and glowed.

"We're going to have to land," she shouted, and Gwen nodded.

"I see it."

Charlotte had always wanted to see the ocean, but she didn't want to be swept out over it, carried far beyond the reach of land. Gwen obviously felt the same because she directed them downward immediately. But just as she did, a large town appeared, nestled on the coast and protected by a vast sea wall.

Both girls cried out at once, and Gwen pulled them up again. Charlotte could see her trying to wrestle them either left or right, but the wind wouldn't cooperate. It was determined to sweep them out to sea.

As they left the land behind, unreasoning terror gripped Charlotte at the vastness that was now apparent in three directions. She knew the sea was big—endless, some said. But she hadn't been able to comprehend the reality.

She wrestled the fear down, however. There was no time to give way to it. Even if it killed them, they couldn't let the wind lay waste to a whole town. And neither was she ready to give up on the two of them. They had to force the wind to bring them back in.

Gwen tried to direct them left just as the wind lurched in that direction. They swerved so violently in response that both girls were nearly unbalanced. But it gave Charlotte an idea.

If she could find a way to communicate it to Gwen, they would possibly have a chance of getting back to land safely without destroying the town. She leaned in, about to shout in Gwen's ear, when a spot of brown caught her eye, followed by a white sail. The wind was sweeping them straight for a fishing fleet—one that was out on the open ocean, far from the protection of the sea wall. On their current course, they would reach them in less than a minute and every one of those ships would be sunk.

There was no time for explanations. Charlotte lunged around Gwen and grabbed the reins. As soon as she had control of them, she held herself in readiness, the reins slack in her hands.

Gwen started to protest, but Charlotte ignored her, all her senses on edge. The second she felt the wind lurch in one direction, she threw the reins the same way, using every bit of her strength.

They swerved so violently that the wind carried them in a half circle, sweeping them back toward the land. Gwen cried out in surprise, but Charlotte couldn't break her concentration to explain.

The wind pulled them sideways again, and she did the same thing, bringing them all the way around in a full circle this time until they faced land again. It happened again in the other direction and then again. And each time they circled, they were closer to the land than they had been the time before.

At last they grew close enough that Charlotte began to consider how to direct them around the town. But before they reached the harbor, the wind cut out as it sometimes did, sending them falling toward the waves. Both girls screamed, but the wind caught them just as their feet broke the choppy surface of the water.

It swept them back up again, only to cut out again. Charlotte's stomach lurched, but she couldn't miss the opportunity. She pulled on the reins in anticipation so that when the wind caught them again—more quickly this time—she was already directing it downward.

They weren't going to make the actual land, but they had a chance at the sea wall. She angled toward it, screaming for Gwen to brace herself.

Charlotte let go of the reins as they skimmed just above the wide wall of stone, throwing herself sideways and landing on the stone with a painful series of bumps. She lay for a minute, listening for the whistle of the wind and hearing nothing.

Sighing in relief, she rolled over to find a young man offering her a helping hand. She took it, glad for the extra assistance since every one of her muscles ached.

"Did you just ride that wind in?" he asked, his eyes wide and his curly hair looking as if it had just been through a hurricane.

Charlotte winced. "Yes, I'm sorry. I hope it didn't hurt you."

"I'm fine," the young man said quickly and offered her a grin. "Just astonished."

Charlotte smiled back weakly, glad the stranger was taking it so well.

"I have a friend," she said as she turned to look for Gwen. "We should—" Her eyes caught on Gwen, sitting frozen a few feet behind them, her eyes on the young man behind Charlotte.

Charlotte turned to follow her gaze and found the young man equally frozen, his eyes fixed on the young woman still sitting on the stones.

"Gwen?" he asked in a breathless voice. "Is that you?"

GWEN

Gwen hit the ground hard and rolled. For a second, she thought she might roll all the way off the wall and drop into the terrifying depth of water on both sides of it. But she stopped in time, her hand somehow still clenched around the now-miniature halter.

She pushed herself slowly into a sitting position, feeling bruised all over in body, mind, and emotions. If it wasn't for Charlotte's intervention, untold numbers would have just died. She had wanted to escape her mother's reach, but she hadn't gone far enough, and now she was bringing calamity to others.

The sound of voices broke through her haze, and she looked toward Charlotte. Someone had approached her and appeared to be offering assistance. Gwen hoped that meant they weren't going to be driven out of the town for bringing the wind in the first place.

The man straightened, Charlotte beside him, and her friend turned toward her, revealing the face of the man at her side.

Gwen's breath caught, everything around her stilling into silence. The face wasn't exactly the one she had been picturing for years, but it was close enough. And the hair was exactly the same, even the messiness of it, as she remembered.

"Easton," she breathed, just as he called her name in tones of equal shock.

Her heart swelled. He was alive. And he hadn't forgotten her.

He ran forward, sweeping her onto her feet and into his arms.

"You did it," he murmured against her hair. "You escaped her!" He pulled back to grin down at her with the same broad smile she remembered. "You escaped by riding the wind? I can't say that option ever occurred to me."

She was too overwhelmed to respond with anything but a smile.

A clearing throat caught her attention, and she turned her head to see Charlotte watching them with amusement.

"How about an introduction?" Her expression suggested she already guessed who the man must be.

Easton let his arms drop and stepped away, and Gwen felt instantly bereft.

"Yes," he said cheerfully, smiling at Charlotte. "I'm curious as well. I don't remember you from the mountain court."

Instant jealousy sunk its claws into Gwen. She had told herself that if only Easton was alive and still remembered her, it was all she needed to be happy. But she had now seen his true adult face and felt his arms around her, and she was already greedy for more.

He might remember her affectionately, but what if he saw her as a friend or younger sister? He might already have a sweetheart or wife. He might like Charlotte more than he liked—

She cut herself off. Charlotte was already married, and Gwen was being ridiculous. If only she could have a few minutes to gather herself after the wild ride and shock of emotion.

"I'm Easton," he said, holding out a hand to Charlotte when it became obvious Gwen was still too overwhelmed to speak.

"I'm Charlotte." She shook his hand. "And I've never been to the mountain kingdom. Gwen took a…detour on her way here."

"I didn't know where you were," Gwen murmured. "I didn't even know you were alive."

Easton's face—the one that still looked as if it had been made only to smile and laugh—darkened.

"This sounds like a conversation for somewhere other than a sea wall," Charlotte said, looking hopefully at Easton.

He quickly agreed, directing them both toward a small home on the harbor. It was tucked just to one side of the sea wall, away from the action of the loading and unloading of boats, but with a breathtaking view of the ocean.

Easton saw Gwen looking at the endless stretch of water and smiled. "I like to be near the sea. It makes me feel free." His face darkened again. "I don't like feeling constrained."

Her insides squeezed as she imagined what sort of restraints her mother might have placed on him and for how long.

"What happened to you?" she whispered, wondering how he could face her after what her mother had done to him.

Somehow they had made it inside the small house,

although she couldn't clearly remember stepping inside, and somewhere along the way Charlotte had disappeared.

"I got angry and confronted her," he said matter-of-factly, not having to specify who he meant. "I should have come to you instead, but I went storming off to her and got myself banished. She made me drink some sort of potion, and when I woke up it was days later, and I was here. My parents were always warning me about what would happen if I ever lost my temper at the palace. I should have listened to them. I just hope she didn't punish them as well."

"As far as I know their only punishment was expulsion from the court. I believe they're living quietly in the city." She paused, unable to stop herself stepping closer to him. "I'm so sorry. It was all my fault."

"What are you talking about?" he sounded genuinely surprised. "I'm well aware where the blame lies, and it's not with you. It's not with me either, not really. But since I was drugged and hauled over the mountains unconscious, I've had no idea how to get back."

"You've been here in—" She stopped, realizing she had no idea where they were.

"It's called Ranost," he said with an amused twitch of his lips. "Rangmere's northernmost coastal town. We fish the northeastern oceans, among other things."

"And you've been here the whole time?"

He nodded. "I've been fortunate enough to build a life here."

"A life?" she asked hesitantly, looking around again. There was no indication in the room that anyone lived in the house other than Easton.

"The years have been kinder to me than they might have been," he said. "I have much to be grateful to the locals for. But it never stopped feeling like I was waiting for my real life to begin." His smile grew warm, his eyes capturing hers. "I never stopped believing you would find a way to stand up to her."

Gwen flushed, soaking in his attention and presence. The reality of him was so much better than her imaginings and being in his presence triggered a flood of memories from their shared childhood. He was just like the companion of those days, and yet at the same time not. She couldn't help noticing how tall he had grown, and how broad his shoulders had become. He filled the space in the house in a way he never had before.

But at the same time, she felt his admiration as a pressure. He believed in her beyond what she deserved. She sat heavily on a nearby sofa.

"I didn't really stand up to her," she said miserably. "I tried to investigate, but as soon as I discovered about becoming a bear and confronted her with it, she locked me up. Honestly, it was luck as much as anything that kept me from dying in my poor escape attempt. If I hadn't accidentally stolen a godmother object from her that turned out to allow me to ride the wind..."

"I'm sorry, becoming a bear?" Easton stared at her, and Gwen flushed darkly. She'd forgotten that the enchantment had begun after she confronted her mother over Easton's disappearance and was locked up. He must have still been in the mountain kingdom somewhere at that point, drugged unconscious, but apparently he hadn't been one of those the queen included in the binding enchantment.

She swallowed. "My mother cast an enchantment, after you...After we..." She sighed. "The queen and I and all her courtiers and guards turn into bears from sundown to sunrise."

Easton rocked back, his eyes growing wide. "That is another surprise."

Gwen watched him closely, but she could see no sign of disgust in his eyes. Catching her scrutiny, he sat beside her. Taking her hands, he smiled at her. "Clearly a lot happened in the years I missed. But what matters is that you found out the truth about her in the end, and you can even ride the wind now! That must be a helpful tool in confounding her. Have you come here for more allies?"

"A...Allies?" Gwen blinked. "I came here to find you. Or at least, that's what I was trying to do. I wasn't coming here specifically because I didn't know you were here."

He smiled, but it didn't quite reach his eyes, overtaken by a quizzical expression instead. "I'm flattered, and I'll help you, of course. I've been waiting for ten years to do so. But I'm not sure how much value I can bring. You'll need more allies than just me to bring her down. Or have you already disrupted her that significantly?"

"I..." She swallowed. "I think you've misunderstood. As soon as I discovered I could direct the wind, I came over the mountains. I came looking for you."

He dropped her hands, his brows drawing together. "But I've heard rumors about traders from the mountains and further tales about people disappearing. The locals might not have put those two things together, but it must be obvious to anyone who knows Queen Celandine. What has happened to her captives? Did you just leave them there? And what about the people in the city? Your people."

Gwen went hot and then cold. After meeting the girl from the city, Gwen had been ashamed of herself for never thinking of the city's inhabitants. But then she had turned around and forgotten about them all over again. Whereas Easton—who hadn't set foot in the mountain kingdom for ten years—still thought of them immediately.

He surged to his feet, striding away from Gwen only to immediately come striding back. He ran a hand through his hair, further disrupting the messy waves.

"You just abandoned them?" he demanded. "But you're the true heir of the mountain kingdom, Gwen! You're the only one who can stand up to her, the only one who can bring her down. How could you just run away?"

All the joy that had filled her on finding him drained out. She leaped up, her hands covering her face. After everything he'd said, after seeing the disbelief in his eyes, she couldn't bear for him to see her tears.

Blindly she ran from the house, fleeing down the harbor, away from the noise and movement toward the quieter section. Distantly she heard him calling after her, but she didn't slow.

Only when the sounds of the town completely fell away did she finally stop. She had reached a bluff that gave a sweeping view across the ocean. A flat rock provided a place for her to perch, and she pulled her feet up onto it, hugging her knees as she looked out over the waves.

The tears had stopped, but the emptiness they had brought remained. At home, she had always felt lonely, the walls of the palace closing in around her. But for a brief window, she had thought herself free. And yet, here she sat in a whole new town, with friends at her side, but just as trapped by loneliness as ever.

Physically, the expanse of the sea stretched out before her while a breeze ruffled her hair. But she felt the enclosing walls just the same, this time made of guilt.

Charlotte's presence only reminded her of the guilt of her

secret. She had betrayed her friend, and her friend had paid the price. And now Easton's presence carried the weight of another betrayal. Everything he had said was true. She was the only other royal in the mountain kingdom, the only heir. She had known others suffered under her mother's hand. And yet, when given the chance, she had fled without a second thought, intent only on saving herself.

She could come up with a list of excuses. She could say she was powerless before her mother. But she had been telling herself that for years, and it was wearing thin. Faced with the one person who had always believed in her and supported her, she was forced to confront the truth.

She had used her powerlessness as an excuse to wallow in weakness. As long as she told herself there was nothing she could do, as long as she passively accepted her mother's control, she didn't have to risk her own safety.

Never once had she truly attempted to best her mother or stand up for anyone else. Even when she finally snapped, she had fought only for her own escape and freedom.

She had done everything Easton had claimed, and now he would never see her the same way again. She had ruined everything.

GWEN

"**Y**ou look like you could use an apple." The kind tones of an older woman interrupted Gwen's despair.

She blinked, wiping away the lingering traces of tears, and scrambled to her feet. The old woman gestured for her to sit again and then sat beside her.

She held out a yellow apple, indicating for Gwen to take it.

Gwen wasn't hungry. Her stomach couldn't possibly take any food given her emotional turmoil, but she didn't want to be rude, so she accepted the fruit anyway.

Only once it was in her hand did she actually look at it properly and realize it wasn't yellow but gold. Actual gold. The metal. It wasn't a fruit at all but a valuable, and amazingly light, treasure.

She looked up. "I can't possibly take this!"

"Whyever not? You need it more than I do. And you never know when it might come in handy. Put it away now, there's a dear."

Gwen blinked, reminded strongly of the affectionate but

"

iron-willed nature of her old nanny. One glance in the woman's eyes told her there was no point arguing.

Bemused, she tucked the golden apple away in a pocket as instructed. The woman gave an approving nod and gazed out over the ocean.

"The castle east of the sun and west of the moon isn't an easy target," she said. "But I think you know that better than most."

Gwen stared at her. She had read that princesses always had godmothers, and she had often wondered if she had one too. She suspected she had just found her.

The apple in her pocket grew heavier as she considered it in a new light.

"That place has already taken more from you than you should have had to give," the godmother continued. "Do you want to be finished with it now? Do you want to walk away?"

She said the words with a look of such sympathy that Gwen nearly started crying again.

"Well?" the godmother asked when Gwen didn't answer. "If I told you that you were free to walk away right now—that I would find someone else to take your place—would you choose to do it?"

"Someone else?" Gwen asked. "Someone better suited for the role?"

The silver-haired woman shrugged. "They might be. Or maybe they would be worse. That isn't something I could say in advance. It would depend on both your decisions and theirs."

Gwen rubbed at her head. She wasn't sure if it was a real option being offered her or just a theoretical exercise, but it was incredibly tempting. She longed to let go of the guilt and walk away from everything.

But could she leave the guilt behind? Who else could fill her role? Who else knew her mother and all the corners of their palace? Who else was known to every member of the mountain kingdom as their heir? Gwen might be a poor heir, but she was the only one they had ever had. Would they accept someone else?

It was all too easy to think of some brave soul facing Queen Celandine, underestimating her, and being struck down. Gwen didn't know if she could ever defeat her mother, but she didn't know anyone else who could either.

How could she hand over something like that and walk away?

"No," she said at last, the word heavy. "I wouldn't."

The godmother smiled as if unsurprised at her choice, although it had surprised Gwen.

"See, you aren't weak," the woman said. "You're just still in the process of finding your strength—and learning who else's strength you can rely on."

"I turned my back and rode away from them all," Gwen whispered.

"So?" the godmother said. "Are you going to ride back?"

"Yes." Again Gwen was surprised by her own answer, this time by its strength and speed.

"In that case," the godmother said, "you didn't truly abandon them."

She sighed, patting Gwen's hand. "In the past you chose weakness because you thought you were weak. But that isn't your fault. You were a child, and the person who should have protected you instead told you every day that you were weak. But now you are a woman, and you have a choice. You can choose to continue believing those words, or you can choose to reject them and believe the words of others instead. If you believe you're capable of standing up to the queen, then you can begin to find the strength to do so."

"Do you truly think that?" Gwen asked.

The godmother raised an eyebrow. "Haven't you been listening? The relevant question is whether you believe it. You let the queen tell you who you are. Are you ready to listen to the people who love you instead?"

Gwen swallowed, thinking of what Easton had just said to her. Did she want to hear what others thought of her? Was there anyone who loved her?

"The High King didn't make you princess of the mountain kingdom by mistake," the godmother said. "You matter to him, and you matter to others."

"Why did he give them Queen Celandine as their queen?" Gwen asked, struggling to completely let go of her bitterness.

"Who said he did?" the godmother asked sharply.

Gwen looked at her with a frown. What was that supposed to mean? How could the High King have made her their princess and yet have had no hand in her mother being queen?

"I can think of one person who might have something to say about who you are and your value," the godmother said with a sudden chuckle. "I think a certain young man is on his way here, bitterly regretting his hasty words." She nodded in the direction Gwen had come, and Gwen caught a glimpse of a familiar figure. Easton was hurrying toward her, his expression intent.

She turned back to question the godmother on what she had meant about her mother, but the rock beside her was empty. She blinked at it for a moment, but the woman was definitely gone.

Climbing slowly to her feet, she considered what her

godmother had said as she waited for Easton. Could she believe she had been chosen? Could she believe she was worthy even after all the mistakes she'd made?

A wave of something that felt more like peace than guilt washed over her, settling deep into her bones. The godmother had said it was up to her to choose whose words she would believe about herself. That meant she could choose this peace. And she could choose to let go of the mountain queen's poison. She could break the walls that closed her in and refuse to ever build them back into place.

"Gwen!" Easton reached her, seizing both her hands and looking into her eyes with frantic worry. "I'm so sorry."

"It's all right." Gwen felt a smile stretch across her face. "Everything you said was true, at least in part. I did run away, but I haven't abandoned them. I realized that while I was sitting out here. I'm going back to free them all. I have to."

She tipped her face up to him, her smile growing. "You're right about the ocean. It's helpful for thinking—and breaking down restraints."

Easton sucked in a breath, his eyes still intent on her face. "You shouldn't forgive me so easily," he whispered. "It only makes me feel worse. I know what you went through in your childhood, but I can only imagine how alone you must have been in the last ten years. I've been living a free life, but you've been under her thumb every moment, trapped in her enchantment, her castle, and her control. And yet, you managed to free yourself! You held onto who you are through it all. You're brave and resilient and incredible, and yet the first thing I did was berate you! You should tell me you never want to see me again. I deserve it."

Gwen's eyes had grown misty as he spoke, but her smile returned at the end of his speech.

"Should I?" she asked playfully.

He looked down at her, his gaze changing as his eyes darkened with an entirely new emotion.

"No," he said thickly. "You shouldn't. You should let me do this."

He pressed his lips down on hers, pulling her into his arms and kissing her as thoroughly as she had always dreamed he one day would.

❧

"I don't think I can steer this time." Charlotte gazed uncertainly at the halter resting in Gwen's palm. "I know I did it last time, but that was a simple matter of getting us back to land. I don't know the way to the mountain kingdom."

Gwen glanced at Easton, a question in her eyes. He just smiled back at her, the warmth in his gaze making her flush while his trust in her ability buoyed her up.

She was the one who had fled the mountain palace. She was their princess. It was her job to lead them back.

"I wish we could take more than three of us," she said mournfully, remembering Easton's talk of allies. "But we could never get an army across the mountains. This will have to be done through stealth, not force of arms. It will be dangerous."

Charlotte propped her hands on her hips. "You should know by now that you're not talking either of us out of it. And while I can't speak for Easton—who looks like he'd follow you wherever you go—I'm not going to the mountain kingdom for you, remember."

Gwen nodded, her flush deepening at her friend's mention

of Easton's devotion. He didn't follow her around, but he had waited for her, and that was more than enough.

"It's time to go home," he said softly, capturing her eyes.

She nodded back. It was time.

"But do we really have to jump off this bluff?" he asked, eyeing the fall to the sea below.

Charlotte snorted. "Think of it as an opportunity to impress your lady love with your courage."

Easton grinned at her. "What if I don't have any?"

Gwen rolled her eyes, grasped both of their arms and pulled them all off the cliff.

Easton gasped and Charlotte screamed, but it seemed to be a scream of delight more than fear. The halter in Gwen's hand grew, the reins appearing in her curled fingers.

She looked back over her shoulder to see the other two lined up behind her. She noticed with smug pleasure that the object had placed Easton behind her. His arms immediately wrapped around her waist, securing them both in position.

"Why am I at the back?" Charlotte complained, and Gwen smiled again. She knew the excitement underlying her friend's words. She was finally on her way to the kingdom where her husband could be found.

They soared high over Ranost, heading for the mountains. But as soon as they hit them, the wind began to fight her.

Her first instinct was to pull against it, as she had before, trying to compensate for its lurching, jerking motions. But she forced herself not to respond on instinct.

Charlotte had shown her the way, and she would need every bit of her strength and concentration to lead them through the more difficult path through the mountains.

She had wanted to follow a low-lying valley to their right, but the wind pulled them left. She scanned the landscape in that direction, comparing it to the maps she had often studied in the palace library. They hadn't included the trails through the mountains, but they had shown the locations of the landscape itself. And from the air, the ground below her looked almost like a map, stretched out for her perusal.

She spotted a crevice that opened into a deep valley. Leaning into the wind's leftward motion, she sailed them into the dark gash in the mountain face. As she had expected, it opened into a valley, the high walls forcing the wind to flow down its length and giving her a chance to breathe.

But all too quickly they reached the end of it, and the wind jerked them wildly again, trying to send them spinning uncontrollably toward the ground. She let it take them downward, waiting until they caught the inevitable cross breeze that flowed along mountain canyons. As soon as it nudged their direction, she leaned into it, pulling upward again until they soared over the first peak.

Charlotte called triumphantly from somewhere behind her, but Gwen didn't respond. Every ounce of her concentration was needed in the life and death wrestle she was undertaking.

And it wasn't only her life at stake. She carried Easton and Charlotte with her, and a whole kingdom depended on them. She would not fail this first challenge.

Valley by valley, crevice by crevice, and peak by peak, she led them through the maze of the mountains, fighting the wind every step of the way. Sweat dripped down her hairline, and she might have slipped from her perch on their wind mount if Easton's arms hadn't held her securely in place.

Exhaustion began to creep in, and she was nearly out of strength when she finally spotted a final, familiar mountain.

"It's over that one," she cried, forgetting all her restraint and yanking the reins in the direction she wanted to go.

But she wasn't the only one who had grown weary. The wind tried to buck, but the movement was light. It wasn't fighting her anymore but losing force entirely. For one breathless moment, Gwen thought it wouldn't make it over the peak.

Then they were past, and it was sinking down the other side. But it didn't matter. They wanted to descend anyway.

She guided it in as accurately as she could, acutely aware that her mother had just battled her through the mountain range and must therefore know of her return. Gwen could only hope the queen was unable to pinpoint the exact location of their dismount.

She aimed for the edge of the city, where they could quickly lose themselves in the streets. As soon as their feet hit the ground, she pushed the miniature halter into her pocket and led the others forward. They both seemed to have realized the danger because they followed her without question.

But once they reached the first intersection, Gwen stopped. She might have spent her whole life in the mountain kingdom, but she didn't know the city at all.

"Psst!" The hissed whisper caught the attention of all three, but only Gwen recognized the girl gesturing urgently for them to join her. It was the fourteen-year-old who had snuck into the palace to complain about the taxes.

She led the others to where the girl was lurking behind a building.

"Are you talking to us?" Gwen asked.

She nodded. "Who else would I be hissing at? I came to get you."

Gwen stared at her in astonishment. "How did you know we were here?"

The girl gave her a scornful look. "You do know you *flew* into the city, right? I've been watching for you so I could hardly miss that."

"You've been watching for me?" Gwen asked, her astonishment growing. "But why?"

"Because they told me to, of course," the girl said impatiently. "Now hurry. We need to get off the streets."

The others looked at Gwen, and she shrugged. They had to find a place to hide, and she would as soon trust this girl whose name she didn't know as anyone else in the kingdom, except perhaps Alma or Miriam.

But as they followed her down a series of dark streets and alleys and finally into a dirty basement, she couldn't resist asking.

"But who told you to watch for me?"

The girl shrugged. "He did, of course. And the others. Everyone who opposes the queen and has been waiting for your return."

Gwen stared at her in even greater astonishment. "There are people waiting for my return?"

"Of course," the girl said. "You're our princess. Who else is going to stop *her*?"

"She's been growing more and more unstable since your departure, Your Highness," said a new voice from the depths of the basement. "She's becoming dangerous on a whole new level. And since the prince returned, she's only gotten worse."

Charlotte pushed herself forward, her face alight. "He's here? Henry's here? Is he in the palace? You're sure he's still alive?"

The man stared at Charlotte, clearly unsure what to make

of her intensity. Gwen felt almost as off balance as the man appeared to be, but somehow hearing the way they talked about her—the certainty in their voices when they talked of her return—made her feel like she could be the strong person they imagined.

"Allow me to make some introductions," she said. "You'll know Easton already."

Easton nodded respectfully, and the man started. Apparently he hadn't recognized him.

"Your parents will be very glad to hear of your safe return," he said, making Easton smile.

Gwen gestured next toward Charlotte. "And this is Princess Charlotte, Prince Henry's wife."

"His wife?" The man's eyebrows rose toward his hairline. "That is likely to cause some problems, considering our plan to marry the prince to you, Princess Gwendolyn."

Easton growled quietly, the sound so low only Gwen heard it. She placed a gentle hand on his wrist and smiled at him. He had to know she was past the point of allowing anyone to bully her into marrying Prince Henry.

"And this," she said finally, gesturing at the man, "is Count Oswin—who is, apparently, not my mother's most trusted advisor after all. I think, together, we might be the heart of the resistance."

TO STEAL THE SUN

PROLOGUE

GWEN

*I*t wasn't hard for Gwen to appear lost and confused as she walked down the street toward the palace. Not only was the route new to her, but she had never walked any street alone in her life.

I'm not really alone, she told herself, calling up the memory of Charlotte's farewell hug, the strength of Count Oswin's handshake, and the look in Easton's eyes as he told her to stay safe.

But the appearance of a squad of guards sent the memories fleeing. The men approached her with steely determination, and there was no one to face them at her side. She *was* alone.

Every instinct told her to run—to flee far and fast. To run until she reached the safety of Easton's arms.

She forced herself to freeze instead, letting go of any hold on her fear and anxiety and giving the emotions free rein to flood through her. By the time the guards reached her, she was visibly trembling. A distant part of her was even impressed at her own performance. The other part was afraid it wasn't a performance at all. But she had assured the others she could be their double agent in the palace, and she was determined not to fail before she even began.

When the guards reached her, she braced herself to be seized by rough hands. But no one touched her at all. Instead, the men formed a protective square around her, their focus on the surrounding streets, as if fearing she might come under attack.

Gwen frowned. What game was her mother playing now?

She licked her lips, her mouth almost too dry to talk. "There's no one following me," she managed to get out.

The oldest guard—the one who seemed to be in charge—turned to give her a sympathetic look. With a flash of recognition, she realized it was the older of the guards she had met at dusk in the gardens. It had only been weeks ago, although it felt like a lifetime.

He had seemed brusque and rough at the time, but she knew now he had been protecting her. And afterward, he had reported to someone other than her mother.

Another shock flashed through her. The guard who led the men intercepting her was one of Oswin's men—a man who, like the count, had changed allegiances over the years, turning against her mother. Her eyes roamed across the other guards. Were they all loyal to Oswin? Was this what he had needed to organize when he had left during the night? Had he somehow maneuvered the situation to send friendly forces to escort her back?

She shook herself. Without confirmation, she couldn't risk so much as a look or gesture that might betray her. She would drive herself mad if she started trying to second guess the loyalties of everyone who lived in the palace.

"I'm ready to go to my mother," she said softly, her voice faltering over the final word.

The guard captain threw her another look but limited his response to a single nod. Even so, within seconds, the group was en route to the castle.

The structure loomed over the city in a way that felt threatening, although Gwen suspected the original builders had intended a different effect. Had they meant the mountain palace to be a protective presence? Perhaps some of them had even dreamed of making it beautiful, like the airy storybook palaces found in children's tales. Gwen had read the Arcadian palace was built in that style.

Whatever the intentions of the original inhabitants, Gwen felt nothing benevolent in the presence of the castle now. Every step closer felt heavier than the last until she wasn't sure if her own feet could carry her all the way inside.

But such thoughts were only a fancy in her mind, and within far too short a time, she was once again within the walls that had been the confines of her whole life. Each time they turned a corner, she looked for any sign of the captive servants. There was none.

She tried not to let her foreboding grow any greater. The count had said they were all still well. Her mother hadn't discovered their involvement in Gwen's liberation, and they had been continuing their duties as normal. She would have liked a glimpse of a friendly face, though.

The guards led her directly to the throne room, but when they opened the doors, the large space held only a single person. The queen sat on her throne in solitary state, as if presiding over an imaginary court.

A shiver ran through Gwen, but her legs carried her forward. She crossed the cavernous space without faltering, registering only faintly that the guards had remained outside.

When she finally reached the stairs that led up to the dais, she stopped and gazed upward, meeting her mother's eyes. Gwen had been afraid that when she came face to face with her mother, she wouldn't be able to conceal the secrets boiling inside her. She had been afraid that her face, her manner—maybe even her words—would spill the truth of her hatred and defiance.

What happened was even worse. Standing in the presence of her mother, a lifetime of habit took over. Her body ceased trembling, and her face became a pleasant mask as she stepped into the role of the dutiful Princess Gwendolyn. She had thought it outgrown, but it fit without a wrinkle, as if it were a second skin.

Shame filled Gwen, although it didn't show on her face. *This is how you survived,* a voice said in the back of her mind. *This is how you can still survive.*

Gwen acknowledged the truth of the thought, but it was soon overwhelmed by another. When she was finished playing her role, how much of her true self would be left to retrieve? If she let herself be subsumed by her mother again, would she lose herself completely this time?

But those thoughts too were followed by another, more final one. *There is no other way.*

CHARLOTTE

One day earlier

"But have you seen Henry yourself?" Charlotte pressed, trying to keep the desperation out of her voice. "Have you spoken to him?"

The man in front of her—the one Gwen had introduced as Count Oswin—hesitated, and her heart contracted. What had the mountain queen done to Henry?

"As far as I know he is well enough," the count said at last. "But I haven't actually exchanged words with him. Queen Celandine has been keeping him in solitary confinement since his abrupt appearance the night before last. I only know he reappeared because a number of us were together at the time, in consultation with the queen."

"You think she would have hidden his arrival if she could?" Gwen asked, and Charlotte tried to focus on their conversation instead of her overpowering fear for her husband.

At least Henry was still alive, and she now knew where he was. Her determination to rescue him had already brought her further than he had believed possible.

"I'm certain she would have preferred to conceal him," Count Oswin said without hesitation. "She's still pretending you're in the castle—in seclusion as you recover from a bout of ill health. But since you're not there, the presence of the prince creates a significant problem for her."

"Because they're supposed to get married," Charlotte said in a flat voice.

The count threw her an uncomfortable look. "Precisely. Of course we didn't know about your existence…" He trailed off, clearly uneasy with the situation.

They all fell silent momentarily, and the count gathered himself, returning to his previous polished air.

"Why don't we all sit down?" He looked behind him at the selection of seating, his face puckering slightly in distaste.

Charlotte echoed his sentiments. The threadbare nature of the furniture didn't bother her, but everything in the basement looked like it needed a good clean.

No one protested aloud, though, so the count quickly had them organized in a loose circle. He sat directly across from Gwen while Easton sat at her side, pulling his chair as close as possible to her. That left Charlotte to fill in one of the gaps with their guide across from her.

The girl—who looked several years younger than Charlotte—gazed unabashedly back at her, clearly fascinated by the young woman who had just been introduced as a princess. Charlotte wished the girl would look elsewhere. Whatever she was expecting from Charlotte, she was going to be disappointed. Charlotte was no princess.

She avoided the girl's gaze, looking around the dim basement. She had spent the journey through the mountains in a state of constant tension. Not only had they been literally riding the wind while it tried to buck and throw them to their deaths, but she had been braced for a dramatic and possibly violent confrontation with the queen on arrival. She hadn't expected to find herself sitting in a basement with no idea what was supposed to happen next.

She refocused on the count. "Do you have a plan? For freeing my husband, I mean."

The count cleared his throat and looked toward Gwen. Charlotte followed his gaze with a sinking feeling. Had the rebels just been waiting, expecting Gwen to arrive with a plan? Because Charlotte was certain Gwen didn't have a plan. Only that morning Gwen had been on her way to Henry's castle to check on Charlotte.

She rubbed her temples. Had it really been less than a day since she had run into Gwen in the forest? Less than two full days since she had lost Henry? It felt like a lifetime. The Charlotte who had returned to the castle on Henry's back, eager to see her husband's face, had been a different woman—one who seemed impossibly young and naive.

Given the way Gwen straightened in her chair, she had also noticed that the count was looking to her. And from the way she was biting her lip, she felt as lost as Charlotte. Charlotte felt a surge of pity for her. If two days of suffering had aged Charlotte, how ancient must Gwen feel?

On impulse, she took her friend's hand. Charlotte had come to the kingdom east of the sun and west of the moon to rescue her husband, but she had also come to help her friend. She wasn't going to let some old man berate Gwen for not having a solution to a problem he hadn't managed to solve in a decade.

GWEN

Gwen looked down at Charlotte's hand, some of the stiffness leaving her body. She didn't deserve her friend's sympathy, but she drew strength from it anyway. The count's expectations were like bricks heaped on her shoulders, but Charlotte gave her support freely, and it lightened Gwen's load to know she wasn't alone.

She didn't have a plan, but she knew what needed to happen. Surely if they all worked together, they could come up with a way forward.

"My mother—" She stopped sharply and drew a firm breath. "No. That woman is not my mother." Some things mattered more than blood. A woman who had spent years using, manipulating, and abusing Gwen without a second thought didn't deserve the title of mother.

It was still hard to look up and meet the eyes of the others, and Gwen braced herself to hear a lecture on what she owed the woman who had given her birth. But Easton's warm hand slid into her free one, giving it an encouraging squeeze at the same time as Charlotte firmly gripped her other hand.

Gwen drew another, freer, breath. Was it really that easy?

The past twenty-three years unrolled through her mind, overshadowed by the constant, looming presence of the queen. Even now, Gwen could feel Celandine's poisonous words burrowed deep in her mind, not yet fully uprooted. No, it hadn't been easy at all, and it wouldn't be easy in the future. But here, encircled by people who saw her as something more than the queen's shadow, she had made a start at least.

She started again. "Queen Celandine has to be stopped. But if you're hoping I flew in here with a plan for how to do that, I'm sorry to disappoint you. I came back because I knew I had to do something to help my people." Her eyes flicked to the young girl on Easton's other side. "I'm sorry that I'm not what you were hoping for or expecting."

The girl shrugged. "He's the one who said we needed you and told me to keep watch." She gestured toward the count with her head. "I could already see how it was that time I went looking for you at the palace."

"Excuse me?" Gwen stared at her, utterly confused.

The girl smiled, a look of combined sympathy and pity that was almost amusing on her youthful face. Almost. Instead, it made Gwen ashamed of what little use she'd made of her extra decade of experience.

"I suppose it's understandable enough," the girl said in a voice that suggested she didn't really understand. "After all, you grew up with *her* for a mother." Her face twisted at her mention of the queen. "And my family appreciated the gold you gave us. My mother is healthy thanks to you." Her eyes slid away. "But it was obvious you weren't going to be good for much else. That's why I found him instead." She nodded at the count. "But then he insisted we had to wait for you. That we needed you." She rolled her eyes and fell silent.

The count gave her a stern look—the kind he must have used many times on his own children and grandchildren. The look of someone whose extra years of experience had been used instead of wasted.

"Of course we need Her Highness," he said. "This is a delicate enough matter as it is. If people think I'm trying to seize power for myself, our side will break into factions and start in-fighting. It will destroy everything we're working toward." He softened slightly, looking between each of the three newcomers. "But I will acknowledge that Natalie is the one who found me. Many among the court have become disillusioned over the years, and I was already their leader, but she's the one responsible for connecting the rebellion at court with the rebels in the city."

Natalie shrugged like it was no big deal, and the count chuckled softly.

"Oh, for the confidence of youth," he murmured.

"You did all that?" Easton gave Natalie an impressed look. She was only a little older than he had been when he had confronted the queen and been banished for his effrontery. Was he wishing he had handled himself more like her back then?

If he had responded differently, he might never have been forced to leave. But at the same time, a small part of Gwen had always warmed whenever she thought of him storming in to confront her moth—no, the queen—on her behalf. She appreciated his passion and loyalty even if she hated the separation it had caused.

"It wasn't as hard as you might think." Natalie shrugged at Easton before turning to Gwen. "Do you remember how those guards were coming our way, and you distracted them so I could sneak out? I was shocked to see guards manhandling the princess like that. And you'd seemed so timid and terrified as we were sneaking out, too. After I got home, I kept worrying about what they'd done to you after I left. So I snuck back into the palace grounds the next day to find out what punishment you'd received. That's the sort of thing people are guaranteed to gossip about. But no one was talking about the incident at all. It was suspicious." She shrugged again. "I found the same guards, and once I'd managed that, I didn't have to follow them for long before they led me to Count Oswin."

"You're the one the guards reported to?" Gwen cried, staring at the count. "That's why my mother never heard I'd been out in the grounds so close to nightfall! Some of the guards are loyal to you over her."

"Thankfully they were the ones to find you that night," the count said. "Of course actually confronting me was a far riskier move than Natalie seems to realize. But happily it turns out we're all on the same side."

"That's not surprising, is it?" Natalie said cheerfully. "The people of the city are on the side of anyone who opposes that woman and her taxes and her bears." She shuddered at the final word.

"I will refrain from pointing out that I'm one of those bears," the count muttered. Gwen shifted uncomfortably. As little as she liked to think of it in those terms, she was one of Queen Celandine's bears too.

"You *were* one of them," Charlotte said, looking unaccountably sad. "The enchantment is broken now."

Instant silence and stillness seized the room as all four of them stared at Charlotte. She blinked back at them.

"Isn't it?" she asked hesitantly. "Henry's enchantment broke, and I thought that was the point of including him in the first place. When it broke for him, wasn't it supposed to break for all of you?"

The count half rose before sinking back into his chair. "The lowlander prince no longer turns into a bear during the day?"

Charlotte gaped at him. "You didn't know?"

He shook his head. "Like I said, he appeared at night, and the queen has had him locked away in solitary confinement since."

"Her specialty," Gwen muttered.

"But wait, are you saying you all still turn into bears at night?" Charlotte gazed wide-eyed between Gwen and the count. "Were you a bear last night, Gwen?"

Gwen shifted uncomfortably. She still wasn't used to the reality of her nightly transformations herself. Her eyes flashed to the count, remembering the deception her mother had perpetrated on the court. He didn't look surprised to hear Gwen also became a bear, though.

"Why do you think I was out in the forest so early when you found me this morning?" Gwen asked Charlotte with a sigh. "It's true I was on my way to your castle, but I had a head start since I spend all my nights outside." She glanced at the dirty half-window in the basement wall. "And talking of nighttime, it must be close to sunset now." She glanced uncertainly at the count.

"You don't need to be concerned," he said calmly. "I sometimes spend the night at my manor in the city, so my absence won't cause any alarm at the palace. And my own people are utterly loyal to me. None of them would dream of mentioning that I didn't spend the night at home."

"But..." Gwen looked uncertainly at the other three. That hadn't been her concern. She had never transformed in front of anyone before, and the idea of doing it in front of Easton made her stomach churn. How could he look at her the same after that?

Charlotte frowned. "I don't understand. Henry definitely turned back into a man. He said he'd never be a bear again. He broke the enchantment. Why are you all still bears at night?"

Gwen forgot her fear for a moment, staring at the count for an answer. He stared back at her, his expression equally blank and confused.

"I was definitely a bear last night," she said slowly. "And you?"

The count nodded, his eyes narrowing in thought. "The idea of including the prince in the enchantment came from the queen, and it obviously didn't work as she intended since it was reversed for the prince—his days as a bear, his nights as a man. I suppose that wasn't the only thing that didn't work to plan."

"No wonder she's been hiding him." Gwen shook her head. "She's already made so many mistakes with these enchantments—each new mistake must make it harder for her to hide her errors."

The count nodded slowly. "Plus, if he's a human all the time now, there's nothing stopping him marrying the princess during the daytime—except for the fact the queen doesn't actually have Princess Gwendolyn stashed in a room at the palace like she claims." Charlotte made a wordless sound of dissent, and he winced. "Well, there's nothing preventing his marriage in the minds of the courtiers. Of course they don't know he already has a wife."

"But how did he break the enchantment?" Gwen asked eagerly, looking toward Charlotte. "If we know that, we might be able to find a way to break ours as well." She carefully didn't look at Easton. Perhaps it would be possible to release herself before he ever had to see her as a bear.

Charlotte's cheeks turned slowly pink. "According to his godmother, the enchantment did need a royal wedding to be broken, but it also took love. He said..." She paused before rushing on. "He said the enchantment would be broken when he looked into his wife's eyes in his human form and felt nothing but love."

The count ran a hand over his head. "Well." He shot a surreptitious glance at Gwen and Easton, who still sat too close together. "Well, then."

It was Gwen's turn to flush, but she resolutely ignored it. "The queen must know that's how the enchantment is broken. She mentioned Prince Henry's godmother to me—about hearing what she said to him—so she must have found a way to overhear when his godmother told him how to break the enchantment." She looked at Charlotte, feeling embarrassed, although she knew she wasn't responsible for the queen's actions. "She was monitoring you somehow. I went into her rooms once, and she had a giant portrait of you and Henry as a bear. She seemed to know he would be returning here soon as well."

Charlotte paled, pressing her hands to her face. "She knew I would..."

She trailed off and went silent, not explaining to the rest of them the terms of the second enchantment—the one that had transported Henry back to the queen. Although the two had broken the original enchantment, they hadn't succeeded in breaking the second one due to Charlotte seeing Henry's human face before the necessary three months had elapsed. Charlotte's visible anguish sent a shaft of pain through Gwen's heart. It hadn't been Charlotte's idea to use that candle, it had been Gwen's. And she still hadn't found the courage to confess it to her friend.

Gwen spoke quickly, trying to distract the others from Charlotte's state. "So the queen's followers believe—"

"Get back!" The count spoke sharply, his words overlapping the sudden itchy sensation that had sprung up beneath Gwen's skin.

She sucked in a sharp breath, her eyes jumping to Easton.

"No. No, no, no," she breathed, frantic but unable to work out what she should do. Should she run out of the basement? Where would she go?

The count surged to his feet, not showing any inclination to scratch the tingling itchiness that must also be sweeping through him. "You all need to stand back." He spoke forcefully, gesturing to the other side of the basement.

Natalie glanced toward the window. "The glass is so dirty, it's hard to tell if it's day or night." She sounded disapproving but unafraid.

Unlike Charlotte and Easton, she showed no bemusement at the count's sudden actions. She must know what was happening. Standing, she stretched out her arms and swept the other two along with her toward the far wall.

"There's no need to be concerned," she said, perhaps in response to their expressions. "They're not actually turning into wild animals. They're just going to become a lot bigger. But they don't always have full control of their movements during the change. If we're too close, we might get hurt."

"You've seen it before?" Charlotte gasped, and it took Gwen a moment to place the emotion in her voice. Was it envy?

"Henry never let me see him change," she added, confirming Gwen's impression.

Gwen's eyes went to Easton again, but the tearing feeling —as if she were coming apart all the way up the center of her body—had already begun, and she couldn't stomach seeing his expression as she changed. She lowered her head, squeezing her eyes shut as she dropped to all fours and waited for the dizziness to pass.

When she opened them again, she saw white fur.

She stared at the other bear across from her. The count had moved back from the chairs, putting space between them, and she was grateful for it because he was huge. Even larger than she was. The sight of his bear form made her instincts twang, shouting at her to run and hide. Her instincts kept forgetting she was a bear as well.

"Gwen?" Easton's tentative question made her wince and turn further away from him. He moved with her, though, circling until he could see her face. "Is that really you?"

He sounded unnerved. How could he not?

Gwen wished she could hide her face in her hands, but she didn't have hands. She had paws. And her face was not her own. The princess Easton loved was gone, replaced by a bear.

CHARLOTTE

"That was amazing!" Charlotte breathed. "I can't believe Henry never gave me the chance to watch!"

"I can," Gwen said in a muffled voice, angling her face away.

Charlotte frowned, moving slowly toward her friend. Easton stood close beside Gwen, but Gwen appeared to be straining away from him.

Charlotte realized the issue and rushed the rest of the way forward. Throwing her arms around Gwen's large, furry neck, she put her mouth near her ear.

"Don't worry," she whispered. "Once I got over the first surprise, I never had trouble with Henry's bear form. I always knew it was him, whatever body he was in. I still loved the man inside. Easton will be the same. I'm sure of it."

Gwen stiffened at first, but the longer Charlotte talked, the more she relaxed. When Charlotte finally stepped back with a last squeeze of Gwen's neck, Gwen shifted, facing them all without flinching.

Easton offered her a smile and tentatively extended his hand. Gwen glanced at Charlotte before looking back at him and visibly swallowing. Only when she nodded her head, did he reach gently forward and placed a hand on her large shoulder.

"It's so soft," he murmured, and Charlotte nodded enthusiastically.

"Isn't it?" she agreed. "I was amazed the first time I felt Henry's fur."

Gwen relaxed even further, and Charlotte was grateful she was present to smooth over the awkward moment for her friend.

"Their fur might be soft, but they also have claws. And teeth." Natalie's voice was hard.

Charlotte threw an inquiring look first at her and then at the count.

"The queen has her guards patrol the city after sundown," the count said. "Anyone fool enough to be caught outside gets scars to remind them of their mistake."

Gwen sucked in an audible breath.

"The queen has no friends in the city," Natalie said. "But there are plenty of people who are too scared to oppose her." She lowered her voice to a mutter. "Cowards."

"Or perhaps they just have more sense than you," the count replied, his tone long-suffering.

Did he resent being forced to work with someone so young? Based on Gwen's brief introduction, he was used to consulting with monarchs.

"Does that mean we're stuck here until sunrise?" Easton asked, his focus on practicalities.

"That would be wisest," the count said. "But don't worry, my grandson will be here soon with food."

Easton raised his eyebrows. "I thought it wasn't safe on the streets at night?"

"My grandson is...distinctive," the count said in a flat voice. "The guards all know him, and none would dare harm him."

Natalie gave a dramatic sigh, in sharp contrast to the count's carefully emotionless face and voice.

"You didn't tell me Emmett was coming," she said. "I would have left before dark if I'd known that."

Charlotte threw her a questioning look, and the girl leaned closer, talking in a loud whisper.

"Emmett is seven. And he has a crush on me." She rolled her eyes.

Charlotte tried and failed to hold back her smile.

"My grandson does not have..." The count sighed, giving up on his denial—either because he knew her claim was true or he knew there was no point trying to reason with Natalie. Charlotte found both options appealingly amusing. It was hard not to like Natalie despite how outrageous she was.

As if on cue, there was a quiet knock on the basement door, giving a moment of warning before it opened. A small figure slipped inside, but his presence was bulkier than his frame warranted thanks to the crutches he maneuvered inside with him. They didn't slow him down, though. He wielded them like someone with long experience.

"Emmett." The deep rumble of the count's bear voice still managed to sound soft and welcoming. The courtier obviously held his grandson in deep affection.

"Did you bring us something yummy, at least?" Natalie asked, her focus on the bag slung over the boy's shoulder.

From the way Emmett's eyes brightened as they fell on her and the way his gaze quickly flitted away from her again,

Charlotte gathered Natalie had been right about the crush. Her mouth tugged upward. Poor boy.

Emmett unhooked the bag and offered it to Natalie. The older girl took it and immediately began rifling through the contents, muttering to herself. When it became obvious she didn't have anything else to say to him, Emmett turned to his grandfather.

"Did she really come back? Is she here?" He glanced doubtfully at Charlotte. Despite the late hour, there was enough light in the basement to clearly illuminate her golden coloring. And while he was apparently unfamiliar with the details of his princess's appearance, he must at least know she was dark-haired.

"I am Princess Gwendolyn," Gwen said calmly, her bear's voice lower than her human one although still recognizable to Charlotte's ear.

Emmett started so badly, he nearly lost his balance. Charlotte's instinct was to rush forward and help, but the boy had recovered before she could move.

"But...you're a bear," he said.

"I hope we can trust you, Emmett," the count said in a heavy voice.

The boy's eyes widened even further, and he cast another look toward Natalie as he nodded vigorously.

"Of course, Grandfather. I would never say anything, you know that." He faltered. "But...why is she a bear? I thought..."

"That I was a princess so pure the enchantment couldn't touch me?" Gwen interjected in sour tones.

Charlotte made a revolted face, knowing Gwen was repeating her mother's words. Gwen might be attempting a façade of calm, but Charlotte knew how deeply her mother had hurt her, and how much Gwen hated being the tool the queen had used against her people.

Emmett stared at Gwen in bewilderment, and Easton drew even closer to her, his air protective. Charlotte couldn't help smiling at the incongruous sight given Gwen's size and current possession of sharp teeth. She had known Easton for less than a day, but he was clearly as devoted to Gwen as the princess was to him.

The thought of the pair's reunion after so many years gave Charlotte joy, but it came hand in hand with an uncomfortable pang. How long would her separation from Henry be? Even if it took years, she would endure it—although she wasn't sure how. She didn't want to think about being separated from him for so long.

"You're a dependable lad, Emmett," Count Oswin said, "but you're still a child. There are a great many things I haven't confided in you."

"You obviously knew," Gwen said quietly to the count. "About me turning into a bear like everyone else."

The count nodded. "Not initially. But my son was the one leading the expedition that brought Prince Henry across the mountains. Although Queen Celandine kept his presence as quiet as possible, she had to allow a few of us into her confidence. We were pressing for a wedding to take place immediately since she had claimed that was what would free us all from the enchantment. She countered by insisting that he needed to be included in the enchantment first. And then when it went wrong and turned him into a bear during the day, she had to explain why the ceremony couldn't be performed at night when he was human."

Natalie had extracted all the food from the bag while he spoke, and she soon had everyone seated in approximation of their previous circle as she distributed the meal. There were a few moments of silence as everyone began eating, but Charlotte was too confused to let the conversation drop.

"Why couldn't the ceremony happen while one of them was a bear?" Charlotte asked, not understanding the issue. "Henry and I were married while he was in his bear form."

The count raised his eyebrows. "Then I can only assume valley weddings are much simpler affairs than mountain ones."

Charlotte suddenly remembered Henry's initial question to her—back when she had only known him as a bear. He had even mentioned that some places had more elaborate ceremonies.

"Among other things," the count continued, "a mountain bride and groom must each wash a dirty shirt belonging to the other."

"Your marriage ceremony includes washing dirty clothing? By hand? On the spot?" Charlotte realized too late that her astonishment might seem rude. Thankfully the count responded stoically.

"As you can imagine, it isn't something that can be done with paws like these. However, it is an essential part of our ceremony. It symbolizes starting a new, fresh future together."

"That's what they say," Easton interjected. "But I'm pretty sure it's an ancient conspiracy to make sure no mountain lady finds herself married to a man who doesn't know how to do his own laundry."

He delivered the words with such a serious air that they surprised a giggle out of Gwen, the vaguely threatening rumble reminding Charlotte of Henry.

Easton smiled back at Gwen, his eyes warm. "I've missed

your laugh," he said softly, his words clearly meant for her ears only.

Charlotte looked away, uncomfortable to be intruding on their moment. Tears built up behind her eyes. She ached for the sense of familiar companionship that existed between Gwen and Easton—the closeness she had experienced for herself for a few short months. She ached for Henry.

"I think it's silly." Natalie wrinkled her nose. "You put on the nicest dress you're ever going to wear in your life and then you have to do laundry?"

"I'm surprised the queen didn't just change the law about weddings," Easton said.

"That assumes she actually wanted us to get married," Gwen said. "But since she had lied about my marriage to a prince breaking the enchantment, the last thing she wanted was to have the wedding actually happen and be proved a liar in front of the entire kingdom. She's been using delaying tactics for the last ten years, so she must have been delighted when it affected Henry differently. She was trying everything possible to delay, hoping something would come up to her advantage, and it did. The reversal in the enchantment for him was a convenient tool for her."

"And now she knows the truth of breaking the enchantment thanks to Prince Henry's godmother, but she still wants the wedding to go ahead," the count mused. "At least she's searching for you as frantically as if she wanted it to. Why is she still committed to the marriage?"

"I don't think that has anything to do with the enchantment." Gwen drew her words out, as if she didn't want to say them. "Or at least, only a little. Our potential marriage has become about what she intends to do after the enchantment is broken."

The count's whole body went still, and it was somehow more intimidating than if he'd made a threat—a reminder that he was currently wearing the form of a very large predator.

"She wants to send you away to Arcadia, doesn't she?" the count asked slowly. "She doesn't intend to ever give you the mountain throne. It's what we've been afraid of for years, but we didn't have any choice. At least we thought we didn't have a choice if we wanted to break the…" His voice trailed off, and his eyes moved to his grandson.

Charlotte frowned. She was definitely missing something here. Possibly multiple somethings.

"Actually, she wants me to marry Prince Henry so I have a claim to the Arcadian throne," Gwen said, eliciting several gasps. "Obviously she intends for us to be puppet rulers, and it doesn't seem like her ambition ends with Arcadia. She sees herself in the role of empress. She talked about her kingdom stretching to the sea."

The count surged upward to stand on four feet. "Queen Celandine dreams of conquest?" A low, menacing growl rolled through the room.

Charlotte gulped, her back straightening. She had never lived in Arcadia, but she had spent years in Northhelm and Rangmere and had met honest, friendly, hardworking people in both places. Were their lives about to be overrun with war? Was Henry's kingdom about to be attacked?

She wanted to jump up and do something, but what could she possibly do? Her best hope to help Henry's kingdom was the same thing she had been aiming for from the beginning— rescue him from the mountain queen.

"So that's it." The count paced the width of the basement, only managing a few strides given his enormous size. "She hasn't been able to move forward with plans of conquest all these years since the enchantment has tied us to the mountains. No wonder she's getting desperate to break it."

Gwen sighed. "Sit down. Please. You're making me dizzy."

To Charlotte's surprise, the count complied. Maybe he really saw Gwen as an authority in the kingdom, and not just as a figurehead. The possibility must be even more overwhelming to Gwen than it was to Charlotte, but there was no question Gwen would make a better queen than her mother.

At least, that fact seemed obvious to Charlotte. But weren't the courtiers supposed to be loyal to the queen?

"Why are you all so desperate to break the enchantment?" Charlotte asked the count. "If you're not interested in conquest yourself, is it so bad to be stuck here or to be a bear if it's only at night?"

Natalie snorted, and Charlotte winced. "I understand why the people of the city must want it to end," she hurried to add, "but is it so terrible for the court? You seem to be fully in control of yourselves still, and you're only bears at night which is much better than it used to be for poor Henry. And isn't your bear form the only reason you're able to get through the mountain passes? What's the reason for the court being so desperate to free themselves?"

"It's me," Emmett said softly, inserting himself into the conversation for the first time. "I'm the reason." He looked down at his right leg where the trouser was pinned up just below his knee.

"You are not the reason," the count said firmly. "You are the miracle." He sighed, looking across at Charlotte with eyes that conveyed the sorrow of years. "Changing nightly appears to have no ill effect on our bodies—even the children who are caught in the enchantment have been able to grow in a normal way. Unfortunately, the same cannot be said for the unborn. We didn't realize initially, but as time passed it became increasingly clear that it was extremely difficult for an enchanted woman to become pregnant. And those babies that did manage to cling to life were harmed somehow in the process of the daily transformations. The effect has been different for each one, but…" He sighed again, glancing at his grandson's missing leg.

"I always wanted a brother or sister." Emmett shrunk in on himself, his food uneaten in his hand.

The count gave a rough growl in the back of his throat. "My son and his wife are desperate for more children but have been unsuccessful all these years. It grieves them greatly, although my daughters consider them fortunate to have even one. Neither of them has managed as much. I expected to have a bevy of grandchildren at my knee by now, but so far Emmett is the only one. And the years keep passing. We have to find a way to break the enchantment before it's too late for them to think of future children. But we cannot allow it to lead to war. I want to save my future grandchildren, but I have no desire to see my children pointlessly slaughtered in the process."

Gwen's mouth fell open, and Charlotte could tell this information was as new to her as it was to Charlotte.

"I understand why you don't want war," Gwen said. "I'm guessing your son would be expected to lead our forces. But the court not being able to have children of their own…How did I not…Is that why I saw so few children at court? I always thought the courtiers were just keeping them away. I never saw Emmett at court, after all."

The count nodded. "We do keep them away. Anyone fortunate enough to have a child tends to be protective of them.

And no one wants to risk one of them saying the wrong thing and—" He broke off and looked at Easton.

"You don't want them to end up like me," Easton said grimly. "And my parents."

"I think your parents might be the fortunate ones," Charlotte muttered. "Didn't the queen exile them from court? Sounds like a reward from where I'm sitting."

"A reward for some, punishment for others," Natalie muttered.

"I think they're nice," Emmett said and then immediately looked mortified, the tips of his ears going red.

Easton looked between them. "Huh?"

Natalie glanced back at him and gave an exaggerated sigh. "They live with us now."

Easton straightened, his eyes widening. "My parents live with your family? Wha—how—?"

"That's a coincidence," Charlotte said lightly, looking between them.

"Not really," the count said. "I'm not denying Natalie did well for a girl her age, but there's a reason she went to the palace in the first place, and why she was able to find and connect with me. She knows a lot more about the palace and court than most fourteen-year-olds in the city."

"My parents are at your house right now?" Easton looked like he wanted to bolt straight out of the door.

Natalie rolled her eyes. "Relax. They'll still be there in the morning."

"But how did they end up—" Easton clearly couldn't relax.

"It used to be the other way around," Natalie said, sounding softer. "When I was very little, my parents both worked in your family's city mansion. Your parents treated them well, and when my mother first got sick they supported her, helped her get early treatment—although the doctors here didn't know how to treat it properly. So when your parents lost everything, my parents took them in without question." Her eyes narrowed. "That's why I've always had to share a room with my younger sister, you know. Our house isn't a mansion like your old one."

"Thank you." Easton held her eyes, his face and voice sincere. "Thank you from the bottom of my heart. I always hoped they were all right, but I feared..." He drew a deep breath. "Thank you. Will you take me to see them?"

Natalie softened even further, giving him a small smile. "I suppose I could manage that. It will be fun actually to see the lost son return." She brightened immediately, bouncing on her seat. "They're going to be so pleased with me for bringing you home. The count kept insisting the princess would return, and of course my parents believed it because they've always put their hope in her, and they wouldn't believe me when I said—" She cut herself off and glanced at Gwen. "Well, never mind that. The point is that no one was expecting *you* to return. They're going to be so surprised." Her grin spread across her face. "I bet our mothers will cook up a feast."

"You can take Easton to see his parents once it's daytime," the count said. "Just make sure he isn't seen by anyone outside the household." He looked across at Gwen. "Easton's parents have been a big part of gathering the rebellion in the city—such as it is. Natalie's home is a central location for our network. No one there will betray us."

"It will be good to see them again," Gwen said with what might have been a tentative smile. For all the remarkable expressiveness of the transformed bears, there were some subtleties of expression lost.

"I said Easton can go," the count said sharply. "Obviously you can't go, Your Highness. You have to return to the palace."

GWEN

There had been debate on the matter, naturally. Easton had taken more offense than Gwen herself over the count issuing her orders. Although his incensed response might have had more to do with the idea of Gwen putting herself in harm's way than any affront to her rank.

Charlotte had mostly stayed silent, but Gwen could read her thoughts in her eyes. She wanted Gwen to go to the palace because that was where Henry was being held. Her only issue was that the count was insisting Charlotte couldn't accompany her. But Charlotte wouldn't speak up, not when going might put Gwen in danger. Instead, she sat silently, leaving the debate to the count.

Natalie had weighed in once—she thought Gwen should do what needed to be done because no one else could do it. It was a sentiment so complete and final that Gwen wasn't surprised when Natalie immediately wandered away, losing interest in the conversation.

The count had plenty of arguments in favor of the plan,

but in the end, Gwen agreed because of Natalie's simple statement. It was the same thought that had taken residence in her mind from the moment the count outlined his plan. Gwen had returned to the mountain kingdom to help her people because she was the heir to her mother's throne and therefore the one most able to help them. What was the point of her return if she shied away at the first hint of danger?

"I'll go," she said quietly. "Of course I will."

Easton went still, looking down at where she sat. He had stood some time ago, facing off with the count's enormous shape.

She could see he wanted to protest, but after a moment of eye contact, he ran his hand through his hair and collapsed back into his seat. Gwen wished she could take his hand.

"I can see why you were originally planning to send Gwen back," he said to the count. "When you still thought she needed to marry Prince Henry to break the enchantment, it made sense. But now we know the wedding isn't the answer, and yet you still want to follow through with the plan for Gwen to return to the palace undercover. What's the point of that when the queen also knows the wedding isn't the answer and even that Henry is already married? You seem convinced she isn't looking for Gwen just to get revenge or to eliminate her, but how can you be sure of that? If Gwen is needed as a spy to gather information, that tells me you don't actually know what the queen is thinking after all. So how can you guarantee Gwen's safety?"

Gwen sighed. The count had already explained his thinking, but Easton was finding it hard to accept. If Gwen was honest, she was as well. It didn't matter, though. She had to confront her mother. She could feel it down to her bones.

"Of course Queen Celandine needs Gwendolyn," the count snapped, his frustration finally breaking free. "That much is obvious. She's the center of all her plans."

Gwen frowned. She wanted to argue, but her mother had said basically the same thing.

The count looked warily between them before sighing. "You're right, there is more to my plan than I've said. I just wasn't sure…It seems obvious, but…"

Easton's eyes narrowed. "What plan?"

The count glanced at Emmett, who had lost interest in their circular dispute and gone after Natalie. The two were involved in some sort of conversation, but the count still lowered his voice.

"From what you've told us, Your Highness, I think the queen will still want to go ahead with your marriage to Prince Henry. She has too many plans for it. She won't hurt you because she needs you to make a public spectacle of the wedding."

"Prince Henry is already married," Charlotte said through her teeth, but the count barely looked her way.

"I hardly think that's likely to stop Queen Celandine from going after what she wants. Nothing has ever stopped her before."

"How will she maintain her position when the wedding takes place but the enchantment remains?" Easton asked. "It doesn't make any sense. She won't even be able to carry out her plans for conquest since you'll all still be tied to the mountains. Gwen marrying Prince Henry is the last thing we want." He glanced at Charlotte before suddenly stiffening. "Or is that your plan?" He swung back to face the count. "You want the kingdom to see that nothing changes when Gwen marries this prince? But even if you don't care about throwing away Gwen's future like that, what about the actual solution to the enchantment? Charlotte said it requires a royal marriage made with love. If you're ever going to be freed, then Gwen needs to—"

"That is exactly my new plan," the count said, watching first Easton and then Gwen with a careful expression, apparently unaffected by Easton's fresh indignation. "The princess returns to the palace and pretends compliance. We encourage the queen to make the wedding as grand and public an event as possible, and then—at the last possible second—we exchange the grooms. The queen has played into our hand by keeping the prince hidden away, and no one knows what you look like these days either, Easton. As long as we find a way to restrain Queen Celandine herself at the crucial moment, none of her loyal supporters will know the difference. And once the marriage is official, the enchantment will be lifted. It will be too late then to take back the marriage. Her plans for conquest will be dealt a crushing blow since you'll have a mountain husband with no tie to any of the lowland thrones."

Gwen's mind went blank. She stared straight ahead, afraid to move in case she caught Easton's eye. For the first time, she was glad she was in bear form since she didn't think bears could blush.

Gwen knew her marriage to Easton would successfully lift the enchantment. If all that was required was for her to look into Easton's eyes and feel nothing but love, then their wedding would be enough. She couldn't remember a time when her heart hadn't been filled with love for Easton.

But that didn't mean he wanted to marry her. He had always held her in affection, certainly, and his kiss back at Ranost suggested his affection had evolved beyond childish friendship. But they had been interrupted by Charlotte, and everything had moved so quickly since that there had been no time to discuss their impulsive moment and what it meant. How could the count just assume…

"You want me to step in and marry the princess?" Easton sounded as dazed as Gwen felt.

"Am I saying you're the king I would have chosen?" the count asked bluntly. "Hardly. But ending the enchantment is more important than choosing a king with connections. And you're not a total disaster. Given your parents' presence in the city, you've acquired an almost mythical status among the ordinary people: the boy who faced off against the queen and lived to tell the tale. You wouldn't believe some of the rumors about where you supposedly are and what you've been doing all these years. The people of the kingdom will accept you as king, and the courtiers will accept anyone who freed them from the enchantment."

Gwen finally looked up and took in the shock on Easton's face. Feeling affection for his playmate Gwen was one thing. Marrying Princess Gwendolyn just as her people conspired to put her on the throne was another matter entirely. She knew Easton loved her as a friend, and he had given her some indication he was interested in her as a woman as well, but that didn't mean he wanted to marry her—not when that meant finding himself jointly responsible for a kingdom in crisis.

He hadn't even explicitly said he intended to relocate to the mountain kingdom. He had a new life in Ranost. What if he had planned to return to it after he'd finished helping her?

She looked around the dirty basement, her eyes skating over her silent, wide-eyed friend and the determined count before resting on her own giant paws. Nothing about the setting was ideal for this conversation. This was not how she and Easton were supposed to talk about their feelings or their future plans.

When she looked up again, she found him looking at her. Their eyes caught and held, and Gwen was doubly glad a bear couldn't blush.

"Well?" the count asked brusquely. "If you marry Easton, will it release us from this enchantment?"

Gwen swallowed, tearing her eyes from Easton to face the other bear. "Yes," she managed to say, the word rough and awkward. As much as she hated the way they were being swept along, the stakes were too high for her to play coy.

She took several steadying breaths before she glanced back at Easton. His expression had changed to one of acceptance and determination, and nausea rose through her. Easton understood the stakes as well as she did. Whatever his personal feelings, he wouldn't refuse the role forced on him by her emotions. And he would never do anything to make her feel bad about it. So how was she ever going to find out his true wishes now?

"If Gwen and Easton getting married will release the enchantment, why don't you have them get married immediately?" Charlotte asked, startling Gwen out of her dark thoughts.

Gwen stared at her, somehow even more shocked than she'd already been. Marry Easton immediately? The idea was at once thrilling and terrifying.

"Why go to the risk of involving the queen and a bunch of subterfuge?" Charlotte continued. "If you do it as soon as it's light out, nothing can prevent the marriage taking place."

The count was already shaking his head before she finished. "If our only aim was to break the enchantment, that would make the most sense. But Queen Celandine is a powerful opponent with a trove of enchantments at her fingertips. If we quietly break the enchantment now, she'll easily take credit for it. That will weaken Princess Gwendolyn's position. As it is, the queen has set our chance up for us. She's the one who built up the princess's position as the kingdom's future savior, and we need to play into that narrative. As soon as the wedding takes place, we intend to put Gwendolyn on the throne—as we were promised—and we need to do everything we can to minimize any opposition."

Gwen swallowed. She had come back to save her kingdom because she was the heir, so she had understood what that meant, but it had felt like a distant and amorphous thing when she stood on the cliff in Ranost. Back in the mountain kingdom, talking specific plans with a senior member of court, it felt entirely too real. If they succeeded, she would become queen.

"So you want the spectacle for more than just the deception," Charlotte said slowly, sounding almost embarrassed at not having seen that for herself.

Gwen wished she could take her friend's hand and give it an encouraging squeeze as Charlotte had done for her. Given her own current feelings, it was easy to read Charlotte's emotions on her face. The girl from the valley had no experience with politics or intrigue and hadn't even known about her new title until two days ago. At least Gwen had always known she was intended to take the throne one day—even if that reality had seemed impossibly distant. How much more lost and out of her depth must Charlotte be feeling?

"But all of this still assumes the queen will go ahead with the wedding," Easton said. "How can we be sure she'll do it, knowing what she does about the enchantment?"

Gwen reminded herself that Easton had always been

against the plan. He was worried about Gwen's safety, not looking for any excuse to get out of the proposed marriage.

"Actually," Charlotte said in a small voice, "I've been thinking about that." She turned to face Gwen. "What does Queen Celandine think of love?"

"Love?" Gwen frowned. "I..." She faltered, unsure how to answer the question.

A lifetime of interactions with her mother unfurled in her mind. Celandine had never shown Gwen a mother's love—she had only experienced warmth like that from Nanny. But it wasn't just Gwen. Celandine had always been there overseeing Gwen's life, but that meant Gwen had observed her mother's life for the last twenty years as well. And Gwen had never seen Celandine show love to anyone. On the rare occasions she had spoken of love, or the relationships of her own past, she had always used a scathing tone as if...

"I'm not sure she believes in love at all," Gwen said.

Charlotte swallowed, clearly uncomfortable. "I wondered if that might be the case. From everything you've said of her, and..." She paused again. "You said she knew about my existence and Henry's marriage, and she knew his godmother had told him a way to free himself from both enchantments, including the one tying him to her. And yet she claimed to know he would be returning soon. It sounded like...like she knew I would fail at the test of trust." Charlotte's eyes shone with unshed tears, but she pushed herself to continue. "But not even I knew that until the last moment. It was a rash decision, not a longstanding one. And the queen doesn't know me at all. That's why I've been sitting here wondering—maybe it has nothing to do with me specifically. Maybe she doesn't think anyone would have that kind of trust—she doesn't think anyone could love like that. And if she doesn't actually believe in love…"

"You think she's discounting that part of the godmother's words as…as meaningless fluff," Easton said thoughtfully.

Charlotte nodded. "If she thinks all that's needed is the actual marriage—followed by the two looking at each other, human eyes to human eyes—she may well believe that marrying Gwen to Henry will break the enchantment. It wouldn't have worked when he was a bear in the day and she was a bear at night, but now that he's free of the enchantment…"

"That lines up with everything I've seen of Celandine over the last two decades," the count said heavily. "She likes concrete realities and doesn't put much stock in emotions." His voice dropped to a mutter. "Sometimes it seems like she doesn't even have them."

"Then that's her mistake," Gwen said fiercely. "She'll never truly understand other people if she discounts emotions, and if she doesn't understand us, maybe she'll underestimate us."

"We're still making a lot of assumptions," Easton said. "We can't send Gwen to face her alone on the back of nothing but guesswork."

"Then what do you suggest instead?" the count asked sternly. "Did you perhaps bring an army across the mountains with you? One that you've previously failed to mention and that won't be intimidated to face a force of giant bears?"

Easton shifted his weight, staying silent.

"I don't want to put anyone at risk, let alone the princess," the count said. "But we can't avoid all risks. The queen has pinned too much on her heir to eliminate her now. I'm confident she won't kill Gwendolyn, no matter how angry she is."

"I agree." Gwen tried not to think of what her mother

might do instead. If she started thinking of small, dark spaces while they were stuck inside the basement, she might lose it.

But even if her mother did lock her up, she would have to endure it. An entire kingdom was depending on her.

Easton fell silent. From the look in his eyes, he still wasn't happy about the plan, but he knew when he was past hope of convincing the rest of them.

"What about me, then?" Charlotte still sounded subdued. "I came here to rescue Henry, but I'm just supposed to sit in this basement instead?"

"Not here." Natalie suddenly reappeared, her nose wrinkling. "This place isn't set up for long term anything. You'll have to come back to my house with Easton." She looked Easton up and down, her lips pursed and eyes narrowed. "But if the plan revolves around no one knowing he's returned or what he looks like, we can't go waltzing through the front door."

"The plan…?" the count asked carefully.

Natalie rolled her eyes. "I was standing on the other side of the room, not down the street. If the plan was supposed to be such a big secret, you shouldn't have talked about it right in front of me." She propped both hands on her hips. "And it's a good thing you've got me anyway. You and the toddler over there will be heading back to your fancy manor soon, and it's going to be up to me to keep these two under wraps."

"Hey! I'm not a toddler!" Emmett protested, but Natalie ignored him.

"We'll have to go before it gets light," she said.

"I thought bears patrolled the streets overnight," Charlotte said cautiously. "Aren't we supposed to stay inside until morning?"

"They do, but come on—they're not on every street at

once." Natalie eyed the window consideringly. "If we leave just before dawn, there will be even fewer because some of the patrols always cheat and head back early. On the other hand, if we wait until after sunrise, the people will flood out of their houses and there really will be someone on every street. If we want to get back unseen, we need to go while it's still dark. It would be one thing if I had brought giant cloaks or something to disguise you all, but I didn't know I'd need to do that."

"Is that really wise?" Easton looked to the count.

He sighed. "It's not ideal, but she might be right. I don't spend a lot of time in this part of the city during the day, but the streets have been busy whenever I've come."

"Relax." Natalie snorted. "I'm not suggesting you hand your plans and your whole future over to a fourteen-year-old. I'm just going to sneak you through five streets and across one square. Then I'll hand you over to the grown-ups."

Something about her tone told Gwen they wouldn't get rid of the younger girl so easily, but she stayed silent. Natalie was Gwen's opposite in so many ways, but Gwen couldn't help wondering if she might have turned out more like the other girl if she had been free of her mother's influence. It was an unanswerable question, but Gwen liked Natalie all the same. At least someone was willing to take bold action and state their opinion without hesitation or pretense.

"If the plan is settled, Emmett and I will head home now," the count said. "I need to make some preparations before the missing princess returns. The rest of you should try to get some sleep. It will be many hours before it's time for Easton and Charlotte to head out. And Gwen, you'll be the last to leave. It's essential you not be seen until you're human again. Most of the kingdom still believe you escaped the enchantment."

"The pure princess who's going to save everyone," Gwen muttered, wishing she could say the words with any kind of conviction.

But it was too late for her to quibble now. She had committed herself to the count's plan, and she would have to see it through.

CHARLOTTE

eaving Gwen alone in the dirty basement felt wrong. Especially when Charlotte was leaving with Gwen's...betrothed? She wasn't sure if that was the right term for them, but they had both agreed to the plan, so it seemed to fit better than anything else. Charlotte just wished she could have had a proper conversation with Gwen about it —one that didn't involve Easton and Natalie listening in.

"Are you sure...Are you sure we should just leave?" Charlotte asked instead, looking reluctantly at Gwen.

Her friend forced out a laugh. "Don't make me say it again! This is the plan. I'll be fine waiting in an empty room on my own."

But from Gwen's face, she was as aware as Charlotte that neither of them were worried about the extra hour or two of waiting. It was the part that came after. She wrapped her arms around Gwen's enormous bear neck and gave her a tight hug.

"You can do this," she whispered. "And you won't be alone once you reach the palace, right? You'll have Alma and the others?"

Gwen twitched beneath her arms, confirming Charlotte's earlier suspicion. She'd noticed her friend hadn't mentioned her alliance with the captive servants to the count, and it hadn't taken much thought to come up with a reason why.

They had arrived in the mountain kingdom mere hours ago, and so far the only assurance they had that the count was telling the truth was Natalie's corroboration. Could they be one hundred percent sure it wasn't some elaborate scheme orchestrated by Queen Celandine? Charlotte couldn't think of a reason why the queen would do something so complex, but that didn't mean she entirely trusted the count either.

She couldn't say anything aloud—not in front of Natalie, and not in front of Easton. If it occurred to Easton this might all be a deception, he would never agree to leave Gwen.

"Don't worry," Charlotte whispered, too quiet for a human to hear, but knowing Gwen's enhanced bear hearing would pick up her words. "I won't say anything about them to anyone. There's no harm in having an extra card to play if something goes wrong."

Gwen nodded almost imperceptibly. "Thank you," she said aloud, and her words rang with sincerity.

Charlotte gave her a final squeeze and stepped back, thinking Easton might want to take her place. He remained where he was, however, merely meeting Gwen's eyes with an intense gaze.

"Stay safe." His voice was low and rough.

She nodded, appearing unable to answer with words.

Charlotte waited another moment, but when neither of them moved, she tugged lightly on Easton's arm. "Come on." It would only get harder the longer they lingered.

At first, Easton didn't budge, his eyes still fixed on Gwen.

But finally he relaxed, bowing to the princess before he followed after Natalie and Charlotte with quick strides.

In the doorway, Charlotte looked back one final time at Gwen. The bear was looking at the small group of them.

"Don't worry," Gwen said with a faint smile. "I'll find your Henry for you."

Charlotte managed a return smile before Natalie pulled her out of the door.

After so long in the stuffy basement, Charlotte should have been glad for the open air and space. But she'd spent too many hours in growing fear of the strange city patrolled by giant bears. Now that she was standing in the street, she felt dangerously exposed.

At least dawn wasn't far away. The deep black of night had given way to dark gray, and regular streetlights broke the darkness even further. Or maybe she should be regretting the presence of streetlights? Weren't they supposed to be in hiding?

Charlotte shook her head. Subterfuge was outside her experience.

"Come on!" Natalie hissed, waving Easton and Charlotte forward. Charlotte wasn't the only one lingering near the door of the basement—although Charlotte suspected Easton had a different reason for being reluctant to move away from the relative safety behind them.

Charlotte reminded herself who she was doing everything for: Henry. If she couldn't even brave a dark street for him, how did she hope to snatch him from the mountain queen?

Scampering after Natalie, she caught up with the younger girl at the closest street corner. Natalie was peering around it, her other hand held up to signal for Charlotte to wait behind her.

Charlotte's nerves thrummed as she waited, wondering what Natalie could see. It was hard to resist the instinct to push forward and see for herself.

Easton's steadying presence arrived at her back, helping to calm her. She felt safer with someone on either side, even though she knew it was just an illusion.

Whatever Natalie saw on the other street must have satisfied her because she gestured them forward. The three crept onto the larger street in single file.

Charlotte tried to step quietly, but Natalie quickly outpaced her. Apparently the other girl was going for speed over silence. Charlotte increased her speed to match, cringing at every footfall.

When they reached the next corner, Natalie's check was much shorter. She had barely peered around the edge before she was gesturing them forward again.

"Wait," Charlotte whispered. "Shouldn't we be more..." She fell silent when Natalie ignored her. Reluctantly, she put on another spurt of speed to catch the other girl instead.

"Natalie!" Easton hissed from behind Charlotte.

She wasn't the only one confused and uncomfortable. Weren't they supposed to be creeping through the streets unseen?

But Natalie didn't pause again until they were on the edge of a cobbled square. This time Charlotte was able to peer over her shoulder, and she caught herself looking for the fountain that usually marked the middle of town squares. Instead of a fountain, however, this square held only the statue of an imposing woman wearing a crown. Charlotte grimaced. She supposed it made sense not to have a fountain in a place where the temperature must often be below freezing. But she would have preferred not to creep right under

Queen Celandine's eyes—even if they were just stone versions.

Natalie glanced quickly up and down the square before shrugging and striding openly across its center.

"Natalie!" Easton hissed again, with more force if not more volume.

The younger girl didn't flinch or look back, though, so after a resigned shrug, Charlotte and Easton both hurried after her. As they crossed the open space, Charlotte flicked glances at the surrounding buildings. It wasn't only stone eyes that watched them but also the closed shutters of too many windows to count. It didn't matter how many times she told herself she was being fanciful—they felt like a real presence tracking the progress of the small group.

"Shouldn't we stick to the edge?" she whispered to Natalie as she finally caught up with the other girl. They had made it more than halfway across the square, but Charlotte's skin was crawling so badly she could barely walk straight.

"I hear something," Easton whispered sharply, and Natalie finally responded.

Grabbing Charlotte's sleeve, she cried, "Run!" without bothering to lower her voice. Pulling Charlotte with her, she veered sideways. Instead of making for the continuation of the main road that had appeared to be their goal, she threw them both sideways toward what looked like nothing but a deep shadow.

Charlotte barely kept herself from screaming as they careened toward the black space. At the last second, she perceived a narrow alley, its entrance blocked by an abandoned cart missing a wheel.

Natalie let go of Charlotte's sleeve, glancing once over her shoulder to check Easton was with them. As Charlotte turned to look as well, Natalie was already leaping up the cart, cresting it in two bounds.

Behind her, Charlotte could hear the local girl hissing for her to hurry and follow, but she couldn't turn back around. Easton was heading their way, and he had obviously taken a few beats to grasp what was happening. He was no longer alone in the square.

Behind him, two large, white figures lumbered across the open space, closing the gap with terrifying speed. Easton saw the look on her face and faltered, turning to glance behind him.

"No!" Charlotte screamed, all her fear forgotten in the panic of the moment.

Their whole plan depended on no one knowing Easton's face. He couldn't let himself be seen.

Her cry brought his face forward again, halting his motion before he had fully turned. She flung herself in his direction. Catching him off guard, she seized the front of his shirt and yanked him toward the alley with all her strength. She used the momentum, sending him behind her while she staggered into the square.

Their positions had now been reversed. Easton was at the base of the cart, being urged by Natalie to "Climb! Climb!" while Charlotte was bringing up the rear of the group.

She spun and dashed to follow him. When he faltered, one foot on the cart, one still on the cobblestones, she screamed at him to go.

He complied, pulling himself up with a grunt. He looked like he was going to stop at the top to help pull Charlotte up, but Natalie must have had the same realization as Charlotte. Her wiry hands appeared out of the darkness, pulling him down the other side of the cart.

Charlotte threw herself the final couple of steps, her hands reaching for the side of the cart. But as they made contact with the round wood, she felt hot breath behind her followed by a tearing pain down her left arm.

She screamed, the cry splitting the night as red splattered across the cart. Immobilized by pain, she froze, but the wiry hands reappeared, pulling her forward. Wrenched into movement, she lurched up, somehow finding the strength to climb the side of the cart.

A change in the air pressure and a panting breath made her duck instinctively forward. The second stroke of the huge clawed paw missed her, hitting the cart instead.

The entire structure crumbled, smashed to pieces by the bear's force. Charlotte tumbled down among the splintered pieces of wood. She twisted at the last moment, landing on her right side to shield her injured left arm.

The shock and pain of the landing held her still as the bear roared and struck at the cart again, reducing it even further into kindling. For a second, her eyes caught on his black ones, and then Natalie was behind her, hauling her to her feet.

"Come on!" she cried. "Run!"

The bear lunged forward, but the alley was even narrower than Charlotte had originally realized. She and Natalie could barely fit down it single file, her shoulders almost brushing the brick wall of the buildings on either side. It must have been a tight squeeze for Easton, who had already disappeared, presumably sent ahead by Natalie.

The bear roared again in frustration, and Natalie urged her to move faster, even shoving her in the back when she slowed. They burst out the other side of the alley onto a new street. Easton waited for them there, his eyes glued to the alley entrance, clearly having been debating if he should go back.

Natalie hissed at him wordlessly and took the lead. Abandoning the last of any pretense at quiet or subtlety, she sprinted down the street and careened around the second corner she encountered.

Easton took one look at Charlotte's injured arm and scooped her off her feet, running after Natalie.

"I can run myself," Charlotte wheezed through the pain. Her injured arm was jammed against his chest, and it was only increasing the agony.

"I know," Easton said through hard breaths. "It's your arm that's injured, not your leg. But there's no time to bind the wound, and we can't leave a trail of blood."

Charlotte fell silent, realizing why he had positioned her in such a painful way. She bit her tongue on the cries that tried to work their way out of her as he ran. She would be in worse pain if they didn't escape the bears.

When they rounded the corner, Natalie was waving them forward from halfway down the street where she stood in what appeared to be a public water trough for the city's horses. When Easton reached her, he dumped Charlotte on her feet in the trough and climbed up after her.

Natalie nodded approvingly and sloshed through the water. When she reached the other end of the long trough, she clambered out again, landing on a long length of rough fabric. Charlotte attempted to follow, only to have her knees give out at a fresh wave of pain, sending her splashing down into the water.

Easton braced her from behind, putting his hands under her arms and lifting her over the edge of the trough in one swift movement. As soon as she had her balance, she shuffled forward on the material, making room for him to follow.

Natalie had already run the length of the material, disappearing down yet another narrow alley. Charlotte gritted her teeth and forced her legs to work, clasping the gash on her left arm with her right in an attempt to keep too much blood from oozing out.

As soon as she'd rounded the corner, she saw the material led to an open door. Natalie stood just inside, waving Charlotte forward with urgency. She half ran the final steps, staggering inside with Easton crowding in behind her.

He seemed to have understood what was happening much more clearly than her, because the second he was inside, he turned and began pulling on the material. Someone behind them seemed to be helping him, because it whisked inside impossibly fast. As soon as the last length made it past the threshold, Natalie closed the door behind them.

"Phew!" she breathed, sinking to the floor and breathing hard. "That was too close." She looked up accusingly. "How are you two so slow?!"

"We need help here!" Easton called down the dark corridor in front of them. "Someone's injured!"

He grabbed a towel off a nearby chair and folded it several times, pressing it to Charlotte's wound. She looked down, planning to take over with her good arm. But instead her head spun, and she nearly collapsed again.

This time Natalie propped her up from behind with an exasperated huff. "The cut didn't look that bad," she muttered, but Charlotte could hear the guilt in her tone.

"What. Was. That?" Easton asked threateningly, his eyes spearing into Natalie.

Charlotte didn't have the energy for his outrage, but she

nodded supportively. "I thought we were supposed to be creeping through the city unnoticed." She wished she sounded more indignant and less exhausted.

"Unnoticed?" Natalie snorted. "I guess you two don't know much about bears. Do you have any idea how well they hear? Well, their hearing is nothing on how well they smell! It wasn't a matter of not being noticed so much as *when* we were noticed. I had to time it so we were most of the way across the square. Thankfully this city has a collection of ridiculously narrow alleys that date from before patrols were done by bears."

Charlotte finally caught up to what must have been apparent to Easton from the beginning.

"The water and the material...that was to throw off our scent trail? So it wouldn't lead them to this house?"

Natalie nodded. "When I first spotted you in the air, I sent word to both the count and my family. My family knew there was a chance I might have to return at night, so they had someone listening out. Thankfully, that fool guard made more than enough noise roaring away at us. So they got the material laid out before we reached the trough." She shook her head. "It wouldn't have been such a close thing if you two had moved a bit faster, though."

"Charlotte is injured," Easton said through his teeth. "And maybe we would have been more prepared if you'd considered *warning us*."

Natalie looked between the two of them doubtfully before shrugging. "Or maybe one or both of you would have refused to set foot out of the basement if you'd known you were about to be chased through the city by a patrol of bears. I don't know you that well, so how could I say?"

"You—" Easton stepped toward her, but the arrival of

several people distracted him from whatever scolding he was intending.

"Someone's injured?" A woman bustled forward, her focus on Charlotte. "Oh, you are too! You poor dear!"

The man moved to Natalie instead, glowering at Easton. Easton met his gaze coolly, not backing down.

"I got the material laid out for you," the man said. "So how did someone end up injured? They're not about to break down our door, are they?"

"I told you, Da," a bored voice said from further along the corridor. "We got it pulled in well before any of the patrols worked out where they were. They're always confounded by those alleys." He had the superior tone of late adolescence, a youth hovering on the edge of manhood.

When he stepped forward into the light, Charlotte could place him instantly. There was no doubting he was Natalie's older brother given the similarity in their coloring and features.

The young man gave his sister a lazy nod, and she narrowed her eyes in response. Apparently his assistance in retrieving the material hadn't won him any points in her eyes. Charlotte could relate to the prickly sibling dynamic.

"Nice to see you helping—for once," Natalie said.

The youth's eyes narrowed. "What was the other option? Let you bring the bears straight to our door? I don't have a death wish, you know."

Natalie's voice turned mockingly sweet. "I know it's just that you love your family soooo much. Admit it! You've been worrying about me all night."

"Ew! Get off me!" The youth tried to fend her off as she surged forward and pulled him into a hug.

Charlotte's heart dropped. The prickly antagonism

between Natalie and her brother was merely one layer of their relationship. But Charlotte's sister's taunts hadn't been a façade for a deeper well of affection.

She swayed, lightheaded. It was a struggle to fight against the pain and not make any embarrassing sounds of distress.

The woman—who must be Natalie's mother—tutted and pressed more tightly on the towel, which only made Charlotte sway again.

"How did you end up injured?" she asked, the question sounding much softer and more sympathetic on her lips than it had on her husband's.

But the reminder caused Natalie's father to throw another suspicious look at both Charlotte and Easton. Another male voice sounded from the end of the corridor.

"Dane, Patti, why don't you bring them in? There'll be time enough to hear how she was injured once they're settled."

Easton stiffened at the sound of the voice. For one lingering second, he continued to match stares with Natalie's father, and then he slowly turned to face the newcomer. "She was injured," he said, "protecting me."

A woman from further inside the house gave a muffled scream just as Natalie's mother removed the towel from Charlotte's arm. Charlotte looked down at the red that spurted from her gashed arm, felt a surge of pain, and blackness rushed over her, claiming all her senses.

CHARLOTTE

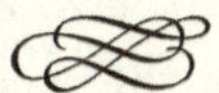

Charlotte came around slowly, grogginess making everything fuzzy for several seconds. Logically, she knew she couldn't have passed out for more than a minute or two, but thankfully someone—or multiple someones—had used that time to move her the rest of the way into the house and lay her down on a sofa.

Natalie's mother—had someone called her Patti?—had even produced some bandages and was in the process of binding the wound properly. She tutted to herself quietly as she secured the final knot.

Charlotte sucked in a breath, but the pain quickly receded to a more manageable throbbing ache now she wasn't being jostled around.

"Does it need stitches?" she managed in a quavering voice.

"You woke up." Natalie stated the fact without emotion, wandering over to gaze down at Charlotte. "For a second, I thought you'd died."

Patti heaved herself to her feet, rolling her eyes at her

daughter. "There's no need to be so dramatic, my dear. Of course she wasn't going to die over a little gash like that."

"Little," Charlotte repeated in the same faint voice, trying to get a proper look at her bandage. "Is it going to need stitches?"

"Don't you worry." Patti gave her a comforting pat. "It's bad enough I thought it might need stitches at first, but now that I've had a good look, I think you'll be all right after all. Which is a good thing since we don't have any doctors on hand. I've seen plenty of gashes in my time, and that one should heal up just fine. I've slathered it in salve—it's one we make ourselves from a plant found only in the high mountains. It's better than anything you have in the lowlands for healing wounds, or so I've heard. Our salve fetches a very pretty price when the traders take it through those new passes."

"Oh." Charlotte felt like her brain was packed with cotton wool.

She tried to pull herself up to a sitting position, and Patti swooped in to help her. Once she was upright, she had to wait a moment for another head rush to die down before she could get a proper look at the room.

She was sitting in a living room of medium size and full of furnishing that wasn't new but instead looked well used and comfortable. Overall it was a welcoming place, but her focus skipped over the room itself to the three people standing several steps away.

Natalie's father and brother had disappeared, so the only one of the three she recognized was Easton. And she nearly didn't recognize him since his back was to her and most of his body was obscured due to the hug he was receiving from the older woman. She had tears running down her face and appeared to have no plans to let go anytime soon.

The man looked equally shaken, standing close and alternating between patting Easton on the back and the woman on the shoulder. He was the only one whose face Charlotte could properly see, and he looked remarkably like—

"Are those Easton's parents?" she asked, feeling a sweeping wave of emotion. No wonder the woman looked like she would never let him go again. They must have spent ten years fearing for him.

Natalie rolled her eyes, but she couldn't wipe the grin off her face. "I knew it was going to be satisfying to bring him home. Aunt Lydia is going to shrivel up after losing all that moisture."

Charlotte gave her a knowing smile. She had talked as if having Easton's parents in her home was a burden, but it was obvious she actually held them in affection.

She cackled. "Uncle Jett doesn't even know what to do with himself." She raised her voice. "Oi! She's awake! Are you finished over there?"

"Oh, leave them be," Charlotte protested, but it was too late.

Easton's mother finally broke off the hug, and Easton quickly turned to face the rest of the room. Charlotte bit back a grin when she saw his look of relieved rescue. He must have shared their concern that his mother was never going to stop crying.

His mother rushed immediately to Charlotte's side, dropping to her knees beside the sofa and warmly clasping her right hand.

"Thank you, thank you," she said wetly. "I heard you protected our Easton. I'm Lydia, by the way." She glanced up at her husband, who had followed her at a more decorous pace. "And this is Jett. You have our gratitude."

Charlotte smiled weakly and extracted her hand. "To be honest, I didn't really do it for him."

Lydia stood slowly, glancing between Easton and Charlotte. "You're not..." When Charlotte looked blank, she gestured between them. "The two of you aren't..."

"A couple?" Charlotte asked, finally realizing what she was trying to imply. "Oh goodness, no. I'm married. To someone else. Of course I didn't want the bears to hurt Easton, but I didn't jump in because of him. I did it for Henry. And Gwen too, of course. It's because the plan hinges on Easton not being recognized."

"The...plan?" Lydia and Jett exchanged a look of bewildered incomprehension.

Easton grimaced. "We hadn't gotten to the explaining part yet."

Charlotte grinned guiltily. "I'm gathering that." She tried to swallow the smile. "The crying part seemed to be lasting a while."

Easton rubbed the back of his neck, and she relented. "Of course it would! You haven't seen each other for ten years! I think you should be the one to explain everything, though."

"Wait!" Patti cried. "We should get Dane and Baden first. Natalie, you run and fetch them."

Natalie looked like she was about to protest but thought better of it and left the room. Within less than a minute she returned with only her father in tow. Her mother looked as if she was going to say something, but when she saw Natalie's defiant expression, she sighed and remained silent.

Natalie sat on the sofa beside Charlotte. "Fetch Baden?

What a joke," she muttered. "When everyone knows he barely tolerates all this stuff." She waved around them.

"The rebellion, you mean?" Charlotte whispered back, eyebrows raised.

Natalie snorted. "He's at that age where he thinks he knows better than everyone. He's convinced we're going to get ourselves killed." She rolled her eyes contemptuously, while Charlotte stared at her.

Baden thought he knew better than everyone? She blinked several times in rapid succession wondering if there was anything to be said in response to such a statement from Natalie. She concluded there wasn't.

"You don't agree with him?" she whispered instead, curious. "You're not worried about the risk?"

Natalie gave her a contemptuous look. "The only thing I can't understand is why it's taken the grown-ups so long. If you want something to change, it's simple. Change it."

Charlotte sat back, not sure whether to laugh or cry. Had she ever possessed the naive certainty that exuded from Natalie? The girl was so clearly young, and yet at the same time, she'd already achieved more in her life than Charlotte had done. Could she really dispute Natalie's philosophy?

While the two of them were whispering, Easton had started the explanation to the older couples. When he got to the part of their plan where he married Gwen and became king, the story broke down, overwhelmed by their exclamations. He eventually had to start again and explain it all to his mother a second time.

"You will be king?" Jett asked, clearly incredulous. "Our son?"

"It wasn't my idea," Easton said, sounding defensive. "But if we want to break the enchantment..." He trailed off, running a hand through his hair. Clearly he lacked the confidence to baldly state that he was the only one Gwen loved and therefore the only one who could break the enchantment with her.

"It's not a terrible idea," Patti said thoughtfully.

Her husband threw her a look, and she shrugged. "You know how the people of the city talk about Easton. And even if their ideas are fanciful, it's true that at only thirteen he had the courage to stand up to Celandine. Who else in the kingdom can say that? And he and his family have suffered at her hands. They have the bloodlines to satisfy the courtiers and the credibility to be accepted by the city folk."

Dane nodded slowly. "As always, you speak wisdom, my dear."

Patti winked at Lydia, who smiled warmly back. "If we have any standing here in the city, it's because of your family's support."

"Support that you've earned," Patti said firmly. "And that you've worked tirelessly to repay. You haven't had an idle day since you came here."

Charlotte stood to her feet, unable to take any more.

"Speaking of idle days," she said. "Are we really supposed to sit around here and do nothing while we wait to see what happens to Gwen?"

As soon as she spoke Gwen's name, Easton tensed.

"No," he said shortly. "Obviously we can't do that."

"If you're going to be accepted as king, we'll need to make some discreet introductions," Dane said. "Let people know you're back."

"No," Charlotte said sharply. "That's the opposite of what we're supposed to be doing. We have to keep his identity—and even his return—a secret."

"A secret from the queen's supporters," Jett said. "But we

have to think beyond the wedding. Just succeeding in the marriage won't be enough. We still need to put them on the throne. And for that we need supporters. We'll be careful and keep the circle small. Just the most influential among the rebels. The people we need to speak up in our support at the crucial moment."

Charlotte bit her lip. His words sounded sensible, but her instincts still protested. The more people who knew, the more likely someone would make a mistake. If this was their only chance to free Henry, then everything needed to go perfectly.

"What about me?" she blurted out instead of the protests she really wanted to make. "What am I supposed to do?"

No one answered, looks of discomfort on their faces. They felt for her situation, but they didn't need her for what they were trying to accomplish.

When they began a conversation about who to introduce first, an unexpected arm slid through hers. "You're with me," Natalie said quietly. "Someone has to plug the rather glaring hole in the count's plan."

"Hole?" Charlotte asked.

Natalie raised an eyebrow. "The bit where the queen is restrained at the crucial moment during the ceremony, of course. Were you thinking that would be easy to achieve?"

Charlotte blinked. "No, I'm guessing not. With so much going on, I hadn't thought yet about—"

"Exactly." Natalie gave a long-suffering sigh. "I'm fairly sure everyone is hoping one of the others will think of a solution for that. So I guess that means it's up to us."

Charlotte shook her head. This was the girl who thought everything was possible. Charlotte should definitely be interjecting some realism into the situation.

Natalie lowered her voice. "I'm thinking we'll need to

sneak into the palace grounds as a starter. We're not going to be able to restrain her without more information on both her and those enchantments she's got locked up."

The protest died in Charlotte's throat. Go to the palace, to Henry? She felt no desire to talk Natalie out of that.

Natalie gave her a sly smile as if she knew exactly what Charlotte was thinking. Internally, Charlotte winced. Natalie had clearly been waiting for a partner in crime as reckless as herself, and a more sensible part of Charlotte knew she shouldn't encourage the other girl.

But it didn't matter what sensible thoughts Charlotte tried to think. Henry was in the palace right now. It had been too long since she'd seen him, and she couldn't bear to sit in Natalie's house waiting for someone else to figure out a way to rescue him. Easton could meet the rebels and make connections. Charlotte was going to do what she'd come to the mountain kingdom to do—she was going after her husband.

GWEN

"So," Queen Celandine said in deceptively gentle tones, "you've returned."

She gazed down from her throne, meeting Gwen's eyes with an outward calm that met Gwen's own. It unnerved Gwen more than anger would have done. She knew her mother was furious with her. She had to be. And yet nothing in the queen's manner gave it away.

Celandine had always been the same—at least for all of Gwen's life. It was the reason Gwen had learned from an early age how to wear a composed mask in her mother's presence. Celandine didn't give way to emotion, and she didn't appreciate others who were unable to do likewise—even small children.

To Gwen it had always made the queen's cruelties more chilling since they were done without the heat of emotion behind them. Celandine didn't lash out in anger or pain, hurting people and then regretting it later. Everything she did was done with calm intention.

The queen rose from the throne in one smooth movement, and it took all Gwen's training not to flinch. Behind her gently upturned lips, she was clenching her teeth as her mother descended the steps toward her.

When the queen wrapped her arms lightly around Gwen and placed her cheek against Gwen's own, she waited for the poisonous words to be whispered in her ear.

They never came. And in the empty room, there was no need for the queen to hide her malice anyway. Anything she had to say she could have said from the throne.

Gwen frowned slightly, too confused to entirely hold herself in. She had never been as good at the skill as her mother.

"You have returned in excellent time," her mother almost purred, and for the first time Gwen wondered if her mother's relief at her reappearance was so great that it outweighed any anger.

A little of the heaviness inside her lifted. If Celandine was that relieved, then the state of the court must be even more fragile than Gwen had realized. Maybe they really could succeed at outwitting the queen.

"I'm sure you'll understand that your actions have destroyed my trust in you," Celandine said silkily. "I'm most disappointed. Naturally you will need to be closely watched."

Gwen's voluminous dress concealed several deep pockets, and she thrust her hand into one solely so she could clench her fingers into a fist. In the process, they brushed against something round and cool. For a second, Gwen forgot to focus on her mother, her mind scrambling to make sense of the object. Then memory returned in a rush.

The golden apple given to her by the godmother. She had forgotten she still had it in her pocket.

Unease gripped her. She should have left it with Easton or Charlotte. Bringing it into the presence of the queen had been foolhardy. Gwen had seen how much Celandine valued godmother objects. She wouldn't hesitate to claim it if she discovered what Gwen had in her possession.

Wrapping her hand around the cool sphere, she drew several calming breaths, trying to slow her racing heart before it gave her away. But the movement proved more distracting than settling.

The moment her fingers closed around the apple, her awareness shifted. She couldn't have said what sense she was using, but she was suddenly gripped by the knowledge that the queen also carried a godmother object in her pocket.

Although she had no memory of seeing it in the queen's display room, she could easily call up an image of it in her mind's eye. The plaited multi-strand length of cord was about six inches long and included several colors along its woven length. To outward appearance, it was a useless item, but Gwen hummed with the awareness of its power. It could—

She frowned. She could feel the awareness almost there, hovering on the edge of her mind, just out of reach.

She let go of the apple, and the awareness of the cord in the queen's pocket immediately vanished. Gwen tried to call its image to mind again, but it was hazy and indistinct.

She blinked, trying to focus on her mother's face and keep her own features steady. When she touched the apple for a second time, the calm façade was difficult to hold, almost overwhelmed as the awareness of her mother's object came flooding instantly back.

At least she had confirmed the new knowledge definitely came from the apple. Did that mean its purpose was to reveal the presence of other godmother objects? Gwen couldn't help a sinking disappointment. For one brief moment when she'd remembered the apple's existence, she had hoped it might turn the tide against the queen. But apparently it was better for little more than a parlor trick.

"Are you even listening to me?" the queen asked, her eyes tightening for the first time.

"Yes, Mother. Of course." The words slid out easily, the product of instinct, but the title left a burning aftertaste. Gwen had rejected Celandine's role in her life only the day before, but it wasn't so easy to reject her to her face.

"Of course," her mother repeated, but the tightness hadn't left her face.

For a moment, they both remained motionless, Gwen barely breathing as she waited to see her mother's next action. It seemed impossible that they weren't even going to mention Gwen's flight, and yet the queen seemed ready to sweep the whole thing under the rug. As if, by returning, Gwen had absolved herself of her past misconduct.

But it couldn't possibly be so easy.

The queen straightened, pulling something out of her pocket. The movement dislodged something else, sending it slipping to the ground.

For a second, Gwen's eyes caught on a multi-colored strand before Celandine swooped down and retrieved it, thrusting it quickly back out of sight. Gwen hadn't missed the shape of it, though. It was exactly like the object she had just seen in her mind. The apple's revelation had been real.

Gwen barely had time to feel the thrill of confirmation before her mother held up the item she had been retrieving from her pocket. A brass key.

Gwen's insides froze, her breath stuttering. She had been

right. Her mother didn't mean to forgive her flight. She was going to punish her. She was going to lock her in the dark. She was going to—

"Come with me," the queen said commandingly, sweeping toward the doors of the throne room.

Gwen trailed obediently behind, her brain still circling around the key and her coming imprisonment. Was the queen leading her somewhere even smaller than the closet where she had spent the days after Easton's disappearance? Would she be confined for an even longer time?

Gwen reminded herself to breathe, only for her head to grow dizzy. She had made the opposite mistake and was breathing much too fast. She would lose her sanity inside whatever tiny hole her mother intended to imprison her in. This time Easton would come for her, but it would be too late. The Gwen he knew would have dissolved.

Her mother stopped in front of a door, and Gwen's brows lowered. It looked...familiar? Her panicked brain took a moment to comprehend what she was seeing. They stood in front of her own room.

"This is..." She didn't finish the sentence before her mother used the key to open the door and then stood aside and gestured for her to enter.

Gwen walked inside without conscious thought, the familiar environment flooding her with relief and reassurance.

"There are matters I must attend to," Queen Celandine said from the doorway with her previous calm indifference. "I'm sure you'll understand why I would like you to await me here." She paused. "You might like to know that the lock has been changed. This is now the only key."

Gwen nodded, still riding high on relief. She was only being confined to her room—her room that had windows and light and more than enough space to move. Her room that had a comfortable bed. She could have thrown her arms around her mother's neck and hugged her.

With a small smile, the queen withdrew, leaving her daughter to stagger over to the window seat, still reeling as the key turned in the lock. The familiarity of the view calmed her, and for a long moment she sat there, absorbing the sunlight that streamed through the glass and enjoying its warmth.

She was safe after all. Her mother hadn't shut her inside the closet. She had only—

Locked her in her room.

Gwen frowned. Her mother had sent Gwen to her room as if she was a rebellious child. She had even locked her in. And Gwen had been thanking her! She had been grateful to her!

A slow tide of fury rose inside Gwen, moving slowly like creeping lava but burning just as hot. The queen had manipulated her. She knew of Gwen's fears, and she had showed her the key purposely to make her think she was being punished. And then she had delivered her to her room instead. If her fear hadn't been overpowering Gwen's mind, she would have been incensed to be locked in her room. Instead, she was relieved and grateful. She had been grateful to her mother! She had even thought of her as her mother again.

Gwen shivered. Celandine wasn't overlooking her rebellion, but her methods were subtle, not overt. She was manipulating Gwen as easily as she had always done, tearing her down and then reassuring her in just the right balance. And Gwen had fallen straight back into her old patterns, just like she had feared she would.

She paced up and down the room, storming and raging silently to herself. She had to be more aware. She couldn't let herself be sucked into her old thought patterns just because she had returned to a familiar environment.

As the hours dragged on and exhaustion set in, Gwen realized her mistake. She had thought her old mask would serve her best, so she had gone along with her mother's pretense of amity between them. But in their old roles, the queen had all the advantages. Gwen was in the process of making herself into a new person, but the familiar environment made it too hard to resist the strength of her old habits. She couldn't stand in the same rooms and interact with her mother in the same way as before and trust that her self-control and determination were enough to carry her through. If Gwen was going to emerge from the palace intact, she had to break free from the rhythms of her past. She had to confront her mother.

The decision to let go of her protective mask felt so momentous that Gwen expected her mother to arrive at her door the moment she reached her conclusion. When the hours dragged on without any sign of the queen, however, Gwen began to grow concerned.

How long was the queen planning to keep her confined? If she intended to lock her up until the moment of the wedding ceremony, Gwen wasn't going to be much use to the rebels' cause.

A key in the lock made her jump to her feet. But the person who emerged through the narrow opening lacked the queen's commanding presence.

"Miriam!" Gwen flew across the room and flung her arms around the young woman.

Miriam startled, barely managing to rescue the tray she was carrying from Gwen's affectionate attack.

"Sorry!" Gwen drew back and took the tray from her, quickly shutting the door with both of them inside.

Miriam regarded the closed door warily.

"I can't believe she let you bring me food!" Gwen continued, not sure if she was marveling more at the food itself or the choice of delivery person. "She really doesn't suspect any of you, then?"

Miriam hesitated before shaking her head.

"Thank goodness." Gwen collapsed onto the nearest chair. "I was worried. I..." She drew a breath. If she wanted to change, she had to start by taking responsibility for her part in the past. "I'm sorry for just running off and abandoning you all. You helped me, and I rushed to save only myself."

Miriam regarded Gwen more steadily than the princess could ever remember the captive servant doing in the past. Eventually, she nodded.

"You did leave," she said, "but now you've come back."

She began unloading the dishes from the tray Gwen held, taking it back from Gwen once it was empty.

"That's all?" Gwen asked with a lightheaded laugh. "I'm forgiven just like that?"

Miriam shrugged. "We don't have so many allies that we can afford to throw them away so easily. And you did come back."

Gwen sobered at the pragmatic response. Sometimes Gwen had forgotten she was a princess and thought of the servants as just her friends. But she doubted they had ever forgotten they were captives. If their plan succeeded, Gwen intended to free the captives as her first act as queen. But at that point, they would likely return home to the valleys.

Some might choose to stay. They had been taken because they were found alone, and some might have no one to return to after so many years in the mountain kingdom. But even if some stayed, Gwen would be their queen. There would always be a barrier and a power imbalance between her and Miriam and Alma and the others.

Gwen owed both duty and affection toward them, but they owed her nothing. If they helped with the rebellion, it would be for the sake of their own freedom. But that was all right. They were allies as Miriam had said, and Gwen could use all the allies she could get.

I suppose this is what it means to be queen, Gwen thought. Gathering allies and weighing how the motivations of others could be used to Gwen's advantage. She wasn't sure how she felt about it. Wasn't it the kind of thing her mother would do?

Even as she thought it, she rejected the idea. Her mother manipulated the motivations of others in order to gain an advantage over them and use them. Allies sought the places where their motivations converged and worked for the good of both parties. Gwen could be an ally to the captive servants and still hold her head high.

She smiled at Miriam. "I would be honored to have you as allies. And in exchange, I guarantee that when I sit on the throne, you will not only be freed, but you will be released with fair compensation for both your captivity and your labor."

Miriam's eyes widened. "You really did come back to challenge the queen, then? You mean to take the throne?"

Gwen nodded. "And I'm not alone." She considered adding more, but caution held her back. Just as she hadn't mentioned the captives to Count Oswin, she wasn't sure if it was safe to mention Easton or the count to Miriam. While she didn't doubt Miriam or Alma, she didn't know all the captives equally well. There might be one willing to bargain with information in exchange for Celandine setting them alone free.

"I need to tell Alma," Miriam murmured. She hurried to the door only to hesitate. "Is there…is there something you want us to do?"

Gwen also hesitated, aware that Miriam's hesitancy reflected the danger she was in from the queen.

"I'll let you know when the time comes," Gwen said at last, hoping her words sounded confident instead of vague.

Miriam accepted them with something like relief, slipping out of the room and locking the door behind her. Was she on her way to return the key to the queen, or had Celandine handed it off to the servants with the intention of keeping Gwen locked away for a long time? With Miriam gone, Gwen kicked herself for not asking such basic questions.

She resolved to be more prepared when one of the servants returned to either collect the tray or deliver another meal. But when the key next turned in the lock, the door was thrust all the way open, and the queen strode in.

For a frozen moment, Gwen was sure she had misjudged Miriam and the servant had already reported Gwen to the queen. But Celandine's expression had a haughty disinterest that didn't fit with that theory, and Gwen's racing heart gradually slowed.

As the queen surveyed the room, Gwen's heart immediately picked up again, however, as she remembered her earlier resolution. The queen might not be angry now, but a defiant attitude from her daughter would likely change that.

Gwen knew she had to act quickly before she lost her nerve. But as soon as she opened her mouth, the queen spoke.

"Come. It is time for you to meet your husband-to-be."

Gwen snapped her mouth shut, her planned words forgotten. Her mother intended to take her to Henry? Charlotte's Henry! Gwen had promised her friend that she'd find him, and now her mother was planning to walk her straight there. Gwen could at least keep her mouth shut long enough to meet the prince and find out where he was being kept.

GWEN

"Yes, Mother." Gwen bowed her head quickly in submission, hoping the queen hadn't seen the surge of excitement in her eyes at mention of Henry.

She expected to be led into the depths of the palace—possibly even to the closet that she had once been trapped in. But Celandine walked only three doors along the corridor before stopping again.

The rooms around Gwen's had been empty for as long as she could remember—silent reminders that her father's death had also taken away the chance of future siblings. Their silent emptiness was so ingrained in Gwen's thinking that it had never occurred to her that Henry might be housed in one of them.

For a horrifying moment, she feared her friend had been mistaken in her husband and that Henry was the queen's guest. Then Celandine withdrew a key, and Gwen's fears receded. Henry was a captive just as she had been.

Gwen of all people knew that a pretty cage was still a cage.

After turning the key in the lock, Celandine paused, stepping back slightly and gesturing for Gwen to open the door. Gwen frowned but couldn't think of any reason to refuse the task.

Cautiously she opened the door and stepped inside. A flash of movement made her startle and flinch away as a solid brass candlestick descended toward her head. By the time she sucked in the breath to cry out, however, the candlestick had veered, missing her by an inch and dropping to the carpet instead.

A tall young man stood staring at her, his chest rising and falling with either exertion or strong emotion. Had he prepared himself for a desperate escape attempt only to pull back when he saw her face? Why?

Gwen had the vague impression he was handsome, but the only feature she absorbed were his piercing blue eyes. They first tightened and then widened as he looked at her.

"You're the princess?" he asked, and then slowly, as if struggling to remember, "Gwen, is it?"

Gwen's heart contracted. Her mother would never have referred to her as Gwen to this foreign prince. To her mother she was Princess Gwendolyn. If Prince Henry knew her as Gwen, then he had heard her name from Charlotte. But how had he recognized her face?

"I see the castle did its job," Queen Celandine entered the room with a satisfied smile. "My daughter is just as beautiful as her portrait, is she not?"

Her portrait? Gwen stared from her mother to the prince in dismay. Like the portrait of Charlotte and Henry that was hidden in her mother's room? Charlotte's description of Henry's castle had sounded concerningly like a mirror for the mountain palace, but this news confirmed it. There had definitely been a link between the mountain queen and Charlotte's home. A link that must have been anchored in the paired portrait that gave her mother a glimpse of Henry and his bride.

Gwen stuffed her hands in her pocket to hide that they were both fisted and trembling. Her mother had no shame and no limits. But she was fooling herself if she thought Henry and Gwen would ever be married.

Her right hand brushed against the apple, reminding her again of its existence. Curious, she wrapped her hand around it and waited to see if the queen still had the plaited cords in her pocket.

Instantly, she was hit with the same awareness as before. The queen's object was still in the pocket where it had been before, still carried on her person. But if last time her awareness of it had been like meeting a new acquaintance, now it glowed with the warmth of an old friend.

If Gwen didn't know better, she would have said her golden apple felt fondly toward the plaited cord that changed someone's shape in order to bind them to the mountains. Gwen blinked. She had known the cord was a godmother object before, but the awareness of its purpose and ability was new.

Apparently her apple was more useful than she'd initially realized. If the queen had possessed it, she would have known the cord's full purpose, and she would never have tried to use it to bind her people to her. Gwen's hand tightened around the apple. If her mother saw it, she would want to possess it, just like she had collected those other objects in her display room.

"Gwendolyn," the queen said in a low warning voice, and Gwen shook herself. She couldn't afford to let her mind wander in front of her mother. She needed all her attention to try to match wits with the queen.

"I thought it was prudent for the two of you to meet before your wedding day," the queen continued, "and clearly I was correct. Hopefully now you will be more cooperative." She gave a satisfied smile, apparently having mistaken Henry's surprise at the sight of Gwen for admiration. "As you can see, I am not attempting to offer you a bad bargain. My daughter is young and beautiful and has been raised as a proper princess. She is a suitable bride for the Arcadian heir."

Henry's eyes narrowed as he looked at the queen. Everything about him was tense, even the surreptitious glances he kept flicking at Gwen. Gwen didn't make the same mistake as the queen, however. He wasn't admiring her, Gwen could tell that much. Instead, she had the distinct impression he was barely restraining himself from asking her something.

"I will not and cannot marry your daughter," Henry said in clear tones. "If you had stopped to listen to me previously, you would know it is impossible. I'm already married."

Celandine made a dismissive sound and gesture. "Any previous ties are inconsequential. Of course you will marry Princess Gwendolyn."

"Inconsequential?" Henry raised an eyebrow, not flinching in the face of the queen's disdain. "I've spent the time I've been gone on research. I know the mountain kingdom was once connected to the Four Kingdoms and made treaties with them. Many generations ago, one of your ancestors closed off the mountain passes, and your kingdom has been all but forgotten. But some of the ancient records still remain, and they were reproduced for me by your handy bell."

The queen's face twisted at his mention of the bell, and he smiled slightly.

"I know that each kingdom agreed to honor contracts and marriages made in the other kingdoms. A marriage in the Four Kingdoms is a legal marriage in the mountain kingdom as well. I am already married and cannot marry your daughter."

Gwen wanted to cheer, but to her dismay, a slow smile spread over the queen's face.

"Officially registered marriages, certainly," she said in sickly sweet tones. "But you were married in the valleys—you must have been since the confines of the enchantment prevented you from leaving the mountains' foothills. So tell me, with which royal family has your marriage been registered?"

Henry's face paled, and Gwen's stomach turned in response.

The queen continued, her smile growing broader. "I assure you I have also not been idle in gathering information, and my teams have been visiting the valleys for years now. From what I understand, the valley officials only make the trek into Rangmere's capital every couple of years. If you wish to play the game of law, I believe you'll find that if a marriage is officially registered in the mountain kingdom earlier than it is officially registered in Rangmere, it is the Rangmeran marriage that will be deemed invalid."

"It may not be on the Rangmeran registry yet," Henry said in a dangerous voice, "but I was married according to valley tradition, and our names were duly recorded. I am already married, and I will not cast my wife aside and enter into another marriage."

The queen's smile dropped from her face, replaced with a dangerous glitter in her eyes.

"Then it seems we must seek a simpler solution. The

validity of your first union will become irrelevant when your bride is dead. As a widower, there will be no bar in any kingdom to prevent you marrying the princess."

Henry went still, not even breathing as he stared at the queen. His hands were fisted at his sides, and Gwen wondered how much control it was taking for him not to attack Celandine.

The silence stretched out until the queen smiled again. "I'm glad to hear you've finished your foolish protesting. We will now continue with our plans for the wedding."

The queen continued to talk about the practical plans she had made for the ceremony, but Gwen barely heard her. She had resolved to stand up to her mother, and now was surely the time. Henry had attempted it and been silenced, so it was Gwen's turn.

But her mind struggled to form the necessary words, her thoughts constantly derailed by the continued glances from Henry. He also didn't appear to be listening to the queen, his whole focus on sending her a silent message unseen by the queen.

Gwen felt foolish and sluggish, unable to grasp what he was so desperately trying to communicate. She needed a moment alone with him, and she certainly wouldn't get one if she picked that exact moment to enrage the queen.

Henry gave a soft sigh, and Gwen could sense her own frustration rolling off him. Before she could attempt her own silent communication, though, his demeanor abruptly changed.

He turned his eyes on Gwen again, but this time his look was open and direct—meant to be seen rather than over-looked. The apparent warmth in his gaze made her squirm given the false note that lay behind it. She stayed silent, however, willing to play along with whatever drama he was enacting for the queen.

"I cannot deny that your daughter is beautiful," he said, aiming his words at Celandine but keeping his eyes on Gwen. "But I don't know if I can bring myself to marry a complete stranger." He finally turned to look at the queen. "May we not have some time alone?"

The queen raised her brows. "I have brought her to you, haven't I? Or are you saying you cannot become acquainted in my company?"

Gwen tensed at the suspicion in her words, but Henry merely smirked.

"There are some types of…acquaintance…that are uncomfortable to achieve in the presence of others," he said smoothly, his eyes returning appreciatively to Gwen.

His words surprised a mirthless laugh from the queen. "I suppose I can allow you a few minutes." She held up a finger, her tone turning to warning. "But a few minutes only. I'm sure I need not remind you that the wedding has yet to take place."

She swept toward the door, pausing at Gwen's side and leaning close to murmur in her ear.

"Take note of this lesson, my dear. For all their protestations, all men are the same. Attempt whatever coyness you like, but allow him a kiss now, and you will yet manage to control him."

Gwen stared at her mother's retreating form in shock. They had suspected her mother was struggling to maintain control in her absence, but even so she had expected more resistance to her return. She hadn't expected her mother to treat it like it had never happened. Before her defiance and escape, one of her mother's last commands to her had been about preparing for her wedding. She hadn't been concerned about the clothes or the ceremony, but rather about Gwen's need to control and manipulate her future husband. And now she was speaking as if that conversation had merely been interrupted by a night's sleep.

Her mother must be more desperate than the count realized if she truly intended to ignore Gwen's rebellion and disappearance. It was like time had rolled back in her mother's mind. Gwen had returned, and it was therefore as if she had never left.

Gratitude filled Gwen that she hadn't spoken up sooner. If her mother truly intended to deny reality, Gwen could use that to her advantage. And she would need every advantage she could manage. A Celandine desperate enough to react in such a way was almost more terrifying than Celandine in her right mind, in full control of every situation. It made her unpredictable and dangerous.

As the door clicked shut, Henry stepped toward her. Grasping her shoulders, he spun her slightly so that his back was toward the door and his body blocked most of hers from view. Leaning close, he positioned his face beside hers.

"Apologies," he whispered, "but if she opens the door, it will look from that direction as if we're embracing."

Gwen nodded, not wanting to waste any of their precious time.

"My wife mentioned you," he said rapidly. "She knew your name. And you seemed to react when you saw me. Have you met her? I don't know how it could be possible, but do you know her somehow?" Fear tinged his voice. "Do you know where she is now? Have you seen her in the last few days? She isn't here in the mountain kingdom, is she?"

Gwen winced, and Henry's face turned ashen.

"No," he whispered hoarsely. "How is that possible?"

"I'm sorry," she murmured, her words falling over each other. "She insisted I bring her here. She's determined to find you. She wants to—"

"Free me," Henry said on a groan. He strode once up and down the room, running an agitated hand through his hair. "I can't protect her if she's here!"

"Then maybe you need to let her protect you," Gwen said firmly.

Henry halted and stared at her. But before she could expand on the topic, he glanced at the closed door and hurried back to position himself in front of her again.

"She isn't alone," Gwen said softly, unable to ignore the pain and worry on his face. "And it isn't just me, either. We have allies. And a plan. There isn't time to explain it all now, but you should just be ready when the moment comes. I'm not working with my mother, and I won't marry you, no matter what she says or does. But we have to play along with her for now. Even if it gets all the way to the ceremony, don't worry. Just be ready to move on my signal."

Henry looked like he was about to argue, but the door clicked behind them. For a half second, Henry leaned even closer to her before a footfall sounded and he started dramatically away.

The queen chuckled. "I'm glad to see the two of you getting along."

Gwen hoped the flush of fury in her cheeks would be mistaken for embarrassment. She kept her face averted from the queen, lest the look in her eyes give her away. Instead, she gazed out the window, waiting for her emotions to calm.

A flash of movement outside caught her eye, and her gaze focused abruptly. There was someone out there, and it wasn't a captive servant or a guard. She recognized the swish of the gown that had disappeared around the corner because it was one of her own—one she had loaned to Charlotte after finding her friend still dressed in her nightgown.

The flush surged back into Gwen's cheeks, this time fueled by a combination of fear and nervous anticipation. She leaned into it, looking from Henry to the queen and then back to Henry before covering her heated cheeks with her hands and fleeing the room.

The queen's laughter chased her out, and as Gwen dashed along the corridor, she caught the distant words as the queen excused her daughter's naivety. Gwen rolled her eyes even while she felt relieved her spontaneous subterfuge had worked. She didn't know how long she had before her mother came looking for her—or set the palace guards to the task—so she couldn't waste time finding Charlotte and sending her away. The last thing they needed was for Queen Celandine to capture her. From what Gwen had seen, Henry would go along with any plan the queen demanded if she had Charlotte under her power.

GWEN

Gwen ran straight to the nearest exit into the garden, weaving through the paths as she rushed toward the spot she had seen her friend. She stayed close to hedges as much as possible, hoping she wouldn't be spotted from any of the palace's windows, and so she nearly missed the two slim figures huddled together in quiet conversation in one of the more secluded spots in the garden.

"Gwen!" Charlotte called, her cry muted, and Gwen swung around.

Racing through the archway in the tall hedge, Gwen came to a stop in front of her friend.

"What are you doing here?" she panted, struggling to catch her breath. "You can't be here. Seriously, I mean it. It's too dangerous."

A militant light came into Charlotte's eyes. "Henry is here." She raised her chin stubbornly. "I won't leave him in danger while I lurk behind in safety."

Gwen huffed in frustration, distantly noting that Natalie

had slipped away. She was too focused on Charlotte to ask what harebrained scheme the two had concocted.

"Henry being here is exactly why you can't be!" she protested, struggling to keep her voice low. "The queen is already threatening you to manipulate him, and that will only get worse if she captures you as well."

Charlotte's eyes lit up. "You've seen him? Is he all right? The queen hasn't hurt him?"

"Not physically," Gwen said, unable to help reassuring her friend. "At least not that I can see. But he's desperately worried about you."

Charlotte smiled softly, a dreamy look in her eyes. "Of course he is. That's very Henry."

Gwen sighed in frustration. Were she and Easton this irritating?

Discomfort filled her as she remembered that she and Easton were far from the position of Charlotte and Henry. The other two were not only married, they had each declared their love already. Gwen still had no idea how she was going to find out Easton's true feelings.

"The best thing you can do for Henry is leave immediately," Gwen said, trying again.

Charlotte shook her head stubbornly. "I won't leave without seeing Henry. There has to be a way to see him. I'm not going to sit around and wait and hope for the best without doing anything."

Gwen frowned. "Don't you trust us?"

Charlotte sighed. "I'm not saying I don't trust the count, but Henry isn't his priority. He's focused on breaking the enchantment, saving your kingdom, and putting you and Easton on the throne. That makes sense, but now that he knows Henry isn't part of breaking the enchantment, Henry has become little more than an afterthought for him."

Gwen sank back and let out a slow breath. She couldn't deny her friend's words. And while she wanted to assure Charlotte that Gwen herself wouldn't forget about Henry's safety, could she really guarantee it? She couldn't even guarantee her own safety.

She sighed. She didn't have the words to convince Charlotte to go back to the city, and neither could she physically force her to do so. In fact, Charlotte would only be in more danger if Gwen didn't get moving soon. Gwen's best hope for helping her friend was to think of a way for Charlotte to safely see Henry. But with Henry locked up and the key with her mother, how could Charlotte possibly get in to see him secretly?

Gwen strode across the small garden and back again, wracking her brains for a solution. As she walked, the apple in her pocket bumped lightly against her leg, causing her mind to briefly wander. With the apple, they could discover the extent of her mother's power. They might even be able to find a weakness they could use to bring her down or an object they could use to restrain her during the wedding ceremony.

But the apple hadn't revealed much the first time it came into contact with the plaited cords. It was as if it needed to get to know the other object first. And that meant if Gwen broke into the queen's display room right now, the apple wouldn't do her any good at all.

She groaned in frustration. Did she really need to break in more than once? The impossibilities only seemed to be mounting. Why couldn't she find solutions instead of more problems?

"What is it?" Charlotte asked, watching her pacing with

concern. "Is it Henry? Is there something you're not telling me?"

"It's not that..." Gwen's voice trailed off as something occurred to her. What if there was one solution to multiple problems?

She turned to Charlotte. "I have an idea."

Charlotte rushed forward to take her hands. "What is it?"

"I've been trying to think how you can get in to see Henry without the queen knowing, but what if you don't try to avoid the queen?"

Charlotte frowned, letting Gwen's hands drop. "I thought you said I had to avoid getting captured at all costs?"

"I'm not saying it's not without risks, but your being here is already a risk. My preference would be for you to agree to leave now..." She looked at Charlotte inquiringly, but Charlotte shook her head, so Gwen continued.

"This is the solution." She drew the apple out of her pocket, extending it on her palm so the late afternoon light caught on the gold.

Charlotte sucked in a breath. "What is that?" she whispered.

"I got it from my godmother, which means it's the bait we can use for the queen. If there's one thing she's obsessed with, it's accumulating godmother objects. They're the basis for her power. If she sees this, she'll want it."

Charlotte frowned. "I don't understand."

"Offer it to her in exchange for seeing Henry," Gwen said simply.

Charlotte stared at her blankly. "Why would she agree to that? Surely she'd just arrest me and steal it?"

"That's the beauty of using this." Gwen smiled triumphantly. "All you have to do is tell her it's one of the objects that stops working completely if it's taken by force. It will only work if given willingly."

Charlotte's mouth dropped open. "That's actually brilliant!" she exclaimed. "Lots of godmother objects do work like that, so she'll likely believe it."

"As long as you make a deal that includes you being free to leave after seeing Henry, she'll have to keep to the terms of the bargain, or she'll lose the power of the object," Gwen added.

Charlotte reached eagerly for the apple, only for her face to darken and her hand to drop. "But I can't take this. It's yours. Your godmother gave it to you. I should use mine." She pulled out a smooth golden ball. "I was given something on the way here as well. If we have to give her a godmother object in exchange for my seeing Henry, it should be mine."

Gwen looked at the ball curiously, but their time was running out. She didn't have the luxury of idle curiosity. She wasn't her mother—she didn't need to own every powerful object she encountered.

"No, it has to be the apple." She pressed it on Charlotte. "I want the queen to have it, and this is a way to get it to her without her suspecting an ulterior motive."

Charlotte put away her ball and slowly accepted Gwen's apple. "Why would you want her to have it?" she asked. "What does it do?"

"It tells the person holding it about the power of other objects," Gwen said, watching Charlotte's face.

Her friend gasped, her eyes flying to Gwen. "I can sense my ball! It's like I can see it in my pocket. Well, not see it. More like I can taste it." She laughed. "No, that's not right. I don't know what sense I'm using, but it's there. And I can feel the golden halter you entrusted to me too." She frowned. "But

I can't tell anything about either one's purpose, just their presence."

Gwen nodded, glad to have her experience confirmed. "That's why we need to get it into the queen's hands. She'll put it in her display room with all her other objects and that's what we need. It seems to need time around another object before it will reveal that object's purpose. We have to give it a chance to warm up to all the objects in that room, so that when we break in there, it's ready to tell us what they each do."

Charlotte shook her head. "Two birds with one stone," she murmured.

Gwen grinned slowly. "Exactly. I'm ready to start solving problems instead of amassing new ones."

Charlotte grimaced. "I know I'm one of those problems. But I can't just walk away from Henry knowing he's right there."

Gwen nodded. For all her initial frustration, she understood. If there had been a way for her to get to Easton anytime in the last ten years, she would have done anything to reach him.

"Don't worry," Charlotte said, determined. "I'll explain everything to Henry and make sure he goes along with the plan."

"Unless you can find a way to get him out immediately?" Gwen challenged, a brow raised.

Charlotte hesitated, her bottom lip gripped between her teeth. "No," she finally said on a sigh. "I won't try that. I know you need the queen to continue planning this wedding." She looked sharply at Gwen. "That is what's happening? She hasn't hurt you?"

Gwen nodded. "She's fully focused on the wedding. Henry

will be safe until then. As long as he doesn't do anything foolish himself."

She didn't say aloud the rest of her thought. Helping Charlotte to make direct contact with Henry was as much about ensuring his compliance as anything else. From his level of agitation earlier, now that he knew Charlotte was in the mountain kingdom—and under open threat from its queen—Gwen didn't put it past him to make some foolhardy attempt at escape before the wedding. But even if he wouldn't listen to Gwen, surely he would listen to Charlotte.

Gwen froze, her ears pricking. Footsteps on gravel sounded from more than one direction, and from the measured cadence, it wasn't courtiers out for a casual stroll.

"Hide!" she hissed, giving Charlotte a light push. "Get out of sight somewhere while I distract them. And then get somewhere close to the palace walls, on the south side. Get the apple out and just throw it around a bit, like you're playing. I guarantee my mother will see you."

Charlotte hesitated for only a moment before nodding decisively and diving into a nearby clump of bushes. Gwen smiled for a fraction of a second at her friend's enthusiastic and literal interpretation of her instructions before she hurried back through the arch.

No guards were in sight yet, but from the sound of the footsteps, she would see them soon. She considered hurrying in the other direction, but after only a moment of indecision, she sank onto the closest bench. As far as the queen knew, Gwen had been overcome with embarrassment and rushed out to cool down. The last thing she wanted was to create the impression she had been attempting to run away.

Slumping down, she leaned her forehead against one hand, breathing slowly.

The footsteps drew closer.

"Your Highness!" The gruff voice made her look up, disappointment rising when she didn't recognize the speaker or his companion. She shouldn't have been surprised, though. Of course her mother would send her most loyal guards to retrieve her recalcitrant daughter.

Gwen stood up slowly, trying to look unaffected.

"Is my mother looking for me?" she asked, careful not to look toward the arch leading into the garden where Charlotte was concealed.

"She merely wants to assure herself of your safety," the guard said, exchanging a quick look with his partner.

Gwen nodded as if that was understandable and started back toward the palace. The guards fell into step, one on either side of her. When the second pair appeared, a silent communication passed between all four guards, and the newcomers fell in behind the existing two.

Gwen expected them to lead her to her mother, but they merely kept pace as she chose her own course. Unsure what else to do, Gwen traced the familiar route back to her room, pausing for a moment in the corridor and gazing down toward Henry's door.

Shaking her head at herself, she pushed open her own door and paused to give the guards a firm look. None of them protested when she shut the door in their faces, and she breathed a sigh of relief. As much as she wanted to go and test Henry's door, she couldn't risk it. Charlotte might already be on her way to the part of the garden closest to Celandine's wing, and Gwen had to give her friend a chance to get to Henry before Gwen disrupted anything else.

She only wished she was as close to being back in Easton's arms again.

CHARLOTTE

Charlotte's heart pounded as she wove her way through the gardens, her ears straining for the sound of footsteps. She wanted Celandine to be the one to find her, not a random pair of guards. They might throw her out of the grounds—or worse, into a cell—without ever giving her the chance to propose a trade with the queen.

She saw no sign of Natalie as she moved. Had the other girl hidden nearby to hear Gwen's plan? Charlotte hoped she had. At least that way the rebels would know what had become of her if everything went wrong. But it was just as possible Natalie had headed out to pursue their original mission—finding more information about the queen's movements.

Charlotte slipped her hand back in her pocket and curled it around the apple. She no longer felt the presence of the golden ball since she had left it buried beneath the bush where she had hidden herself along with the golden halter. She didn't want to risk carrying either one into Celandine's presence. They were already handing over one object to her. There was no need to make it three.

In the garden with Gwen, the plan had seemed solid, but the closer she got to the castle, the faster Charlotte's heart beat. What if the queen didn't see her? Or what if she wouldn't agree to the trade? If she had no interest in the apple, or decided to take her chances and seize it by force, Charlotte would be left helpless and with nothing to use to buy her freedom.

Charlotte shook her head, focusing her thoughts on Henry instead. It would all be worth it if she could see him. And she didn't intend to be tricked into giving Gwen's object away for a mere few minutes either. If Celandine would be bound by their agreement, Charlotte intended to bargain well.

When she reached the south side of the building, she approached close, peering into the windows she passed. The largest showed an expansive room furnished as a study and lined with bookshelves. An elegant woman wearing a glittering circlet sat at the large desk, her head bent over a stack of papers.

Charlotte immediately pulled back, her heart pounding. She had found the right place, but she needed to stage herself better if she was going to outwit the queen.

Strolling casually in front of the window, she didn't glance toward the glass. Instead, she gazed out at the city, which stretched below the palace, choosing a place to sit on the grass and angling her body so she could keep her apparent focus on the view while giving the queen a clear line of sight to Charlotte's profile.

As soon as she was seated, she pulled out the apple and threw it into the air. Tracking its flight, she smiled at the way the lowering sun caught on the gold, making it shine. Perfect.

It landed in her palm with a dull thunk, the weight of it nearly catching her off guard. She quickly flicked it up again, watching its rise and then descent. It was taking all her self-control not to look toward the window, but she didn't want the queen to know she was aware of her presence, and if their eyes locked…

It flew up again and then a fourth time. When she fumbled the catch, the apple dropped to the grass and rolled a short way. Charlotte retrieved it with her best approximation of a carefree laugh. It barely squeezed through her throat, though, the semblance of calm difficult. She wasn't sure if she was more terrified of the coming confrontation with the queen or more elated at the prospect of being reunited with Henry. Within minutes, she might be at his side, held in his arms. Waiting was both painful and never-ending. Minutes had never moved so slowly.

She'd lost track of the number of times she'd thrown the apple when a shadow fell across her. Shielding her eyes with one hand, she gazed up at the queen.

Gasping theatrically, she scrambled to her feet and dropped into an instant curtsy.

"Your Majesty," she said, glad her voice trembled only a little. "I apologize for disturbing you. I didn't know…"

The queen's eyes were trained on the apple, her expression hinting at the greedy desire Gwen had been sure she would feel. But at Charlotte's words, she tore her gaze away and looked at Charlotte's face.

Her eyes widened, a crease appearing between her brows, and Charlotte remembered Gwen had once mentioned a portrait.

"What are *you* doing here?" the queen breathed. "*How* are you here?"

Charlotte stayed silent, reminding herself that it didn't matter if the queen recognized her. She would have realized the connection as soon as Charlotte suggested her bargain anyway. But she needed to choose her words carefully.

"There's nothing I wouldn't do to be reunited with my husband," she said. "Nothing I wouldn't give."

"Even in my youth I wasn't so foolish," the queen said, but she looked pleased. "However, if that is truly your heart's desire, maybe I can help you."

Charlotte didn't have to feign her eagerness as she looked up, meeting the queen's eyes. "You know where Henry is? You can take me to him?"

The queen cocked her head. "Give me that apple, and I will do so."

Charlotte looked down at it, drawing it back against her body, as if uncertain about the trade.

The queen's eyes followed the object. "You said you would give anything. Surely you would not begrudge such a bauble."

Charlotte drew herself up, pretending to gather her courage. "If one such as Your Majesty desires it, it must have value."

The queen's eyes narrowed. "You know who I am. With a word I can have you arrested and take everything you possess."

Charlotte held her ground. "The old woman who gave it to me said it won't reveal itself if taken by force. She said it can only be used by someone who has received it as a gift, freely given."

Celandine let out a sharp breath, and Charlotte had to suppress a smile. Their gamble had worked. The queen believed it.

For all I know, it might actually be true, Charlotte thought.

"If I give it to you," Charlotte continued, "I want more than to just be taken to Henry."

The queen's brows rose, but Charlotte thought she detected amused respect beneath the disbelief. Celandine thought she had the unassailable upper hand, so she was willing to play along with Charlotte's game. Now Charlotte had to turn that to her advantage.

She'd spent her time waiting on working out a strategy, so the words came easily. "It's nearly sunset. In exchange for this object, I want to spend the whole night with Henry. Just the two of us alone."

Another smile flickered across the queen's mouth. "Just one night?" she asked, the words almost mocking. But Charlotte knew she had to walk a fine balance. If she asked for too much, the queen might decide to risk taking the apple.

"One night undisturbed with Henry." She lifted her chin. "And in the morning, you let me walk away from the palace and its grounds alone and unharmed."

The queen let out a laugh. "You're a bold one. Are you sure he's worth it?" The amusement danced in her eyes, inviting Charlotte to doubt her husband. But she met the queen's gaze unflinching. She wouldn't fall into the same trap again. She trusted him.

"That's my bargain," Charlotte said. "I get tonight with Henry, and in the morning I walk away. If the conditions aren't met, the object will cease to work and become an ordinary apple. Assuming we can believe the old woman's words."

She could see the sour note in Celandine's gaze. She didn't want to give authority to the godmother, but she also understood the futility of trying to deny it. She had a whole room full of their objects, so she couldn't deny the High King's power.

Charlotte gave a final small toss of the apple, letting it wink in the fading light.

"Well?" she asked.

The queen glanced at the approaching sunset, her jaw setting. Then something shifted in her eyes, and she looked back at Charlotte and laughed.

"If you will willingly walk into the spider's lair, who am I to deny you?" she mocked. "It's a bargain."

Charlotte moved the apple to her left hand and thrust out her right. After only the smallest pause, the queen took it and shook, her face twisting. But Charlotte didn't care. Her heart was singing. She was about to be reunited with Henry.

The queen pulled her hand free of Charlotte's as soon as possible and held it out, palm upward. Charlotte dropped the apple into it, glad she had thought to bury the other objects.

Celandine gazed down at her new treasure, her expression gloating. But before long she looked up again, glancing once more at where the sun hung low in the sky.

"Come," she said, her tone cold and commanding.

Charlotte hurried behind her, barely able to keep up with the queen's long strides. Everything had gone as Gwen had predicted, but it was hard not to feel a shadow of dread as she stepped inside the palace. If Gwen had miscalculated or Charlotte had misread the queen, everything could be about to go terribly wrong.

The queen opened a door and ushered Charlotte inside. She hurried in, full of excitement, only for her heart to plummet as soon as she saw the empty space.

"Where—" she cried, turning back to the queen.

"It is not yet night," Celandine said curtly, cutting her off. "Your bargain was to spend the night with your prince. You will be guided to him after sundown."

Charlotte tried to protest, but Celandine had already left, closing the door firmly behind her and turning a key in the lock. Charlotte blew out a long breath. It wasn't what she had been hoping for, and after the heady expectation of only moments before, it was bitter to find herself still parted from Henry. But the situation hadn't exploded yet. She had always expected the queen to do as little as the bargain would allow—it was why she had tried to word it carefully. She only needed a little more patience and she would be with Henry again.

At least the room she was confined in had a small window, allowing her to watch the sunset. The sun had never descended so slowly, but finally—finally—the last of it slipped beneath the horizon and the sky darkened.

She ran to the door and banged on it. When no one answered, she tried the handle, aware of the futility of the attempt. To her surprise it twisted beneath her hand. When had it been unlocked?

She pulled the door open tentatively, peering at the corridor outside. A large white bear filled her view, startling a screech out of her. But the bear made no aggressive moves, and after a moment she calmed, embarrassed at her outburst. She had seen Gwen and the count change the night before, and she had spent months' worth of days with Henry in his bear form. She even knew the palace was full of bears at night. She shouldn't have been so startled.

The bear didn't respond to her outburst, waiting patiently for her to exit the room. She did so cautiously, examining the bear for any sign of its human identity.

The only thing she could tell, however, was that it wasn't Henry. His bear form was familiar to her, but she didn't know how to distinguish anyone else. For all she knew, it could be Queen Celandine herself.

Charlotte doubted it, though. Something about the bear's air didn't match the queen's commanding arrogance. Charlotte wasn't going to risk making assumptions, however.

"Where's Henry?" she asked, keeping her words to a minimum.

"Follow me," the bear said in a deep, gravelly voice.

Charlotte nodded and waited for the bear to start down the corridor. Trailing behind, she felt the earlier anticipation sparkling through her veins again. It didn't matter who was leading the way—she was going to Henry.

They crossed several corridors before the bear stopped in front of a wooden door. He remained silent, indicating it with his head.

Charlotte brushed past him, her breath catching as she saw the key sticking out of the keyhole. It was really happening. Her husband was waiting on the other side of that door.

Forgetting all about the bear, she turned the lock and slipped through into the luxurious bedchamber on the other side. She forced herself to shut the door behind her and lock it from the inside before turning to scan the room for Henry.

"Henry?" she called, her voice quavering.

There was no response. Frowning, she stepped further into the room, her eyes drawn to the large four-poster bed. It was strangely early for him to be asleep, but a human form was visible beneath the blankets, a riot of dark hair on the pillow catching her eye.

She ran to the bed, her steps faltering as she took in the features of her husband. Comfortable familiarity laced through with love washed over her. She had only seen his human face for a few brief minutes, but his appearance was burned into her mind.

"Henry," she said again, tears escaping her eyes and

tracking down her cheeks. "I came for you, just like I said I would."

He didn't stir, and the first tendrils of concern unfurled in her mind.

"Henry!" she said again, louder, but he still didn't stir. Leaning forward, she shook him by the shoulder, her movement growing more and more rough as he didn't respond.

It made no difference. Her husband lay in the bed like one dead.

CHARLOTTE

Fear rolled through Charlotte, hot and slow and then swift and overwhelming. Something was wrong with Henry.

She held her breath as she leaned over him, placing her cheek in front of his lips. When she felt his soft breath against her skin, her knees nearly collapsed. She grasped the bedcovers to keep herself upright, sucking in sharp gasps of relief. He was alive.

She cupped the warm skin of his face in her hands, calling him softly to wake. She shook his shoulders so hard that his body rolled from side to side in the bed. She even shouted, her fear and anger growing as she commanded him to wake up.

The more vigorous efforts made him groan and roll away from her, but nothing made his eyes open. Henry was deeply, impossibly asleep.

Charlotte dashed away the tears on her cheeks, her anger burning hot. The queen had betrayed their agreement. But even as she thought it, Charlotte was kicking herself. She had thought to demand the whole night and to specify they had to be alone, but she had made a mistake. It had never occurred to her to require him to be conscious. The queen had stolen her night with Henry, and now she had Gwen's apple.

Charlotte squeezed her hands into fists, feeling her nails dig into her palms. She forced herself to relax her muscles, releasing her fingers and holding for a moment before squeezing them back into fists again. She completed the exercise over and over until her mind calmed.

It wasn't a total disaster. Gwen had wanted the queen to have the apple, so at least Charlotte had delivered it in a way that allowed the queen to believe herself the victor.

The calm, rational thoughts were hard to maintain, though. It felt to Charlotte too like the queen was the victor, and defeat was a bitter taste in her mouth.

At least I've seen him, she told herself. *At least I can see he's physically unharmed—apart from the sleeping, that is.*

The day before, she would have given much for a mere glimpse of him, but it no longer felt like enough. Perhaps there was still hope, though. Whatever enchantment the queen had used on him might run out before morning. He might wake up at any moment, and they still had hours before them. Charlotte would keep watch, ready for the first sign of his waking.

But sitting by the bed, so close and yet so far from him, was unbearable. She climbed in beside him, slipping beneath the covers and curling at his side where she could feel the reassuring warmth and solidity of him. She would still stay awake and keep watch, she would just do it from the bed.

But staying awake became harder and harder as the night hours wore on. The pillow was soft and the mattress comfortably firm, and more importantly, Henry's breaths were steady and reassuring, setting the rhythm of Charlotte's own breathing. She had lain beside him for so many nights, reassured by his presence, and her body remembered those nights despite her mind's efforts to stay alert.

Eventually she couldn't resist any longer, and she slipped into the welcoming embrace of sleep—the deepest since she had lost Henry.

She woke to spears of sunlight and turned her head sideways. For the first time ever, she had a morning view of her husband still in bed beside her. A rush of joy filled her, only to immediately be doused by the memory of where they were. They weren't in their castle in the forest. They were in the mountain kingdom, and Henry was a prisoner under an unnatural sleep. She flung off the covers, crawling over to shake him again.

She had slept the night away, and now morning had already arrived. She had to wake him before it was too late. The queen's guards could burst in at any moment—she was surprised they hadn't already arrived.

"Henry! Henry!" she cried, fresh tears streaming down her cheeks.

He stirred in response, groaning and running a hand over his face, his eyes shut.

"No," he grumbled, his voice rough with sleep. "I want to stay in this dream. Lottie's here."

Charlotte's tears fell more thickly, blurring her vision. "Wake up, wake up!" she cried. "I'm really here, but we only have a moment. Wake up!"

His eyes sprang open, and for a silent second she stared down into the piercing blue eyes that had haunted her every moment since he'd disappeared. Then he surged into a sitting position, his arms sweeping around her and bundling her onto his lap where he held her tightly against his chest.

"Lottie," he said thickly. "Lottie."

Pressed against his strong chest, safe within the circle of his arms, her tears turned into full sobs. She knew she needed to regain control—that they had important words to exchange—but she couldn't do anything but revel in the moment.

He was the one to recover first, pulling back slightly to look down at her.

"Wait," he said, his clarity returning by the second. "What are you doing here? You can't be here, Lottie!"

She wiped at her cheeks, trying to remember what she needed to say.

"I'm so happy to see you again," she managed instead. "I missed you so much."

His arms tightened again, his eyes piercing into hers, devouring her face.

"It seems impossible." He cupped her face gently in his large hands, his eyes slipping down to her mouth. "I didn't think I'd ever see you again."

Charlotte angled her face up invitingly just as he pressed his lips down, meeting hers in a fervent kiss. She sank into it, absorbing all his longing and relief and desire and returning it in equal measure.

The door banged open, startling them apart. Awareness rushed back to Charlotte, and she gasped. She had been given two precious minutes, and she had spent them crying and kissing him.

"Wait," she cried as the queen swept into the room, a line of guards behind her.

She tightened her grip around Henry's neck, leaning forward to murmur in his ear. "I only bargained for the night. I'll be safe, but only if I leave now. You have to play along and do what Gwen says."

His head moved as he looked toward the queen, and Charlotte could feel the horror in every line of his body.

A guard seized her from behind, prying her away from Henry. When she didn't let go, another guard came forward to help.

The second she ripped free, Henry leaped from the bed, fists raised, fury on his face.

"No!" Charlotte lunged forward, surprising the guards enough that they momentarily lost hold of her.

She placed both hands on Henry's chest in a restraining gesture. "You can't fight them." She captured his eyes with hers, holding them with determination. "You have to let me go. I told you I have to leave now. I said I'll be safe."

The guards leaped forward again and took hold of her, dragging her away from Henry. He swayed toward her, his hands still fisted, and she shook her head frantically. Reluctantly, he looked at the massed guards and then the queen and remained in place.

"And the other thing!" Charlotte cried as she was dragged backward from the room. "Promise me, Henry. Promise me!"

She caught the moment of acceptance and begrudging acquiescence in his eyes just before she was pulled out into the corridor. As soon as they stepped sideways away from the door, the guards stopped, holding Charlotte in position, just out of sight of those in the room.

She looked toward the door, presuming they were waiting for the queen, but Celandine didn't appear. Instead, Charlotte heard Henry's voice, the angry rumble too low for her to catch the specific words, and then the queen's response, colder and higher, easy to decipher.

"I told you before," she said, "and I'll tell you again. There is an easy solution to any legal dispute. And as you can see, such an action is well within my power. If you want that girl to live, then you will cease any useless attempts at defiance."

Charlotte went cold all over. It was just like Gwen had said. Celandine was using Charlotte to control Henry.

She wanted to scream and fight, to run back in there and tell him to ignore the queen's words. But she knew it would do no good. She would never convince him not to protect her over himself. She had thought she was so clever, tricking the queen, but she was the one who had been tricked. Everything had played right into Celandine's hands.

Even the few extra moments past dawn that had been granted them had been done with a purpose. She was taunting them, reminding them who was in control, and making sure that Henry saw for himself that Charlotte was there, within the queen's reach.

Charlotte wanted to kick and punch at the guards around her, just for the satisfaction of unleashing the rage inside her. But she couldn't give way to it. She couldn't give them any excuse to violate the rest of the bargain.

The queen stepped out of the room, making a show of shutting and locking the door behind her. At her appearance, Charlotte shook off the guards' hold. They let her do so, stepping back.

Charlotte met the queen's eyes, barely reining in her anger to speak calmly.

"Call off your guards," she said. "The bargain was that I walk out of here unharmed and alone."

The queen gestured down the corridor. "By all means. No one is stopping you."

Charlotte narrowed her eyes, disliking the slight smile that hovered around the queen's eyes and mouth. But there was nothing left for her to do except take the offered chance to escape. A direct confrontation with the queen wouldn't achieve anything good. Not yet, anyway.

She held her head high as she spun on her heel and walked down the corridor. She wanted to sprint as fast as she could run, but she had specified that she be allowed to walk out of the palace, and she wouldn't risk changing a single aspect of the bargain in case it provided the queen with a loophole.

At walking pace, it seemed to take an eternity to find a door that opened to the outside, but she finally stepped out into the morning air. The gravel paths of the gardens stretched before her, and she picked up her pace slightly. Every time she glanced over her shoulder, there was no one in sight, and by the time she was halfway through the grounds, she concluded she wasn't being followed. It seemed impossible that the queen was just going to let her walk away, but apparently the pull of the godmother object was as strong as Gwen had claimed.

She still jumped at every minor sound, flinching away from every moving shadow. She wouldn't be safe until she'd made it back to Natalie's family.

She had been too distracted by Henry all night to spare a thought for the younger girl, but she remembered her guiltily as she traversed the gardens. Surely Natalie had returned home before dark rather than risk being caught in the streets at night.

Charlotte's hand moved to her arm where thin bandages still lay beneath her sleeve. The salve had worked wonders already, but Charlotte could feel the ache of it whenever her mind quieted.

The outer edge of the garden approached, and Charlotte's attention shifted to the streets beyond. As predicted by Natalie back in the basement, there was a steady trickle of traffic on every street within view, although the ones nearest the palace moved about their business quickly, their eyes averted from the looming structure.

Charlotte's family had traveled through Rangmeros when they moved from Northhelm to the valleys. It was her only visit to a capital city, so she still remembered it vividly. She had been nervous because the other kingdoms considered Rangmere to be a cold, hard place, but the city had bustled with life, and she hadn't sensed any of the fear that radiated from the mountain people.

Charlotte's shoulders hunched, her senses on high alert. Everything about this place put her on edge.

She stepped onto the cobblestones of the closest street, taut with tension. Her heart lay behind her in the palace, and her mind was leaping ahead to her destination, but a prickle in the back of her neck placed her firmly in the moment.

Her eyes darted to various side streets, her mind instinctively looking for routes she could take to escape nonexistent pursuers. Her measured steps took her further into the street as she remembered she didn't have to walk anymore. She could run all the way back to Easton and Natalie if she wanted.

No sooner had the thought occurred to her than doors opened in several directions. Guards poured out of the surrounding buildings, streaming toward her from every direction she had just scoped.

Charlotte froze, spinning to look behind her. Guards had even appeared from the gardens, closing off her retreat.

"Nonononononono." The syllables poured out of her in a constant stream as her eyes and brain scrambled to find a solution. She couldn't allow herself to be captured and used against Henry.

The guards closed in, not bothering to run given they had her surrounded. She backed toward one of the few buildings that hadn't disgorged guards.

"Here!" a high voice called, dragging her attention upward.

A hand was hanging down from the portico above the front door, gesturing for her to approach.

"Hurry!" the voice said again, and Charlotte thought she recognized it.

Leaping the rest of the way to the house, Charlotte jumped onto the rim of one of the large clay pots that flanked the door with decorative flowers. Taking the hand held out to her, she gripped the other person's wrist while they did the same to hers, securing the firmest hold they could manage.

The person above hauled upward while Charlotte jumped and caught the edge of the portico with her free hand. Her legs waved helplessly for a moment while the person above her grunted and pulled. Then she was high enough to get the forearm of her other arm over the edge of the roof, allowing her proper purchase.

Shouts from behind made her redouble her efforts, grunting as she scrambled inelegantly onto the small stretch of roof that jutted out over the door. As soon as she had her knees under her, she looked up and met Natalie's eyes.

"Totally predictable," the other girl said with rolled eyes. "You need to learn to word your bargains better. You're lucky I was hiding nearby to hear what happened and could easily see how it would all end." As she talked, she climbed onto a protruding window ledge above them and from there up to the two-story roof of the house, using a vine that wound down the stone for purchase.

Charlotte winced and tried to hurry after her. The guards were already on the ground below them, attempting to climb up without assistance from above. It wouldn't take them long to manage it.

She scrambled from the bottom of the window ledge to the thin lip above the window, wobbling dangerously as she clutched at the ivy around her. The greenery began to tear away from the building, and she screamed as her body swayed backward away from the wall.

Before she could topple far enough to lose her foothold completely, however, Natalie's slim, firm hand grabbed the shoulder of her dress. A seam somewhere in the material tore, but the dress itself stayed in place, and Natalie's intervention steadied Charlotte.

With a helping hand, she managed to pull herself all the way onto the roof. Once she had both feet under her, she breathed a sigh of relief, careful not to look toward the edge.

"Come on," Natalie said shortly, sprinting off across the sloped surface.

Charlotte's face paled, but she followed at a slower pace. She didn't want to escape the queen's guards only to fall and break her neck.

When they reached the edge of the house, Natalie didn't slow. Taking a running leap, she flew across the narrow gap between the house they were on and the one behind it.

Charlotte gulped, eyeing the narrow alley that lay between the houses. But she couldn't stop. The angry cries behind her had already reached roof level.

Backing up a couple of steps, she ran forward, pushing off against the edge of the roof and sending her body flying into the air. For a heart stopping moment, she soared, certain she was going to slip when she hit the other side and bounce her way to the ground below.

She landed on her feet, falling to her knees but remaining firmly on the new roof.

"See, it's not that hard," Natalie said from where she had paused to check Charlotte's progress.

A chuckle burst out of Charlotte. "It was actually sort of fun." A glance over her shoulder quickly sobered her. "But please don't tell me we have to do a lot more of those before we get to your house. And I definitely can't jump over the width of a full street."

"We'll never make it to my house via rooftop," Natalie said undaunted. "But we don't need to stay up here much longer anyway. We just needed to get you out of that trap."

She took off running sideways, skipping across a row of connected houses. Charlotte followed, finally finding her gait on the rooftops as she got the hang of how to keep purchase on their surface.

The last house in the row stood on a corner of two minor streets, and a balcony wrapped around the front and side of the building. Natalie slid down the roof, dropping onto the balcony below. Charlotte followed her, feeling the rush of free falling, her heart soaring into her throat. Despite their situation, she landed with a smile on her face.

Natalie had already disappeared, so she hurried to follow her down the trellis that stood against one end of the balcony. After their route so far, the trellis seemed as secure and simple as a staircase, and both girls reached the ground in less than a minute.

"And now," Natalie said, tucking her head down, "we run."

Charlotte didn't have time to catch her breath before they were both off. Pumping her legs as hard as she had ever done in her life, Charlotte flew down the street behind Natalie.

They wove in and out of foot traffic, carts, and carriages as they crossed the city's streets.

When a small dog turned unexpectedly, putting itself in her path, she didn't even break stride. Leaping over it in one smooth motion, she immediately had to duck beneath a giant crate being carried by a man two steps further down the street.

"In here," Natalie panted, turning into yet another narrow alley.

Charlotte followed, acutely aware that their pursuers were in human form this time. A narrow alley wasn't going to foil them.

But the guards had fallen behind, slowed by the need to clamber up and down roofs to follow where the girls had gone. So when they darted out of the alley into another street, there was no one visible behind them.

Natalie looked over her shoulder, checking the street behind them was clear before she swerved suddenly into yet another alley. Charlotte followed, nearly colliding with her three steps in.

Instead of the usual hodgepodge of walls and doors that lined most of the alleys, this one contained one smooth, unbroken wall as if the whole length bordered a single property.

"What—?" she asked, but Natalie was already moving again.

Climbing onto a crate, she strained upward, just managing to reach the top of the wall. "Give me a boost!" she whispered, and Charlotte rushed forward, offering her laced hands as a foothold.

Natalie stepped into her fingers, pushing off and hauling herself over the edge of the wall. Charlotte stepped toward the crate, ready to follow her—or at least attempt to do so—but Natalie's head was still poking over the wall, now on the other side.

"Go further down," she hissed. "I'll meet you there."

Charlotte hesitated, struck with the irrational anxiety that Natalie meant to abandon her. But the girl had been the one to lie in wait for her with a plan for their escape. Charlotte would trust she knew what she was doing.

Running down the alley, she heard footsteps keeping pace on the other side of the wall, reassuring her that Natalie was still with her. As she reached a small door in the stretch of wall, it swung open. Charlotte slid to a stop, panting.

Grabbing at the edge of the wood, she pulled herself through and slammed it closed behind her. Her breaths rasped in and out as she stared at Natalie, the two girls now safely on the other side of the wall together. Laughter bubbled up inside her, pushing its way out, and she doubled over, giggling.

Natalie stared at her doubtfully before giving in and laughing along with her.

"L…Latch it," Charlotte managed to force out, and Natalie leaped into action, securing the door behind them.

They both quieted down, the emotional release giving way to labored breathing that slowly calmed.

Charlotte looked around. "Where are we?"

They stood at the end of a stretch of greenery that was denser and less sculpted than the palace gardens. Some distance away, a large house rose above the green, its crisply painted walls shining in the morning light. Charlotte didn't remember many details of Natalie's family home, but it definitely wasn't this mansion.

"I told you," Natalie said. "My house is too far. This is Count Oswin's city home."

Charlotte whistled softly. "He really is important!" She glanced around, uneasy. "But will he be angry that we turned up like this? What if we led the guards to his house?"

Natalie shrugged. "I checked before we dashed in here. There wasn't anyone in sight."

Charlotte frowned, not quite satisfied. "They might ask around. Someone might have seen us."

"The people of the city won't help Celandine's guards," Natalie said dismissively. "I'm not saying they'd risk their hides to help us, but not getting involved is the safest option anyway, so they'll all say they didn't see anything and get away from the guards as quickly as possible."

Charlotte sighed, having to accept Natalie's greater understanding of the city and its people. She still didn't like involving so many other people in her own folly, though.

She didn't regret the time with Henry, and at least she'd sent Gwen's apple where it needed to go. But in every other regard…She sighed again.

"There's no need for the count to know anything about it, anyway," Natalie said carelessly. "We can just wait here in the garden until the guards give up and go back to the palace and then slip out again."

"No." Charlotte shook her head decisively. "We're here now, and we should go in and find the count. He said everyone in his household is trustworthy, so we don't have to worry about being seen."

Natalie gave her a doubtful look, but Charlotte held firm.

"Thinking I could foresee and control all the variables is what got me into this trouble," she said. "I'm not making the same mistake again. We need to tell him what happened and the danger that someone might trace us here."

"I suppose—if you insist," Natalie said a little sourly. But she made no further protest, leading the way through the garden to the back door of the mansion.

When she went to open it, Charlotte leaned around her with a warning look and knocked on the wooden panel instead. Natalie rolled her eyes but stepped back, crossing her arms and waiting silently.

It didn't take long for footsteps to sound from inside. When the door swung open, the footman on the other side regarded them both with raised brows.

"We don't usually get visitors to the back door," he said.

Charlotte smiled as sweetly as she could manage. "I'm guessing most of your visitors don't come over your back wall."

The footman's brows drew together.

"We're here to see Count Oswin," she hurried to add. "He's not expecting us, but he'll know who we are. You can tell him Charlotte and Natalie are—"

An instant change came over the footman's face when he heard the names. Leaning out, he pulled them both inside and shut the door behind them.

"They'll be glad to see you," he said with an easy grin that took her by surprise. "Come on, I'll show you the way."

GWEN

Waiting for sunset in her room, wondering what was happening to Charlotte, was torturous. But she couldn't go out with the sun so low on the horizon. Being seen around the palace in her bear form would not only enrage her mother but also damage the plans of the rebels.

Gwen had escaped the mountain kingdom and then ridden the wind back to save it, but both sides still wanted her to play a false role as the pure princess—someone whose apparent virtue seemed to involve sitting around waiting and doing nothing at all.

She paced up and down, her thoughts alternating between Charlotte—was she with Henry now?—and Easton—was he thinking of her as much as she was thinking of him? Every now and then she stopped and looked around her room in wonder. It should look different. After all the changes in her, it should look different.

But everything was exactly the same as she'd left it. This was the danger she had recognized earlier. Trapped in the same environment, the new Gwen wavered before the old one.

Walking slowly over to her bureau, Gwen stared down at the various jars, bottles, brushes, and handheld mirrors arranged on its top in an orderly fashion. Half in a dream, she reached out one arm and swept it all off with enough force to send some of the smaller items hurtling into the wall.

They fell with various crashes, bangs, and tinkles as glass smashed and liquid sloshed onto the carpet. The cacophony drove back the dreamlike feeling, and a burst of energy took its place.

She stared at herself in the mirror, a smile growing on her face as she reached up and tugged at the mirror's edges. For a second it resisted before pulling sharply free and crashing against the surface of the bureau. Buzzing, Gwen moved to the wardrobe, ripping its doors open so violently that one of them pulled free of its lower hinge.

She seized the contents in large armfuls, tossing the garments over her shoulder and seizing more until the wardrobe was empty. But it wasn't enough. Bracing one shoulder against the side of the robe, she shoved with all her strength. At first it resisted, but she gritted her teeth and shoved harder. It wobbled once and then crashed over with a muffled thud.

She swept on, upending the bedside cabinet and pulling out all its drawers, tipping over the table and chair where she had eaten countless meals. Gripping the curtains of the bed in both hands, she pulled, reveling in the feeling of them ripping free and collapsing to the ground around her.

As she looked around for something else to overturn, she felt the now familiar itchy tingling, followed by the tearing sensation. She squeezed her eyes shut, waiting for the change to finish. When she opened them again, she looked down at enormous paws and sharp claws and her smile returned.

Turning on the bed, she unleashed her bear strength, ripping through the pillows until feathers floated through the room in all directions. She tore at the bedspread and even the mattress underneath, leaving them in ribbons.

The curtains on the windows came next, and the upholstery on the chairs. Then she turned her claws against the walls themselves, ripping long gouges down the wallpaper.

It felt good to be reckless and even better to use the full strength of this new form. In the days since she had stopped taking the drugged drink each night, she had been so careful and so restrained whenever she was a bear. But now she felt her muscles stretching and straining, and it felt good.

Part of her worried guiltily about destroying items that still had use in them. Some had even been beautiful. But at the same time, she knew she could never sleep in that bed again or sit in one of those chairs. She had been obediently doing so for twenty years, and now they represented nothing but captivity of both her body and mind.

She sat back on her haunches and surveyed the destroyed room with satisfaction. Princess Gwendolyn would never have dared do anything so dramatic and defiant. This was no longer Princess Gwendolyn's room, and Gwen was no longer surrounded by a familiarity she didn't want. Everything about this scene was sharp and uncomfortable and confronting.

She had been ready to endure an uncomfortable night amid the ruin of her room, but her bear self was as comfortable on the carpeted floor as she had been in the forest of Charlotte's valley. She curled up, surrounded by feathers and torn material, and slept as easily as she had under the stars.

Gwen woke, sore and disoriented. It took her a moment to

make sense of the ruin around her, memory returning slowly. Morning had arrived some time ago, and her human body was much less comfortable on the floor than her bear one.

She rose slowly, rubbing at the shoulder that ached from pushing against the wardrobe the evening before. She didn't regret anything, though. It would have been much more terrible to wake in her bed, thinking for those first bleary moments that she was back in her old life as Princess Gwendolyn.

Looking at the window, she realized again that the first hours of the morning were already past. She needed to find out what had happened to Charlotte.

Choosing simple clothes from a bureau drawer that had survived the night's rampage, she dressed and tried her bedroom door. To her relief, it opened. More than anything, that freedom confirmed her mother's retreat into the past—an option Celandine apparently preferred to facing a reality that no longer conformed with her plans.

Gwen's stomach rumbled as she hurried down the courtyard, and her steps turned instinctively for the kitchen. She didn't correct them. If she needed information about any dramatic events in the palace, the captive servants were the best place to start.

Pausing on the threshold, Gwen breathed in the delicious smell of roasting food and baked treats. She admired the bustle of activity, wishing she didn't have to disrupt it. She had always loved the kitchen as a child, going there often with Easton. But she had been restrained to only the most occasional visit in the past ten years—a rule enforced by Alma. Since Alma sought to protect the captives from the queen's wrath, Gwen couldn't argue with her strictures. It had been yet another loss, though.

Thinking of the risk if she was seen by a courtier, Gwen stepped all the way inside, out of clear sight from the corridor. The movement attracted attention, and a ripple spread through the servants as they looked in her direction and whispered among themselves.

Gwen cleared her throat. "I missed breakfast."

A cook offered her a seat at the well-scrubbed wooden table that ran down the center of the room. As she sat, a young man slipped out the kitchen door, taking off at a run.

Sure enough, she had barely started on the food laid before her when Alma appeared, puffing slightly. Her brows rose when she saw the princess, but she took a moment to catch her breath before speaking, giving time for multiple other servants to slip in behind her, mingling with the crowd already in the kitchen.

"So you really are here," Alma said at last. "I suppose I shouldn't be surprised."

A rush of affection filled Gwen at sight of the older woman. She hadn't realized how much she needed a friendly face. But she also didn't want to forget the realization she had come to with Miriam.

She put down the piece of bread in her hand. "I'm sorry. I didn't mean to cause trouble by coming here, I just—"

"No." Alma said the word firmly. "Miriam told us everything. You came back for us, Your Highness, and we can brave more than this. This is our chance." Her face darkened. "Some of us have been waiting a very long time for any sort of chance."

Gwen hoped she didn't look as terrified as she felt. So many people were relying on her, unaware that Gwen had very little idea what she was doing.

"I came to find out if there was any news of Charlotte," she said.

Alma frowned and glanced around the kitchen. She was met only with blank stares and shrugs.

"Is that someone from the city?" she asked. "I don't think there's a courtier named—"

"No, she came with me from the valleys," Gwen said. "She's the lowlander prince's wife."

Another murmur swept through the room at that. The captives might not have heard of Charlotte, but they knew something about Henry.

"Have you been taking him food?" she guessed.

Alma hesitated. "We've been preparing it, but the queen delivers it herself." She paused. "We've heard rumors that he's cursed."

It was clear from the captives' faces that they didn't know what to make of that suggestion. Gwen almost told them it was the opposite—he was the only one to have freed himself —when it hit her like a bolt.

The captives were as ignorant as she had once been. They knew something happened in the mountain kingdom at night but not what. They didn't know about the transformations.

Gwen didn't hesitate. If they were going to join the rebels, they had to know what they faced.

"Actually," she said, "it's not the prince who's cursed, it's me." A gasp of surprise swept around the room. "Me, and my mother, and all the courtiers and guards. We are tied to these mountains because at night we turn into large, white bears."

"You—what?" Alma asked in a dazed voice.

"At sundown I turn into a bear," Gwen repeated calmly. "And at sunrise I turn back again. I'm still myself in my head the whole time, though. We don't turn wild or anything."

"I…" Alma collapsed into a nearby seat. "We've come up with lots of theories over the years, but I can't say anyone came up with that. Every one of us was drugged for the journey across the mountains, so we never saw…"

"It does explain it, though," the cook said. "We wondered how they made it across."

"And some of the messes we've had to clean up make more sense too," a younger woman muttered. "Remember those gouges high up on the wall of the green sitting room? None of us could work out what could have made them."

Gwen thought guiltily of her room. "If any of you have the job of cleaning my room, please skip it today. And tomorrow. And—actually, you can forget about it all together."

Alma raised an eyebrow. "Do I want to know what you've done?"

Gwen smiled. "I'm going with no."

"I thought *you* were going to marry that prince." The cook regarded Gwen skeptically. "We've all been worked off our feet preparing for it. So how can he have a wife?"

Gwen grimaced. "My mother isn't used to having her plans foiled. She's determined to go through with it, and for now at least, we're playing along." Her voice turned firm. "I will not be marrying Prince Henry, however."

Yet another stir ran through the crowd.

"But please continue with your preparations in line with the queen's commands," she said hurriedly. "We'd rather not tip our hand yet."

Facing only Miriam, it had seemed sensible to say nothing. But with the captives massed before her, she couldn't bring herself to treat them with suspicion. They had been stolen from their homes and turned into slaves for the mountain queen—some for almost ten years. The queen had no allies in this room.

"So this Charlotte is part of your plans?" Alma asked shrewdly. "But she's crossed the queen somehow?"

Gwen grimaced. It was a little more complicated than that, but the sentiment was close enough to the truth.

Alma exchanged a look with the cook, waiting for him to nod before turning back to Gwen. "We haven't heard anything about an unknown girl," she said briskly, "but the orders for the prince's food changed late yesterday. We were instructed to deliver a drugged drink, just as we used to do for you."

She gave Gwen an apologetic look as she said it, but Gwen had long forgiven the captives' role in her previous life. They hadn't done any of it by choice.

"He was drugged all night?" she asked, heart sinking. That must mean Charlotte had succeeded in bargaining for a night with Henry. And the queen had found a way around the bargain's terms. Did that mean she'd also found a way around the terms intended to protect Charlotte?

"There definitely hasn't been any talk of preparing food for another captive?" she asked.

The cook and Alma both shook their heads. Did that mean Charlotte had succeeded in getting out of the palace or just that she hadn't been fed yet?

Sighing, Gwen rose. She was going to have to find her mother after all.

Before leaving, she faced Alma and the cook. "Miriam asked what you could do."

They both tensed.

"Please let me know if the queen ever asks you to drug any food or drink again," she finished, and they relaxed. It wasn't a huge request, but it might prevent a future calamity like Charlotte's attempted night with Henry.

Gwen left the room, heading for her mother's study as she considered how to get access to Henry again. If he hadn't spoken to Charlotte, then it was up to Gwen to give him further reassurance and stop him from doing anything foolish.

She arrived at the door of the study only to hear the tromp of boots behind her. Glancing back, she saw a weary-looking squad of guards heading in her direction. She stepped to the side, allowing the two in the lead to enter the study ahead of her. They were both rigid and tense, apparently too distracted to even notice her.

The rest of the guards remained behind in the corridor, at least half of them openly gawking at her. But they didn't make any move to restrain her or question her presence.

"You what?" the queen cried from inside the room, and Gwen flinched instinctively.

The guards flinched even more, however, and Gwen made up her mind, slipping into the room. No one noticed her entrance.

"One girl," the queen said in lower but equally threatening tones. "You only had to detain one girl. Exactly how many men did you take with you?"

Both guards shifted nervously.

"There was another girl waiting for her," one said. "She helped—"

"A single other girl?" the queen demanded. "Is that supposed to be an excuse?"

"Without our bear senses," the other one tried, "we couldn't follow."

"I see." The queen's voice was ice. "So you have allowed

your nightly forms to become a crutch and an excuse. Clearly it is time for the royal guards to get in shape. I want every guard not on active duty to report to the training yards. Sunup to sundown. And you will train there every day until I deem you are no longer a disgrace to me."

The men's eyes widened, but neither protested.

"Yes, Your Majesty." The first one bowed low, and the other quickly followed.

Gwen kept her face impassive but inside she was crowing. Not only had Charlotte managed to escape—with Natalie's help from the sound of it—but the queen's reaction had played even further into their hands. An exhausted, distracted guard force could only help the rebel efforts.

The elation died as she finally noticed the man standing to one side and slightly behind her mother's desk. He was half in shadow, barely noticeable beside the commanding presence of the queen. But he had noticed her.

Gwen shivered at his gaze. What was Lord Rafferty doing here where she might once have expected to find Count Oswin? Before her escape, he had leveraged a moment of surveillance of Gwen into inclusion with her mother's inner circle of courtiers. Apparently, in the weeks since he had made fast use of that opportunity.

The feel of his eyes made her want to flee. But her mother had finally spotted her.

"My daughter," Celandine said smoothly, her manner changing completely.

Both the guards threw Gwen an alarmed look before bowing again toward the queen, a third time to Gwen, and hurrying out of the room.

"Where have you been?" Celandine asked, although she sounded distracted.

"In my room, of course," Gwen replied. "Resting."

The queen relaxed a little at her answer. "You should get all the rest you can now. After the wedding, matters will proceed quickly."

"Matters?" Gwen asked, her eyes flicking to Lord Rafferty.

"The matters we spoke of previously," the queen said in a voice that shut down any further conversation. "But that is not something you need to think of. I will manage the situation."

"Yes, Mother," Gwen said meekly, a little relieved her mother hadn't expanded on her words. Did that mean Lord Rafferty wasn't yet included in all her plans?

If the queen was edging out Count Oswin and replacing him with someone of Lord Rafferty's ilk, then they couldn't make their move fast enough. The queen had enough ambition of her own without listening to someone who obviously had just as much as her.

CHARLOTTE

Exchanging surprised looks, Charlotte and Natalie both followed the count's footman without comment, allowing him to usher them into a brightly lit sitting room filled with people. Charlotte faltered on the threshold, trying to make sense of the gathering.

"Natalie!" Patti rushed to her daughter's side, throwing her arms around her neck.

"Really, Mother!" Natalie sounded disgusted, but Charlotte caught the pleased light in her eyes. She was at that age where she still wanted her mother's affection but wasn't willing to admit it.

"Charlotte! What a relief." Easton crossed more calmly to Charlotte's side, his parents trailing behind him.

"Well, this is good timing," the count said, not sounding altogether pleased. "I was about to head to the palace to see if I could get any word of you."

"How could you leave without telling us?" Patti scolded Natalie. Dane stood at her side, giving his daughter equally disappointed looks.

"We were going to be back by sundown," Natalie replied, seeming unaffected by their disapproval. "But then Charlotte got herself into trouble. Since she came with Princess Gwen and is supposedly married to that lowlander prince at the palace, I figured you wouldn't want me to abandon her to be captured by the queen." She shrugged.

"It's true," Charlotte rushed to say. "Natalie appeared in the nick of time and saved me. I owe her a debt of gratitude."

A soft snort in the background drew her eyes to Natalie's brother.

"Always has to be the hero," Baden muttered, earning himself a fiery look from Natalie.

"I suppose in that case..." Patti seemed torn between indignation at her daughter's behavior and pride at her success.

"Were your meetings with the rebels a success?" Charlotte asked Easton softly while Patti and Dane continued to affectionately chide their daughter.

"I'm afraid the reality of me and my last ten years doesn't quite live up to their imaginings," he said with a self-deprecating grin.

"Nonsense!" Lydia said firmly, her gaze bright as she watched her son. "They loved you."

Jett cleared his throat. "Perhaps not quite that. But they were more than pleased that the time has finally come to move against the queen. And some of them were quite enthusiastic at the prospect of Easton as king. After ten years, they see our family as belonging to the city more than the court, so they're pleased to think of one of their own on the throne."

Easton ran a hand through his hair, and Charlotte could easily recognize the concern on his face because it was the same concern she felt whenever she thought about Henry's true role. Most of the time it was easy to focus on the crisis in front of them, but every now and then she remembered what would happen if they succeeded, and she wanted to run and hide. She had no qualifications to become Crown Princess Charlotte.

Easton lowered his voice, angling himself toward Charlotte. "Did you see Gwen?"

Her lips twitched as she looked at him. "You are aware that everyone here already knows the two of you are in love, right? Our entire plan is literally built around it. You don't have to whisper."

Easton flushed, and she regretted teasing him. The poor man's entire life had been overturned without warning. It was no wonder it took a bit of getting used to.

"I did see her," she said softly. "And she looked well. Unharmed, anyway. And plotting how to work against her mother. She had an object from her godmother." She proceeded to explain about the apple and what she had exchanged it for.

At some point in the story, the rest of the group drifted over, listening as she outlined her failed night with Henry and their escape across the rooftops.

The count shook his head. "That was a very foolish risk."

"I know," Charlotte said quietly. "I'm sorry."

"There's no use trying to tamp down the fervor of youth, Oswin." Jett clapped him on the back. "We'll never succeed at that, so we'll have to content ourselves with channeling it in useful directions."

"I had a chance to speak to him briefly, at least," Charlotte said. "And he promised he'd play along and assist Gwen. So hopefully that was enough..." She trailed off, wishing she'd had time to tell him more of their plans. It would take strong nerves for him to play along all the way to the middle of the wedding ceremony.

"We're relying on the princess, then," Oswin said. "Hopefully she's managing to hold firm against her stepmother."

Charlotte's thoughts snagged on his final word. "Her what?"

The count gave her an odd look. "Queen Celandine, of course."

"No, I know who you mean," Charlotte said. "I just thought…are you saying she isn't Gwen's birth mother? She isn't any blood relation at all?"

Easton also gave her an odd look. "No, she isn't. But she doesn't let anyone talk about it at court and especially not anywhere around Gwen. I didn't even know myself until I was thirteen and overheard my parents mention it. They hadn't told me because they were worried I would tell the princess." His mouth twisted. "I was so incensed that everyone was lying to her that I flew straight off to confront the queen, setting off this whole situation."

"None of it is your fault," his mother murmured, but Easton ignored her, still focused on Charlotte.

"But I'm surprised Gwen didn't mention it to you," he said. "It's the reason she finally defied her mother and escaped."

Charlotte's frown deepened. "I don't think so. It was finding out about being drugged every night and being a bear that pushed her to escape. She's always talked as if Celandine is her…" She trailed off as she reviewed their conversations, skimming over them in her mind, her certainty growing. "Gwen thinks Celandine is the woman who gave birth to her," she said with confidence.

"No, that can't be right," Easton cried. "I'm sure she said…" He too trailed off into thought, and when he spoke again, he sounded uncomfortable. "Or did I just assume she'd found out the same thing I did?"

"What are you both talking about?" the count asked. "I heard her say it with my own ears. Back in that basement hideout, she plainly said Celandine isn't her mother."

"She did say that." Charlotte drew out the words. "But I interpreted it to mean she was rejecting Celandine's role in her life. Don't you remember how nervous she was to say it? Like she was anxious over the rejection." Charlotte's feelings about her own parents had seesawed often enough for her to have recognized the high emotion of the moment.

"You're right." Easton sounded horrified. "She could easily have meant that. And the rest of us just assumed…"

"How is that possible, though?" Charlotte asked. "Why is Celandine queen if she's only a stepmother, and how could it possibly have been kept a secret from Gwen? What has been going on in this kingdom?"

"What hasn't been going on?" Baden muttered, and for once Natalie nodded in agreement.

"I suppose you don't know anything about our history or laws, do you?" Lydia asked.

Charlotte winced apologetically. "In the Four Kingdoms, the mountain kingdom is seen as a myth, if it's thought of at all. I didn't even know it was a real place until Gwen said she came from here."

"Our succession laws are a little complicated," Lydia said. "The oldest child of the previous monarch inherits the throne, but if they marry, they rule jointly with their spouse."

"So if they die, their spouse just becomes the monarch on their own?" Charlotte asked doubtfully.

"Not exactly." Lydia sighed. "If the next heir in line is an adult, the throne passes immediately to them. But if they're a child, then the spouse continues to rule as before until the child comes of age and is able to take the throne themselves."

"Like a regent?" Charlotte asked.

Jett nodded. "But without the limitations of a regency."

"Celandine must have married Gwen's father when Gwen was very young if she doesn't remember anything about it," Charlotte said, trying to puzzle it all out.

"Sadly, Gwen's mother died in childbirth," Lydia said. "Gwen never had the chance to know her. And when Gwen was three, King Isander became ill. The royal doctors could do nothing to prevent his decline, and the king—who loved his daughter very much—decided to take her to spend some time away from court before the end."

"I thought you were all trapped in the mountains?" Charlotte queried.

"They didn't go far," Jett clarified. "Just to a lodge belonging to the royal family that's on the very edge of our valley. In the past, it was used frequently by the royal family as a retreat where they could spend time together without the pressures of court. But it's fallen into disuse since Celandine took the throne. She said too many bad memories resided there for her to take the princess back." He fell silent, and his wife continued the story.

"While they were at the lodge, King Isander's health deteriorated faster than expected, and he died there. The princess was brought back to the castle by Celandine, who claimed to be her stepmother and the queen."

"What?" Charlotte cried, startled. Whatever she had been expecting, it wasn't that. "But everyone at the palace knew her, right? She'd gone down there with them?"

Lydia shook her head. "She met the king during his final weeks at the lodge. He sensed his death was coming sooner than anticipated and proposed marriage so his daughter wouldn't be left alone without a parent. He wanted her to have a proper monarch to take the pressure from her shoulders during her childhood and youth. She had the marriage certificate and the proper seals, and the servants and guards who returned from the lodge all corroborated her story."

Lydia shrugged. "I was busy with a young son at the time, but it seemed just like Isander not to want to abandon his daughter to so many years in a regency. I only wish he had made a better choice for his new wife. He had no idea what misery he was condemning the poor princess to."

"So Celandine turned up, claimed the throne, and then made everyone pretend she was Gwen's real mother?" Charlotte gaped at them. "How is that possible?"

"The loyal guard force she brought with her were persuasive," the count said dryly. "And those of us closest to the king scrutinized the documents closely. There was nothing out of order." He sighed. "If we'd known how it would go, we might have fought harder, but she was charming and persuasive back then, before she'd consolidated her power. And King Isander had consistently refused to name a regent. It had all of us worried, concerned about what would happen in the case of a sudden decline. It made sense to us that he had held off because he had another plan in mind, and none of us relished the power struggle that would eventuate if we had to choose a regent instead. We let it happen, and by the time Celandine made a move—evicting those members of the court most loyal to Isander and replacing them with her own people, her hold had become far too strong to be challenged."

"But someone did eventually challenge it," Jett said ruefully. "A thirteen-year-old boy. And she responded by binding the court to her with an enchantment. No one knew what we were facing twenty years ago."

"That is one massive loophole she exploited," Charlotte breathed. "But Gwen's been an adult for years. Why is Celandine still queen?"

The count sighed. "Celandine has always ruled with the expectation that she would eventually hand over to Gwendolyn. That was part of the reason she was initially accepted. But she has played the enchantment to her advantage, always coming up with a plausible excuse for why Gwendolyn isn't ready to take the throne. Marriage to a prince, along with the destruction of the enchantment, was supposed to be an end to any possible excuses. She'll have to step down. Or at least, she should be forced into it. Knowing her, though, I'm sure she has some further plan to delay the handover of power."

"Something Gwen said gave me the impression she did mean for Gwen to take the throne after her wedding," Charlotte said thoughtfully. "She meant to install her as a puppet queen. I guess she had to make sure Gwen was sufficiently beaten down before taking that risk."

Easton winced, his face lined with pain. He had been gone for the past ten years, but he must have seen enough in the ten years before that to know what Charlotte was talking about.

"And we just sent her back there," he murmured under his breath. "Alone. And now it turns out she doesn't even know the truth. Celandine has never acted as a true mother to her, and she didn't birth her either. Gwen has no ties to her and owes her no loyalty. But Gwen is the only one who doesn't know that."

He blew out a breath, straightening. "I have to go to her."

"No!" his mother cried. "It's too risky! What if the queen sees you?"

"I don't care," he said, his voice granite. "I'm not abandoning her to that place for a second time. Not knowing the truth makes her vulnerable. I should have gone to her and told her the truth immediately after I found it out. I've spent ten years regretting that, and I'm not going to regret making the same mistake again. I have to find her and make sure she knows everything."

He scanned the room. "If none of you will help me, at least don't try to stop me."

"I'll help you," Charlotte said quietly.

Gwen had helped her get to Henry, and now she would help Gwen's beloved find his way to her.

GWEN

This time, Gwen didn't return straight to her room. She couldn't bear to be shut up in there for endless more hours, just waiting. But neither did she want to endanger the servants by seeking them out. Which left her once again alone, walking the corridors she had roamed so often.

But these weren't just halls she had once walked alone. They were also the play spaces where she had run with Easton, and she chose to think of him as she walked instead of dwelling on the painful, solitary years. Without him and Nanny, her life would have been only one long stretch of bleak darkness. The two of them had saved her, and now she was choosing to return to the Gwen they had helped form. The Gwen she wanted to be.

When her steps finally circled back to her room, she slipped inside with a soft sigh. She couldn't avoid the mess she'd made forever.

The chaos assaulted her vision, distracting her enough that she missed the flash of motion from one side. A hand clamped over her mouth, stifling her scream, and a strong arm circled her shoulders, pulling her firmly back against a solid chest.

She thrashed, trying to maneuver her teeth for a bite until the words in her ear permeated her brain.

"Gwen! Gwen! It's me. It's Easton."

She stilled instantly. Easton? Was it possible? She had spent half the day dreaming of him, so was it possible she was dreaming this too?

But she could feel the solid warmth of him, goosebumps rising where his breath brushed behind her ear. He was real. He was there.

She slumped in the circle of his arm, her eyes welling with tears. Easton immediately dropped his arm, instead taking her shoulders and spinning her so he could see her face.

"Gwen?" His voice was rough and his face drawn. "What is it? What's wrong? Are you hurt?"

She managed a tremulous smile, drinking in the sight of him. His face was somehow afraid, angry, and achingly beautiful all at the same time. She had never seen such a welcome sight.

"I'm sorry," she managed to choke out. "I'm fine. Really. Just glad to see you."

Easton glanced around the room, his eyes coming back to hers. "I didn't dare wander the palace looking for you, but when I saw what had happened here..." He shuddered. "I've been going out of my mind waiting in this room!" He pointed at one of the walls. "Those are claw marks, Gwen! Don't try to claim they aren't."

Gwen bit her lip guiltily. "That was me. In a fit of...defiance? Rejection of my past? It wasn't exactly rage, but..." She shrugged.

Easton finally let go of her shoulders, falling back a step

and laughing. "It was you? You did this?" He looked at the mess with new eyes, his lips twitching. "I approve. I just wish I'd been here to join in. I always hated this room. I hated the thought of you stuck in here all the time."

Gwen smiled. "But it brought you to me today. You knew where to find me." Her smile fell away as reality intruded. "But what are you doing here? You shouldn't be here!"

Easton swallowed, the light dimming from his eyes. "I had to see you. There's something I have to tell you."

Gwen's heart seized. Was he here to tell her that being king was a burden too heavy for him to accept? Was he going to say he was pulling out of the plan?

He stepped forward and took both her hands in a gentle grip. She wanted to prod him to hurry up and say what he was going to say, while at the same time she wanted to beg him not to say it.

When he hesitated, she nearly pulled her hands away, unable to bear the tension. But he gave her fingers a squeeze, and her heart calmed. Easton of all people wouldn't desert her. Somehow they would find their way through this—whatever it was.

"Ten years ago, I made a horrible mistake," he said. "I learned something about the queen—about you—and I went to her to confront her instead of coming to you. I've regretted it ever since."

"You said that back in Ranost," Gwen said, frowning. "Surely you don't think I blame you for that?"

He let one of her hands go, raking his fingers through his hair. "When I said that in Ranost I thought—I assumed—you'd discovered the same truth I discovered ten years ago. But I just learned from Charlotte that you probably don't know it after all." He swallowed. "I couldn't leave you here believing a lie. After everything that woman has done to you, I couldn't leave you even the tiniest bit more vulnerable to her."

Gwen frowned, utterly lost. "What are you talking about? What did you find out ten years ago?"

"She isn't your mother." Easton spat out the bald words. "Celandine is your stepmother, not your birth mother. It's just another one of the secrets she forced the court to keep from you."

Gwen's mouth dropped open. "What are you talking about? Are you saying I'm not really the princess?"

"What? No!" He groaned. "I'm fumbling this. Your parents were king and queen when you were born, but your mother died in childbirth. Celandine was King Isander's second wife."

"I..." Gwen's head spun. "I don't..."

She staggered and Easton rushed to right a toppled chair for her. Its upholstery was torn, but Gwen sank onto it anyway, raising a hand to her head.

"Celandine is my stepmother." She said the words slowly, like she was trying to absorb them. "My father's second wife." She looked up at Easton, lost. "Why would she lie about something like that?"

He shrugged uneasily. "To ensure your loyalty maybe? She's obsessed with loyalty."

"Is that why she didn't come with us to the lodge?" she muttered. "Did my father leave her back at the castle because she wasn't my real mother?"

"What?" Easton frowned at her.

It was her turn to shrug. "It's a little thing, really, but I always wondered. I don't have any memories of my father before his final illness—I was too young. I don't remember anything from before that at all. My earliest memories are of that trip to the lodge, so I've thought of it often since. I remember his death so clearly. I guess it's the sort of thing that sticks with you." She shivered.

Easton didn't say anything, his expression turned soft and compassionate, so she kept talking. "I was so excited to be by myself with him, but at the same time I was terrified because I somehow knew he was going to leave me. I don't think anyone had told me directly, but I knew. When he died, I cried and cried. I thought I was going to be left all alone in the world. I can still remember the relief when Celandine walked into the room and picked me up."

She scrubbed a hand over her eyes. "She used to get so angry when I tried to bring up that time and those memories, so I quickly stopped talking about it altogether. But I always thought it was a little strange. I remember the relief of her arrival so vividly, but it wasn't attached to any feelings of love. I wasn't glad to see her specifically, I was just glad someone was there." Her voice dropped. "I thought there must be something broken inside me because what sort of small child doesn't love their mother? I tried so hard to find memories of her from before the lodge trip, sure I would feel the love in those, but I could never recall anything from before. And all the time, I wondered why she wasn't on the trip with us. If she had been, I would have remembered her, and that meant so much to me—to remember my mother from before."

She sighed. "I have this memory of Count Oswin—a much younger version of him—telling me how much my father wanted to spend time just with me. It made me feel so guilty. I was the reason my mother missed out on my father's final weeks. And I always wondered if maybe I'd been the one to insist she didn't come—because I didn't love her the way I loved my father. Maybe that's why she's always been so cold toward me ever since."

"I remember how hard you tried to love her when you were a child." Easton stared at her. "I couldn't understand it given the way she treated you. Is that why?"

Gwen nodded. "But this information changes those memories completely. The love wasn't there because I didn't even know Celandine. She wasn't my mother, she was almost a stranger!" Her brow creased. "But when did she marry my father? They must have been newlyweds. How could he have left her behind?"

"Your memories must be mixed up," Easton said. "Celandine was there at the lodge—that's where you both met her. They were married at the lodge only a week or so before King Isander's death."

Gwen stared at him, fresh shock washing through her. "Are you saying she wasn't part of the court?"

"Apparently not. My parents said they'd never heard of her before she appeared after the king's death with you in tow."

Gwen swallowed, her mind whirring. "She appeared at court and claimed to have married my father on his deathbed and *everyone just believed her?*" Her voice rose at the final words, and concern sprang into Easton's eyes.

Gwen leaped to her feet. She was shaking again, but she no longer felt weak. Instead, she blazed with fury.

"She had their marriage certificate and all the relevant papers," Easton said uneasily. "And while there were minimal servants and guards at the lodge—that's its purpose—the ones who were there all backed up her story. The count said…" He trailed off, brows lowering further and further as he watched her face.

"I told you I have no memories of court from before my father's death," Gwen said slowly and carefully, "but I clearly remember the weeks at the lodge. I've gone over and over those memories a thousand times in the years since. My father was desperate to spend every minute with me. He had a little bed set up by the window of his room so we never had to be parted. I was with him every moment, except when his manservant was helping him wash. *And I never saw Celandine until she walked into the room after his death.*" She enunciated each word of her final sentence carefully and clearly.

"Are you saying…" Easton began, and Gwen finished for him.

"If Celandine didn't marry my father *before* we went to the lodge, she never married him at all."

Easton fell back several steps, his face paling. "So it's…all a lie? The whole thing? Not just being your birth mother but being the queen? Everything!"

Fresh fury ripped through Gwen. "No wonder she wouldn't let me talk about my father's final weeks and refused to ever take us back to the lodge! And no wonder she had everyone lie to me. She must have been terrified about what I might say. She must have either bought off the servants and guards at the lodge or used an object to enchant them, but I was the one witness she couldn't buy."

"So instead she tried to undermine, silence, and manipulate you." Easton's fury now matched her own. "If only we'd had this conversation ten years ago. We could have confronted her together in front of the court and—"

Gwen suddenly deflated, the righteous anger draining out of her. "And what? You said she has papers and witnesses and what do I have? I have no proof."

"But still! How could she—"

Gwen took his hands, silencing him. "Thank you," she said simply. "Thank you for coming here. Thank you for understanding how important the truth would be to me. You don't know how much it means to me that you came despite the risks. That woman has never been a nurturer to me, and so I've been trying to cut the remaining ties in my mind, trying not to think of her as my mother, but…" She sighed. "It's been hard. I'm fighting so many years of ingrained habits. But now I know it's not only her treatment of me that disqualifies her. She's not my birth mother either, and nor is she even my step-mother. She's literally just a usurper who has spent twenty years stealing the people, relationships, and position that should have been mine."

"Gwen…" Easton looked down into her face, his eyes growing warm. "I—"

Gwen's hand flew to his mouth, silencing him as her eyes grew wide.

"Did you hear that?" she whispered, glancing around frantically for somewhere to hide. "There was a step!"

The door handle rattled, and her heart stopped. Pushing Easton violently to the floor, she scooped up a long, torn curtain and flung it over him. She had just pulled the corner over his left boot when the door was pushed open.

She straightened and spun toward the new arrival, hoping it was Alma or Miriam.

It wasn't.

GWEN

Queen Celandine—the usurper—strode into the room and faltered. Her eyes widened as she surveyed the chaos. Gratitude flooded Gwen that she had so effectively destroyed her room. She could never have hidden Easton in time otherwise.

And the physical evidence of her defiance no longer mattered. Given what she had just learned, there was no way she could have faked her old self and called Celandine mother. She could barely even look at her.

"What happened here?" Celandine stared from the mess to Gwen.

Gwen shrugged. "I did some redecorating."

"*Redecorating?*" Celandine's eyes narrowed. "Are you trying to tell me something, Gwendolyn?" she hissed.

Gwen met her eyes steadily. "I suppose I am. I'm telling you I don't want any of this from you. All I want is my throne."

Celandine's nostrils flared, but for once she didn't have a ready quip.

"I'll go ahead with this wedding you have planned," Gwen continued, "and then I'll take the throne that is owed me." She paused and smiled sweetly. "Unless you think the wedding isn't such a good idea after all?"

Celandine let out a heavy breath. "Is that what this is about? You think if you throw a tantrum, I'll cancel the wedding? Do you really have so little ambition? Arcadia could soon be yours, and the rest of the Four Kingdoms after it."

"Don't you mean yours?" Gwen asked. "The Four Kingdoms will be yours. Why would I want that?"

Celandine threw her eyes toward the ceiling. "You'll be the one sitting on the throne with every luxury you can ask for! Don't talk as if I'm planning to lock you in a dungeon."

She looked ready to do just that, so Gwen moderated her tone, aware that she was not only walking a fine line, but that Easton was one wrong step away from discovery. She needed to get Celandine out of her room.

"And why should I believe that?" Gwen asked. "I'm twenty-three, and so far you've done nothing but talk about me sitting on the throne one day."

Celandine relaxed the slightest bit, and Gwen felt a surge of satisfaction from knowing she had said the right thing.

"This time is different, my dear," the queen said. "I held off in the past only because I was waiting for the perfect moment. And that perfect moment has now arrived. You will free our people and then lead them to their glorious future. No one will dare challenge us then."

Her eyes lit with fervor, and Gwen felt an unfamiliar pang of sympathy for her. Celandine was broken in ways Gwen hadn't been able to recognize as a child. And although they had lived side by side for twenty years, Gwen would probably never know what pain from her past had broken her.

But that new awareness changed nothing. Celandine had destroyed countless lives, and there was no place for her in the mountain kingdom. A deep weariness gripped Gwen. She wished it could have been different—that Celandine could have broken the cycle of pain instead of inflicting it on Gwen. But all Gwen could do was resolve that she would be the one to forge a different future. If she was blessed with children one day, she would make sure they knew every day that they were loved and valued.

"Fine," she said, injecting the word with the youthful petulance she had never dared show in her younger years. "But if you're not true to your word this time, you won't like the results."

Celandine looked like she was barely refraining from rolling her eyes as she assured Gwen of the glorious future before her.

"I'm tired," Gwen muttered, staring pointedly at the door.

Celandine's eyes narrowed, but she seemed to think better of whatever rebuke hovered on her tongue. Instead, she swept silently out of the room.

Gwen watched her go in astonishment. She had always been the one restraining herself in her mother's presence. It was surreal to see that reversed.

When the door closed behind the queen, she waited a breath and then two and three. But the door didn't swing back open, the footsteps retreating away down the corridor.

"You can come out," she said on a long exhale.

Easton burst up from the floor, sucking in gulps of air. "I was afraid to even breathe in case she saw the curtain moving. I've been doing a delightful experiment on just how shallow you can make your breaths without passing out."

Gwen winced. "Sorry. I'm just glad we managed to hide you in time. That was way too close."

"Do you have a key for your door?" He eyed the lock dubiously.

"Sadly, no. I used to, but she changed the lock while I was gone."

Easton surveyed the room as if looking for a more comfortable hiding place. Unfortunately Gwen's destruction of the room had removed most of the options.

"Wait!" she said. "How could I forget?" Walking across to the wall, she pressed on a spot at hand height, revealing a hidden latch.

Easton's eyebrows rose. "How did I never notice that door? It's just like all the storage cupboards around the palace corridors—designed to blend in with the wall but not so well disguised as to classify as a hidden room. But why would the princess have a storage cupboard in her bedchamber?"

Gwen smiled wistfully. "We used to love playing spies in those cupboards. This room isn't for storage, though. It's the sleeping space for a servant. When I was a child, Nanny slept in here so I was never alone." She stepped involuntarily back as she remembered what it had been used for after Nanny's death.

Easton stepped into the small space, peering around. When Nanny had been alive, Gwen had loved to sneak in there and burrow into Nanny's bed, insisting she read her stories or brush her hair. But after Nanny died, the queen had used the space for Gwen's punishments, and she hadn't volun- tarily stepped inside for years. Once she had become so compliant the punishments had stopped, she had managed to push the memory of the room almost completely from her mind.

"It's not much bigger than those storage cupboards," Easton noted, and Gwen felt a rush of guilt. "There's barely room for a cot in here."

As a child it had merely seemed cozy, and she'd never questioned why she had such an excessively large room while Nanny had a tiny one. It was only after the woman was gone, when Gwen was older, that she started asking questions like that.

Easton smiled and held out a hand to her. "We can talk in here. That way if anyone comes, you only have to dash out and close the door on me."

Gwen reluctantly stepped inside, waiting for the panic to overtake her. But it didn't come. With the door open and Easton at her side, the space had transformed back into the cozy haven of her young childhood. She breathed a sigh of relief.

"I still miss Nanny sometimes," Easton said with a sigh. "She was always as kind to me as she was to you."

Gwen swallowed against the looming tears. "I miss her all the time. But I'm also glad she wasn't around to see what happened with my mo—Celandine. She would have been heartbroken at the way she treated me. And if she had spoken up in my defense and Celandine punished her, I would have been beside myself."

"I always felt that way when she punished you," Easton said, his voice soft and warm and laced with regret. "I used to dream of racing in to rescue you, but…"

"You did rescue me." Gwen took his hand, raising it to her cheek. "You were everything to me."

His cheeks warmed beneath her touch, his eyes riveted on her face. "You were the beautiful princess from a fairy story and also my best friend. It never felt quite real to me," he whispered. "There isn't a day that's gone by since we were parted when I haven't thought of you."

"Me either," she whispered back.

"Gwen." The word sounded torn from him.

It hit her heart with a shot of pain. For her, being back in his presence was nothing short of beautiful and miraculous. Every moment felt precious.

But he sounded broken and unsure. If he truly didn't want the life here, she couldn't tie him to it because of his feelings for her. If she let him do that, he would come to resent her and that would be the worst thing of all.

So how could she be sure of his true feelings? He would never want to hurt her, and neither would he abandon an entire kingdom—his kingdom.

He wouldn't lie to you, a voice said inside, and she recognized it instantly as the truth. If she wanted to know how he truly felt, she only had to ask. But that required the courage to hear the answer.

She drew a breath, willing herself to say the words, but his eyes were no longer on hers. They had dropped to her lips, and Gwen could no longer remember the sentence she was trying to form in her mind. All she could think about was their close proximity, the warmth of his hand against her cheek, and the way his eyes darkened as they looked at her.

Here in this private, close space, it felt like the rest of the world had disappeared. Like their problems no longer existed, and there was only the two of them and the vast ocean of love and belonging that tied them together.

"Gwen," he murmured again, his voice even more ragged, although this time it was a different sort of torment in his voice.

"Easton," she breathed back, angling her face up toward him.

He sucked in a breath and bent to press his lips to hers, his free hand circling her waist while his other one continued to cup her face.

Their first kiss had burned bright and hot, the culmination of years of separation and longing. It had shaken Gwen's carefully guarded heart apart. This second one filled her, mending the lost and lonely corners inside her. With Easton, she was never alone. With Easton she belonged.

She wanted it to go on forever, but he broke it off, his chest heaving with sharp breaths as he leaned his forehead against hers.

"Gwen," he whispered for a third time, and this time it was warm and loving. She wanted to hear him say her name like that every day for the rest of her life.

Awareness rushed back in as she remembered the unsettled matters between them, the unspoken topics that needed to be discussed. She had already known Easton felt enduring affection for her and also desire. But she needed to know if that was enough for a future. She didn't have the luxury of choosing her career, and neither would her husband. They would both be chained to a demanding role that they could never put down, never rest from.

Gwen gently pushed him away, knowing she needed distance if she was going to manage the conversation that had to happen. Easton's brows drew together, his expression bereft. He reached for her, but she shook her head.

"Easton, I have to know," she said. "And I'm trusting that you won't lie to me."

His jaw flexed. "I would never lie to you," he replied, and she believed him.

"I know. I trust that." She drew a deep breath. "And that's why you have to tell me the truth—even if you think it will hurt me. Even if you think others might suffer for it."

"Gwen, you're scaring me." He tried to step toward her again.

She shook her head, and he froze, watching her with concern.

"I know you care about me, Easton." She hated the wobble in her voice. "But that doesn't mean you should be forced into marrying me—forced into becoming king—before you've even had a chance to properly consider the matter. We hadn't been reunited for even a full day before you were being asked to commit to me for life. That's too much! I know it's too much. And I'm afraid you'll say yes because you know how much it matters to the kingdom. But I can't bear to see you tied to me because of that."

"That's what's been bothering you?" He laughed, relief and something less certain in the sound. "Gwen, I knew I wanted to grow up and marry you when we were thirteen. I just didn't think anyone would let me, given you were the princess. I've spent ten years wishing there was a way to come home to my family—home to you. You are home to me, Gwen, and I care about that far more than I care about what I do or what role I fill. If you needed me to build a house for you and bring home wood every day for our fire, I would do it without a second thought. And if you need me to put on a crown for you, I'll do that with equal gladness. One thing the years in Ranost taught me is that I can find experiences to enjoy and fulfilling tasks anywhere and in any job. But without the people I love, they'll always feel a little empty."

He gave a low laugh. "You're asking me to become royalty, Gwen! It might be a burden, but it's not a hardship. I love this kingdom, and I would gladly serve it even if it wasn't you asking it of me."

A weight lifted off Gwen, and she felt so light she wondered at the fact she didn't float straight out of the door and bob around on the ceiling of her bedchamber.

"It's you I'm worried about," he said in a low voice, bringing her back to the ground. "You answered the count so quickly, so certain of your feelings for me, and I can't help but wonder…"

He hesitated, and she waited, having no idea what he could be concerned about. Her feelings for Easton had never wavered.

"You loved me when we were children, but you barely know me as a man! The queen kept you so isolated that it's no wonder you clung to the memory of our friendship. How do you know your feelings aren't just childish leftovers that will wither and die under the pressure of daily life?"

Gwen wanted to instantly protest, but she forced herself to consider the question. It was a valid one.

"You're right that we missed a lot of years," she said softly. "And there are so many things to relearn about each other—things I want to know about your life in those missing years. But even one day was enough to see that you were still you. And I never loved you just because you were the only boy I knew. Back then you were honest and loyal, and you still are. You're still brave and outspoken—but you won't hesitate to apologize when you know you're in the wrong. I've watched the court for enough years to know what a rare combination that is. You're confident without pushing yourself forward, and you're always thinking of me." She gave a cheeky smile. "I'm only human. I can't help but find that attractive."

Easton laughed, the sound freer than it had been before. "If you keep going with that list, you're going to make me blush."

"How about you kiss me instead?" Gwen suggested, her eyes sparkling. "Because as far as I'm concerned, this is the true moment of our engagement."

Easton wrapped both arms around her waist, but he continued to lean back, gazing down at her face.

"You're really sure, Gwen? It still feels a little hard to believe. You really want me?"

She nodded, emotions rising up to clog her throat.

"In that case," he murmured, "will you marry me, most beautiful of princesses?"

"Of course," she said on a shaky laugh.

"There," he said with satisfaction. "*Now* we're truly engaged."

She wrapped her hands around the back of his head, standing on her tiptoes and dragging his lips down to hers. He came without protest, and for a long time they stayed lost in each other.

But when the warm light on the floor of her chamber crept all the way to the door of their hidden room, she reluctantly stepped back from his arms.

"It's getting late," she said. "And you need to leave."

"Gwen," he sounded dazed and reluctant, and she understood his distaste at the idea of parting. But she wouldn't put him in danger.

"It's too dangerous for you to stay here," she said firmly. "And you can't travel through the city at night. You need to go now while you can still creep out safely. Once everyone turns into bears, someone might smell you."

He grimaced but didn't protest again. And at least she was able to accompany him through the corridors, checking around each corner for him and guiding him to the nearest door. He told her not to come outside, though, pointing out that he could more easily creep unseen through the gardens alone.

She had been the one to insist he leave, but it was still painful to watch him go. Words to call him back kept rising to her tongue, nearly escaping. But she bit down on them and held them inside. They were in a desperate fight for their future and their happiness, and she couldn't let a moment's weakness ruin everything.

CHARLOTTE

They had returned to Natalie's house, but Natalie herself had disappeared somewhere. As Patti plied them all with endless cups of tea, Charlotte tried not to worry about what trouble the girl was getting into.

Charlotte felt out of place, aware that she was being treated more frostily since she had returned from the palace without Easton. But her diversionary efforts had only been required to help get him into the building. He had assured her that once inside, he knew every corridor, cranny, and hiding place. That didn't mean she would breathe easily until he returned safely, however—preferably with good news about Gwen. She didn't even blame his parents for assigning her some of the blame for his foolhardy decision to breach the palace. They had only just been reunited, and now he had placed himself straight into danger again.

She had positioned herself in a corner, as out of the way as possible, while she watched Patti and Lydia work together seamlessly, ferrying hot drinks and preparing the evening meal. Lydia in particular fascinated her. Lydia had once been a courtier, but she seemed to have adjusted to life as an ordinary citizen. Could Charlotte do the same in reverse? Would she one day be as comfortable in a palace—on a throne—as Lydia was in a kitchen?

The sound of the front door banging open made her sit up, half-hopeful, half-scared. But the sounds that emerged from the front hall were welcoming, and she sank back against the sofa.

Easton appeared in the sitting room doorway, still slightly out of breath, as if he'd run through half the city to get to them before sunset. He endured exclamations, hugs, and scoldings from both Lydia and Patti before he noticed Charlotte sitting quietly in the corner. He gave her a meaningful nod, his face serious but his eyes bright, and a further knot of tension released inside her. He wouldn't look like that unless Gwen was all right.

His safe return changed the tone in the whole house. No one sent her looks of recrimination anymore, and further new arrivals—including Count Oswin, his son, and numerous rebels Charlotte didn't recognize—only increased the buzz in the atmosphere. And best of all, Charlotte even saw Natalie slip in, unnoticed in the chaos except by Charlotte and Baden.

"Thank goodness," Baden muttered to his sister. "Mother was starting to talk about sending me out to look for you."

Natalie rolled her eyes. "As if you would have been able to find me."

"That's what I tried to tell her," he replied, unoffended by her response.

Patti finally noticed her daughter's arrival, pulling her in to help with the evening meal, and Charlotte went with them. In the kitchen, surrounded by women who worked around and over each other, their voices and hands overlapping as they prepared a last-minute feed for a crowd, she could almost pretend she was back home in the valleys. The mountain people might be the stuff of fairy tales, but they gathered together and shared meals to mark significant occasions just as the valley folk did. She only wished Henry was there with her. As it was, she kept looking over her shoulder, half-expecting to see him. Without him present, something essential was missing.

When the count and his son transformed into bears, there was only a small ripple of unease among the rebels present which spoke of how much the two of them were trusted. And when everyone had eaten their fill, they gathered back in the sitting room, faces turning serious. There weren't enough seats for everyone—especially with the count and his son in their bear forms—so Charlotte wedged herself into a corner, content to sit on the floor. This had been their fight long before it was hers, and while they were allies, they had different final goals.

As quiet finally settled on the room, everyone having found a place, Charlotte noticed the way everyone's attention turned to Easton. He was a recent arrival just like her, but he belonged here in a way she didn't. Already the rebels were looking to him as much as Count Oswin as their leader. Clearly they had accepted the idea of him as future king.

"I spoke to the princess," he said, his voice grave. "And I learned something important." He paused and everyone stayed silent, attentive. "Celandine's reign is illegitimate. She never married King Isander. She was never truly queen."

Murmurs and exclamations swept the group. Charlotte felt no great surprise, though. She had only heard the story of the king's marriage earlier that day, and unfettered by years of accepting it as truth—especially knowing what they did now of Celandine—the whole tale had sounded implausible to her.

"Does the princess have proof?" asked a rebel Charlotte didn't know.

Easton shook his head, his expression grim. "Unfortunately not. She only pieced it all together today after finally discovering Celandine isn't her mother. She knows the story isn't true because she remembers their visit to the lodge. She was with her father the whole time, and Celandine wasn't there like she claimed she was. But twenty-year-old memories aren't proof."

"They're proof enough for me," someone muttered, and several people called out agreement.

"It's enough for me, too," Easton said. "But it isn't enough to march into the palace right now and remove her from the throne. I hope we can use the information, though. It's another tool to sway the court when we make our move."

Heads nodded in all directions.

"I also got confirmation that the wedding is planned for the day after tomorrow," he said. "Which means we need to start planning how we get ourselves into the palace. From what I've learned, we won't want to leave it until the last minute. At the moment, the queen is busy punishing her guards for failing to catch Charlotte."

Heads briefly turned in her direction, and she managed an awkward smile.

"She has them training from sunup to sundown," Easton continued, "which means there are only the standard patrols in the gardens, and they're tired and making sloppy mistakes. But it will be different on the wedding day itself. Every guard will be on duty, watching the perimeter of the gardens and the palace. And they'll all be on high alert since they'll be released from the extra training if the wedding goes smoothly."

"So we need to get in the day before," Jett said, leaning forward. "Tomorrow. We need our whole force concealed in the palace before sundown the day before the wedding."

"Is that even possible?" Dane asked doubtfully.

Count Oswin exchanged a look with his son. "I think I can help with that. It can be done."

"Wait." Jett held up his hand. "Don't say any more details now. I trust you know what you're doing, and the less we all know ahead of time the better."

He cast a look around the group, and Charlotte expected to hear protests or at least looks of discontent at the implication they weren't trustworthy. But all she saw were grim nods of approval. Apparently after twenty years, the rebels were past personal affront, their focus only on the success of their mission.

They discussed who would be present and how large a force they would need, the conversation washing over Charlotte since she recognized none of the names. The rebels who lived nearby started leaving, willing to brave the city at night if they lived in the neighboring streets.

As each one left, Easton and the count took them aside, murmuring at what time and from which direction they should enter the palace grounds the next day. From the occasional overheard whisper, Charlotte gathered they would be trickling in forces all day rather than risk a larger group attracting attention.

Others—those who lived in different parts of the city— were staying the night. They still gave their farewells and received their information, however, departing for the beds prepared for them on the upper story.

Eventually, Charlotte was once again alone with the original core group.

"Is it really that simple?" she asked.

The count sighed. "I imagine the reality will be anything but simple, but there's only so much we can prepare in advance."

"Talking about preparing in advance..." Patti hauled herself to her feet. "We'd better do some preparations for the morning meal now." She gave her husband a significant look before seizing an arm of each of her children. "You can all help me."

Both Natalie and Baden protested, but she swept them firmly from the room, her husband trailing behind. Charlotte threw a confused look at Easton, but it was the count who explained.

"They're going to stay behind tomorrow," he said. "If something goes wrong, we need someone left who can coordinate whatever rebel forces remain."

"Jett and I want to be with our son," Lydia said softly, "but Natalie is only fourteen, and Rebecca is even younger. Patti and Dane want to keep their children here safe, and we understand that."

"And we're needed more than they are, anyway," Easton said. "None of the city rebels know the palace like me and my parents do. We'll be the ones to meet each incoming pair and lead them to the hiding place." He looked at the count. "Which means we need to know where it is."

"My son's apartment," the count said immediately. "It's large enough to fit everyone."

"And it won't be suspected?" Easton asked skeptically.

"You wouldn't be aware since you haven't been here," the count said, "but this is the first time my son has been at any rebel meeting. He's been part of our cause from the beginning, but the queen has been starting to grow suspicious of me—something I have long feared was coming. In preparation for such an eventuality, my son and I have cultivated the appearance that we've fallen out and barely tolerate each other. Most of the court believe we only maintain any contact because of Emmett. Everyone knows I wouldn't do anything to risk losing contact with my grandson. As a result, while Celandine has started excluding me where possible in the last weeks, my son still holds his position of respect as the leader of the trading groups that cross the mountains."

Charlotte turned a disapproving look on the younger man who had been almost silent the entire evening. She didn't appreciate working with someone responsible for snatching innocent valley folk to become slaves for the queen. Easton was regarding him with the same cold look and visible shame washed over the nobleman.

"I'm not unaware of my own wrongdoing," he said in a low voice. "In the early days, I thought..." He sighed. "It doesn't matter what I thought. But I came to realize my mistake and —" He turned to Easton. "Ask your princess. She can confirm there haven't been any new captives for a long time."

"Except for Henry," Charlotte said, ice in her voice.

The count's son—whose name she didn't even know, she realized—looked at her guiltily.

"That's different," he said. "He wasn't intended as a long-term captive. We thought he would break the enchantment and allow us to free everyone—the mountain people and the valley captives—from the queen. We didn't know—" He glanced at Easton and grimaced.

"We've done the best we can," the count said firmly. "And, more importantly, we're doing our best now to fix our mistakes. If you want to insist on retribution anyway, we all might suffer."

Charlotte deflated, her cheeks flushing. She was the last person who should be raking someone over the coals for past mistakes. The pressure of Henry's arms around her and the feel of his lips on hers filled her mind. When he had woken to find her with him in the palace, there had been no lingering trace of judgment in his eyes for her own colossal mistake.

Easton nodded. "If the mountain kingdom is going to have a new future, we can't begin with a pointless game of assigning blame. Celandine is the problem, and we all need to be focused on removing her and her loyal guards from power."

"What about the remaining loyal members of court?" the count's son asked, his voice tentative. Charlotte wondered how many of them were his friends.

"The newest piece of information about the illegitimacy of Celandine's reign should help in their case," Easton said. "I believe that when they realize they were tricked, it will be enough to sway them into accepting the reality of the change of power."

Both Count Oswin and his son relaxed. Had they been worrying about a bloodbath after Gwen took the throne? If so, they didn't know her very well. Charlotte herself had only known Gwen for a short time, but she knew such vengeful violence wasn't in her nature. Gwen had cared for Charlotte from the moment they met, even when they were virtual strangers.

"What about the queen?" Jett asked. "Do we have a way to restrain her during the change in the ceremony? Because without that..."

"Actually, Gwen has a plan for that," Charlotte said,

thinking of the apple. "She's found a way to make use of her stash of godmother objects."

"Excellent," the count said briskly. "In that case, we'll find a way to make contact with the princess once everyone is safely hidden in the palace. We would have needed to do that anyway."

"There's one last matter," Jett said. "We didn't want to mention it with the broader group in case anyone became overenthusiastic and started spreading hints too early. But it would be best if we can include the people of the city in the changeover of power—and not just the prominent citizens invited to the wedding. I'm picturing a crowd who could burst into the palace in support of Queen Gwendolyn at the optimal moment."

The count and his son exchanged a look, brows knit. Rousing the inhabitants of the city was outside their area of influence.

"We can help with that!" Natalie burst into the room, dragging Baden with her.

The rest of the adults gave her disapproving looks, but Charlotte just grinned. Of course Natalie had been lurking in the corridor, listening. Was there anything surprising in that? The girl didn't believe in limits.

"And how could you help?" Lydia asked, somehow making the words sound kind rather than dismissive.

"We'll send out word for the youth to gather. Since we gather whenever the boredom gets overwhelming, it won't raise any suspicion. And no one would betray us to the adults." She wrinkled her nose, as if such an act was unthinkable. "Once everyone is there—right when the wedding is happening—we'll let them know why they're really there and send them home to rouse their families."

Easton looked thoughtful. "That might actually work."

"Of course it will work," Natalie said.

Charlotte suppressed another laugh. Natalie had an impressive ability to be both infuriating and likable.

"In that case, we have our plans." The count rose. "And now these old bones need to get to a bed. Once upon a time, I could function on little to no sleep, but those days are long behind me, regardless of my form."

Lydia led him and his son out, and Charlotte was left to wonder if there was any chance everything would go as they'd planned.

GWEN

The night had passed easily despite Gwen's fears. She was still worried for Easton, but after their conversation, she felt a warm glow whenever she thought of him. And it was easy to drift asleep to the memory of his arms around her.

When she woke, her focus turned to one thing. There had been more than enough time for the apple to warm up to every object in Celandine's collection. Now Gwen needed to find a way to sneak in there and steal whichever of them would let the rebels restrain the queen for the length of the wedding ceremony.

Timing was crucial. If she did it too early, the queen might discover the theft. But if she left it too late, Gwen might be swept up in wedding preparations and be unable to get away. Unless it would be better to assign the task to someone else? But who could get all the way into the queen's bedchamber other than her supposed daughter?

Gwen's mind went round in circles, and she still hadn't finalized a plan when a team of seamstresses descended on her in a whirl of material, scissors, and tape measures. They took one look at the mess in her room and bore her off to an empty meeting room to complete the final fittings and measurements for her wedding gown.

Knowing she would be wearing the outfit when she married Easton, not Henry, Gwen couldn't help taking an interest in the elegant concoction of ivory satin with a gossamer layer over the top. Looking at herself in the full-length mirror held up by one of the women, Gwen felt for the first time that she could be both a princess and herself. Princess Gwendolyn had been a mask, but perhaps it was possible for Queen Gwendolyn to be her true self.

When she finally made it back to her room, it was long past time for the midday meal. She was rewarded with the sight of a tray—the food cold but still edible. She consumed it ravenously and was still finishing the last bites when her door opened, the movement too tentative to herald Celandine's arrival.

Gwen gulped down the final mouthful and stood to face Miriam. The captive's face lifted when she saw Gwen.

"Oh thank goodness! Officially I'm here for the tray, but I've been checking every half hour, wondering when you'd return. I was starting to worry about someone seeing me popping in and out of here like a jack-in-the-box."

Gwen's lingering good humor from the gown and her full stomach instantly evaporated.

"What?" she asked. "What is it?"

"We've received another order from the queen." Miriam gathered up the dishes as she talked, placing them back on the tray. "We're supposed to drug Prince Henry's evening meal again, just like last time."

Gwen sucked in a breath. "Charlotte must have used her ball to make a second deal! She should have told me!"

"Maybe she's relying on you to handle it even without a conversation," Miriam suggested, and Gwen felt warm at the suggestion of confidence in her abilities.

She nodded decisively. "And I will handle it. You'll need to serve the drink, of course. We don't want the blame coming back to any of you. But I'll find a way to talk to Henry and warn him not to drink it."

Miriam looked relieved, although whether at Henry's potential escape or their own lack of involvement, Gwen wasn't sure. Either way, she thanked the princess and hurried out of the room.

Gwen sighed and sank into the single upright chair. Plans to break into her mother's collection of objects would have to be put on hold. It was more urgent to find a way to talk to Henry.

If only she could burrow straight through the walls. She wouldn't have to break through very many before she reached the room holding Henry. Unfortunately, even in her bear form, solid stone walls presented a problem.

It would be easier to walk straight through his door. But Celandine was the only one with a key.

Or was she? Gwen sat up straighter. Her mother had specifically told her that she had changed Gwen's lock while Gwen was gone. But surely she hadn't changed every lock in the palace. Henry's door could probably be opened with a master key, and Gwen knew from experience that copies of that could be obtained if you had the right access.

She stood. The guards were all busy doing exercises all day, leaving their barracks deserted. She smiled. Perfect.

Both the head housekeeper and the captain of the guard

had a copy of the master key, and both had a healthy fear of doing anything that might bring them negative attention from Queen Celandine. They had long ago made an arrangement to keep a spare copy of the key hidden in case either of them ever lost theirs and needed to replace it quickly. Easton had been the one to discover this fact and steal the spare fourteen years ago. The captain had assumed the housekeeper had needed it and promptly had it replaced. There was every like-lihood the replacement—or another subsequent version—was still in the same place.

She walked through the palace as if she belonged there, aware that hurrying would only attract attention. And she had walked the corridors aimlessly so many times that no one she encountered spared her a second look.

Her heart was still pounding when she reached the barracks, however. They were connected to the main palace by a single door, and once she had passed it, she would have no excuse for her presence.

Lingering would only increase the risk, though, so she pushed inside. Her gaze darted around the room, and she expelled her held breath. It was empty just as she'd hoped.

She hurried through the communal room and past doors leading to smaller bunk rooms, only stopping when she reached the captain's office. Standing on tiptoes, she sighed with relief when she found the key to the room still hidden above the doorframe. The encircling mountains that trapped them away from the other kingdoms also protected them from serious threats, making it difficult for the guard force to remain vigilant for decades on end.

She let herself in and raced to his desk, her fingers fumbling as she used the same key to unlock the third drawer on the right. She pushed aside some papers and finally caught sight of it. The key.

She stuffed it in her pocket, pushing the door closed and running out again, moving even more quickly than on her way in. She flew past the bunks and out again into the main palace. She didn't stop until she was several corridors away, the key seeming to burn in her pocket.

Gwen stopped and rested her back on the cool stone wall, sucking in lungfuls of air. The key wasn't really hot, and it didn't blaze with light to attract the attention of anyone who saw her. There was nothing to indicate its presence in her pocket.

Even so, she didn't have the nerves for any more waiting. She would go straight to Henry.

She retraced her steps, seeming to reach Henry's door much more quickly than she had managed the route in the other direction. She almost missed the lock on her first try, but eventually the key slid in and turned with a satisfying clunk.

She didn't make the mistake of rushing straight in, though. Opening the door only a crack, she put her mouth against it and whispered into the room, "It's Gwen! Don't attack!"

Only then did she push the door the rest of the way open and step warily inside, looking for candlesticks despite her warning.

Henry stood several steps away, his arms crossed and his shoulders tense. At least he made no move to attack her.

"Don't worry," he said. "I wouldn't dare attack anyone. Not when the queen might have Charlotte in her clutches."

Gwen shut the door behind her, her eyes softening. "Don't worry," she said hurriedly. "She got away. If you've seen guards running laps outside or sparring endlessly all day, that's punishment for letting her slip past them."

Henry staggered back, sinking into a chair and covering his face. "Oh, thank goodness," he murmured.

"I'm sorry I didn't manage to come to you sooner," Gwen said. "It was a risk, so I didn't…But I should have…"

Henry looked up, the momentary weakness of his relief already passed. "So why are you here now if not to reassure me? Has something happened? Do you need me to do something? Charlotte made me promise to listen to whatever you said and help you."

Gwen felt another surge of gratitude for her friend's trust.

"I think Charlotte must be coming back," she said, making Henry's eyes brighten and then dim again.

"She shouldn't risk that," he said harshly.

Gwen grimaced. "I'm afraid she didn't discuss it with me, so I didn't have an opportunity to talk her out of it. But the queen had you drugged last time Charlotte made a deal to spend the night with you, and now she's given the order for you to be drugged again."

"Drugged?" Henry's eyes narrowed. "Is that what happened? I woke up to Charlotte at my side, but we didn't have time for her to explain anything. I've been utterly confused as to what happened."

"She was with you all night," Gwen said softly. "But you were drugged so she couldn't have woken you."

Gwen turned away from the expression on Henry's face, feeling as if she were intruding on his private emotions.

"She lay at my side all night?"

She turned back at the soft smile in his voice.

"The sleeping draft will be in the drink," she said. "You have to pretend to drink it and then pretend to fall asleep. The servants won't say anything about taking away a full glass, but if you can find a way to drain it somehow that would be even better."

He was nodding as she spoke, his face creased in concentration.

"If you can avoid being drugged, you'll have the whole night together," Gwen continued. "And Charlotte will know more about the rebel plans than I do. She can tell you everything that's going to happen and what they need you to do."

The more she thought about it, the more she thought that must be the reason Charlotte had made a second bargain. There must be important information the rebels needed to pass to Henry. She just wished there was a way for her to talk to her friend and get more information herself.

"So all I have to do—" Henry started only to break off as the door was thrust violently open.

Gwen flinched, but there was no time to attempt to hide. By the time she'd even processed what was happening, Celandine was standing in the doorway, looking between them.

"Well, well, well," she said. "I'd like to say I'm surprised, but that wouldn't be true."

Gwen's mind raced, trying to think of an excuse for her presence, but her thoughts kept tripping over each other as she wondered how long the queen had been out there. How much had she overheard?

"So you came to warn the prince not to drink his drugged drink tonight," Celandine said coolly. Her eyes narrowed. "I'm disappointed in you, Gwendolyn. I gave you a second chance, despite my better judgment, and this is how you repay me?"

"How—" Gwen gaped at the queen, despair filling her as she realized she had no way to fix the situation.

Henry stepped forward, his attitude menacing now he knew Charlotte wasn't in the palace. But the queen glanced at him with such dismissal Gwen felt sick.

"Oh, stand down, brave boy," she drawled. "Your precious Charlotte may have slipped through my hands last time, but I'll have her soon enough."

Henry froze, his muscles stiffening.

Celandine's eyes went back to Gwen. "That's right. I know all about the rebels' plans. There are still some people left in this city who know where their best interests lie."

Gwen's heart sank. A traitor among the rebels? She forgot all about Charlotte for a moment, her mind full of Easton. If only she had some way to warn him!

"What I didn't know," the queen continued, "was whether my servants were part of the conspiracy. And so I set up this little test."

Gwen gaped at her. It had all been a test? The servants had warned her about the queen's command because Gwen had asked them to. She had kept them a secret from the count and his rebels only to betray them directly to the queen.

Tears burned her eyes, her breath catching. Whatever happened to them now was her fault.

"Your mistake, Gwendolyn," the queen said with venom in her voice, "was looking to anyone other than me. You will only let others down and betray them. It's in your nature."

Gwen sunk in on herself, her mind shrinking inward as the queen's words reverberated in her head. But deep inside, she found something different.

There were other voices inside now. Easton's words of love and confidence. Charlotte's words of friendship and trust. Even the count's as he declared he had been waiting for her because she was the queen they needed. When there had been no voice but Celandine's, Gwen had been unable to push her words out, no matter how hard she tried. But now there were other words filling those spaces instead. The hollow inside Gwen was no longer empty, and it had no room for Celandine's lies.

She raised her eyes, her shoulders straightening.

"No," she said firmly, the word complete and final in itself.

The queen's eyes widened, and a flash of fury crossed her face, the emotion seeming to catch Celandine off guard as much as it did Gwen.

She stepped forward and grabbed Gwen's ear, twisting it until Gwen cried out. When she pulled, Gwen had to follow, the pain forcing her limbs to comply.

Henry tried to intervene, but Celandine had Gwen out of the door too fast, shutting it in the prince's face and turning the key in the lock.

Tears leaked from Gwen's eyes as Celandine dragged her down the corridor.

"I will deal with the servants soon enough," she hissed. "But first I'm going to deal with you."

CHARLOTTE

Easton had suggested Charlotte could stay behind with Patti and Dane, but he didn't argue when she refused. He must have already known the attempt was futile. There was no way Charlotte was remaining in the city while the false queen attempted to marry Henry to Gwen. And if everything went wrong, she would be the only one thinking of Henry first.

The count had commanded them to wait until the end— the last of the rebels to arrive in the palace grounds. Easton had protested that, reminding them he was supposed to help guide the other arrivals. But the count insisted Jett and Lydia could manage the task, pointing out that Easton was the most important of all of them. As the man Gwen loved, he was the only one who could free the mountain court from their enchantment.

Easton had reluctantly agreed, and Charlotte had been assigned as his companion. The two of them would creep in together, and they wouldn't need a guide. But as soon as everyone else had departed, they made a slight adjustment to their plan. Instead of going straight to join the other rebels, they would find Gwen first. They were both desperate to see her for their own reasons, so neither needed much convincing.

They wore cloaks pulled up high over their heads as they strode through the streets in the waning light, keeping to shadows wherever possible. The afternoon was already wearing down, and the city's people had started dispersing to their homes. If they'd left their departure much later, they would have stood out on the nearly deserted streets.

It wasn't their first time making the same trek together, but Charlotte had never felt so tense as they crept into the palace gardens. Last time, when they saw a patrol in the distance, Charlotte had made enough noise to draw their attention before fleeing back into the city before they could see her identity.

This time they both needed to make it inside. But Easton must have been right about the guard numbers. They didn't even encounter a patrol as they wound a circuitous route through the gardens, staying out of sight of the palace windows. Charlotte even grew bold enough to stop and dig up her golden ball and Gwen's harness. Who knew what need they might have for the objects before the next sunset.

Inside the building, Easton took the lead. But as they walked the corridors, something nagged at Charlotte. The route felt strangely familiar. A door came into view, and she instinctively slowed, half a beat before Easton did.

When he also slowed, stopping at the door, Charlotte's eyes widened. The gardens and furnishings were so different that she had nearly forgotten the palace was the original version of her and Henry's castle. And Gwen had the same room she and Henry had shared in the other version.

Chasing away a shiver, Charlotte slipped into the room behind Easton. As soon as he stepped aside, she gasped.

Someone had torn the room to pieces, leaving shredded stuffing, loose feathers, and torn material everywhere she looked. In one corner smashed glass and broken bottles lay shattered across the floor, and even the wardrobe had been toppled.

Her hand flew to her mouth. "What happened to Gwen?" she cried.

"What?" Easton whirled, his pale face fixing on her. But a moment later he relaxed. "Oh, you mean the room? She did it herself."

Charlotte's brows rose. "Wow. She really…" She shook her head. But part of her felt proud of her friend. Had it felt as cathartic as it looked? "That's all right, then," she added. "I thought someone must have attacked her."

"I thought that at first too. But where is she now?" Easton looked around uneasily. "The state of the room doesn't mean anything, but she's not here. I thought she'd be here this late. Her bear form is supposed to be a secret."

Charlotte shrugged, trying to chase away the tendrils of panic that stirred on the edges of her own mind. "We knew it wasn't a guarantee we'd find her here. It isn't quite sunset yet. And we can't go blundering around the palace looking for her. That would be asking to be caught."

Easton reluctantly nodded, but his body didn't relax, the lines of his muscles remaining tense.

Turning abruptly, he strode to one of the walls and fumbled with something out of Charlotte's view.

"It's locked," he said, clearly frustrated. Banging his fist on the wall, he raised his voice. "Gwen? Gwen? Are you in there?"

"Shhh!" Charlotte hissed. "What are you doing? Do you want someone to hear us?"

Easton slumped. "It didn't used to be locked."

"Is that a door?" Charlotte said, able to see the lines of it now she was paying attention. It wasn't entirely hidden, but it had been designed to blend in with the wall. "I'm sure if she's in there, she would call out and let us know."

"We both wanted to speak to her," Charlotte continued, "but it's not essential to the plan. We should get to the others so they know we're safe, and then we'll come back at night when we know for sure she'll be here. The count said we had to make contact with her."

She could still read the reluctance on his face, and she suspected she knew the reason. The count wanted a rebel to make contact with Gwen, but it didn't have to be Easton. Once they joined the others, it was unlikely Easton would be allowed out again until the crucial moment. But his importance was the reason they couldn't put off going to the specified apartment any longer. If the rebels thought something had happened to Easton, they would risk going out into the palace to look for him.

Easton knew the realities as well as she did, and he finally sighed and nodded. "Let's go, then."

Charlotte winced sympathetically, staying quiet since she knew any words of hers would be meaningless. She felt the same tension in her own belly, urging her to run off and find Henry. But she had already done that once with nearly disastrous results. This time she was going to follow the plan.

Easton's pace had slowed, but he still led them steadily down corridors and around corners, presumably making for the apartment of the count's son.

"It's just up ahead," he murmured at last, gesturing to the nearest corner.

But before they rounded it, they both pulled up short, exchanging looks. The tramp of boots sounded in the distance. Not the measured tread of a routine guard patrol or the casual stroll of a courtier—multiple people in heavy boots were running full pace in their direction.

Charlotte had only had time to panic when the running feet stopped. She didn't even finish her breath of relief before the fear returned, however. The sound of an aggressive fist pounding on wood reached them.

"Open in the name of the queen!" a man called.

Charlotte and Easton exchanged horrified looks, both still frozen in place.

The fist banged again and then the creak of the door opening.

"What is the meaning—" the voice of the count's son started in cold tones, but the first voice cut him off.

"Don't bother, traitor," he snapped. "You're surrounded."

Instant chaos broke out just out of sight, shouts, cries, screams, and pounding feet. It sounded like furniture was being overturned, and Charlotte could barely breathe, let alone move.

Easton sprang into action, however. Dragging Charlotte with him, he pulled open a narrow door that was almost hidden in the paneling of the wall, just as the one in Gwen's room had been. He shoved her inside. Following behind, he pulled the door closed.

Enough light came in around the door for Charlotte to identify their location as a storage cupboard. Easton bent down at an awkward angle and pressed one eye against the wall. Charlotte stared at him in confusion until he pulled back and gestured impatiently for her to go to the other side of the door.

There was just enough room for her to fit, so she obeyed, eyeing him as he bent over again. From the new angle, she could see he was pressing his eyes against a tiny circle of light. A peephole!

Searching the wall in front of her, she found another point of light and bent toward it. She didn't know how long she could maintain such an uncomfortable position, and she couldn't imagine why anyone would put peepholes at such a level. Charlotte was short, so if it was uncomfortable for her, it wouldn't suit anyone but a child.

Understanding dawned. Of course. Easton and Gwen had spent their childhood roaming these halls. Apparently spying from storage cupboards had been part of their childish adventures. No wonder Easton had known just where to go.

She positioned herself so she could see out into the corridor beyond. It was empty, but the distant sounds of a scuffle were dying down now, replaced with barked orders and the occasional muffled cry. They didn't have to wait long before a line of people came into view.

The rebels had their hands on their heads, their expressions ranging from terrified to resigned. A line of guards marched on either side of them, swords gripped in their hands and faces stern.

Charlotte had to clap her hand over her mouth to keep from crying out when she saw Jett and Lydia marched past, and Easton went rigid beside her. But the worst was the very end of the line. The final figure was much too short, his movement out of step with the others due to the crutches beneath his arms.

Behind him, two guards hauled a man who wasn't

marching but instead struggling with his captors. When his face flashed in their direction, Charlotte recognized the count's son—Emmett's father.

"My son is not part of this," he said in heated tones. "I don't even know why he was home. He's only seven!"

Emmett flinched, and it was easy to guess he and his mother had been sent away for safety but he had snuck back. The clack of his clutches didn't falter, though, his head high as he followed in the line of prisoners.

The guards at the back were all turned toward the struggling nobleman, but he twisted in the direction of the storage cupboard, facing directly toward their hiding place.

Easton straightened, and before Charlotte knew what was happening, the door had flashed partially open before immediately closing again.

The count's son went slack at the brief glimpse of Easton, his eyes fixed on the now closed door. Several of the guards also turned that way, following the direction of his gaze. There was nothing left to see, however, thanks to Easton's quick movement, and the count's son quickly resumed his struggles, distracting them.

"What was that?" Charlotte hissed at Easton, as quietly as she could.

He shrugged. "I saw an opportunity, and I took it. At least now they know we're still free. And that we know what happened to them."

"But how do we know they're not all being marched off to be executed?" Charlotte whispered as the sound of their marching line faded from her hearing. Tears of panic and horror pricked at her eyes, and she could only imagine how much worse it had to be for Easton.

Easton slid slowly down to sit on the floor, his hands fisted and eyes blazing but the lines of his body broken and weary.

"We can't know for sure, but I doubt it. That isn't the queen's style. She won't want to just eliminate her enemies. She'll want to make sure no one else tries the same thing. She's making a grand spectacle of this wedding—even some of the more prominent people from the city have been invited— so I don't think she'll miss the chance to make a show of this as well. Whatever she intends to do to them, it will happen tomorrow, in front of the wedding guests."

"Tomorrow," Charlotte said slowly. It was only a small reprieve, but it was better than thinking of all those people already dead.

"And surely she wouldn't execute Emmett in front of a crowd," she murmured. "That would hardly garner sympathy."

"We can only hope so," Easton said roughly, and Charlotte guessed he was thinking of his parents.

"She isn't going to execute anyone," she said in a bracing voice. "We're still free, and we'll find a way to rescue them."

Easton gave a bark of humorless laughter. "How are we going to do that?"

Charlotte straightened. "We're not. I am."

Easton frowned.

"I know you don't want to hear this," she said firmly. "But the count already told you how important you are. Your role is to appear in the middle of the wedding. No matter what else happens, we can't let that fail. And that means you need to stay right here in this cupboard."

"You want me to just sit here while—"

"Yes," she said, cutting him off ruthlessly. "I know I'm asking the hardest possible thing. I know it's the last thing you want to do. But this is what is needed from you, Easton."

"How can you save them on your own?" Easton shook his head. "Alone, and a stranger here no less."

Charlotte drew herself up. "I won't be alone. There's someone else who knows this palace almost as well as you do."

Easton scrambled to his feet. "We don't even know where Gwen is. And if it's too dangerous for me to get involved, it's several times more dangerous for her." He groaned and scrubbed a hand over his face. "If the queen somehow knows our plans, she must already know Gwen is involved as well. Who knows what she's done to her."

"Stop!" Charlotte commanded. "Stop thinking like that, or you'll drive yourself mad. Believe me. I have reason to know."

Easton subsided, apparently remembering how long the queen had been holding Charlotte's husband a prisoner.

"There's someone else who knows these corridors and rooms," Charlotte said more softly. "Or at least, a copy of them. Henry. Just give us a chance."

Easton hesitated for a moment before he groaned and sank back to the floor. "Who has more experience at waiting than me?" he asked bitterly.

"I'm sorry." Charlotte hesitated, but the best reassurance she could offer was to succeed at rescuing the other rebels. "I'll come back for you as soon as I can. Promise you'll still be here?"

He nodded, not looking at her, and she had to accept it.

Stooping to check the peephole, she confirmed the corridor outside was still empty before leaving the cupboard. She scanned the corridor, locking each distinguishing feature in her mind so she could find the place again.

Drawing the golden ball out of her pocket, she stared down at it. The godmother who had given it to her had said it would help her find her true love. She still didn't know how it was supposed to work, but it was all she had.

She placed it gently on the ground and, feeling foolish, whispered, "Please take me to Henry."

Nothing happened, and her sense of foolishness grew until suddenly, without visible impetus, the ball began to move. It rolled down the corridor, following after the departed prisoners, and she hurried in its wake. She was relieved the ball was leading her in the opposite direction to the apartment used by the rebels. It seemed likely there would be guards stationed there still, waiting in case she and Easton appeared.

But soon she didn't have thoughts for anything except the task of following the ball. It moved at pace, and she worried about losing it every time it rounded a corner—almost as much as she worried about it leading her straight into a squad of guards or a group of courtiers.

But almost as if it knew, the ball led her only down deserted corridors, or through empty rooms. When it finally rolled to a stop, it bumped gently against a concealed door that looked almost identical to the one on the storage cupboard half a palace away.

She frowned at the ball. Henry was concealed inside a storage cupboard now? Tentatively she tried the door, and it opened without resistance. Peering inside, she saw only similar supplies to those that had filled the last cupboard, although these appeared to be finer in quality, the pillows and blankets soft and luxurious.

She went to shut the door, but the ball rolled inside. Confused, Charlotte followed. When she bent to retrieve it, it zipped away from her, rolling just out of reach. She stepped closer to try again, and it did the same thing.

Throwing her hands up, Charlotte cried, "Fine!"

Closing the door behind her, she crossed her arms. "I'll stay in here if that's what you want."

The ball immediately rolled forward and bumped gently against her boots.

Charlotte retrieved it without trouble this time, considering what she should do. She could leave now that she had the ball secured, but where would she go?

Spotting the circle of light from a peephole, she bent to peer through it. Maybe it was worth watching for a while to see what happened.

CHARLOTTE

The minutes stretched long, and Charlotte began to regret her plan, her back spasming from the awkward position. She was about to give up and straighten when a sound caught her ear. Pressing her eye closer, she forgot the discomfort.

A door almost directly opposite her opened, and a subdued pair of women emerged. For a moment, disappointment speared her until she spotted what was in the hands of the woman in the lead. Draped over her arm was an unfinished but elaborate outfit—the kind that might be worn by a male at a wedding or similar celebration.

She sucked in a breath as the woman turned to her younger companion. "Those measurements should have been done two weeks ago. We'll be lucky to have this done on time, even with the whole team working all night. You lock up and return the key, and I'll get this straight to the others."

The younger woman didn't look happy with the arrangement, but the other was already hurrying away. With a slight tremble in her hand, the remaining seamstress fit the key in the lock and turned it.

Charlotte could barely breathe at the opportunity before her. "Good ball," she whispered, stroking it as if it was a sentient creature. "Good ball!"

She waited until the woman turned to go and then flung open the door. Barreling out into the corridor, she clutched the woman from behind, one hand over her mouth. The seamstress hadn't even had time to scream.

As she had expected from her earlier demeanor, the woman immediately went limp, shaking all over.

"Please don't hurt me," she sobbed against Charlotte's hand.

Charlotte winced, but she couldn't falter. Using the hand that wasn't covering the woman's mouth, she wrested the key from her slack fingers.

Looking around, she found a door with a keyhole and pushed the woman toward it. The seamstress stumbled forward on faltering feet, still not putting up any significant fight. Did she think Charlotte had a weapon?

Opening the door, Charlotte glanced inside at the untouched bedchamber. It was too pristine to be in regular use, so she released the woman and gave her a hard shove from behind. The seamstress staggered into the room, dropping to her knees.

Before she could turn around, Charlotte whisked the door closed, sighing with relief as she turned the key in the lock. As she'd hoped, she was now in possession of the master key Gwen had mentioned.

"Sorry!" she called through the door, feeling another spurt of guilt at the muffled sobs from the other side.

But she had the key in her hand! She ran to the door the woman had closed, thrusting the key into the lock and turning it. Bursting into the room, she closed the door behind her.

"Forget to measure the length of one of my fingers?" a sardonic voice asked from the window, its owner not turning to look at her.

"Henry," she said, half sob, half word.

He whirled, his blue eyes finding her instantly, his whole face transforming.

"Charlotte!" He ran to her, and she ran to him, the two of them colliding in the middle of the room.

"I found you! I found you!" she cried, tears running down her cheeks.

"Oh, my love," he murmured, wiping them away and gazing at her in wonder. "How can you be here? The queen…"

Charlotte sniffed, trying to pull herself together. "She captured the rest of them. Or almost all of them. Do you know where Gwen is?"

Henry's face twisted. "She came to warn me about something, but it turned out it was a test the queen had set up. Celandine dragged her away."

"Oh no!" Charlotte stared at him in dismay. "Everything really has gone wrong."

"It's hard to believe that when you're standing here with me," he said.

"Oh Henry! I keep messing everything up, but this time I need to save everyone. We need to save everyone."

"Slow down," he said. "I've been locked in here the whole time with only the occasional, confusing snippet of news. What's been going on out there?"

Charlotte's whole body buzzed with energy, and she would have paced the room if she could have brought herself to leave Henry's arms. But he had wound one arm around her middle, and she wouldn't have pried herself away for anything.

Speaking as slowly as she could manage, she explained everything that had happened so far, sticking only to the necessary facts.

"So the queen is still progressing with this wedding," he said when she finished. "And that's a good thing—but only as long as we can make the swap in the middle."

Charlotte nodded, her hands creeping up to grasp the front of his shirt. "I'm not letting her marry you off to Gwen or anyone. You're already mine."

He smiled affectionately down at her. "Do you think I would marry anyone else? I already have a wife. A delightful—if occasionally exasperating—one."

She giggled and hiccupped at the same time, a final tear leaking out.

"Henry, I'm so, so sorry," she said. "If I'd just trusted you and waited…"

He bent to kiss the tear off her cheek. "Charlotte, you made a mistake, but it was an understandable one. I forgave you immediately. And look what you've managed since! I never thought you could actually find a way to come here. But you're not only here, you have the whole kingdom in open rebellion."

Charlotte gave a watery chuckle. "I definitely can't take credit for that."

Henry smiled down at her. "Maybe not, but it does seem like we can be of some help. So maybe we're right where we're supposed to be?" He sighed, his arm around her tightening.

"I'm the one who never properly apologized for involving you in all this to begin with. I married you without telling you the truth, knowing I was caught up in an enchantment worked by a dangerous woman. You were wronged by me more than I ever was by you."

Charlotte shook her head stubbornly. "Now that I know everything, if I had my choice again, I would still marry you in a heartbeat. You are worth every moment of pain."

"I had no idea how well my heart picked when I saw you in the woods," he murmured before lowering his mouth to hers.

Charlotte returned the kiss eagerly. Her husband felt utterly familiar—home in a way no place had ever been—but this part was still new. Feeling his arms around her, his chest firm against hers, his mouth moving on hers was exquisite and wondrous and almost too much.

When he pulled back, she made a soft sound of protest, and he groaned and almost pulled her close again. But he stopped with his mouth a whisper from hers.

"Don't we have some people to save?" he whispered.

Charlotte squeaked, memory rushing back as her cheeks flushed.

"One day soon," Henry said with a grin, "I'm going to find a castle in the woods where the two of us can be alone together without any bears. But for now, I think we have a kingdom to help save."

"I'd like to find Gwen, if we can," Charlotte said. "But the queen will have to bring her to the ceremony, at least. She's too important to Celandine's plans for her to do anything too drastic. So it's probably more important for us to find the rebels before she decides to start executing people."

"Do you have any idea where they're being kept?" he asked, stepping away from her, all business.

She sighed softly at the cold air between them before turning her mind to the job ahead.

"Unfortunately, no," she said. "But this palace is just like your castle. You spent much more time roaming around it than I did—all those days as a bear before I arrived. Were you able to tell just from the layout and position of the rooms what they were supposed to be for? Could you guess where a large group of people might be kept?"

Henry frowned. "I could guess, but that wouldn't mean I was right."

"At this point, an educated guess is better than wandering around blindly and hoping we trip over them."

Henry winced. "There's really no one else who could help them?"

"That would lead us back to finding Gwen first. Do you have any idea where she's being kept?"

"Unfortunately, I don't know that either. They might even be together."

Charlotte tried not to let panic overwhelm her. She had been so certain that if she could just find Henry, the solution would be simple. Now she wondered how much of it had been her own emotions talking.

Henry instantly picked up on her mood. "Don't worry," he said sounding more confident than he could possibly feel. "We'll find them. The two of us together can manage anything."

Even though she knew the words were only meant to bolster her confidence, somehow they worked.

"What about a guard hall or...or barracks or something? Do you remember anywhere that looked like it could have been that?"

His eyes brightened. "Actually, yes! There was a small wing

joined to the rest of the building by only a single door. I noticed that some of the rooms had brackets in the walls that looked like they were intended for bunks."

"We should start there," Charlotte suggested, grateful to have somewhere to begin. "Even if they're not there, we might manage to overhear something or follow some guards to their prisoners."

She didn't mention the difficulty of getting into the guards' barracks without being seen. The job already felt overwhelming, so they should tackle one thing at a time.

Henry nodded and took her hand, winding his fingers through hers as he led her toward the door. She looked down at their joined hands, a smile stealing up her face despite the circumstances. Another thing they couldn't do before.

When Henry stepped out into the corridor, he drew a deep breath as if the air was fresh and clear instead of just like the air inside his chamber. How many hours had he spent staring at that door, wishing he could walk through it?

He pulled her to their left, but she froze, pulling back against him. Tugging her hand free, she whispered, "Wait," and dashed back to the door.

Pulling the key out of her pocket, she locked the door behind them. Henry watched her, confused.

"What's the point of that?"

She put a finger to her lips, and he fell silent. Hurrying back to the room where she had left the seamstress, she slid the key beneath the door.

A gasp on the other side told her the woman had been sitting watching the door.

"His door has been locked again," Charlotte called through.

"Thank you," came the wobbly reply.

Dashing back to Henry, she seized his hand and took off

running, pulling him with her. As soon as he'd recovered from his initial surprise, he easily kept pace, quickly outstripping her and tugging her along behind.

Once they were several corridors over, she stopped, bending over to catch her breath. Henry stopped as well, gazing down at her with a quizzical expression, barely out of breath himself.

"What was that?" he asked.

"One of the seamstresses," Charlotte explained. "Now she can return the key like nothing happened. And when someone comes in the morning to bring you food, they'll find the door locked and you mysteriously vanished. No one will be able to say exactly when in the night it happened or that it had anything to do with the poor seamstresses."

"Was that wise?" Henry's brows furrowed. "She might go straight to check if I'm in there and then run to the queen."

Charlotte shrugged. "I suppose it's possible, but you didn't see her. She might be a lovely person, but she is not what you'd call courageous. I'd be willing to bet a lot that she goes straight on as if nothing happened, hoping the whole time that no one ever connects her to any of it." Her mouth twisted. "I'm sorry, Henry, but she was just so terrified. I couldn't abandon her to take all the blame."

He smiled down at her, his face softening. "I wouldn't expect anything else from your soft heart."

She made a face at him.

"It's too late to worry about it anyway," he added. "The best we can do is get moving quickly."

She nodded agreement, and they began moving again, although this time at a more sustainable pace.

"Does it seem normal to you that the corridors are so

empty?" she asked after several more turns without anyone coming into view.

Henry grimaced. "I'm afraid the servants were implicated in the rebels' plans. I suspect the queen has confined them all somewhere. And the guards must be busy rounding up and guarding the rebels. As for the courtiers…"

"Even the ones uninvolved must have worked out something is going on," Charlotte agreed. "If it was me, and I lived in Celandine's castle, I'd be lying low, too."

Henry glanced at the darkness out of a window they passed. Charlotte couldn't remember when night had arrived, but even the traces of sunset were gone.

"There's something else to consider," he said. "Anyone we encounter at this point won't be…human."

"They won't have a human body," Charlotte said reprovingly. "They're still people underneath."

Henry smiled lovingly at her. "It always amazed me how easily you saw me for me, even when I wore a bear's body. But in this instance, I'm more worried about their teeth and claws. And size."

"I think it's actually their ears and noses we should be most concerned about." Charlotte put her hand on her arm where she still wore a slim bandage beneath her sleeve.

Henry's eyes followed the movement, and he frowned. "What is it? Were you hurt somehow? Did one of the bears—"

His voice rose, and she shushed him urgently. "Do you hear something?"

He froze instantly, his head cocked as if listening. His eyes grew wide.

"Yes," he hissed. "Run!"

Grabbing her hand again, he sprinted, pulling her behind him almost too fast for her to keep her feet under her. She found a rhythm and tried to pull her hand free, but he held on tight. She stopped fighting and focused on running, her breath sawing in and out of her lungs.

Pounding steps sounded behind them accompanied by heavy breathing that didn't sound human. They ran harder.

They reached a strangely shaped intersection, two corridors branching off. Henry pulled her in one direction, but a bear appeared in the distance. It stopped, its head coming up in alert at the sight of them.

Charlotte backtracked, dragging Henry with her as she took the other direction. He seemed almost reluctant, though, his eyes frantically darting all around them.

They careened around a corner, and Charlotte discovered the source of his reluctance. They had reached a dead end.

She barely managed to stop herself from running headlong into the smooth stone wall.

"A window?" she rasped out, struggling to catch her breath.

A low growl rumbled down the corridor, building as two voices overlapped. She spun around, her knees nearly giving out at the sight of two enormous white bears prowling toward them.

Her arm throbbed in memory, and she whimpered. Henry stepped in front of her, his face determined, and it galvanized her into action, strengthening her knees. She looked around, but the windows here had crossed panes. She didn't think she could smash them if she tried.

"We surrender!" she called quickly, raising both hands.

The bears didn't pause, continuing to pace toward them. Henry had never lost his human side, and Gwen had claimed to be the same. But these bears looked like predators to her, their eyes dark and fixed on their prey. Were they lost in the hunt?

Henry backed up, pushing her behind him, but all too soon, her back hit the wall and his hit her. They both stopped.

"If only I was still a bear myself!" Henry muttered, and for the first time Charlotte wished his bear form back. Without it, it looked like they were about to die.

GWEN

Celandine dragged Gwen along the corridor, but they didn't go far. When she reached Gwen's room, she pushed her inside, finally releasing her ear. Gwen staggered, rubbing at it.

As soon as she regained her balance, she lunged for the door, but the queen moved quicker. Grabbing one of Gwen's arms, she twisted it behind her, immobilizing her.

Gwen panted, desperation fighting with her desire not to give Celandine the satisfaction of seeing her break.

"I thought you had finally learned your lesson," Celandine snarled. "Learned that you're nothing without me. Why else would you come crawling back?"

"I came back because someone had to stand up to you," Gwen snapped. "You've plagued this kingdom long enough!"

Celandine snarled again and thrust Gwen toward the wall. Too late Gwen realized what she was doing. She must have prepared because the door to the servant room was propped open, the small space inside a looming darkness.

Gwen cried out, grabbing with her free hand at the edge of

the doorframe. But Celandine twisted her other arm, angling Gwen so that her precarious hold slipped free, and she stumbled into the room. Again she turned and lunged for the door, and again Celandine moved too quickly for her, this time slamming the door in her face. Gwen collided with the solid surface, slamming her nose against it.

She fell back, her eyes stinging with more than pain. It couldn't be happening. Not all over again.

Distantly, she heard a key turn in the lock. Holding herself together by the barest thread, she stumbled over and tried the handle anyway. It had to open. It had to open.

It didn't open. She slumped to the floor, a sob tearing from her throat. She had come so far. She had finally found her strength and defied Celandine to her face, and yet here she was back where she had begun.

The darkness pressed on her like a physical force, and with the barest whimper, Gwen's senses slipped away from her. She could see nothing, hear nothing, feel nothing except the presence of her panic, sliding down her throat and up her middle and coating her hands. She buried her head in her hands, trying to drown it out, to hide from it.

A scream burned up her throat, but it came out like a whimper, her chest unable to expand enough for any volume.

Dark. Dark. Dark. Dark. Dark. Alone. Alone. Alone. Alone. Alone.

The words echoed in her mind until they had no meaning. She was going to die here. She would grow hungry and thirsty —so thirsty—until the pain stopped gnawing at her and consumed her whole.

She would never even see the light again. She had thought Celandine had already stolen everything from her, but now she had even stolen the sun. Gwen would die in darkness.

She curled in on herself, time losing all meaning.

At one point, something echoed distantly. Some outside sound or presence. Her brain reached for it, but it was too far away to properly grasp. A pounding perhaps. Or even her name?

Gradually, too gradually, it permeated into her brain, pushing back the darkness. Had she only imagined it, or was someone there?

She staggered to her feet, her muscles contracting strangely, as if they'd forgotten how to work. Someone was there, and they would rescue her.

"Please!" she called, pounding on her side of the door. "Please! Is there someone there?"

She was greeted only with silence. She had taken too long to respond, and whoever had been there must have left.

Tears dripped unheeded down her cheeks, and shame filled her. She was a grown woman, and all that was needed to reduce her to this was to be locked in a small space. It made no logical sense. She knew that. But she couldn't fight the sheer terror that had her in its grip, her younger self rising to swallow the new her.

She pounded again and again until her hands hurt, but no one responded. She was alone once again.

She slid down to sitting again, but she had regained some measure of calm. It was dark in here but not nearly as small as that dreaded closet where she had been confined for days after Easton's banishment. She could move and stretch out. Even lie down when she got tired.

It was surprising the queen had put her in such a large space, even if it was conveniently close.

Remembering the sequence of events that had led her here wasn't pleasant, but it helped her cling to the grip of her sanity. She had endured worse. She could endure this too. She could endure until someone came to rescue her. This time Easton would come for her.

And then the tingling started. Gwen fell forward, her mind seizing as the tearing sensation began. She was growing bigger, so much bigger, and the space was growing smaller. The walls really were closing in on her. And they wouldn't stop. They would keep going until Gwen was squeezed to death, her bones and muscles sandwiched flat, and her life extinguished. There would be no need to wait for the hunger and the dehydration.

The scream fought its way out, coming out as a terrifying baying, howling growl that sounded horrifyingly inhuman. She would never be herself again, never be held by Easton again. She was alone. It was dark, and she was alone.

She thrashed around, no longer conscious of what she was doing, just desperate for an escape from the darkness around her and her own mind. Coherent thought had fled, and she had only wordless impressions and fear, fear, fear. So much fear.

Gwen had no idea how much time passed in that state. She had no more sense of its passage than she had rational thought. But eventually, a single image intruded.

Easton. His face appeared in her mind's eye, driving back the darkness. He was coming to the palace to face the queen, and if Gwen stayed stuck here, he would face her alone. Another face appeared. Alma, followed by Miriam. What was her mother doing to them while Gwen remained trapped here?

Other faces crowded in. Charlotte. Natalie. Easton's mother, who had always been kind to Gwen and now apparently lived in the city. Even Count Oswin.

The queen had tormented Gwen for years, but she had also tormented these people. If Gwen gave in completely to her panic, Celandine won. And yet…And yet…

Gwen put her head in her hands, only to find she was reaching up with paws instead of fingers. She froze, closing her eyes against the terrifying, encroaching black around her, and thought of nothing but her body. She could feel its unfamiliar shape, the pulsing strength of her muscles, and the sharp points of her claws and teeth.

Her mother thought Gwen was a victim. She shut her away thinking she would buckle and collapse. And Gwen had nearly done exactly that. But Gwen was finished being a victim. She hated the dark, and she would never like small places, but this room wasn't her tomb. She had strength still. And it was time to use it.

With a growl that built in volume and strength, she turned to where she knew the door was. Rearing back on her hind legs, she fell forward with her full force against the wood, claws extended. It cracked. She reared back again and fell forward, paws swiping as she descended. The door splintered, one of her paws breaking through, and light burst in.

She blinked, her eyes stinging at the sudden illumination. Shutting them, she lowered her head and rammed the shards of the door. It teetered and collapsed outward, sections of the wood snapping completely.

Gwen staggered through the opening into the untouched chaos of her bedchamber. The room had never looked so beautiful to her.

She collapsed, sucking in long, sweet breaths as her eyes adjusted to the light. Then she lumbered to her feet, shaking herself. While she would always avoid small, dark places if possible, they would never have the same hold on her again—not now she had fought her way free.

She breathed in, sucking the air through her nose, and froze. Easton and Charlotte. She easily picked their scents from everything else—fresh but not immediately so. Someone had been there! It was his voice she'd heard!

But where were they now? She tensed, the lingering fear still bubbling through her veins, convincing her they must be in trouble.

The door to her room was ajar, allowing her to easily push through. *I'm coming,* she thought silently, lifting her snout to sniff the air.

Easton's scent was fainter out here, harder to pinpoint. But Charlotte's seemed fresh. Gwen followed it to the door of a random, unused bedchamber on the opposite side of the corridor. She frowned. What could Charlotte have been doing there?

She didn't seem to have gone inside, though. Her scent continued down the corridor toward Henry's room instead, which made far more sense. Gwen followed, the physical activity driving out the remaining trembling and weakness in her limbs.

She stopped outside Henry's room. Should she try to open the door? But Charlotte's scent lingered in the corridor, and it was joined by a new one. Gwen frowned, considering. Unlike Charlotte and Easton, she had never smelled Henry while in her bear form. But something about the new scent felt vaguely familiar. If she had to guess, she thought it was him.

Intrigued, Gwen hurried faster, following the scent of the two of them. It wasn't part of the plan for Charlotte to free Henry at this point. What had been happening in her absence?

A third scent appeared, triggering a low growl. The new

one was unfamiliar, but it screamed of a threat. Here in the palace, an unknown bear could only mean one thing. Charlotte and Henry were being pursued.

Gwen broke into a lumbering run, bumping against walls as she rounded corners, her ears picking up the distant sound of overlapping growls. She pushed herself still faster.

She reached a familiar intersection, the sounds and smells coming from the dead end on the left. She didn't hesitate as she raced around the final corner.

Several things reached her consciousness at once.

Charlotte and Henry were trapped against the wall, and Charlotte's arms were raised in surrender. The two bears weren't stopping, however. They advanced on the two smaller figures, their growls threatening.

Had they lost their minds? Or had the queen ordered that Charlotte was to be killed if found? Henry was likely to die attempting to protect her if so.

Fury ripped through Gwen. A growl she didn't know she could produce thundered down the corridor, and she leaped forward, claws flashing.

She raked the rump of the bear on the left. He whined, falling sideways away from her. She leaped again, flying through the opening he had created and stopping just short of her friends' astonished faces.

Spinning, she lowered her head, her ears pinned back as she growled a warning.

The other two bears responded in kind, but their eyes showed confusion. They had no idea who she was.

The uninjured one tried to lunge forward, and Gwen slashed at him, her movement so quick her eyes couldn't follow. A trail of red down his arm was left in her wake. He pulled back, his gaze growing even more wary.

Gwen peeled her lips back and growled in satisfaction. The guards liked using their bear forms to terrorize the city, but they weren't used to facing another bear.

"Don't touch them!" she said in a low, threatening voice.

"Gwen!" Charlotte cried in recognition. "Oh, thank goodness."

The two guards froze, exchanging looks. Their confusion had overtaken whatever bloodlust or order had driven them. Like the rest of the palace and city, they had no idea their princess turned into a bear at night just like them.

"Yes, that's right," she said, her words clear despite her gravelly bear voice. "I'm your princess, and I order you to stand down. Now!" She roared the last word, and they both fell back, looking terrified.

Gwen smiled, feeling a different kind of strength coursing through her. She was not only finished being a victim, she was finished being the pure princess who hid in her room and earned her supposed virtue through inaction. She was done cowering and hiding. No matter what her form, Queen Gwendolyn would stand in the breach for the weaker members of her kingdom every time it was needed.

"A...apologies," the guard with the injured rump stammered, clearly not knowing what to do with her.

She wasn't their queen, but they did think she was their queen's daughter, and they knew she would soon sit on the throne. It was no surprise when they both turned tail and ran.

"Gwen!" Charlotte ran forward, tears in her eyes, and flung her arms around Gwen's neck.

"Thank you, Your Highness," Henry said more carefully. "You arrived at just the right moment."

Gwen leaned into Charlotte's hug for a moment, catching her breath.

"We should get moving," she said. "I don't know who those guards are going to report to, but word will get back to Celandine soon that we're here."

Henry grimaced. "We were hoping to keep my escape secret for longer."

"Never mind that," Charlotte said. "We need to take Gwen to Easton. He's worried sick."

"Easton?" Gwen's eyes lit up. "You know where he is?"

Charlotte nodded. "The queen caught all the other rebels, but Easton and I had gone looking for you, so we weren't there yet. I made him hide, and he promised he'd stay there." She smiled brightly. "And now he's about to be rewarded for his superhuman forbearance."

"Wait, Celandine caught the others?" Gwen cried, dismayed. "All of them?"

Charlotte winced. "I'm afraid so. Even Emmett."

"What?" Gwen stared at her, her mind racing. What was going to happen to the plan now?

"Come on," Charlotte said. "I might need the two of you to help me find the way. I'm fairly sure I remember the place, but..." She smiled, the expression not quite reaching her eyes. "We can work out what to do once all four of us are together."

CHARLOTTE

Thankfully, Gwen was able to lead the way to the section of the palace that contained the apartments of the count and his adult children. Once in that more familiar environment, Charlotte was confident in bypassing the dangerous apartment and leading the others straight to the storage cupboard.

She opened the door with a flourish, more relieved than she wanted to admit when Easton blinked up at her from a seated position on the floor. He raised his hand against the light, and Charlotte beamed at him.

"You're welcome," she said, standing back and gesturing toward Henry and the bear in the corridor.

Easton leaped to his feet. "Gwen!" He rushed to her side, relief lighting up his face. "You're here! Charlotte found you!"

"As promised," Charlotte said smugly before her face twisted a little. "I haven't found the others, though. At least not yet," she added hastily.

"We'll find them together." Gwen leaned her head against Easton's side.

He put an arm around her head, and she looked like she could have started purring with satisfaction. Charlotte hid a smile. Henry used to look like that sometimes in the library in their old castle when she scratched behind his ears or in other hard to reach spots.

"We should find somewhere less open," Henry said tensely. "We're not all going to fit in that cupboard."

Gwen shivered, and Charlotte was glad she had Easton at her side. Whatever had happened to Gwen after she got dragged away by the queen, she clearly hadn't fully recovered from it.

"This way." Gwen led them to a door one corridor over.

Easton turned the handle for her and stepped into a deserted sitting room.

"No one comes here during the day, let alone at night," Gwen said.

"What about our scent?" Charlotte asked. "Couldn't they track us?"

"Actually, I think I can do something about that," Henry offered.

Charlotte raised her eyebrows. She only hoped they weren't going to have to slop through any water troughs.

"Give me a minute."

He was gone for far longer than a minute, and when he returned, Charlotte wrinkled her nose in disgust. A highly unpleasant aroma clung to him.

Gwen, on the other hand, gagged, turning away with disgust.

"What do you think?" He directed his question at Gwen.

"Real bears probably think that smell is normal, right?" she asked. "Unfortunately my bear senses and human mind are working together in a terrifying alliance. It's like the most awful stench you've ever smelled amplified ten times."

Henry nodded with satisfaction. "I got rid of it all before I came in, so this is only a minor version of how it smells out there and all down the surrounding corridors."

"Is that horse manure?" Easton asked tentatively.

Henry smiled with satisfaction. "From the stables. I'm just glad I won't be responsible for cleaning your palace when this is all finished, Your Majesties."

Easton made a choked sound, his eyes bulging, and Gwen gagged again. Charlotte laughed, however. "Brilliant!"

"Hopefully this buys us some time," Henry said. "I'm not convinced we want to do anything too hastily."

Everyone shared what had happened to them in the last few hours, Easton drawing even closer to Gwen when she gave an emotionless recitation of her time in the small room.

"We were right there!" Easton cried in a tortured voice. "If we'd just stayed a little longer, or if I'd called for you a little louder..."

"It's my fault," Charlotte said, misery washing over her. "I told you to lower your voice and said we had to leave. I didn't think you were actually in there, Gwen."

"No!" Gwen's voice came out unexpectedly strong. "You were doing what you thought would be best for me. I understand that. And I'm actually glad you didn't find me. I needed to break free myself."

"You're always so gracious," Charlotte sighed, wondering if she would be the same after years of being a princess. Was it something you learned by being a royal?

Gwen drew a deep breath, sounding so distressed that Charlotte frowned at her.

"Actually," she said, "I think I should take this chance to

confess something—before you and Henry risk yourselves even more for me."

"What are you talking about?" Charlotte asked. "Of course we're going to help you. We're not just going to run away and abandon you."

"But you don't know everything," Gwen said. "You think it was your parents that came up with the idea of using their candle to get a look at Henry's face, but actually..." She finished on a rush, "Actually, it was me. When they took me out to their stables, I put all sorts of doubts about Henry in their heads and suggested the idea of the candle."

She turned to Henry. "I'm so sorry! I had no idea who you were. I thought you were working with the queen. I even thought you might have been the one to give her the bear enchantment in the first place."

Charlotte stared at her, her mind whirring. "It was you?" she cried. "Why didn't you say anything?"

Gwen winced. "When I tried to express doubts at first, you were so certain about Henry. I was worried about you, thinking you were another person being fooled and trapped by my mother. We'd only just met, so I thought you would be more likely to listen to your parents than to me. So I set up a chance to speak to them, and I poisoned their minds against Henry. It's all my fault."

"No," Charlotte said slowly. "I'm the one who took the candle into that room and lit it. Half of my anger toward my parents was because I was actually angry at myself." She sighed. "What a mess. You were right that I listened to my parents, and that was another mistake of mine. I let myself be swayed by their concerns even though they don't have a history of good judgment or decision-making." She sighed again. "You can love someone and know not to trust their judgment. I should have known better than to let myself be swayed by them. But their proposed solution lined up so exactly with what I wanted to do myself."

She looked at Henry, apology all over her face. "At the end of the day, I'm the one to blame. Everyone else—even you, Gwen—have the excuse that you were acting out of concern for me. But I was driven by curiosity and impatience."

Henry gave her a reassuring smile, taking her hand and threading his fingers through hers. She turned to Gwen with a smile.

"Henry has forgiven me my much bigger crime. You don't even need to ask if I can forgive you. Of course I can. It's already forgotten."

Gwen's expression lightened, her whole body suffused with relief. "I'm sorry I didn't tell you sooner. I should have told you straight away when we met after Henry's disappearance. But I thought...I thought..." Tears welled, making it difficult for her to speak.

"I'm glad that's resolved," Easton said, clearly trying to hide his tension. "But I think we should talk about what we do next. Gwen, do you have any idea where the queen might have taken the rebels? If she wants to keep them locked away until the wedding, where would they be?"

Gwen sat back, clearly considering the question. "The guards have cells of various sizes, of course, but none of them are big enough for so many."

"Would she think it was dangerous to keep them togeth-er?" Henry asked. "If they could work together, they might find a way to escape."

"Together..." Gwen murmured, seeming struck by a thought. "Actually, there's one place. The servants all get locked in together every night. It's a series of connected storage rooms. They're in the basement level, and there aren't even any windows. The servants have been in there as a group for nearly ten years, and they haven't found a way to break out."

"And she thinks they're rebels as well," Henry said, catching up with her idea. "She's probably got them all locked in there together."

"Do you know where the door is?" Easton asked. "And how we can get the key?"

Gwen looked down at her paws and then back at him. "We might not need a key."

Easton grinned. "If you're suggesting you could break down the door with pure force, I believe you. But if we don't want to bring people running to investigate the commotion, we might want to find a subtler method."

"And I think we need to wait for morning anyway," Henry said. "The guards' sense of smell and hearing are too great an advantage when they're bears. We won't manage to creep around unseen or sneak into the basement rooms if they can smell or hear us from half a palace away."

Easton looked like he wanted to argue, but just like Charlotte, he'd never been a bear. She was inclined to agree with Henry, and doubly so when Gwen quickly nodded her agreement.

"Does that window open?" she asked, nodding at the largest window in the room. "I think we're all going to need some rest at some point tonight, but we'll need to take turns staying up on watch, and we should have an escape route planned. They may decide to search this whole area room by room if they guess we're the source of that stench."

Henry strode over and tested the latch on the window, peering outside. "It opens, and the jump isn't too big."

"We don't need to take watches," Gwen said. "I should do it the whole time. I'm the only one with bear senses, and I actually slept well the last couple of nights."

Charlotte and Henry exchanged a look.

"You can do most of the night," he agreed, "but you need to get a few hours' sleep. We don't know what tomorrow will be like yet, but the wedding was planned for the late afternoon, I believe, so it will likely be a long day."

"So what is our plan?" Charlotte asked. "Is the queen really going to try to go through with the wedding in the middle of all this?"

"That has been her plan, but when she realizes Henry is gone, the plan is going to have to change," Gwen said.

Henry frowned. "Should I go back to my room?"

"No!" Charlotte cried, thankful when the others stayed silent. "That is not happening. We're together now, and we're going to work this out together. No more prisoners, no more separation."

Gwen nodded, Easton a beat behind her.

"She can't have a wedding," Gwen said. "Not unless she can recapture us both and somehow force us to comply." She was carefully not looking at Easton as she said it. "But she won't want to admit weakness. And she'll still want a spectacle. The invited guests from the city and even the loyal courtiers will likely still turn up at the appointed time. Celandine will be telling herself she can recapture us in time, or else she'll plan a big demonstration with all the rebels instead, thinking that will restore order and her power, at least in the short term while she works out how to fix things. That's been her strategy until now, always a temporary fix, keeping things going while she gets herself further and further into trouble."

"So we'll still have our audience," Easton said thoughtfully.

Gwen nodded.

"In that case," he said, meeting her eyes. "We need to give them what they came to see."

"A wedding!" Charlotte cried in delight, clasping her hands together. "With no need for last minute switches. Just the two of you, getting married. As long as we can keep the queen and her guards occupied, the courtiers won't protest. They don't even know what Henry looks like, remember."

"But how do we keep the queen and her guards occupied?" Henry asked.

"We lock her up." Gwen looked surprised by the ferocity in her own voice.

"Is that even possible?" Charlotte asked.

"She isn't superhuman," Gwen replied. "She doesn't have the strength of a bear during the day."

"What about her godmother objects?" Easton asked.

"She keeps them in a hidden room," Gwen said. "The only one she carries continually on her person is the one tied to the bear enchantment. And that won't help her get out of a locked cell. Her strength comes from fear and intimidation and her guards. Stripped of those, she's just a human woman with the strength of a human woman. She can't batter down a door."

Henry slowly smiled. "So we lock her up, and then we lead her guards on a merry chase so they don't have the chance to properly look for her."

"It doesn't have to last forever," Charlotte said. "Only long enough for the captives to do their job."

"The captives?" Henry looked at her, confused.

"The wedding!" Charlotte cried, rolling her eyes at his obliviousness. "Do you think a function like that is going to magically come together on its own? The queen was planning to put on a show, but now it's our show, and we can't look less impressive than her. We have to somehow convince the captives to play the role of servants one more time and set everything up."

"So the rebels will have to lead the chase," Henry said thoughtfully. "You and I can help with that."

"The bride and groom will have to stick with the wedding preparation." He looked at Easton with a small smile, and Charlotte almost laughed. It was obvious which he thought was the better assignment, despite the danger.

From the pained look on Easton's face, he agreed. After the way they had all been treated, everyone wanted a piece of Celandine and her people. But the plan made the most sense that way, and nobody tried to argue.

Charlotte was certain she wouldn't be able to sleep. But when she lay on one of the broad sofas with Henry pressed against her back and his arms around her, she drifted off faster than she would have liked.

She was jerked awake by a frantic whisper from Gwen in the small hours.

"Quick! Someone's coming," she said.

"Wha…" Charlotte sat up, bleary-eyed and confused.

Henry woke behind her, instantly alert. "Out the window, then. I left some manure there earlier."

Easton pushed it open, and Gwen climbed through first, scrabbling with her paws for purchase before heaving herself over the ledge. Charlotte tried to hold back her impatience, glancing constantly between the door and the window, just waiting for someone to thrust the door open.

"Climb through," Gwen called back quietly. "Straight onto my back."

"Gwen!" Easton exclaimed, pausing halfway over the sill. "You can't carry three of us!"

"Yes, I can," she said stubbornly. "I'm not an ordinary bear, you know. I'm bigger, for one. And I don't have to carry you far. Just far enough to confuse them. My scent will be unfamiliar to them, especially since most of them don't even know I'm a bear at night. And I'll walk through the manure. If you're on my back, it will make it much harder for them to smell where you went."

"Come on," Charlotte said to Easton, giving him a light push. "Just do what she says."

Still grumbling, Easton dropped carefully onto her back and slid forward as far as he could go. Charlotte followed next, Henry lifting her over the sill and placing her on Gwen's back with ease. He followed last, barely fitting behind Charlotte, although he somehow managed to not only balance there but also lean back to close the window behind them.

Gwen took off at a careful walk, heading for the closest patch of concealing trees. Once out of sight, she angled toward the stables.

"If we're throwing them off with the scent of manure..." she murmured in answer to the question no one had voiced aloud.

She walked all the way into the stables, and Charlotte expected the horses to start screaming and whinnying in terror. But they must have grown used to the presence of bears in their vicinity because they barely reacted at all.

Gwen stopped below a ladder that led up to the hay loft. They took turns stepping straight onto it, climbing one at a time. When they had finished, Gwen rubbed her side against the lower rungs, hopefully covering their scent.

"But what about you?" Easton leaned over the side, looking down at her.

"There's an empty stall on the end. I'll sleep there," she called quietly back.

Easton twisted to look at Charlotte and Henry, and she could read his thoughts on his face. Thankfully, Gwen spoke before Charlotte needed to.

"You stay up there," she told him. "Don't even think about coming down to join me."

Charlotte gave him a sympathetic look as he nodded with resignation. She felt selfish, but she was glad it wasn't Henry down there, so close and yet too far. After so many stressful days apart, she wasn't ready to have him more than an arm's length away.

CHARLOTTE

It took her longer to fall asleep the second time, but she managed it in the end. And when she woke, the first brush of the morning was already past.

She bolted awake, staring from Henry to where Gwen now slept beside them. Easton sat to one side, keeping watch over her.

"What are we still doing here?" She gasped and lowered her voice. "Aren't there grooms down there by now?"

Henry shrugged. "No one came. I guess the grooms are all captives."

Gwen stirred, nodding sleepily at Henry's comment.

"We needed to give Gwen a chance to rest," Easton said. "She was awake all night keeping watch over us."

"But now we need to get to the basement." Charlotte's stomach rumbled on cue, making her flush. "Ignore that. I don't need to eat."

"We should eat." Gwen sat up and stretched, yawning. "I'm sure the grooms have something stashed in their office. Let's go check."

They found a whole basket of apples and a large hunk of cheese that they divided four ways.

"I'll admit, I feel a lot better after that," Henry said, and Charlotte nodded agreement.

The day before, it had been easy to sneak through first the grounds and then the palace. In hindsight, it had been too easy, the way cleared for the rebels to walk into the trap.

Now, the grounds teemed with guard patrols. They were everywhere, even if their steps lagged, and they kept rubbing their eyes as if they'd already been on duty all night.

"Thank goodness they're all so tired," Easton whispered as they once again dove into a clump of bushes to hide. "Otherwise we'd have been caught by now for sure."

They finally made it into the actual palace, but that only meant substituting empty rooms and storage cupboards for bushes. By the time they reached the entrance to the basement level, Charlotte's nerves were stretched so tight they were about to snap.

Two guards stood on either side of the door. Their attitude was far from alert, but they were awake, and they had swords at their sides.

"There's no way to sneak around those two," Gwen said. "There are only two doors down to the basement level, and if this one is guarded, the other one definitely will be. This is the back entrance."

Charlotte looked Henry and Easton up and down. "You're a prince, Henry, and you were a courtier's son at least until you were thirteen, Easton. Do you both have combat training?"

The two men exchanged a look before nodding simultaneously.

Charlotte shrugged. "Then I think we'll need a direct

confrontation this time. There are only two of them, and they won't know what either of you look like, so they won't be sure who you are at first."

"I'd rather not leave dead bodies in our wake," Gwen said queasily.

"We can raid the last storage cupboard and look for something to use to gag and secure them," Charlotte suggested, and Gwen reluctantly nodded.

Henry and Easton exchanged another look and another nod before striding forward together.

"Come on, hurry." Charlotte pulled Gwen toward the cupboard, but Gwen resisted.

"Let me get the supplies," she said. "You stay here in case they need backup."

Charlotte grimaced, unsure what backup she could possibly provide, but Gwen was already darting away. And since Gwen knew her own palace better, it did make sense to let her go.

"You there!" Henry called in an imperious voice, pointing toward the guards.

They straightened instinctively, recognizing the casual note of command in his voice and bearing that marked him as someone with authority.

"What is going on?" Henry continued. "There are guards everywhere, and my wife couldn't sleep for half the night from all the commotion. We're supposed to be attending a wedding today, but—"

One of the guards interrupted. "This area is off limits. We're going to have to ask you to leave."

Henry and Easton kept advancing, and the guards looked warily at each other before the first one drew his sword and the other followed suit. But they'd left it too late and let Henry and Easton draw too close.

Breaking into a sprint, the two men rushed the guards, lashing out with fists and feet. Charlotte gasped, her heart in her throat, but before she could even think about moving forward, it was all over. The two guards lay on the ground groaning, and the swords were in the hands of their attackers.

Henry looked back and motioned her forward, and she rushed over.

"Gwen went on her own to get something to use as rope," she said, and Easton looked up, alarmed.

But before he could go off in search of her, Gwen appeared, having managed to procure actual rope and several long stretches of torn material for gags. Henry and Easton made quick work of securing their defeated opponents, dumping the two men in a nearby room.

"Let's hope we don't have to do that too many times," Charlotte said, eyeing the closed door uneasily. Easton had tied the ropes with a seaman's knots, but there was still no telling how long it would take the defeated guards to get free.

Thankfully, they met no more guards on the basement level. Apparently, only the doors had been left guarded in order to free the others up to patrol the grounds and castle corridors.

Gwen led the way to the relevant set of rooms, having explained that while she'd never been inside, she had been to the door before. Since Gwen was no longer in her bear form, it was a good thing she'd remembered that she still had her stolen master key in her pocket. Celandine hadn't remembered to confiscate it when she'd dragged Gwen away.

"I could have just unlocked the door and walked out." Gwen looked down when she said it, apparently embarrassed.

Easton put a hand on her arm. "Didn't you say what you went through in there was important? And you don't know if this key would have worked anyway. The queen changed the lock on your room, so she might have changed that one too."

"That's true." Gwen brightened. "Both of those things are true."

"But let's hope it works on this door," Charlotte added nervously. Without a bear among them, it would take a long time to beat down such a sturdy door. She took the key out of Gwen's hand since her fingers were trembling slightly after the reminder of her recent imprisonment.

The key slid in and turned. She threw a relieved look back at the rest of them, pushing the door open and stepping forward.

"No!" Gwen and Henry called at the same time.

Henry lunged forward and caught hold of the back of her dress, yanking her backward. A length of wood, being wielded as a baton, flashed down hard on where her head had just been.

Henry gave a sigh of relief and pulled her into a quick hug.

"How did you know that was going to happen?" Charlotte blinked up at him.

He gave a guilty look in Gwen's direction. "I nearly did the same thing to Gwen when I thought she was the queen."

Someone peered out the door and then turned to shout back into the room. Charlotte tried to pull away now that the prisoners had seen the identity of the arrivals, but Henry held on.

"I think we should let them come out here," he said. "I don't fancy all of us getting trapped in such a secure location."

Easton and Gwen nodded fervent agreement, so Charlotte stayed in place, watching as people began to file out of the door. Most of them she didn't recognize, but when Lydia and Jett emerged and rushed to their son's side, she smiled, watching the reunion with pleasure. And when Emmett's crutches appeared, the boy following a swing later, she almost cried to see him unharmed. His father hovered at his shoulder, his eyes meeting Charlotte's.

He nodded at her, gratitude on his face, but she gestured with her head toward Gwen and Easton, who were already surrounded. He should save his gratitude for his future king and queen.

But when Count Oswin appeared, she hurried to his side. He hadn't been in the line of prisoners who had paraded past her hiding place, so she hadn't known to expect him there. He must have been arrested separately.

She was glad to see him, though. If he was there, they only needed to convince one person of the rebels' new role in the day's events.

The count clasped her hand. "It's good to see you. More than good. When my son told me he'd had a glimpse of Easton, I hoped...But I wasn't sure..." He glanced at his grandson and stopped, seemingly overcome with emotion.

"Of course we had to come rescue you," Charlotte said warmly. "But we're not just here to save you."

The count looked at her sharply. "We're still going ahead with the plan? How is that possible?"

Charlotte grinned. "There have been a few amendments..."

With the help of the count and his son, they got the grateful crowd separated, the servants heading down the corridor in one direction, while the rebels followed Henry and Charlotte several yards the other way.

After they'd explained the situation, the count surveyed

the small crowd. "Anyone have any objections? Anyone want out?"

The group stayed silent.

Henry gave the count a disapproving look as he stepped forward to address the group. "We only want people who are actual volunteers. You've all had a highly distressing experience, and if you need to withdraw, we won't take it as a reflection on your commitment to the cause."

Still no one spoke up.

Charlotte stepped forward as well. "In that case, does anyone have any suggestions about how we can lure the queen into a secure location? Somewhere we can lock her in?"

The rebels who had snuck in from the city gave each other blank looks. But some of the freed prisoners were courtiers whose allegiances had shifted, and several of them narrowed their eyes in thought.

"I have an idea," Emmett piped up.

His grandfather stepped forward, but Charlotte motioned for him to wait and let Emmett speak.

The boy looked back toward the room they'd just left. "Why not use that?"

Charlotte raised an eyebrow. "How do you propose we get her in there?"

"She's already planning to come," he said, gaining enthusiasm. "I spent the night talking with some of the servants."

"Captives," Henry said, and Emmett flushed.

"Yes," he amended. "The captives. They said the only reason the queen hadn't slaughtered them already was that she needed them."

The count scoffed. "That's what comes of replacing every single one of your servants with captive slaves."

Emmett shifted uncomfortably, and Charlotte motioned for him to continue.

"Apparently, she was going to come back today and collect some of them so they could finish preparing her big event. The others were going to be left here, under guard."

"She was going to threaten them in order to make the others comply," Henry said thoughtfully, clearly turning Emmett's suggestion over in his mind.

"But will she come herself?" Charlotte looked to the count as the one who must know her best. "Won't she just send some guards to collect them?"

"She'll come," he said confidently. "She'll want to make a big show to intimidate them, and she won't trust that to any of her people. It's one of her weaknesses that she surrounds herself almost entirely with subservient people. The old captain of the guard is more interested in not attracting her attention than showing any initiative. He doesn't have the personality for chilling speeches or spreading fear by his mere presence."

His son nodded. "Prince Henry and Princess Gwendolyn have both escaped her grasp. She knows she's hanging onto the situation by a thread. She won't want to risk anything else getting out of control."

"In that case..." Charlotte grimaced. "How well does she know her own guards?"

"I'm going to guess not well at all," the count said, looking bemused. "They aren't loyal to her because of a personal connection. Only because she gives them power and gold."

Charlotte surveyed the group, pointing at one man and then another. "You and you." She turned to Henry. "What do you think? I think they're the closest matches we've got."

He narrowed his eyes, examining the two men before agreeing.

"How do you feel about playing guards for a little?" Charlotte asked them.

The two looked to the count, who redirected their attention to Charlotte.

"The door down to this level had two guards when we arrived," Henry explained. "We...removed them. You'll find them tied up in a room just upstairs. You'll need to strip them and use their uniforms. Here's one of their swords." He handed the weapon over. "We'll retrieve the other one from Easton."

"The queen will likely use the main entrance," the count said. "But if she does appear, just keep your heads bowed in respect and attempt not to say anything. Hopefully no one will notice you're not who you're supposed to be."

Charlotte handed the master key to the count's son. "You go with them. The guards are locked away. Once they have the uniforms, lock them up again and bring the key back down. We'll need it here."

The three men moved off, a couple of others following to assist them.

"Won't the queen notice something is wrong when she opens the door and the room inside is deserted?" Charlotte asked.

"That's why I need to be in there," Emmett said, rejoining the conversation.

"Absolutely not," his father said instantly, and the boy rolled his eyes.

"I'm not a baby, Father. And obviously you'll need to be with me. But look at me! I'm a child, and also—" He gestured at his leg. "Do I look like a threat? I'll be in the first room, lying down without my crutches. The queen will send some guards in first to make sure no one tries what we did earlier, so when I see them, I'll start crying and wailing, saying I've been abandoned and the others are all hiding in the back rooms. But the moment the queen comes inside herself—all the way inside—Father will leap up and grab me and sprint us straight out of the room. The rest of you can be ready to shut the door the second we're out." He beamed around at them. "And if I get a chance on the way out, I'll snatch the key right out of her hand."

"I can see some things that could go wrong with that," Henry said through the side of his mouth.

Charlotte winced in agreement. But the idea did have some merits. It was true that no one else among them could possibly be as disarming and non-threatening in appearance as Emmett.

"What if it's not just his father hidden in there with him?" she suggested.

Henry gazed at the amassed rebels. "Some of you are courtiers," he said. "Do any of you have experience fighting with a blade, preferably of disarming a bladed opponent without a blade yourself?"

Four men shouldered their way through the crowd to stand before them. One had a roughly bandaged left arm, and another had a gash along one cheek.

"We can do it," one of them said.

"And would welcome a chance," added another in a low growl.

"We wouldn't have been taken so easily back there," the first added, "if they hadn't gotten a knife to the boy's throat."

Emmett looked down at the ground, reminding Charlotte of what she had overheard the evening before. He wasn't supposed to have been in the apartment at all. No wonder he was desperate to have a part in making up for his mistake. Charlotte could relate to the feeling.

"It's fairly dark in there," she said. "We should be able to conceal all five of you in there with him. You can be ready to burst out and fight your way out if necessary. The queen's not going to send her entire guard force in ahead of her."

The count tried to protest, but surprisingly it was his son who restrained him. "We have to let him do this," he said quietly in his father's ear. "If he walks away from this feeling like he was weak and helpless and at fault, it might destroy the rest of his life. He already has enough battles of that kind to fight."

Both men glanced at the boy's missing leg.

Charlotte watched them, impressed. She hadn't expected so much insight from the count's son. It was reassuring, though, after his actions earlier in his life. Maybe he really could prove a support to Gwen in the future.

Once the plan had been decided on, it didn't take long to get everyone organized. Gwen and Easton led the captive servants away, taking them out through the back door that was now guarded by their own people in disguise.

Some of the rebels went with them to hide on the next level up and wait, splitting their forces. There were only so many people who could be helpful in a single corridor.

Once Emmett and his various protectors were hidden inside, the rest of them crowded through the next door down, hiding themselves out of sight from the corridor. Once the queen arrived, they would have to move fast.

It seemed like they'd hardly settled out of sight before Charlotte heard marching boots, and someone hissed, "She's here!"

CHARLOTTE

Charlotte would have preferred to have longer to catch her breath before Celandine's arrival, but at least it sounded like she was coming from the direction of the main door. She wouldn't have passed their people in that case.

Charlotte strained her ears to hear the key turn in the lock and the door open. As expected, the first steps to enter sounded like the boots of guards.

Some low, surprised murmurs drifted out, presumably at the discovery of the empty room. Then Emmett started whimpering, his cries pathetic and weak. He spoke amid the blubbering, but Charlotte was too far away to catch his words. More footsteps sounded, and then Celandine's imperious voice demanding to know what was going on.

"Now!" Charlotte whispered and raced out of the door. Henry was a step ahead of her, two burly men from the city ahead of him.

The four of them lined up along the wall behind the open door to the prison rooms, staying as quiet as possible. A shout rang inside the room, and then the sound of a scuffle broke out. Charlotte recognized a fist hitting flesh and more shouts before the count's son raced from the room, Emmett in his arms. He didn't stop, continuing down the corridor toward the back exit. Emmett looked back over his shoulder and met Charlotte's eyes, grinning broadly. He held up his prize—the queen's key—and Charlotte saluted him.

One of the other rebels came next, walking backward, a sword in his hand and a bruise already blooming under one eye. Two of the queen's guards followed him, both on the attack, and behind them came a crush of people that was hard to distinguish, some rebels, some guards. Charlotte struggled to complete her head count of the rebels, ensuring they had all emerged. But she reached the correct number at the same time as she noted the other important point—the queen still hadn't emerged.

"Close it!" she yelled, and the two rebels against the wall heaved together, pushing the door ahead of them.

One of the guards shouted in protest, trying to throw himself into the closing gap, but Henry darted forward and shoved him hard enough to send him staggering all the way inside. The two rebels gave a final push and slammed the door closed, leaning against it to keep the guards still remaining inside from opening it again.

Charlotte darted between the struggling bodies, inserting their key and turning it before dashing away, heading further down the corridor in the direction of Emmett and his father.

From the other direction, the remaining rebels streamed out of their hiding place, joining their comrades and easily subduing the guards with their superior numbers. Charlotte counted heads again, not relaxing until she had confirmed her original count. Everyone on their side was accounted for, along with many of the guards.

She could hear screaming and shouting from the other side, but the wood was the thickest she had ever seen, and the hinges were on the outside. The guards who had ended up locked inside with the queen could pound on it for hours without breaking it down.

"Do they have any weapons left in there?" she asked one of the rebels who had been hidden inside.

"We disarmed most of them," he said. "They might have a dagger or two, but they won't get through that door in a hurry with only that."

"We're fortunate that once we sprung into action, most of them leaped to form a shield in front of the queen," another added. "It meant they unintentionally blocked her exit."

A piercing scream cut through the wood of the door. "Why don't we move upstairs?" Charlotte suggested, happy to put distance between her and the enraged queen, even if Celandine was locked away.

"What about this lot?" a rebel asked, indicating the subdued guards.

"We can take them upstairs with us. There's rope up there, and we can tie them up with their comrades."

"There must be others who knew the queen was coming down here, though," the count said. "If they come looking with a key…"

"They'll have to come through us." All four of the volunteers who had identified themselves as experienced fighters stood before them, now armed. "In a corridor like this, the captain of the guard would have to bring his entire force—split and attacking from both directions—to get through us."

A grin spread over Charlotte's face. "Then it's our job to make sure the entire force isn't available, even if they do work out where she is."

The four of them grinned back, moving to take up positions by the door. The rest of the rebels dragged their new prisoners with them up the stairs, finding a crowd on the other side of the door. The remaining rebels rushed forward to help secure the guards, having already found the rope Gwen left.

"What about Gwen and Easton and the others?" Charlotte asked one of them.

She shrugged. "They didn't stick around."

Charlotte nodded, hoping that meant the other part of their plan was succeeding as well. If the captive servants all decided they were taking their freedom and left without helping, the later parts of the plan would falter.

"You all know what we have to do now," the count said loudly. "Split up and find weapons if you can. Pair fighters with someone less experienced if possible, and I want at least one member of the court in each group. The guards will hesitate to do any serious damage to a member of the court without direct commands to do so. Our goal is to sow chaos and confusion. Find guards and then lead them on a chase for as long as you can. Keep them running and confused. We can't let them gather into a force of any size or give them time to stop and seek proper command. If you see someone else has been captured, free them if you can."

A chorus of agreement sounded, and the group spread out, breaking into smaller clumps. Charlotte looked at Henry with a smile.

"What about us?"

"We're a pair," he said. "And I don't think we need anyone else." He held out his hand, and she put hers into it.

"I've still got that master key," she said. "So I think we can get up to enough mischief on our own."

It took them several minutes of running to find their first pair of guards. The two men strolled leisurely across their field of vision until one of them recognized Charlotte and let out a shout. Charlotte and Henry took off running immediately, Henry taking the lead as they led the soldiers around in circles. When he darted through a door, he led Charlotte straight through the receiving room on the other side and out through a door in the opposite wall. He closed it behind them and gestured at the keyhole.

Charlotte locked it, and the two of them dashed back around to lock the other door while the protesting soldiers were still trying the handle of the locked one.

"There are windows, so I don't know how long it will keep them," Henry said.

"Long enough for now." Charlotte grinned back. "Let's go and find some others."

With Henry's knowledge of the castle and their master key, they managed to pull the same trick on ten different soldiers, strolling away each time to the sound of shouts and curses.

Charlotte grinned up at Henry. "Is it terrible that this has been kind of fun?"

The thrill of being chased was both terrifying and exhilarating, and if it wasn't for the exhaustion setting in to her legs, she could have gone on much longer. She glanced out a window, noting the lowering sun. They had passed several other rebel groups in the last few hours, even rescuing one as they were being escorted back toward the guard barracks. She hadn't seen Gwen or Easton or any of the servants, though. The rebels had purposely been trying to keep the guards away from the section of the palace that included the throne room.

Were the wedding preparations finished? Had the ceremony started? She wished she could be there to see her friend married, but she knew her role was too important to worry about being a guest.

Thought of guests made her wonder how the arriving wedding guests had gone. Had any of them spotted a rebel group being chased by royal guards? Had some of the guards been available to guide guests in? She hoped some of the intended guests had made it through the chaos to be the witnesses Gwen and Easton needed.

"Do you think it's—" she started to say to Henry, but a figure jumped out behind him, making her words falter.

Before he could respond to her horrified expression, the enormous guard had his arms around Henry from behind, pinning his arms to his side and holding a knife to his throat.

A sneering courtier stepped out from the shadows, another guard at his side.

"Shall I restrain her, Lord Rafferty?" the second guard asked, looking toward Charlotte.

"I don't think that will be necessary," he said in an oily voice that sent a shiver up her spine. "I think she'll be most well-behaved." He looked toward Henry and smiled again.

Henry shook his head, but even that small movement made the knife tip prick his skin. Charlotte gasped.

"Don't listen to him," Henry choked out before his captor tightened his grip.

"All I want from you is that key in your pocket," Lord Rafferty said. "I can't find the captain of the guard, but I know you have a master key. Don't bother trying to deny it. I just watched that neat little trick you pulled. If you want this fellow here to live, hand it over now."

Charlotte's mind moved faster than seemed possible, heightened by the danger to Henry and all their plans. If this lord was after the key, he must know or guess where the queen was. But she couldn't just stand by and watch Henry be killed.

She glanced again at the window. The sun was even lower. Soon it would be kissing the horizon. She had to trust they had held out long enough.

"Fine." She drew the word out, keeping her expression downcast and fearful. Slowly she plunged her hand into her pocket and drew it out. But as Lord Rafferty reached for it, she flicked her arm back and then whipped it forward, sending the key sailing over his head and down the corridor.

He cursed, and the second guard raced after it. But Charlotte's eyes were on Henry. As the guard holding him turned to watch the hunt for the key, Henry's eyes flickered down to the man's left arm.

Charlotte jumped at him, biting hard into his left arm. The man screamed and pulled it away, shaking her off. But the second he loosened his grip, Henry's own left arm broke free, snapping up and pulling the wrist holding the knife away from his throat.

The whole thing took only a second, and Henry was free. A line of red dribbled down his neck, but he brushed it away, appearing unharmed in any serious manner. He kicked the guard in the shin, and when he shouted and doubled over, he punched him hard in the stomach. The man went down, winded, and Henry took Charlotte's hand.

For what felt like the hundredth time that day, they ran.

"Never mind them!" she heard the lord screaming behind them. "We have the key. That's all that matters."

"Should we try to get down there first?" Charlotte gasped out between panting breaths. "Try to stop them?" But when she glanced back, four more guards ran up to join them.

"I think it's too late for that," Henry said.

Charlotte nodded. "I just hope we managed to give them enough time. Should we head to the throne room in case Gwen and Easton need help?"

"Actually," Henry said. "If the queen is about to be free, I think there's somewhere else we need to be."

GWEN

As people poured out of the basement prison, the captive servants turned toward Gwen's familiar face. Alma and Miriam pushed to the front of the group, and Gwen could have cried to see the smiles on their faces. She had been afraid they would resent her after her request had exposed them to the queen.

"I told you she'd come for us," Alma said in a loud, satisfied voice, eyeing off the rest of the group.

"Thank you for your faith," Gwen murmured, tears pricking at the back of her eyes. "I just hope you're willing to have a little more because I have a final request for you."

She led the way a short distance down the corridor, relieved again when the captive servants followed her, separating out from the rebels who had clustered around Charlotte and the count.

She raised her voice slightly so they could all hear her. "I came here to rescue you, and if you want to walk away now, I understand. You don't owe me anything."

"The mountain kingdom owes *us*!" a discontented voice shouted from the back.

Gwen nodded. "I agree. And that's why if you walk away now, I'll understand. But the reality is that while you're freed from that room, you're still trapped here in a kingdom controlled by Celandine. All of us are. If any of us are going to be truly free, then we need to remove her from the throne. And I'm hoping you'll be willing to help with that."

"So that you can sit on it instead!" another scornful voice called from the middle of the crowd.

Miriam whipped around, glaring. "You all know what she told me! The princess isn't like her mother. She's not only going to free us, she's going to send us off with compensation." She turned back to Gwen. "Right?"

"Absolutely!" Gwen said firmly, remembering the chests of gold in her mother's hidden room. "I even have a way to get you home." If she had to fly each of them across the mountains individually, she would do it.

Murmurs swept through the group at that, everyone turning to their neighbor and exchanging whispers. Gwen didn't try to catch individual words, instead listening to the sound as a whole, tracking its mood. It had started with astonishment and a tone of disbelief, but as they conferred, she heard it change. A note of determination crept in before taking over completely. Alma had said they were waiting for their chance, and apparently she had been right. The captives were ready to seize the opportunity offered to them.

"How dangerous is this task you want from us?" Alma asked.

"Hopefully not dangerous at all," Gwen said. "But it's something you know best how to do. If I tried it on my own…" She grimaced. "The queen planned for this afternoon to be a grand spectacle of her power. We're planning to turn it into something else, but we still need the grand spectacle. We need to show the courtiers and the people of the city that we are just as capable and powerful as the old queen."

"You want us to set up the ballroom?" Alma sounded disbelieving.

Gwen nodded. "Down the corridor, you'll see the rebels gathered. They're going to keep the guards and the queen occupied, so I'm hoping there won't be anyone to disturb your efforts. In fact, it's likely the guards aren't even keeping up with the constantly changing situation. If they see you working and preparing in your previous roles, they won't even realize anything is wrong. I don't expect them to harass you."

"And after we've finished?" Alma pressed. "Will we be expected to prepare your evening meal when all of this is over?"

"If this day ends with me as queen, you will be free," Gwen said firmly. "It will take a bit longer to distribute the compensation, and even longer to ferry anyone who wants to go across the mountains. But I'll do it as quickly as is possible in the middle of everything else." She drew a breath, feeling like she was taking a risk. "And if anyone wants to remain in the mountain kingdom—either in the city or in a paid role in the palace—I would love for you to stay. By choice or not, this has been your home for years now, and I won't take it from you forcibly like your last home was taken. From this point on, each of you gets to choose."

She gazed over the faces, reading in the expressions that she'd said the right thing.

Alma rubbed her hands together, her face setting into lines of determination. "All right then, we have work to do."

No one argued.

"Well done," Easton murmured in her ear, his approval warming her. "You sound like a queen."

She threw him a grateful look, but there was no time for a proper conversation. The same was true with Charlotte, although from the look on her face and the brief squeeze she gave Gwen's hand, everything had gone smoothly on their end as well. The captives were ushered out the back way, some of the rebels going with them.

When she walked through the door and saw the two guards back in position, her heart seized. But they grinned jauntily and gave her an elaborate bow, and she relaxed again. They weren't the old guards but rebels wearing guard uniforms. Charlotte had even managed to find rebels who looked similar to the men who had previously held the post.

Once they were all out of the basement level, Miriam approached Gwen with a grin she'd never seen the captive woman wear before. Something had changed in her, and she was no longer tentative in Gwen's presence.

"Come on, then, Your Majesty, we have lots of work to do." She gave Gwen an exaggerated look of appraisal, running her eyes up and down her body and wrinkling her nose. Four women stood behind her, two of them chuckling.

"And you're with us, Your Majesty." An older woman and two men appeared beside Easton.

He looked at Gwen in alarm. "I'm happy to help with the preparations of the throne room in any way I can, but I'm staying with Gwen."

Alma stepped up, tutting and shaking her head.

"The preparations you need aren't in the throne room. If we're putting on a show, don't forget that you two are the star players. If you want to present an image of glory and power, it's going to take a *lot* of work."

Gwen flushed, wanting to protest, but when she looked down at herself, the protest died unspoken. She had slept the night in the stables and before that in her ruined room. She probably had feathers in her hair, and she couldn't remember the last time she'd washed. It had definitely been before the manure. With horror, she looked across at Easton's dirty, disheveled appearance. He hadn't spent hours in a state of total panic and cold sweat in the recent past, so what did Gwen herself look like?

Easton looked back at her, his expression bemused but his eyes laughing. When she held his gaze, his look turned soft and loving, his message clear. He didn't care what she looked like.

Her panic receded but only a little. Alma and Miriam were right. She couldn't appear before the court and city in this state and claim to be their rightful queen.

She still hated being separated from Easton, but neither of them complained further as they were carried off in different directions. The servants didn't need to be told not to take Gwen to her own room, instead easily locating unused rooms closer to the throne room for their purpose.

The women around Gwen came and went over the following hours, but Miriam was always with her. They prepared a bath, somehow producing fragrant soaps for both her body and hair and lotions for her to use after. And when they'd wrapped her in a soft robe, they began on her hair.

The woman who took the lead was one Gwen knew only a little, and she'd had no idea of the woman's skill. It took a long time, but when she finished, Gwen's hair was twisted into an elaborate pile on her head, full of curls and artful tumbles.

Pearls and small flowers hid in the creases, and a tiara of silver and pearls nestled at the front. Gwen had never seen anything so elegant.

They helped her into the frothy layers of her wedding gown after that, and the gown was even more breathtaking than when Gwen had worn it for the final fittings. In the back of her mind, she couldn't forget that Charlotte and Henry were out there somewhere, doing battle with the queen and her guards on Gwen's behalf. But neither could she help losing herself in the moment, thinking of Easton, who was somewhere nearby being helped into the wedding outfit originally intended for Henry. Was someone desperately making last minute adjustments, perhaps sewing it while he modeled it for them? She had to stifle a laugh at the idea of poor Easton forced to stand still for hours or risk being poked with a needle.

She had thought the afternoon would drag, her worry making the hours interminable, but instead they passed shockingly quickly. When Alma appeared to say it was time, Gwen started and flew to her feet.

"What do you mean? It can't be!" She looked out the window and realized the sun was lowering toward the horizon after all. "Did any guests arrive? Did they still come?"

Alma grinned with satisfaction. "We requisitioned those two rebels dressed as guards and added a few of our own to their number. We've had *guards* escorting guests from the edge of the palace grounds for the last hour. It looks like most of the courtiers had fled to their city homes—even they could tell something strange was going on in the palace—but none of them dared miss the wedding. The seats are full."

Gwen drew a long breath, fear fluttering through her. But it was balanced by a sense of certainty. This was the role she had been born for, the one she was supposed to fill. Whatever happened next, she was doing the right thing.

She turned to Alma and nodded, face serious. But Alma just gazed at her before smiling in an almost motherly way. "You look beautiful, Your Majesty."

Tears welled again, and Gwen quickly blinked them away. "Thank you, Alma. Thank you for everything. Your kindness meant everything to me in those lonely years after Easton's banishment."

Alma gave her another, sadder smile. "I always felt sorry for you, Princess Gwen. Some of the others thought it was foolish since you were the princess, but at least the queen didn't keep any of us close by her side day after day."

Gwen swallowed and nodded. "Just so you know, she isn't my mother. She isn't even my stepmother. She's no relation of mine in any way, just a usurper. And it's time for her to go."

Alma held out her arm. "In that case…"

Gwen took it, allowing Alma to lead her out of the room, Miriam coming behind to fix her train. She would have liked Charlotte beside her, but she knew she was working out of sight to clear the way for Gwen and Easton's moment. And it felt fitting, somehow, that it was just the three of them.

When they reached the door of the throne room, she heard the gentle swell of music from inside as the doors ponderously opened. She gasped at the sight before her.

Rows and rows of white seats ran down both sides of a long velvet carpet. Greenery and the first of the spring flowers had been woven into the chairs closest to the aisle as well as around the columns that lined the room. Gauzy white material, like the top layer of her dress, hung from the ceiling in graceful folds, and at the end of the aisle stood Easton. His messy brown curls had been tamed for once, a golden circlet holding them in place, but his eyes were the same as ever as they stared back at her, blazing with love.

"Ready?" Alma asked softly, and Gwen nodded, unable to speak.

A rustle of movement filled the large room as Gwen stepped in on Alma's arm. She heard the faint murmur of query and alarm—presumably coming from the loyal courtiers in attendance. They had been expecting her to enter on the arm of Queen Celandine, not a woman most of them wouldn't recognize.

But Count Oswin himself—a noble who had been a close advisor to both King Isander and Queen Celandine—stood at the front of the room with the man they all assumed to be Prince Henry. And false guards stood in ceremonial positions between each pillar, their spears straight and their faces serious. The crowd settled.

The aisle felt simultaneously long and short, the moment stretching on too long and then over too soon. Alma put Gwen's hand into Easton's and the sense of homecoming was overwhelming. Trouble was coming for them—it might be almost at the door—but still this moment was exactly what it should have been.

The count began to speak, his measured voice serious and unhurried as he said the traditional words. Gwen wanted to whisper for him to hurry, but she only smiled at Easton instead. It was their wedding, but it was also a drama being enacted for the people of the kingdom, and they had to play their parts properly.

Part of her remained tensed, watching the double doors of the throne room out of the corner of her eye. Someone had closed them, but they had no bar or key.

But the other part of her still managed to lose herself in

the moment and in Easton's wonder-filled eyes. He gave no outward sign of remembering their precarious situation, his heart apparently full of Gwen and their marriage.

At one point, she glanced at the audience, and her eyes caught on Lydia and Jett, standing at the back of the room. She smiled at them, glad they had managed to leave the rebels to be present at their son's wedding. And surely it was a good sign about the success of the rebels' mission.

She didn't falter when the count instructed them to face each other and weave their right arms together, circling three times with their joined arms at the center. Her eyes remained fixed on Easton's the whole time as the count spoke of the joining of their lives and futures.

Her voice didn't waver when the count asked her if she promised herself to this man as her husband and had her repeat a series of vows. She had attended plenty of court weddings, but the words had never hit her so forcefully before. And she had never been so glad that tradition dictated their names were used only at the end. Most of the audience still believed they were watching her marry Prince Henry.

When two people each carried a washtub onto the dais, she almost laughed aloud, however. In the past, she had accepted it as part of the tradition, but now all she could think of was Natalie's scorn. The girl was right. Even as a princess, Gwen had never worn such a beautiful dress. It wasn't what she would have chosen to do laundry in.

With exaggerated care, she bent over the tub, Easton mirroring her to her left. Had Easton washed his own shirts in the long years of his banishment? Gwen was relying on the hasty lesson given her when Miriam dumped several shirts into Gwen's bathwater and showed her how to scrub them.

Gwen tried not to splash her dress, even as she scrubbed as

quickly as possible, her eyes on the horizon. The sun was creeping lower and lower, and at any moment, the queen might appear and ruin everything. Gwen couldn't bear if all this led to nothing, the wedding interrupted before the marriage was official.

Finally, she held up the dripping shirt that apparently belonged to Easton. It was white and clean. Easton also held up hers, and the crowd cheered. They let the clothes drop back into the water and stood, turning to face each other and clasp hands.

They were close, so close.

"You have woven your futures together," the count said, his loud voice echoing through the room like a proclamation. "You have made your vows, and you have washed each other clean, I therefore—"

Both doors crashed open. "Stop!" The queen's scream rent the room.

Chairs scraped and heads twisted as everyone turned astonished faces to the furious woman in the doorway. Guards streamed past her, racing for Gwen and Easton. Easton's fingers tightened on Gwen's, and he tugged her toward him.

"Stop this treason instantly!" the queen shouted again.

Count Oswin met her eyes across the distance of the room and shouted even more loudly into the shocked silence of the crowd.

"I therefore declare Princess Gwendolyn, daughter of King Isander, married to Easton, of the mountain kingdom. What is done cannot be undone."

As he spoke the traditional words—the ones that made the marriage final—several things happened at once.

Celandine screamed her anger, the shrill cry cutting

through the crowd and making Gwen shiver. The guards along the walls sprang into motion, pouring forward to block the path of the queen's guards. The sun slipped all the way below the horizon, and Gwen looked into Easton's eyes—the eyes of her husband.

The familiar tingling itch began, but she barely felt it, her heart welling with love for the man who had stood by her through everything. The man who had just promised to stand by her forever.

And the tingling faded, dropping away into nothing. No tearing started, and no transformation followed. Night had fallen, but Gwen was still a woman.

The arrival of the queen and disruption of the wedding had shocked the crowd into silence. But nightfall sent the courtiers surging to their feet, shouting and calling. Gwen turned her head and saw people falling on each other, tears streaming down faces as they embraced or collapsed from shock and relief.

The count called again in the same booming shout.

"The enchantment is broken! All hail Queen Gwendolyn and King Easton! All hail!"

"No! No!" Celandine screamed, still in the doorway, but louder still came the roar of the crowd.

"Hail! Hail! Hail!"

Gwen turned fully to look out at them, her earlier certainty and strength returning in response to their cries.

"Hail! Hail! Hail! Hail!"

The shout seemed to swell and grow impossibly loud until Gwen realized the voices inside the hall had been joined by a roar from outside. A mob of people burst in behind Celandine, Natalie at their lead. They streamed around the queen, who stood alone, like an island in the rippling sea of people. The crowd from the city filled every spare space in the room, their enthusiastic cries of support filling the air with a thundering noise.

The grappling of the guards had been swept away by their arrival, and Gwen was relieved to see none of Celandine's guards attempted violence against the new arrivals. They had already been confused by their unexpected opponents—dressed in identical uniforms which made it hard to tell friend from foe—and the roar and unity of the growing crowd appeared to have provided the final piece of intimidation.

Gwen held up her hands, and the shout slowly faded, expectant silence slowly gripping the crowd. Celandine still stood straight, however, her eyes spearing into Gwen's.

"This is treason!" she cried, her words whipping over the distance between them.

"No," Gwen said back, her voice projecting across the room. "Yours is the treason. You stole the throne, enchanted my people, and abused me. It ends now."

"How dare you speak those words to your mother!" the queen cried, and a soft murmur reminded Gwen that Celandine still had supporters in the crowd.

But other voices murmured back, hostile and defensive. Celandine might have her supporters in the room, but Gwen had more.

Her eyes hardened, her hands clenching. "You are not my mother. Neither are you my stepmother. If you had been, you would have given me my throne when I came of age, as the law requires." Another murmur, and this time there was only sympathy and approval for Gwen. "I was with my father every moment until his dying breath. He never married you. He never even met you. You are nothing but a usurper, and your time is finished."

A shocked cry rose at her words, heads turning between Gwen and Celandine. Brows lowered and voices raised as the mood in the room turned ugly.

Celandine fell back one step and then another, horror twisting her face as she surveyed the angry crowd. Gwen stood steady, not removing her gaze, and Celandine was the first to look away. Turning, she fled.

Gwen looked at Easton, wishing Celandine's desertion was the end. If only the woman would run and not stop running. If she disappeared into the mountains, it would all finally be over.

But Gwen knew her too well to believe she would give up so easily. Celandine's guards and position had not been her only source of power. She had one last move to make.

"She'll go to her objects," she said to Easton. "We have to stop her."

He nodded, the same anxiety she felt showing in his eyes. It wasn't over yet.

Gathering up her skirts in both hands, Gwen leaped down from the dais and ran after Celandine.

INTERLUDE

CELANDINE

Celandine ran, hatred and anger and fear twisting in her gut and burning in her throat. She had to get to her objects. She had to let them drain away the awful emotions. Once her mind was clear and sharp, she would see her way out of the mess the ungrateful princess had created.

There would be a way out. There had to be. Celandine had worked too hard and for too long to see everything stripped from her. She would destroy everyone rather than become weak and vulnerable again.

A man jumped out to block Celandine's path, and she recognized him. How dare her own courtiers turn against her! She had given this man everything, and yet his wife had smiled to Celandine's face while behind her back she whined endlessly about babies. Being pregnant, having a baby—they were things that made you vulnerable. Didn't the woman realize Celandine had done her a favor?

No matter what she did for them all it was never enough. They were always poised, ready to betray her, ready to seize power for themselves. Just like that brat.

The man lunged for Celandine, but her fury lent her strength. She sidestepped him, spinning as he passed, and smashed her fist into the back of his skull with all the force she could muster.

He went down, hitting the floor hard, and she resumed her flight. As she ran, she shook her hand, which pulsed with pain. She should have drawn her dagger instead of lashing out with her fist. This was exactly why emotions were dangerous. It was too hard to think clearly while in their grip.

She reached the door to her exclusive wing of the palace and slowed. There was no sign of the guard always stationed there. Fresh fear gripped her. Her standing command was that no matter what happened in the rest of the palace, that post was never to be deserted. Seeing it empty was a fresh blow.

She quickened her pace again, not quite to a run, but she couldn't keep herself to an appropriate cautious speed. What if the rebels were already ransacking her objects?

Celandine reached for the closed door of her bedchamber only to be grabbed from behind.

"You're under arrest for treason to the crown," a rough voice said, this one unfamiliar.

She drew her dagger in one fluid movement and stabbed backward. It plunged into some part of her captor. She didn't care which part since all that mattered was that he let her go, staggering backward. She released the hilt and reached for the door instead.

Someone else was behind her—shouting angrily and rushing to help the injured man—but she didn't care. All she could think of was her objects.

She shut the door behind her, her eyes flying to the tapestry. It had been pulled back, revealing the portrait. She snarled at the sight of it, taunting her. She should have slashed it to pieces days ago. From the moment Henry broke his enchantment, the image had changed. It now showed his human state, smiling out at the world with his arm around the golden-haired girl. But worse than the two of them were the new arrivals in the portrait.

The portrait of the mountain princess had disappeared along with the castle that was a mirror of the mountain palace. But instead of ceasing to exist, the image had appeared beside the happy couple. And now, the mountain princess was no longer alone. One of her arms twined around the waist of the traitor, Easton. The boy she should have killed ten years ago.

While she stared at the image—fresh, dangerous fury rippling through her—someone spoke.

"We thought you might come here." Prince Henry stepped out of the shadows to stand in front of his portrait.

His wife stepped forward to join him, the two of them mocking her with their double appearance.

"It's over, Celandine," she said. "Gwen is queen as she should have been long ago. But she's nothing like you, so if you surrender now, she'll show you mercy."

Celandine growled, eyeing the hidden latch. If she lunged for it, could she get it open before they stopped her? Could she get to her objects?

"Is this portrait the only information you had about us?" the girl asked, apparently unable to help herself.

Celandine refocused on her. Why was she wasting both of their time on such irrelevant questions?

"I didn't need any other information," she said coldly, trying to regain her usual manner. "I saw when the prince found himself a foolish girl to become his wife, trying so hard to free himself from my enchantments." She laughed, but the sound was weak and thin.

The girl's brow furrowed. "Then how did you know? How did you know I would betray him and look at his face before the three months?"

Celandine laughed, the sound fuller. "You really have to ask that? The more infatuated you clearly became, the more obvious it was."

"But...why?"

The girl must be even more foolish than she appeared.

"Because trust is as much an illusion as love," Celandine snapped, her eyes drifting back to the hidden latch on one side of the portrait. "No one truly trusts any other person. Of course you would want to see his face—to be sure he was who he said he was. Love and trust are both illusions that make you weak and vulnerable—and easy to manipulate."

The girl paled and stepped back, but the prince caught her around the waist, steadying her.

"You're wrong." He looked at Celandine without flinching. "Fear is what cripples us. Fear is what makes us vulnerable. Love is what gives us the strength to throw off fear. You discounted love and trust and that has been your undoing. Gwen and Easton never wavered, and now they have taken back everything that is rightfully theirs."

Celandine cried out, feeling his words like a dagger straight to her chest. Done with analyzing, she threw herself forward, her fingers reaching for the latch.

She found it, tearing the portrait open and revealing the dark space beyond. The prince shouted and tried to grab her, but she slipped from his grasp, darting forward into her most treasured place.

She didn't hesitate, her hands reaching for the object that would destroy them all.

CHARLOTTE

Somehow Celandine slipped through Henry's grasp and fell into the room behind the wall. Charlotte cried out, both of them scrambling to follow. They had been trying to find that latch when they'd heard Celandine's arrival. If only they'd known where it was, they might have been able to intercept her before she got inside.

Night had fallen outside, but enough light came through the room's windows and spilled from the lanterns in the bedchamber beyond to illuminate the scene before them.

The chests that overflowed with gold lay neglected along the walls, the focus of the room on the many plinths that were scattered through the middle of the room. Each one held a different object, except for the empty plinth in the middle where Celandine stood. Her hand was clasped around something that looked like a short scepter, and her mouth was turned up in a smile that held no true emotion.

All the anger, fury, and fear that had danced over her face earlier were drained away, leaving her terrifyingly cold and empty. How was it possible to change so quickly? Was it due to the object in her hand?

Both Henry and Charlotte stopped warily just inside the room, but Henry began to advance slowly forward again, his eyes on the deposed queen.

"There's no point to any of this," he said. "Put down the object, and we can report that you cooperated."

Celandine laughed, mirthless and high. "You have no idea how hard I worked for the power I hold. I will never choose to lay it down."

Henry took another step forward, his eyes on the object in her hand.

"What is that?" he asked, his voice reasonable and calm, although Charlotte knew him well enough to recognize the underlying note of tension.

"I was going to flatten the path before Gwendolyn with this," Celandine said. "She claims I'm so awful, but I was going to give her everything. I was going to flatten the mountains for her."

Charlotte gulped, staring at the winking jewel on the tip of the scepter. Could that small thing really do so much?

"But Gwendolyn doesn't want what I can offer," Celandine said. "And she has turned my people against me. Now she will see what happens when I turn the mountains against her."

"You can't do that," Henry said. "You *shouldn't* do that."

"You think I'm lying?" Celandine's lips curled upward, and she thrust the scepter toward one of the windows. "This object can do even more. She thinks the sunset saved her, but I will steal the sun away. See who will follow her when the sun never returns."

As she spoke, dark clouds rolled across the sky, too quickly to be natural, stealing the last of the dusk light and obscuring the stars and moon. The only light left in the room was the lamplight coming in from the bedchamber.

Charlotte shifted uneasily, staring at the stark blackness out the window. Surely Celandine's words were empty boasts. She couldn't really steal the sun, could she?

Celandine cackled. "First the sun, and now I'll take her precious mountains. I was going to flatten them for her, but instead I'll send them crumbling on her head."

Henry lunged toward her, reaching for the scepter, but she jumped backward out of reach. A rumble began outside. It sounded like thunder except it built and built until Charlotte could feel it rattling through both the stones beneath her and her bones.

She staggered toward the window, gripping the sill and trying to peer outside. Were the mountains collapsing toward them? It sounded like it.

Henry lurched, the ground beneath them shaking and disrupting his footing as he tried to chase Celandine through the plinths. She evaded him, her knuckles and fingers white around the scepter.

The rumble grew until Charlotte pressed her hands to her ears, her eyes watering. Celandine was going to destroy them all, not caring that she would destroy herself in the process. And what about the valleys and the kingdoms beyond them? Celandine would destroy everything if she blocked the sky and brought down the mountains.

Charlotte dropped her hands, using them to brace herself against the wall instead as she took in the room. Celandine was dashing between the plinths, Henry in pursuit. But somehow she always slipped from his fingers. Should Charlotte help? If she tried to circle from the other direction, they might be able to trap her and force the scepter from her hand.

Or maybe Celandine would bring the ceiling down on their head before they could. The palace was already creaking alarmingly, and they were three stories up. If the wing collapsed, none of them would survive.

Her eyes swept over the room until a beam of lamplight coming through the open portrait caught on a round, smooth golden surface. The one familiar object in the room of plinths. The golden apple.

With a jolt, Charlotte remembered the moment Gwen had first placed it in her hand and her explanation of its purpose. Gwen had arranged for it to be placed here with intention. If there was something in this room that could stop Celandine, the apple would tell Charlotte what it was.

She pushed off from the wall and ran toward the apple, swerving to avoid Celandine's path on the way. Thankfully, the deposed queen swerved to avoid her as well, unaware of Charlotte's intentions.

She staggered the final steps to the plinth, the floor unsteady beneath her. Her fingers fell on the apple, and even before she had fully picked it up, her mind warmed with the awareness of multiple familiar objects all around her. It was nothing like her previous experience with the apple, not only because of the affectionate familiarity she felt toward the objects but because of their number. They overwhelmed her mind.

She gasped, whirling to look at all the objects with her eyes, trying to match them with the sense of their presence in her mind. Her eyes landed on a small golden whip, sitting alone on a plinth near the door. As she focused on it, her awareness of the other objects in the room muted, receding slightly to bring this one to the front of her mind.

It was the pair to the golden halter in her pocket, the tool

Celandine had used to fight Gwen's travel on the wind—a tool that had leveled a village and nearly sunk a fleet. It was no good to her inside the room when the halter wasn't in use, but it called to her because it was familiar.

She tore her eyes away, forcing her mind to the next object along. But there were too many objects in the room, and the rumbling was growing even louder. She could barely hear anything above its sound now. If she examined the objects one by one, she might not find anything of use in time.

Instead, she squeezed her eyes closed and filled her mind with the apple's awareness. Even with her eyes closed the objects floated in her mind, no longer attached to their plinths. She let her mind drift over them, releasing her conscious thoughts to let the instinctive layer of her mind take control.

There! Something flashed past her awareness, and she seized on it, focusing in. The object was a jewel, cut to fine points and polished to a high sheen. Its outside was cold and hard and clear, but inside it roiled and pulsed with an intensity that took Charlotte's breath away. Anger, sadness, love, joy, hatred, envy, excitement, anxiety, disgust, all mixed together and contained beneath the smooth surface of the jewel.

And Charlotte knew—thanks to the apple—the meaning behind what she sensed. This object removed emotions, sucking them from anyone who touched it and storing them inside the jewel instead.

Charlotte had noticed the change in Celandine after she entered the room and wondered if the scepter was responsible. But Celandine must have touched the jewel on her way past. How often had she come into the room to hold the jewel? From the store of emotions inside it, she must have come countless times.

Celandine didn't believe in emotions—she had made that clear. She saw them as weaknesses, so it made sense she wanted to purge them from her system. But that meant she had never learned to deal with them, to feel them. She had never learned how to let them wash over her and recede. If Charlotte could break the jewel, would the emotions return to their original owner?

Her eyes snapped open, and she scanned the room, looking for a jewel that matched the one in her mind. Her gaze caught on a red stone thanks to the lamplight that made it gleam.

She ran toward it, ducking past Celandine as she went. Celandine was in the middle of lunging away from Henry, and her body slammed into Charlotte's arm, knocking the apple from her grip. It flung halfway across the room, rolling out of sight. But it didn't matter now. Charlotte already knew what tool to use.

She reached the plinth and snatched up the jewel. Instantly her body calmed and her mind felt clearer and easier, the terror and anxiety she had been feeling sucked away. She could see why the object had been appealing to the former queen. But it had become a crutch.

Lifting it over her head, Charlotte threw the jewel with all her might at the closest wall. It sailed through the air, winking as it arced high. It caught the attention of the others, and they both paused, turning to look. Celandine let out a wordless cry of protest, but it was too late.

The jewel hit the stone wall and smashed, shards flying in all directions. A wave of fear and anxiety hit Charlotte so strongly she staggered backward as her fear returned to its original owner. Gasping, she barely kept her balance, spinning to find Celandine.

If the returned emotions had hit Charlotte so hard, what would they have done to Celandine, who had stored decades' worth of every emotion in there?

Celandine's head was thrown back, her face twisted with heightened emotion, her eyes wide and staring. She fell backward, colliding with a plinth and taking that down too, its object toppling off and bouncing away in one direction while the scepter flew from Celandine's hand in the other.

Celandine curled into a ball, sobbing. Her arms wrapped so tightly around her knees it must have hurt, her sobs turning into a keening that rose higher and higher.

It was hard to turn away from the horrible effect of twenty years' unchecked emotion, but the floor was still shuddering, the rumble in the air still vibrating in Charlotte's bones. The scepter had flown in her direction, so she dropped to her hands and knees, searching the floor for it.

"There!" The tip showed from between two chests, fallen gold coins lying atop and around it, obscuring its presence.

She stretched out, wrapping her fingers around it and pulling it back toward her. The second she touched it, her mind expanded, taking in not just the room or the palace but the mountain range in every direction and the sky above her. Holding the scepter, she could shape her environment however she wanted. The thrill of power ran through her, but following behind was the fear. It was too much. No one person should be capable of re-forming the land itself.

Charlotte nearly flung the scepter away from her, only just stopping herself. Her fingers remained wrapped around it, but she looked up, pleading wordlessly for someone to help her.

A figure holding a lantern appeared in the open portrait, another dark shape behind her. Charlotte's mouth fell open at the magnificent sight of Gwen in an enormous wedding dress, the filmy layers falling around her and the train disappearing behind, her hair piled high and the tiara on her head winking in the light.

Gwen paused for one second as she took in the room—Celandine balled up and keening with Henry hovering beside her, and Charlotte sprawled across the floor on the far side of the room, a scepter gripped in her outstretched hand and terror on her face. She met Charlotte's eyes, seeming to read the plea for help there, and handed her lantern to Easton behind her.

But she didn't run toward Charlotte. Instead, she gathered her skirts and darted in a different direction, stooping to retrieve something fallen on the ground.

For a stupefied minute, Charlotte's consciousness hovered between the mountains outside—whose peaks were beginning to crumble, enormous boulders rolling down their sides—and her friend. Was Gwen retrieving the object Celandine had just knocked loose? Charlotte hadn't even seen what it was, but surely it wasn't important in the middle of such danger.

But when Gwen straightened and turned toward Charlotte, it was the apple gripped in her hand. She ignored Celandine and the plinths and the rumbling outside and walked straight toward Charlotte, the apple gripped in her palm and her eyes on the scepter.

Understanding washed through Charlotte, followed by

relief. If Gwen had the apple, she would know how the scepter worked. She would know how to wield it and how to undo the damage Celandine had already done.

Charlotte pulled herself to her knees, holding the scepter toward Gwen. When her friend reached her, she dropped to her knees at her side. But when she wrapped her hand around the scepter, she didn't pull it away from Charlotte.

"Two will be better than one," she shouted over the rumbling. "It will only respond to strength. We have to force it to obey us."

Charlotte could feel Gwen beside her through her normal senses, but she could also sense her through the expanded awareness the scepter gave her. Charlotte tried to follow Gwen's lead, forcing her will on the scepter, instructing it to roll back the clouds and rebuild the mountains.

It groaned, the sound more felt than heard beneath the volume of the thunderous rumble. But it didn't obey. More of the mountain tips crumbled, the broken boulders rolling further down, heading toward the city in the valley below.

"No!" Gwen shouted. "I will not let her destroy our mountains! I will not let her steal even one more bit of light from me."

Gwen's will merged with Charlotte's, their unified voices commanding the same thing. Together they shouted into the deafening noise and chaos around them, building a mental picture of a clear sky and whole mountains and forcing the shape of that command onto the scepter.

"You. Will. Obey. Us," Gwen choked out, speaking through gritted teeth.

The rumbling quieted.

Charlotte drew a gasping breath, her fingers squeezing

forcefully around the scepter. The rumbling quieted further and then still further. New light stole into the room as the sky cleared, revealing the moon and the last of the light from the sunset.

In the distance, blocked by the walls, Charlotte sensed the boulders rolling back uphill. The mountain peaks re-formed as if they had never been touched, even the life on their slopes returned to its original state.

She slumped down, every muscle trembling with the after-effects of her exertion. They had done it.

Gwen swept her into a hug, crying into her shoulder and croaking out her thanks. A shout sounded behind them, followed by running feet, a crash, and then a high-pitched scream that made her blood stop.

The girls pulled apart and looked across the room. Henry was taking the final two strides toward a broken window. He looked back at them with a pale face.

"I tried to catch her," he said, "but..."

"She moved too fast." Easton's voice shook. "We were both watching you, and..."

Gwen stood, swaying on shaky legs. Easton hurried to her side, putting an arm around her for support, and she leaned against his shoulder.

"Perhaps, she..." She swallowed and tried again. "When I fell from an upper-story window, the wind—"

Henry poked his head through the broken window, careful to avoid the remaining shards of glass. When he pulled back into the room, his face was drawn and he shook his head.

"I'm sorry, Gwen. There wasn't any wind to catch her."

Gwen swallowed. "I could have...I should have..."

"No." Charlotte stood more slowly, speaking the word with force. "You were busy saving entire kingdoms—busy undoing the work that woman set in motion. Everything about her life was a tragedy, but none of it was your doing." She moved around to meet her friend's eyes. "This isn't your burden to carry, Gwen. You'll have enough burdens undoing the damage she caused in your kingdom."

"Listen to Charlotte," Easton said. "She's right. At the end, Celandine made her own choice. It wasn't your fault she wasn't in her right mind."

Charlotte looked sadly toward the plinth that had supported the jewel. "I'm not sure she had been for a long time."

She looked down, realizing she still held the scepter. She wanted to drop it. She wanted to never touch it again. But she couldn't risk anyone else getting their hands on it. She gripped it in both hands, raising it high and pulling up one knee. But just before she brought it down, she paused, the scepter hanging in midair.

Her eyes slowly rose, meeting Gwen's.

"Perhaps," she said, "there's one thing…"

Gwen's blank look transformed to understanding, and a smile spread over her mouth. "Just one," she said.

She stepped forward and gripped the scepter along with Charlotte for one final time. Connected through the scepter, Charlotte knew they had indeed had the same thought. Together they bore down on the scepter, forcing their will on it.

Distantly, the sound of grating stone drifted through the night air, making Henry turn back to the window. But there was nothing to see in the gray dimness of early night.

Within a minute, both girls relaxed, grinning at each other.

"A small change like that won't do any harm to the mountains or their environment," Gwen said, letting go of the scepter.

"But it will do us a lot of good." Charlotte smiled.

Once again gripping the scepter's length in two hands, she raised it up and brought it down hard on her knee. It snapped in half with a sound like brittle wood.

She looked down at the two lifeless shards she held in each hand and nodded. No one could touch the mountains now.

Gwen nodded approvingly, and Charlotte let the pieces fall to the ground, overwhelmed by a rush of exhaustion. Henry's arms slid around her from behind, and he guided her back against his chest. She collapsed against him with a sigh of gratitude, letting her eyes drift shut.

"What did you do?" Henry asked. "At the end there?"

Charlotte didn't open her eyes although a smile curved up her lips. "Nothing too significant."

"We just made sure we'll always be able to visit each other from now on," Gwen said.

"You made a permanent pass?" Easton asked eagerly. "One that doesn't require bear form?"

"The mountain kingdom isn't cut off from the other kingdoms any longer." Gwen sounded satisfied. "And I won't have to fly the captives home one or two at a time. We can set up proper trading routes too."

"An excellent first act as ruler," Easton said, sounding a little awed.

"I thought so," Gwen said smugly before sighing, her voice turning rueful. "I'll have to explore the rest of these objects later. I think there are some wedding guests who are waiting to see us."

Charlotte's eyes flew open, taking in her friend's appearance for a second time.

"Your wedding!" she cried. "Did it succeed? Are you married?"

Gwen nodded almost shyly before looking up into the face of her new husband and beaming. "Celandine tried to stop it, but she was too late. And I exposed her as a usurper before everyone."

"We broke the enchantment, too," Easton said.

Charlotte gasped. "Of course you did! You're not a bear, Gwen!"

Gwen gave a relieved laugh. "I'm very pleased to know I never will be again. I'm quite happy to keep my normal human body from now on, even if I can't break down doors with my hands."

"I'm so happy for you both." Charlotte wasn't sure if the tears in her eyes were from joy, relief, or exhaustion. "I just wish I could have been there."

"It was beautiful," Gwen said. "The captives outdid themselves."

"*You* look beautiful," Charlotte said.

"We weren't able to be there for Gwen and Easton's wedding," Henry said, "but I hope Queen Gwendolyn and King Easton will grace our wedding with their presence."

Charlotte pulled away, twisting to look up at him. "What are you talking about? We've been married for months."

"In the valleys," he said. "But Celandine pointed out to me that it might be more than a year before Master Harold registers it officially with the Rangmeran authorities. And in the meantime, she was convinced I could register a different marriage elsewhere. So as soon as possible, we will be married again and officially registered here in the mountain kingdom. I don't want anyone to ever question that you're my wife again."

Charlotte laughed. "Are you expecting a steady stream of people trying to force you into unwanted marriages?"

"Maybe I just want to give my beautiful bride the wedding she always deserved." He smiled down at her.

Charlotte had only one answer to that. She reached up on her tiptoes and kissed him.

EPILOGUE

CHARLOTTE

Charlotte stared at herself in the full-length mirror. Her dress wasn't as elaborate as Gwen's had been, but it was far fancier than the dress she had worn at her first wedding. And—more importantly than either fact—it suited her perfectly. The clean lines of the satin gown exuded an elegance befitting a princess without overwhelming the woman inside the dress.

She met Gwen's eyes in the mirror, and her friend smiled knowingly.

"It's hard to see yourself as a princess—or queen—and also yourself. But it's possible. If I can get there, so can you."

Charlotte smiled tremulously. Gwen of all people knew exactly what she was going through. She could never have guessed that the woman in the portrait would become her best friend and the most amazing support. She was only glad that the mountains were no longer a barrier between them.

"Promise you'll come and visit," she said, trying not to sniffle.

"Of course I will!" Gwen hesitated. "Although I understand

you'll have your sisters with you in Arcadia. You might not have as much need for—"

Charlotte shook her head firmly, turning to give her friend a pointed look. "You've met my sisters. While I'm glad I can offer them a new life in Arcadia—the kind of life they've always wanted—their presence can't make up for your absence."

Gwen's smile grew stronger. "I'm actually curious to see Arcadia. I've read about it in books, and it sounds beautiful."

Charlotte glanced out the window at the mountains. They were visible from any direction, their peaks white with snow despite the warm sun that shone into the enormous valley housing the mountain kingdom.

"I'm going to miss the mountains," she said. "I've gotten used to having them always there in the distance. There's something solid and calming about their presence. It was one of the things I liked about my old life in the valleys."

"Do your parents love the mountains as well?" Gwen asked. "Is that why they're not going with your sisters to Arcadia?"

Charlotte hesitated. "I don't think it's the mountains exactly." She sighed. "My father dreams of new horizons and new frontiers. He loves the idea of building a life from nothing. So how could he turn away now that a true new frontier has opened up?" She gestured at the mountains outside.

Gwen grimaced guiltily. "I suppose we only made that worse by having the first courier through the new pass go straight to his door with instructions to bring your family here without delay."

Charlotte chuckled. "Maybe a little. He already has grand plans for the trading route he's going to set up. But Henry and I appreciated it so much."

Gwen laughed along with her. "Poor Henry was so impatient. He could barely wait for your family to get here as it was. I almost pulled out the halter to get them here more quickly."

Charlotte's eyes widened. "Do not let my father get word of the possibility of riding the wind!"

Gwen nodded solemnly. "Noted."

Charlotte relented. "My relationship with my family was so broken at my first wedding, and they won't be part of my daily life in Arcadia going forward. I couldn't have a second, proper wedding without them. Henry understands."

"Have you really forgiven them for everything?" Gwen asked, and Charlotte could hear the echo of another question behind it. Had Charlotte really forgiven Gwen for her role in the candle disaster?

Charlotte smiled. "I have forgiven them for everything. I don't want any resentment hanging over the new life I'm about to start. But I haven't forgotten. Henry and I have already discussed it, and we're going to set my sisters up in a comfortable house in the Arcadian capital but not in the court itself. They're family, and I want to do what I can to support them in building a fulfilling life for themselves, but I can't build my own new life with them too close."

"What about your mother?" Gwen asked. "Is she upset your father is insisting they stay?"

Charlotte considered the question. Her family had only arrived the day before—thanks to Henry's determination to have a proper wedding as soon as possible. But she had spent the evening with them, and her mother had seemed content with the plans being made.

"I think she would like Arcadia," she said. "But she would never leave my father, despite his flaws."

She and Gwen's eyes met, and they shared a look of silent understanding. They were both newlyweds themselves, and they understood what it meant to enter a marriage. It was inevitable there would be times when one member of a couple would have to compromise for the other. That was part of being a team.

"Their new house disappeared, you know," Charlotte added, trying not to laugh at the thought. "It was created for them by the bell, so when Henry broke his enchantment and the castle and bell disappeared, everything else it had created disappeared with them."

Gwen's eyes widened, but Charlotte continued to smile. "I think it worked out for the best, though. They fled to my aunt and uncle's house, and since the last of my cousins has just become betrothed, my mother and aunt realized they enjoy living together. Henry is going to give them the gold he originally promised, and they plan to use it to expand my aunt and uncle's house. When my father—and probably my uncle with him—are traveling through the mountain pass, my mother will still have company. I think she'll be happy enough in that life."

"And you'll be happy having some distance from them," Gwen murmured.

Charlotte grimaced, not denying it. "Some relationships improve with some distance. We'll be very happy to see each other when we have a chance to visit." She hesitated. "My family is far from perfect, and they've hurt me, but I know it doesn't compare to your situation. Even if Celandine had been your true birth mother..." She hesitated, shaking her head. "Some relationships can't be salvaged."

Gwen's smile didn't waver. "Don't be sad for me. Not on

your special day. I have a new family now. Lydia and Jett are already the parents I always wished I could have."

Charlotte impulsively embraced her friend, and Gwen hugged her back. She wished she could have Gwen as her attendant, but she understood that Gwen's new role as queen precluded it. At least Gwen and Easton would be present in the front row, which was better than Charlotte had managed for their wedding.

She had been prepared for her sisters to throw fits at not being included in the wedding themselves, but they seemed to accept the excuse that there was no time to organize the necessary outfits. It probably helped that they were still in shock at the discovery of Henry's true identity and the coming changes in their lives.

"Are you ready?" Natalie bounced into the room, looking beautiful in a gown of deep gold. "I had no idea it took so long to get ready for a wedding!"

Gwen threw a speaking look at Charlotte. "Are you regretting your choice of attendant yet?"

Charlotte stifled a laugh. "Never."

Natalie joined her beside the mirror, surveying herself with satisfaction. "How could she regret it? I was clearly born to wear a dress like this."

Gwen and Charlotte exchanged looks of concern at the disturbing light in Natalie's eyes. There was something both terrifying and exhilarating about never knowing what outrageous plan the girl would get into her head next.

At least her inclusion in the event had succeeded in raising her spirits. Ever since the revelation that her brother Baden had been the one to reveal the rebels' plans to the queen, she had been unnaturally downcast. Charlotte was just glad the job of sorting out that particular delicate situation fell to Gwen, not her.

Natalie herself was above reproach. Even without her brother's assistance, she had managed to rouse the city's youth, leading them to gather their families and storm the palace in support of Gwen, arriving at the crucial moment.

Natalie finished her perusal of her reflection. "Well? Are you ready, Charlotte?"

"She is," Gwen said with a smile. "She's perfect."

Charlotte laughed. "Perfectly happy, perhaps."

"Come on, then." Natalie opened the door. "You don't want Henry to think you're not coming."

Gwen shook her head. "I think Charlotte, of all people, has proven her devotion. She came all the way to the mountain kingdom to find Henry. She's not going to run away now."

"Will you really let me visit you in Arcadia?" Natalie asked Charlotte as they walked through the corridors toward the throne room.

"Of course," she said before hastily adding, "Once you're a bit older, and if your parents give permission."

Natalie nodded absentmindedly, but Charlotte wasn't sure she'd actually heard the last part.

They reached the double doors of the throne room and found Charlotte's father waiting for them, a beaming smile on his face.

He leaned in to kiss her forehead, his eyes gleaming. "I've never been so proud of you, Charli-bear."

She smiled back. "Just don't let Henry hear you using that nickname. I think he's had enough of bears for a lifetime."

Her father laughed back. "If anyone deserves to become a crown princess, it's you, my daughter."

Charlotte shook her head but didn't protest aloud. It was

no use trying to convince her father how unqualified she was for the role. He believed in her, and she would have to believe in herself as well.

As Natalie took up her position in front of them, ready to enter first, Charlotte caught a considering look in her eye. When Charlotte glanced at Gwen, she saw she'd noticed it too, but whatever Gwen's thoughts on the matter, they were clearly swept away when Easton appeared, the golden circlet from his own wedding glinting among his brown curls. His eyes moved quickly over Charlotte to land on Gwen.

They lit up at the sight of his wife, regal in frothy layers of deep blue. Charlotte sighed and smiled. In just moments she would be standing at Henry's side. She couldn't wait to see the same look in his eyes as Easton wore when he looked at Gwen.

The doors creaked open, and Easton offered Gwen his arm. She accepted it, and the two of them walked into the throne room. The audience rose at their entrance, bowing or dropping into curtsies, sending a rippling wave through the room in line with their progress.

Only when they were seated at the front of the room did everyone else resume their seats, craning their heads toward the door as the wedding music began.

Natalie stepped out confidently, making her way slowly down the aisle. Charlotte took her father's offered arm and let him lead her behind her lone attendant. She had insisted that the room's decorations be kept simple, given all the tasks facing the palace in the wake of the transfer of power. But just the presence of Henry was enough to make the whole room beautiful in her eyes.

He didn't take his gaze off her from the moment she

appeared, and as soon as she reached him, he squeezed her hands.

"You're beautiful," he murmured.

She smiled back, forgetting both the pain of their past and the anxiety of her future role. In that moment, she was free to do nothing but celebrate this reminder of their vows. They had already promised with both word and action to be loyal and to love and be loved. But she couldn't wait to make the same promises again.

Some elements of the ceremony were unfamiliar, but she succeeded in weaving their arms together and circling without tripping over her small train, grateful for their several practice runs the day before. But when they brought out the tubs for washing, she made the mistake of meeting Natalie's eyes.

The look on the younger girl's face made it almost impossible not to break out into giggles, and Charlotte spent the entire time she was scrubbing trying not to let them burst free. Henry kept shooting her amused glances as he struggled through the task himself. He had more experience than most princes his age, but apparently scrubbing shirts wasn't part of his skill set.

Eventually they both had the garments clean, however, holding them up proudly and enjoying the cheers of the crowd. When Count Oswin proclaimed the final words of the ceremony, declaring that what had been done could not be undone, Henry and Charlotte gazed into each other's eyes, feeling the special weight of the words. No one could dispute their marriage now.

Henry pulled her close and kissed her, leading to more cheers, and Charlotte's cheeks were flushed by the time she pulled back. Henry grinned down at her unrepentant, though.

He hadn't stopped smiling since she had entered the room and just seeing him gave Charlotte a swell of happiness. How long would it be before she stopped feeling that way every time her eyes fell on his tall form?

The party following the ceremony continued long into the night. Charlotte and Henry had allowed Gwen and Easton to choose the guest list, knowing they wanted to make use of the invitations. There was far too much politics involved in setting up their new court to miss such a valuable opportunity.

Charlotte didn't mind all the unfamiliar faces. Her family was there, along with the new friends she had made, and Henry was at her side. Nothing else mattered.

But when Gwen had finally finished circulating—having needed to talk to every one of the guests—she collapsed into a chair beside Charlotte.

"Did I know being queen would be so exhausting?" she moaned.

Charlotte grinned back. "If you're trying to terrify me, know that nothing will ruin my mood today."

Gwen straightened in her chair. "Of course I'm not trying to do that! I'm sure you'll love making polite talk with every single person at all those future Arcadian parties."

Charlotte snorted but didn't retort since Natalie bounded up to them at that moment, her eyes concerningly bright.

"I've been thinking," she said ominously.

Gwen and Charlotte exchanged a look.

"What are you planning now?" Gwen asked in an even more exhausted voice.

"Charlotte said I can visit Arcadia in a few years, but why stop there?" Natalie gazed into the distance dreamily.

"What do you mean?" Charlotte asked warily.

"It hit me during the ceremony," Natalie said. "You're a queen, Gwen."

"Queen Gwendolyn to you," Charlotte said sternly. "At least in public."

Natalie waved a hand dismissively. "But you were born a princess, so it's not surprising. But Charlotte on the other hand…She's going to be a queen one day too, but she was born into a family just as ordinary as mine."

Charlotte winced. Was Natalie's introduction to Charlotte's family responsible for sparking this train of thought?

"So if Charlotte can become a queen, then I'm going to become a queen too," Natalie finished cheerfully.

"You're going to become a queen?" Gwen asked incredulously. "How would that work, exactly?"

Charlotte could see the connection, though. "By marrying a crown prince, I suppose," she said.

Natalie nodded. "Exactly. Did you know the old crown historian is one of the guests today? He's absolutely ancient, but he's the one who's been updating the official records since the traders reestablished contact with the Four Kingdoms. I've just had a very interesting talk with him."

"Don't tell me…" Gwen said weakly.

Natalie continued on, unheeding. "It turns out," she said triumphantly, "that Crown Prince Frederic of Lanover has a son who is sixteen years old and who will one day be king of Lanover."

Charlotte wracked her brains, trying to remember the royal family trees she had learned as a child in school. "You mean Prince Leo?" she asked.

"That sounds right," Natalie said. "Or Leon, or Luca, something like that. Anyway, as soon as I'm eighteen, I'll come to

Arcadia to visit you, Charlotte, and then I'll continue straight on to Lanover. It's perfect."

Gwen and Charlotte stared at her, rendered equally silent by the matter-of-fact plans. Natalie eyed them both as if they were the strange ones before shrugging and bounding off again, perhaps to regale someone else with tales of her glorious future.

"You don't…You don't think there's any chance she might actually succeed, do you?" Gwen whispered in the silence after her departure.

"Let's hope not—for Lanover's sake," Charlotte said back with feeling, and then both of them dissolved into helpless laughter.

Their laughs had finally subsided to the occasional chuckle, and they were wiping at their eyes when Henry appeared, eager to steal his bride.

Gwen sent them off with a wave, and Charlotte went joyfully. As lovely as the day had been, she couldn't wait until it was just the two of them again as it had been all those weeks in their castle.

Henry pulled her into a shadowed corner and wrapped his arms around her, gazing down into her face. "I talked to Easton. He and Gwen are lending us their lodge for two weeks. He said it's their wedding present."

Charlotte's face lit up. "The one right on the edge of the valley?"

Henry nodded. "I told them we don't need any servants. I think we can survive two weeks on our own, even without the bell."

Charlotte nodded fervently, overwhelmed at the thoughtful offer from their friends. As happy as she had been already, the knowledge they would leave so soon for Arcadia had been a slight shadow. Knowing she would have some time alone with Henry before she had to face his family and the Arcadian court made the whole prospect easier to bear.

She sighed and leaned against him.

"It will be nice to have some time to ourselves before we head home," Henry said, echoing her thoughts. "And I hope you don't mind, but I suspect we'll have to have a third wedding when we do eventually reach Arcadie. I am their crown prince, after all, and you'll be their queen one day. We might be well and truly legally married now, but my people will want their own celebration."

Charlotte swallowed. She didn't mind another ceremony. It was what it signified that scared her.

"How can I be a queen one day? I'm just an ordinary girl."

Henry threw back his head and laughed. "An ordinary girl? You are far from ordinary, my beautiful wife. Who else could find their way to the palace east of the sun and west of the moon? Who else has ridden the wind, stolen back the sun, and helped defeat the mountain queen? I've never met anyone less ordinary." He paused. "Unless it's my mother. You know she was born a woodcutter's daughter, right?"

Charlotte nodded, the vague memory of Alyssa's history coming back to her. But everyone said the Arcadians loved Princess Alyssa—or Queen Alyssa as she must now be. Was it possible they could accept Charlotte in the same way?

Henry smiled down at her, reading her thoughts on her face. "They're going to love you just like they love her. You're not only beautiful, you're intelligent, kind, and considerate of others. And my mother will love you most of all. You don't have to worry. Queen Alyssa is going to approve of the newest princess of Arcadia."

EPILOGUE

GWEN

Gwen's stiff smile remained in place until the door closed behind the latest supplicants. Some days it felt like their time consisted of nothing but meetings from sunup to sundown. Hands appeared on her shoulders, firmly kneading at the knots. She closed her eyes and sighed, welcoming the momentary release of pressure.

"It won't be so bad once everything is more settled," Easton murmured. "At least that's what my parents have assured me, and the count agrees."

Gwen opened her eyes and smiled up at him. Reinstating Lydia and Jett to the court had been an easy decision, and they had already turned out to be better advisors than most of the people who held the title. She was thinking of giving them the official appointment soon.

She stretched, bending her head from side to side in an attempt to erase the crick in her neck. Charlotte and Henry's current days at the royal lodge were looking more and more idyllic with every passing hour. But Gwen and Easton had promised each other they would have their own visit there once matters settled down in the mountain kingdom. She just hoped it didn't take much longer.

At least both the court and city had accepted Count Oswin's reinstatement as Chief Advisor thanks to the combination of his longstanding position at court and his role in the rebellion. Unfortunately, the new positions given to Patti and Dane weren't so uncontested.

Gwen sighed again. It was only a minority who insisted the whole family should take the blame for Baden's treachery, but their last meeting had contained several of their number. Of course it had also included a few who represented the majority—people who argued in favor of the valuable role in the rebellion undertaken by Patti, Dane, and even Natalie. Thus why the conversation had been heated.

Thankfully, those who were wavering in the middle had been mostly convinced by Natalie's participation in Charlotte's wedding. Seeing she still held royal favor had swayed all but the most entrenched. But those who were most entrenched in their opinions were also usually the most vocal.

And she and Easton would have to make a decision about Baden himself soon. She had been putting it off for Patti and Dane's sakes—and to a lesser extent Lydia and Jett's. As betrayed as they all felt, they had argued passionately that he had only done it out of fear for his family, believing the old queen too powerful to be overthrown. They had pleaded for clemency, and Gwen and Easton had put off any decision at all, not wanting their reign to begin with something so contentious.

Celandine's guards had been easier to manage, at least, since no one had spoken in their defense. Those known to have committed casual cruelties in the city were handed over to be tried as civilians, and the others had already been marched through the new mountain pass. According to Easton, there were sea captains who would be both willing to take them and capable of keeping them in line. Some of them might even become productive citizens.

"Do you think they accepted Patti and Dane's new roles as spokespeople for the city?" Easton asked, gazing at the closed door. "Even if they didn't like it?"

"They certainly didn't like it," Gwen agreed. "But there's no one we could appoint who would be loved by everyone. I'm sure they'll come around when they see what a good job they do." She groaned. "But what are we going to do about Baden?"

"Actually, I've been thinking about that," Easton said. "And for once, maybe we can follow in Celandine's footsteps."

Gwen's head snapped around to face him. "What?"

"She misused her power, but she did manage to maintain it in the face of opposition for twenty years. She knew something about balancing opposing interests. And when faced with a rebellious youth whose parents had influence, she chose banishment over a more confronting punishment."

"You only challenged her!" Gwen cried indignantly. "You didn't put anyone's life at risk. You weren't a traitor to your own family and people! Her reaction was outrageous."

He shrugged. "That's a matter of perspective. Celandine certainly thought of me as a traitor. I'm sure if she'd had her free choice, she would have executed me for daring to challenge her. But she recognized the effect that would have on every parent in the court. So she solved the problem by removing me from view."

Gwen forced herself to consider the option with an open mind. "If Baden is banished from the mountain kingdom, he'll be out of sight, and hopefully mind, of everyone baying for his blood. But his parents and sisters will know he's physically unharmed and able to build a life for himself."

"Exactly," Easton said. "I, of all people, know it's possible to do. And he's three years older than I was when I was banished. He's certainly old enough to work and provide for himself in a town like Ranost. I've had several long talks with him, and I agree with my parents. He did it out of fear for his family's safety. He won't be a danger to anyone else if we set him loose in Northhelm."

Gwen's shoulders slumped. "Patti and Dane won't exactly be happy, but you're right. I think it's the best we can do. And now that the mountain pass is open, they can probably pay him some quiet visits in a few years' time, which is better than your parents could hope for."

"You don't feel the punishment is too light?" Easton asked curiously.

Gwen rubbed her temples. "He's still a youth. Of course we can't ignore something so big, but I don't want us to start our rule by handing out harsh punishments. These weeks have been difficult enough as it is." She groaned. "I can't say I thought I would be taking Celandine's example in anything, though."

"No one is completely wrong all the time," Easton said. "Just like no one is right every time. I've been spending every spare minute reading the histories, trying to absorb all the records of how past monarchs handled the issues that arose. I haven't found one who was perfect yet, but there's always been something to learn from each of them."

"And this is why you are just the husband I need." Gwen stood and wrapped her arms around him. "I think you're better at this than I am."

He shook his head. "No, we just make a good team."

He leaned down to kiss her, but a knock on the door made them pull reluctantly apart. Alma backed inside, a tray held in her hands.

"I knew you'd need something substantial after that lot," she said, placing it on the enormous desk. "So don't even think about starting another meeting until you've eaten everything on there."

She fixed them both with a stern look, and they grinned back at her. Gwen had already said farewell to Miriam and most of the other captive servants, but she had been beyond delighted when Alma decided to stay.

Gwen had immediately given her the official role of housekeeper, and Alma had already sourced paid servants for most of the needed roles. From what Gwen had seen, she was training them thoroughly and ruling with a firm but fair hand. Gwen was just relieved she didn't have to attempt the task herself. She had enough on her plate already and very little idea of the daily practicalities of running a palace building.

"What would we do without you, Alma?" Easton asked, settling in to eat with enthusiasm.

"That's what I asked myself," she said, watching him eat with satisfaction. "What was the point of returning to North-helm when there was no family waiting for me? That was why I was snatched in the first place, after all. Here, on the other hand, there's plenty needing my attention."

"And you have family here now," Gwen said firmly.

When they had both eaten, and Alma had taken the tray away—having watched them sternly the whole time—Gwen finally sank back into Easton's arms.

He managed to kiss her successfully this time, but when he

pulled back, they both sighed simultaneously. Their stolen moments were always too short.

"After our trip to the lodge, I want to take a trip to Ranost," Gwen announced. "I want to learn more about your life in those years when you were gone."

Easton smiled. "And I want to share all my stories with you. I think you'll love the sea as much as I do if you get the chance."

He glanced toward a locked drawer in the desk. A drawer whose only key was on a chain around Gwen's neck.

"In ordinary circumstances, I would say we won't have the opportunity to get away very often," he said. "But thankfully I married a queen who can ride the wind. We can manage a day trip to Ranost if that's all the time we have."

"Oh yes, let's!" Gwen said instantly. "Surely we can manage at least a single day away soon."

"We'll be able to visit Charlotte and Henry more easily with your halter too," Easton said. "The more I think about it, the more advantages there are. I'm sure there will be plenty of difficult decisions in our future, but at least we'll always be able to manage brief trips away to clear our heads."

Gwen smiled at him and turned her face up for another kiss. "Just having you at my side is enough for a happy life. After everything we've been through, it isn't something I'll ever take for granted."

"I want more for you than just me," Easton protested, his eyes soft as he smiled at her. "And thankfully that's true already. And we'll continue to build even more together." He nodded decisively. "I think we can have a very happy life riding the wind together."

To find out if Natalie succeeds at becoming a queen, read To Ensnare a Prince: An Entwined Prince and the Pauper Retelling.

Or if you missed discovering the Four Kingdoms, try the rest of the Four Kingdoms books, starting with the very first book, The Princess Companion: A Retelling of The Princess and the Pea. Or you can skip ahead and meet Charlie as a child in the final book in Return to the Four Kingdoms, The Abandoned Princess: A Retelling of Rapunzel.

The Four Kingdoms duology marks the end of the full-length adventures in the Four Kingdoms. I'm so grateful to all the readers who have joined me on that journey. But while those adventures are now drawing to a close, new fairy tale adventures will be beginning. If you enjoyed the Four Kingdoms stories, discover the new fairy tale kingdoms found in Kingdoms of Legacy, where not only the characters, but the kingdoms themselves, are shaped by classic tales. Beginning with Legacy of Roses: A Beauty and the Beast Tale.

To be informed of my new releases, as well as new bonus shorts, please sign up to my mailing list at www.melaniecelli er.com. At my website, you'll also find an array of free extra content in my Four Kingdoms world.

Thank you for taking the time to read my book. I hope you enjoyed it. If you did, please spread the word! You could start by leaving a review on Amazon or Goodreads or Facebook or any other social media site. Your review would be very much appreciated and would make a big difference!

ACKNOWLEDGMENTS

This is my first fairy tale to be split across two books and to follow two separate heroines as they discover adventure, loss, love, and strength. It's been an enjoyable challenge to try something a little different, and I hope my readers also enjoy the variety in format.

Family—both the one we're born into and the ones we find later in life—is central to so much of who we are and who we grow into. As Charlotte and Gwen's stories wrestle with the meaning of family and loyalty, I find myself incredibly grateful for my own family—my family of origin, the family I married into, the family my husband and I have created, and the friends of my heart who have become as dear as family. You are all a gift and a joy, not least because of your willingness to continuously choose love over hurt or offense. It is my prayer that anyone who wasn't born into such a family will be able to find them later in life.

In my case, my family have also been an integral support in my publishing journey, and I am so grateful to my mum, my dad, my sister, Deborah, my brother James, and my husband, Marc, for beta reads, edits, website design, tech support, last minute calls, flexible schedules, and lots of conversations about the ins and outs of publishing. I appreciate you all more than I can say.

The same goes to my amazing beta reading friends,

Rachel, Greg, Ber, Priya, and Katie. And to my editor Mary who is far more supportive and flexible than I deserve.

Another big thank you to the amazing Karri—I love the covers for this duology so much!

And, of course, thank you to God who teaches us the true meaning of love, devotion, and family.

ABOUT THE AUTHOR

Melanie Cellier grew up on a staple diet of books, books and more books. And although she got older, she never stopped loving children's and young adult novels.

She always wanted to write one herself, but it took three careers and three different continents before she actually managed it.

She now feels incredibly fortunate to spend her time writing from her home in Adelaide, Australia where she keeps an eye out for koalas in her backyard. Her staple diet hasn't changed much, although she's added choc mint Rooibos tea and Chicken Crimpies to the list.

She writes young adult fantasy including books in her *Spoken Mage* world, her *Mage's Influence* world, and her various *Four Kingdoms* and *Kingdoms of Legacy* series that are made up of linked stand-alone stories that retell classic fairy tales.

www.ingramcontent.com/pod-product-compliance
Lightning Source LLC
Chambersburg PA
CBHW050558170726
48283CB00001B/19